The Littlest Matchmaker

USA TODAY Bestselling Author
Marie Ferrarella

&

Nikki Logan

Previously published as *Diamond in the Ruff*
and *Slow Dance with the Sheriff*

HARLEQUIN® MUST LOVE DOGS

ISBN-13: 978-1-335-69087-6

The Littlest Matchmaker

Copyright © 2018 by Harlequin Books S.A.

First published as Diamond in the Ruff
by Harlequin Books in 2014 and
Slow Dance with the Sheriff by Harlequin Books in 2012.

The publisher acknowledges the copyright holders
of the individual works as follows:

Diamond in the Ruff
Copyright © 2014 by Marie Rydzynski-Ferrarella

Slow Dance with the Sheriff
Copyright © 2012 by Harlequin Books S.A.

Special thanks and acknowledgment are given to Nikki Logan
for her contribution to The Larkville Legacy series.

Recycling programs
for this product may
not exist in your area.

Printed in U.S.A.

www.Harlequin.com

CONTENTS

USA TODAY bestselling and RITA® Award–winning author **Marie Ferrarella** has written more than two hundred and seventy-five books for Harlequin, some under the name Marie Nicole. Her romances are beloved by fans worldwide. Visit her website, marieferrarella.com.

Books by Marie Ferrarella

Harlequin Special Edition

Matchmaking Mamas

The Montana Mavericks: The Great Family Roundup

The Fortunes of Texas: The Secret Fortunes

Visit the Author Profile page at Harlequin.com for more titles.

DIAMOND IN THE RUFF

Marie Ferrarella

To
Rocky and Audrey
who made my life so much richer
in their own unique way.

Prologue

"You don't remember me, do you?"

Maizie Connors, youthful grandmother, successful Realtor and matchmaker par excellence, looked at the tall, handsome, blond-haired young man standing in the doorway of her real estate office. Mentally, she whizzed through the many faces she had encountered in the past handful of years, both professionally and privately. Try as she might to recall the young man, Maizie came up empty. His smile was familiar, but the rest of him was not.

Ever truthful, Maizie made no attempt to bluff her way through this encounter until she either remembered him or, more to the point, the young man said something that would set off flares in her somewhat overtaxed brain, reminding her who he was.

Instead, Maizie shook her head and admitted, "I'm afraid I don't."

"I was a lot younger back then and I guess I looked more like a blond swizzle stick than anything else," he told her.

She didn't remember the face, but the smile and now the voice nudged at something distant within her mind. Recognition was still frustratingly out of reach. The young man's voice was lower, but the cadence was very familiar. She'd heard it before.

"Your voice is familiar and that smile, I know I've seen it before, but…" Maizie's voice trailed off as she continued to study his face. "I know I didn't sell you a house," she told him with certainty. She would have remembered that.

She remembered *all* of her clients as well as all the couples she, Theresa and Cecilia had brought together over the past few years. As far as Maizie was concerned, she and her lifelong best friends had all found their true calling in life a few years ago when desperation to see their single children married and on their way to creating their own families had the women using their connections in the three separate businesses they owned to find suitable matches for their offspring.

Enormously successful in their undertaking, they found they couldn't stop just because they had run out of their own children to work with. So friends and clients were taken on.

They did their best work covertly, not allowing the two principals in the undertaking know that they were being paired up. The payment the three exacted was not monetary. It was the deep satisfaction that came from knowing they had successfully brought two soul mates together.

But the young man before her was neither a professional client nor a private one. Yet he *was* familiar.

Shrugging her shoulders in a gesture of complete surrender, Maizie said, "I'm afraid you're going to have to take pity on me and tell me why your smile and your voice are so familiar but the rest of you isn't." Even as she said the words aloud, a partial answer suddenly occurred to her. "You're someone's son, aren't you?"

But whose? she wondered. She hadn't been at either of her "careers"—neither the one involving real estate nor the one aimed at finding soul mates—long enough for this young man to have been the result of her work.

So who are you?

"I was," he told her, his blue eyes on hers.

Was.

The moment he said that, it suddenly came to her. "You're Frances Whitman's boy, aren't you?"

He grinned. "Mom always said you were exceedingly sharp. Yes, I'm Frances's son." He said the words with pride.

The name instantly conjured up an image in Maizie's mind, the image of a woman with laughing blue eyes and an easy smile on her lips—always, no matter what adversity she was valiantly facing.

The same smile she was looking at right now.

"Christopher?" Maizie asked haltingly. "Christopher Whitman!" It was no longer a question but an assertion. Maizie threw her arms around him, giving him a warm, fond embrace, which only reached as far up as his chest. "How *are* you?" she asked with enthusiasm.

"I'm doing well, thanks." And then he told her why he'd popped in after all this time. "And it looks like we're going to be neighbors."

"Neighbors?" Maizie repeated, somewhat confused.

There'd been no For Sale signs up on her block. Infinitely aware of every house that went up for sale not just in her neighborhood, but in her city as well, Maizie knew her friend's son was either mistaken or had something confused.

"Yes, I just rented out the empty office two doors down from you," he told her, referring to the strip mall where her real estate office was located.

"Rented it out?" she repeated, waiting for him to tell her just what line of work he was in without having to specifically ask him.

Christopher nodded. "Yes, I thought this was a perfect location for my practice."

She raised her eyebrows in minor surprise and admiration.

"You're a doctor?" It was the first thing she thought of since her own daughter was a pediatrician.

Christopher nodded. "Of furry creatures, large and small," he annotated.

"You're a vet," she concluded.

"—erinarian," he amended. "I find if I just say I'm a vet, I have people thanking me for my service to this country. I don't want to mislead anyone," he explained with a smile she now found dazzling.

"Either way, you'll have people thanking you," Maizie assured him. She took a step back to get a better, fuller view of the young man. He had certainly filled out since she had seen him last. "Christopher Whitman," she repeated in amazement. "You look a great deal like your mother."

"I'll take that as a compliment," he said with a warm smile. "I was always grateful that you and the other ladies were there for Mom while she was getting her treatments. She didn't tell me she was sick until it was close to the end," he explained. It was a sore point for him, but under the circumstances, he'd had to forgive his mother. There hadn't been any time left for wounded feelings. "You know how she was. Very proud."

"Of you," Maizie emphasized. "I remember her telling me that she didn't want to interfere with your schooling. She knew you'd drop out if you thought she needed you."

"I would have," he answered without hesitation.

She heard the note of sadness in his voice that time still hadn't managed to erase. Maizie quickly changed the subject. Frances wouldn't have wanted her son to beat himself up over a decision she had made for him.

"A veterinarian, huh? So what else is new since I last saw you?" Maizie asked.

Broad shoulders rose and fell in a careless shrug. "Nothing much."

Habit had Maizie glancing down at his left hand. It was bare, but that didn't necessarily mean the man wasn't married. "No Mrs. Veterinarian?"

Christopher laughed softly and shook his head. "Haven't had the time to find the right woman," he confessed. It wasn't the truth, but he had no desire to revisit that painful area yet. "I know Mom would have hated to hear that excuse, but that's just the way things are. Well, when I saw your name on the door, I just wanted to drop by to say hi," he told her, adding, "Stop by the office sometime when you get a chance and we'll talk some more about Mom," he promised.

"Yes, indeed," Maizie replied.

As well as other things, she added silently as she watched Christopher walk away, anticipation welling in her chest. *Wait until the girls hear about this.*

Chapter 1

Okay, how did it get to be so late?

The exasperated, albeit rhetorical, question echoed almost tauntingly in her brain as Lily Langtry hurried through her house, checking to make sure she hadn't left any of her ground-floor windows open or her back door unlocked. There hadn't been any break-ins in her neighborhood, but she lived alone and felt that you could never be too careful.

The minutes felt as if they were racing by.

There was a time when she was not only on time but early for everything from formal appointments to the everyday events that took place in her life. But that was before her mother had passed away, before she was all alone and the only one who was in charge of the details of her life.

It seemed to her that even when she was taking care of her mother and holding down the two jobs that paying off her mother's medical bills necessitated, she had usually been far more organized and punctual than she was these days. Now that there was only one of her, in essence only one person to be responsible for, her ability to be on top of things seemed to have gone right out the window. If she intended to be ready by eight, in her mind she had to shoot for seven-thirty—and even that didn't always pan out the way she hoped it would.

This morning she'd told herself she would be out the door by seven. It was now eight-ten and she was just stepping into her high heels.

"Finally," she mumbled as she grabbed her bag and launched herself out the front door while simultaneously searching for her keys. The latter were currently eluding detection somewhere within the nether regions of her oversize purse.

Preoccupied, engaged in the frantic hunt that was making her even later than she already was, Lily wasn't looking where she was going.

Which was why she almost stepped on him.

Looking back, in her defense, she hadn't been expecting anything to be on her doorstep, much less a moving black ball of fur that yipped pathetically when her foot came down on his paw.

Jumping backward, Lily's hand went protectively over her chest to contain the heart that felt as if it was about to leap out of it. Lily dropped her purse at the same time.

Containing more things in it than the average overstuffed suitcase, the purse came down with a thud, further frightening the already frightened black ball of fur—which she now saw was a Labrador puppy.

But instead of running, as per the puppy manual, the large-dog-in-training began to lick her shoe.

Since the high heels Lily had selected to wear this morning were open-toe sandals, the upshot was that the puppy was also licking her toes. The end result of that was that the fast-moving little pink tongue was tickling her toes at the same time.

Surprised, stunned, as well as instantly smitten, Lily crouched down to the puppy's level, her demanding schedule temporarily put on hold.

"Are you lost?" she asked the puppy.

Since she was now down to his level, the black Labrador puppy abandoned her shoes and began to lick her face instead. Had there been a hard part to Lily's heart, it would have turned to utter mush as she completely capitulated, surrendering any semblance of control to her unexpected invader.

When she finally rose back up to her feet, Lily looked in both directions along the residential through street where she lived to see if anyone was running up or down the block, frantically searching for a lost pet.

It was apparent that no one was since all she saw was Mr. Baker across the street getting into his midlife-crisis vehicle—a sky-blue Corvette—which he drove to work every morning.

Since it wasn't moving, Lily took no note of the beige sedan parked farther down the block and across the street. Nor did she notice the older woman who was slouched down in the driver's seat.

The puppy appeared to be all alone.

She looked back at the puppy, who was back to licking her shoes. Pulling first one foot back, then the other, she only succeeded in drawing the dog into her house because the Labrador's attention was completely focused on her shoes.

"Looks like your family hasn't realized that you're missing yet," she told the puppy.

The Lab glanced up, cocking his head as if he was hanging on her every word. Lily couldn't help wondering if the animal understood her. She knew people who maintained that dogs only understood commands that had been drilled into their heads, but she had her doubts about that. This one was actually making eye contact and she was *certain* that he was taking in every word.

"I have to go to work," she told her fuzzy, uninvited guest.

The Labrador continued watching her as if she was the only person in the whole world. Lily knew when she'd lost a battle.

She sighed and stepped back even farther into her foyer, allowing the puppy access to her house.

"Oh, all right, you can come in and stay until I get back," she told the puppy, surrendering to the warm brown eyes that were staring up at her so intently.

If she was letting the animal stay here, she had to leave it something to eat and drink, she realized. Turning on her heel, Lily hurried back the kitchen to leave the puppy a few last-minute survival items.

She filled a soup bowl full of water and extracted a few slices of roast beef she'd picked up from the supermarket deli on her way home last night.

Lily placed the latter on a napkin and put both bowl and napkin on the floor.

"This should hold you until I get back," she informed the puppy. Looking down, she saw that the puppy, who she'd just assumed would follow her to a food source, was otherwise occupied. He was busy gnawing on one of the legs of her kitchen chair. "Hey!" she cried. "Stop that!"

The puppy went right on gnawing until she physically separated him from the chair. He looked up at her, clearly confused.

In her house for less than five minutes and the Labrador puppy had already presented her with a dilemma, Lily thought.

"Oh, God, you're teething, aren't you? If I leave you here, by the time I get back it'll look like a swarm of locusts had come through, won't it?" She knew the answer to that one. Lily sighed. It was true what they said, no good deed went unpunished. "Well, you can't stay here, then." Lily looked around the kitchen and the small family room just beyond. Almost all the furniture, except for the TV monitor, was older than she was. "I don't have any money for new furniture."

As if he understood that he was about to be put out again, the puppy looked up at her and then began to whine.

Pathetically.

Softhearted to begin with, Lily found that she was

no match for the sad little four-footed fur ball. Closing the door on him would be akin to abandoning the puppy in a snowdrift.

"All right, all right, all right, you can come with me," she cried, giving in. "Maybe someone at work will have a suggestion as to what I can do with you."

Lily stood for a minute, studying the puppy warily. Would it bite her if she attempted to pick it up? Her experience with dogs was limited to the canines she saw on television. After what she'd just witnessed, she knew that she definitely couldn't leave the puppy alone in her house. At the same time, she did have the uneasy feeling that the Labrador wasn't exactly trained to be obedient yet.

Still, trained or not, she felt as if she should at least *try* to get the puppy to follow her instructions. So she walked back over to the front door. The puppy was watching her every move intently, but remained exactly where he was. Lily tried patting her leg three times in short, quick succession. The puppy cocked its head, as if to say, *Now what?*

"C'mon, boy, come here," Lily called to him, patting her leg again, this time a little more urgently. To her relief—as well as surprise—this time the puppy came up to her without any hesitation.

Opening the front door, Lily patted her leg again— and was rewarded with the same response. The puppy came up to her side—the side she'd just patted—his eager expression all but shouting, *Okay, I'm here. Now what?*

Lily currently had no answer for that, but she hoped to within the hour.

"Hey, I don't remember anyone declaring that this was 'bring your pet to work' day," Alfredo Delgado, one of the chefs that Theresa Manetti employed at her catering company, quipped when Lily walked into the storefront office. She was holding a makeshift leash, fashioned out of rope. The black Lab was on the other end of the leash, ready to give the office a thorough investigation the moment the other end of the leash was dropped.

Theresa walked out of her small inner office and regarded the animal, her expression completely unfathomable.

"I'm sorry I'm late," Lily apologized to the woman who wrote out her checks. "I ran into a snag."

"From here it looks like the snag is following you," Theresa observed.

She glanced expectantly at the young woman she'd taken under her wing a little more than a year ago. That was when she'd hired Lily as her pastry chef after discovering that Lily could create delicacies so delicious, they could make the average person weep. But, softhearted woman that she was, Theresa hadn't taken her on because of her skills so much as because Lily's mother had recently passed away, leaving her daughter all alone in the world. Theresa, like her friends Maizie and Cecilia, had a great capacity for sympathy.

Lily flushed slightly now, her cheeks growing a soft shade of pink.

"I'm sorry, he was just there on my doorstep this morning when I opened the door. I couldn't just leave him there to roam the streets. If I came home tonight and found out that someone had run him over, I wouldn't be able to live with myself."

"Why didn't you just leave him at your place?" Alfredo asked, curious. "That's what I would have done." He volunteered this course of action while bending down, scratching the puppy behind its ears.

"I normally would have done that, too," Lily answered. "But there was one thing wrong with that—he apparently sees the world as one giant chew toy."

"So you brought him here," Theresa concluded. It was neither a question nor an accusation, just a statement of the obvious. A bemused smile played on the older woman's lips as she regarded the animal. "Just make sure he stays out of the kitchen."

Lily gestured around the area, hoping Theresa would see things her way. This was all temporary. "Everything here's made out of metal. His little teeth can't do any damage," she pointed out, then looked back at Theresa hopefully. "Can he stay—just for today?" Lily emphasized.

Theresa pretended to think the matter over—as if she hadn't had a hand in the puppy's sudden magical appearance on her pastry chef's doorstep. After Maizie had mentioned that their late friend's son was opening up his animal hospital two doors down from her real estate office and went on to present him as a possible new candidate for their very unique service, Theresa had suggested getting Christopher together with Lily.

She'd felt that the young woman could use something positive happening to her and had been of that opinion for a while now.

The search for a way to bring the two together in a so-called "natural" fashion was quick and fruitful when, as a sidebar, Cecilia had casually asked if either she or Maizie knew of anyone looking to adopt a puppy. Her dog, Princess, had given birth to eight puppies six weeks ago, and the puppies needed to be placed before "they start eating me out of house and home," Cecilia had told her friends.

It was as if lightning had struck. Everything had fallen into place after that.

Theresa was aware of Lily's approximate time of departure and had informed Cecilia. The latter proceeded to leave the puppy—deliberately choosing the runt of the litter—on Lily's doorstep. Cecilia left the rambunctious puppy there not once but actually several times before she hit upon the idea of bribing the little dog with a large treat, which she proceeded to embed in the open weave of the welcome mat.

Even so, Cecilia had just barely made it back to her sedan before Lily had swung open her front door.

Once inside the catering shop, the puppy proceeded to make himself at home while he sniffed and investigated every inch of the place.

Lily watched him like a hawk, afraid of what he might do next. In her opinion, Theresa was a wonderful person, but everyone had their breaking point and she didn't want the puppy to find Theresa's.

"Um, Theresa," Lily began as she shooed the puppy

away from a corner where a number of boxes were piled up, "how old are your grandchildren now?"

Theresa slanted a deliberately wary look at the younger woman. "Why?"

Lily smiled a little too broadly as she made her sales pitch. "Wouldn't they love to have a puppy? You could surprise them with Jonathan."

Theresa raised an eyebrow quizzically. "Jonathan?" she repeated.

Lily gestured at the Labrador. "The puppy. I had to call him something," she explained.

"You named him. That means you're already attached to him," Alfredo concluded with a laugh, as if it was a done deal.

There was something akin to a panicky look on Lily's face. She didn't want to get attached to anything. She was still trying to get her life on track after losing her mother. Taking on something new—even a pet— was out of the question.

"No, it doesn't," Lily protested. "I just couldn't keep referring to the puppy as 'it.'"

"Sure you could," Alfredo contradicted with a knowing attitude. "That you didn't want to means that you've already bonded with the little ball of flying fur."

"No, no bonding," Lily denied firmly, then made her final argument on the matter. "I don't even know *how* to bond with an animal. The only pet I ever had was a goldfish and Seymour only lived for two days." Which firmly convinced her that she had absolutely no business trying to care for a pet of any kind.

Alfredo obviously didn't see things in the same light

that she did. "Then it's high time you got back into the saddle, Lily. You can't accept defeat that easily," he told her.

Finding no support in that quarter, Lily appealed to her boss. "Theresa—"

Theresa placed a hand supportively on the younger woman's shoulder. "I'm with Alfredo on this," she told Lily. "Besides," she pointed out, "you can't give the dog away right now."

"Why not?" Lily asked.

Theresa was the soul of innocence as she explained, "Because his owner might be out looking for him even as we speak."

Lily blew out a breath. She'd forgotten about that. "Good point," she admitted, chagrined by her over-sight. "I'll make flyers and put them up."

"In the meantime," Theresa continued as she thoughtfully regarded the black ball of fur and paws, "I suggest you make sure the little guy's healthy."

"How do I go about doing that?" Lily asked, completely clueless when it came to the care of anything other than humans. She freely admitted to having a brown thumb. Anything that was green and thriving would begin to whither and die under her care—which was why she didn't attempt to maintain a garden anymore. The thought of caring for a pet brought a chill to her spine.

"Well, for starters," Theresa told her, "if I were you I would bring him to a veterinarian."

"A vet?" she looked at the puppy that now appeared to be utterly enamored with Alfredo. The chef was scratching Jonathan behind the ears and along his nose, sending the Labrador to seventh heaven. "He doesn't look sick. Is that really necessary?"

"Absolutely," Theresa answered without a drop of hesitation. "Just think, if someone is looking for him, how would it look if you handed over a sick dog? If they wanted to, they could turn around and sue you for negligence."

Lily felt hemmed in. The last thing she wanted was to have to take care of something, to get involved with a living, breathing entity.

Eyeing the puppy uncertainly, Lily sighed. "I should have never opened the door this morning."

"Oh, how can you say that? Look at this adorable little face," Theresa urged, cupping the puppy's chin and turning his head toward Lily.

"I'm trying not to," Lily answered honestly. But Theresa was right. She didn't want to chance something happening to the puppy while it was temporarily in her care. Emphasis on the word *temporarily,* she thought. "Okay, how do I go about finding an animal doctor who's good, but not expensive? I wouldn't know where to start," she admitted, looking to Theresa for guidance since the woman had been the one to bring up the matter of a vet to begin with.

Theresa's smile bordered on being beatific. "Well, as luck would have it, I happen to know of one who just opened up a new practice a few doors down from one of my best friends. She took her dog to him and told me that he performed nothing short of a miracle on Lazarus." The fact that Maizie didn't have a dog named

Lazarus, or a dog named anything else for that matter, was an unimportant, minor detail in the grand scheme of things. As a rule, Theresa didn't lie, but there were times—such as now—when rules were meant to be bent if not altogether broken. "Why don't I call her to get his phone number for you?" she suggested, looking at Lily.

That sounded like as good a plan as any, she supposed. "Sure, why not?" Lily replied with a vague shrug, resigned to this course of action. "What do I have to lose? It's only money, right?"

Theresa knew that times were tight for the younger woman. She saw what she was about to propose as an investment in Lily's future happiness.

"I tell you what. We've had a great month. I'll pay for 'Jonathan's' visit," she offered, petting the eager puppy on the head. The dog stopped roaming around long enough to absorb the head pat and then went back to sniffing the entire area for a second time. "Consider it my gift to you."

"How about me?" Alfredo said, pretending to feel left out. "Got any gifts for me, boss?"

"I'll pay for your visit to the vet, too, if you decide you need to go," Theresa quipped as she retreated into her office.

Once inside, Theresa carefully closed the door and crossed to her desk. She didn't care for cell phones. The connection was never as clear as a landline in her opinion. Picking up the receiver, she quickly dialed the number she wanted to reach.

Maizie picked up on the second ring. "Connors' Realty."

"Houston, we have liftoff," Theresa announced in what sounded like a stage whisper to her own ear.

"Theresa?" Maizie asked uncertainly. "Is that you?"

"Of course it's me. Who else would call you and say that?"

"I haven't the vaguest idea. Theresa, I mean this in the kindest way, but you've definitely been watching too many movies, woman. Now, what is it that you're trying to say?"

Impatience wove through every word. "That Lily is bringing the puppy to Frances's son."

"Then why didn't you just say so?"

"Because it sounds so ordinary that way," Theresa complained.

"Sometimes, Theresa, ordinary is just fine. Is she bringing the puppy in today?"

"That's what I urged her to do."

"Perfect," Maizie said with heartfelt enthusiasm. "Nothing like being two doors down from young love about to unfold."

"I don't see how that's any different from Houston, we have liftoff," Theresa protested.

"Maybe it's not, Theresa," Maizie conceded, not because she thought she was wrong, but because she knew Theresa liked to be right. "Maybe it's not."

Chapter 2

The first thing that struck Christopher when he walked into Exam Room 3 was that the woman was standing rather than sitting. She was clearly uneasy in her present situation. The puppy with her appeared to have the upper hand.

Smiling at her, he made a quick assessment before he spoke. "This isn't your dog, is it?"

Lily looked at the veterinarian, stunned. "How can you tell?" she asked.

All she had given the receptionist out front was her name. The dark-haired woman had immediately nodded and told her that "Mrs. Manetti called to say you'd be coming in." The young woman at the desk, Erika, had then proceeded to call over one of the veterinary aides, who promptly ushered her and Jonathan into an exam room. As far as she knew, no details about her nonrelationship to the animal she'd brought in had been given.

Maybe she was wrong, Lily realized belatedly.

"Did Theresa tell you that?" she asked.

"Theresa?" Christopher repeated, confused.

Okay, wrong guess, Lily decided. She shook her head. "Never mind," she told him, then repeated her initial question. "How can you tell he's not mine?" Was there some sort of look that pet owners had? Some sort of inherent sign that the civilian non–pet owners obviously seemed to lack?

Christopher nodded toward the antsy puppy who looked as if he was ready to race around all four of the exam room's corners almost simultaneously. "He has a rope around his neck," Christopher pointed out.

He probably equated that with cruelty to animals, Lily thought. "Necessity is the mother of invention," she told him, then explained her thinking. "I made a loop and tied a rope to it because I didn't have any other way to make sure that he would follow me."

There was a stirring vulnerability about the young woman with the long, chestnut hair. It pulled him in. Christopher looked at her thoughtfully, taking care not to allow his amusement at her action to show. Some people were thin-skinned and would construe that as being laughed at. Nothing could have been further from the truth.

"No leash," he concluded.

"No leash," Lily confirmed. Then, because she thought that he needed more information to go on— and she had no idea what was and wasn't important when it came to assessing the health of a puppy—she went on to tell the good-looking vet, "I found him on my doorstep—I tripped over him, actually."

The way she said it led Christopher to his next conclusion. "And I take it that you don't know who he belongs to?"

"No, I don't. If I did," Lily added quickly, "I would have brought him back to his owner. But I've never seen him before this morning."

"Then how do you know the dog's name is Jonathan?" As far as he could see, the puppy had no dog tags.

She shrugged almost as if she was dismissing the question. "I don't."

Christopher looked at her a little more closely. Okay, he thought, something was definitely off here. "When you brought him in, you told my receptionist that his name was Jonathan."

"That's what I call him," she responded quickly, then explained, "I didn't want to just refer to him as 'puppy' or 'hey, you' so I gave him a name." The young woman shrugged and the simple gesture struck him as being somewhat hapless. "He seems to like it. At least he looks up at me when I call him by that name."

Christopher didn't want her being under the wrong impression, even if there was no real harm in thinking that way.

"The right intonation does that," he told Lily. "I'll let you in on a secret," Christopher went on, lowering his voice as if this was a guarded confession he was about to impart. "He'd respond to 'Refrigerator' if you said it the same way."

To prove his point, Christopher moved around the exam table until he was directly behind the puppy. Once there, he called, "Refrigerator!" and Jonathan turned his head around to look at him, taking a few follow-up steps in order to better see who was calling him.

His point proven, Christopher glanced at the woman. "See?"

She nodded, but in Christopher's opinion the woman appeared more overwhelmed than convinced. He had been born loving animals, and as far back as he could remember, his world had been filled with critters large and small. He had an affinity for them, something that his mother had passed on to him.

He was of the mind that everyone should have a pet and that pets improved their owners' quality of life—as well as vice versa.

"Just how long have you and Jonathan been together?" he asked. His guess was that it couldn't have been too long because she and the puppy hadn't found their proper rhythm yet.

Lily glanced at her watch before she answered the vet. "In ten minutes it'll be three hours—or so," she replied.

"Three hours," he repeated.

"Or so," she added in a small voice. Christopher paused for a moment. Studying the petite, attractive young woman before him, his eyes crinkled with the smile that was taking over his face.

"You've never had a dog before, have you?" The

question was rhetorical. He should have seen this from the very start. The woman definitely did not seem at ease around the puppy.

"It shows?" She didn't know which she felt more, surprised or embarrassed by the question.

"You look like you're afraid of Jonathan," he told her.

"I'm not," she protested with a bit too much feeling. Then, when the vet made no comment but continued looking at her, she dialed her defensiveness back a little. "Well, not entirely." And then, after another beat, she amended that by saying, "He's cute and everything, but he has these teeth…"

Christopher suppressed a laugh. "Most dogs do. At least," he corrected himself, thinking of a neglected dog he'd treated at the city's animal shelter just the other day, "the healthy ones do."

She wasn't expressing herself correctly, Lily realized. But then, communication was sometimes hard for her. Her skill lay in the pastries she created, not in getting her thoughts across to people she didn't know.

Lily tried again. "But Jonathan's always biting,"

"There's a reason for that. He's teething," Christopher told her. "When I was a kid, I had a cousin like that," he confided. "Chewed on everything and everyone until all his baby teeth came in."

As if to illustrate what he was saying, she saw the puppy attempt to sink his teeth into the vet's hand. Instead of yelping, Christopher laughed, rubbed the Labrador's head affectionately. Before Jonathan could try to bite him a second time, the vet pulled a rubber squeaky toy out of his lab coat pocket. Distracted, Jonathan went after the toy—a lime-green octopus with wiggly limbs.

High-pitched squeaks filled the air in direct proportion to the energy the puppy was expending chewing on his new toy.

Just for a second, there was a touch of envy in her eyes when she raised them to his face, Christopher thought. Her cheeks were also turning a very light shade of pink.

"You probably think I'm an idiot," Lily told him.

The last thing he wanted was for her to think he was judging her—harshly or otherwise. But he could admit he was attracted to her.

"What I think," he corrected, "is that you might need a little help and guidance here."

Oh, God, yes, she almost exclaimed out loud, managing to bite the gush of words back at the last moment. Instead, she asked hopefully, "You have a book for me to read?"

Christopher inclined his head. He had something a little more personal and immediate in mind. "If you'd like to read one, I have several I could recommend," he conceded. "But personally, I've always found it easier when I had something visual to go on."

"Like a DVD?" she asked, not altogether sure what he meant by his statement.

Christopher grinned. "More like a *P-E-R-S-O-N.*"

For just a second, Lily found herself getting caught up in the vet's grin. Something akin to a knot—or was that a butterfly?—twisted around in her stomach. Rousing herself, Lily blinked, certain that she'd somehow misunderstood the veterinarian.

From his handsome, dimpled face, to his dirty-blond hair, to his broad shoulders, the man was a symphony of absolute charm and she was rather accustomed to being almost invisible around people who came across so dynamically. The more vibrant they were, the more understated she became, as if she was shrinking in the sunlight of their effervescence.

Given that, it seemed almost implausible to her that Christopher was saying what it sounded as if he was saying. But in the interest of clarity, she had to ask, "Are you volunteering to help me with the dog?"

To her surprise, rather than appearing annoyed or waving away the question entirely, he laughed. "If you have to ask, I must be doing it wrong, but yes, I'm volunteering." Then he backtracked slightly as if another thought had occurred to him. "Unless, of course, your husband or boyfriend or significant other has some objections to my mentoring you through the hallowed halls of puppy ownership."

Her self-image—that of being a single person—was so ingrained in her that Lily just assumed she came across that way. That the vet made such a stipulation seemed almost foreign to her.

"There's no husband or boyfriend or significant other to object to anything," she informed the man.

She was instantly rewarded with the flash of another dimpled grin. "Oh, well then, unless you have any objections, I can accompany you to the local dog park this weekend for some pointers."

She hadn't even been aware that there was a dog park anywhere, much less one here in Bedford, but she kept that lack of knowledge to herself.

"Although," the vet was saying, "I do have one thing to correct already."

Lily braced herself for criticism as she asked, "What am I doing wrong?"

Christopher shook his head. "Not you, me," he told her affably. "I just said puppy ownership."

She was still in the dark as to where this was going. "Yes, I know, I heard you."

"Well, that's actually wrong," he told her. "That phrase would indicate that you owned the puppy when in reality—"

"The puppy owns me?" she guessed. Where else could he be headed with this? She could very easily see the puppy taking over.

But Christopher shook his head. "You own each other, and sometimes even those lines get a little blurred," he admitted, then went on to tell her, "You do it right and your pet becomes part of your family and you become part of his family."

For a moment, Lily forgot to resist experiencing the exact feelings that the vet was talking about. Instead, just for that one sliver of time, she allowed herself to believe that she was part of something larger than just herself, and it promised to ease the loneliness she was so acutely aware of whenever she wasn't at work.

Whenever she left the people she worked with and returned to her house and her solitary existence.

The next moment, she forced herself to lock down

and pull back, retreating into the Spartan world she'd resided in ever since she'd lost her mother.

"That sounds like something I once read in a children's book," she told him politely.

"Probably was," Christopher willingly conceded. "Children see the world far more honestly than we do. They don't usually have to make up excuses or search for ways to explain away what they feel—they just *feel,*" he said with emphasis as well as no small amount of admiration.

And then he got back to the business at hand. "Since you can count the length of your relationship with Jonathan in hours, I take it that means you have no information regarding his rather short history."

She shook her head. "None whatsoever, I'm afraid," she confessed.

Christopher took it all in stride. He turned his attention to his four-footed patient. "Well, I'm making a guess as to his age—"

Curious about the sort of procedures that involved, she asked, "How can you do that?"

"His teeth," Christopher pointed out. "The same teeth he's been trying out on you," he added with an indulgent smile that seemed incredibly sexy to her. "He's got his baby teeth. He appears to be a purebred Labrador, so there aren't any stray factors to take into account regarding his size and growth pattern. Given his teeth and the size of his paws in comparison to the rest of him, I'd say he's no more than five or six weeks old. And I think I can also safely predict that he's going to be a *very* large dog, given the size of the paws he's going to grow into," the vet concluded.

She looked down at the puppy. Jonathan seemed to be falling all over himself in an attempt to engage the vet's attention. No matter which way she sliced it, the puppy *was* cute—as long as he wasn't actively biting her.

"Well, I guess that's something I'm not going to find out," she murmured, more to herself than to the man on the other side of the exam table.

Christopher watched her with deep curiosity in his eyes. "Do you mind if I ask why not?"

"No."

"No?" he repeated, not really certain what the answer pertained to.

Her mind was *really* working in slow motion today, Lily thought, upbraiding herself. "I mean no, I don't mind you asking."

When there was no further information following that up, he coaxed, "And the answer to my question is—?"

"Oh."

More blushing accompanied the single-syllable word. She really was behaving like the proverbial village idiot. Lily upbraided herself. What in heaven's name had come over her? It was like her brain had been dipped in molasses and couldn't rinse itself off in order to return to its normal speed—or even the bare semblance of going half-speed.

"Because as soon as I leave here with Jonathan, I'm going to make some flyers and post them around town," she told the vet. She was rather a fair sketch artist when she put her mind to it and planned to create a likeness of this puppy to use on the poster. "Somebody's got to be out looking for him."

"If you're not planning on keeping him, why did you bring him in to be examined?"

She would have thought that he, as a vet, would have thought the reason was self-explanatory. She told him anyway.

"Well, I didn't want to take a chance that there might be something wrong with him. I wouldn't want to neglect taking care of something just because I wasn't keeping it," she answered.

"So you're like a drive-by Good Samaritan?"

She shrugged off what might have been construed as a compliment. From her point of view, there was really nothing to compliment. She was only doing what anyone else in her place would do—if they had any kind of a conscience, Lily silently qualified.

Out loud, she merely replied, "Yes, something like that."

"I guess 'Jonathan' here was lucky it was your front step he picked to camp out on." He crouched down to the dog's level. "Aren't you, boy?" he asked with affection, stroking the puppy's head again.

As before, the dog reacted with enthusiasm, driving the top of his head into the vet's hand as well as leaning in to rub his head against Christopher's side.

Watching the puppy, Lily thought that the Labrador was trying to meld with the vet.

"Tell you what," Christopher proposed after giving the puppy a quick examination and rising back up again, "since he seems healthy enough, why don't we hold off until after this weekend before continuing with this exam? Then, if no one responds to your 'found' flyers, you bring Jonathan here back and I'll start him out on his series of immunizations."

"Immunizations?" Lily questioned.

By the sound of her voice, it seemed to Christopher that the shapely young woman hadn't given that idea any thought at all. But then she'd admitted that she'd never had a pet before, so her lack of knowledge wasn't really that unusual.

"Dogs need to be immunized, just like kids," he told her.

Somewhere in the back of her mind, a stray fact fell into place. She recalled having heard that once or twice. "Right," she murmured.

Christopher smiled in response to her tacit agreement. "And," he continued, "if you don't get a call from a frantic owner by this weekend, why don't we make a date to meet at the park on Sunday, say about eleven o'clock?" he further suggested.

"A date," she echoed.

Given the way her eyes had widened, the word *date* was not the one he should have used, Christopher realized. It had been carelessly thrown out there on his part.

Very smoothly, Christopher extricated himself from what could potentially be a very sticky situation. "Yes, but I have a feeling that Jonathan might not be comfortable with my advertising the situation, so for simplicity's sake—and possibly to save Jonathan's reputation," he amended with a wink that had her stomach doing an unexpected jackknife dive off the high board—again, "why don't we just call the meeting a training session?"

Training session.

That phrase conjured up an image that involved a great deal of work. "You'd do that?" she asked incredulously.

"Call it a training session? Sure."

"No, I mean actually volunteer to show me how to train Jonathan—provided I still have him," she qualified.

"I thought that part was clear," Christopher said with a smile.

But Lily had already moved on to another question. "Why?"

"Why did I think that was clear?" he guessed. "Because I couldn't say it any more straightforwardly than that."

She really *did* need to learn how to express herself better. "No, I mean why would you volunteer to show me how to train the dog?"

"Because, from personal experience, I know that living with an untrained dog can be hell—for both the dog and the person. Training the dog is just another name for mutual survival," he told her.

"But aren't you busy?" she asked him, feeling guilty about taking the vet away from whatever he had planned for the weekend. Grateful though she was, she wondered if she came across that needy or inept to him.

Christopher thought of the unopened boxes that were throughout his house—and had been for the past three months—waiting to be emptied and their contents put away. He'd moved back into his old home, never having gotten around to selling it after his mother had passed away. Now it only seemed like the natural place to return to. But the boxes were taunting him. Helping this woman find her footing with the overactive puppy gave him a good excuse to procrastinate a little longer.

"No more than the average human being," he told her.

"If the dog is still with me by the weekend," she prefaced, "I still can't pay you for the training session. At least, not all at once. But we could arrange for some sort of a payment schedule," she suggested, not wanting to seem ungrateful.

"I don't remember asking to be paid," Christopher pointed out.

"Then why would you go out of your way like that to help me?" she asked, bewildered.

"Call it earning a long-overdue merit badge."

She opened her mouth to protest that she wasn't a charity case, but just then one of his assistants knocked on the door.

"Doctor, your patients are piling up," she said through the door.

"I'll be right there," he told the assistant, then turned to Lily. "I'll see you at the dog park on Sunday at eleven," he said. "Oh, and if you have any questions, don't hesitate to call. I can be reached here during the day and on my cell after hours."

"You take calls after hours?" Lily asked him, surprised.

"I've found that pets, like kids, don't always conveniently get sick between the hours of eight and six," he told her, opening the door.

"Wait, how much do I owe you for today?" she asked, forgetting that there was a receptionist at the front desk who would most likely be the one taking care of any and all charges for today's visit.

Christopher started to head out. He could hear his next patient barking impatiently from all the way down the hall. Without breaking stride, he told Lily, "I don't charge for conversations."

He was gone before she could protest and remind him that he *had* given Jonathan a cursory examination.

Chapter 3

Lily was certain she hadn't heard the man correctly. Granted, Jonathan hadn't received any shots or had any specimens taken for a lab workup, but the veterinarian *had* spent at least twenty minutes talking to her about the puppy and he *had* looked the Labrador over. In her book, that sort of thing had to constitute an "office visit."

Didn't it?

While she was more than willing to do favors for people, Lily had never liked being on the receiving end of a favor because it put her in the position of owing someone something. She was grateful to the vet for taking an interest in the puppy that was temporarily in her care and she was happy that he'd offered to instruct her on how to maintain a peaceful coexistence with the ball of fur while the puppy *was* in her care, but she wasn't about to accept any of that for free.

It wouldn't be right.

Taking a breath, Lily extracted her checkbook from her jumbled purse and then braced herself for her next confrontation with the puppy.

Doing her best to sound stern, or at least authoritative, she looked down at Jonathan and said, "We're going out now, Jonathan. Try not to yank me all over this time, all right?"

If the puppy understood what she was asking, then he chose to ignore it because the minute she opened the door, he all but flew out. Since the rope she had tethered to the Labrador was currently also wrapped around her hand, the puppy, perforce, came to an abrupt, almost comical halt two seconds later. He'd run out of slack.

The puppy gave her what seemed to Lily to be a reproving look—if puppies could look at someone reprovingly.

Maybe she was reading too much into it, Lily told herself.

Still, she felt compelled to tell the puppy, "I asked you not to run."

Making her way out to the front of the clinic, Lily saw the receptionist, Erika, looking at her. She flushed a little in response. "You probably think I'm crazy, talking to the dog."

Erika's dark eyes sparkled. "On the contrary, most pet owners would think you're crazy if you didn't. They understand us," she explained with easy confidence, nodding toward Jonathan. "They just sometimes choose not to listen. In that way, they're really no different than kids," Erika added. "Except that pets are probably more loyal in the long run."

"I'm not planning for a 'long run,'" Lily told the receptionist. "I'm just minding this puppy until his owner turns up to claim him," she explained. Placing her checkbook on her side of the counter, she opened it to the next blank check, then took out her pen. All the while, Jonathan was tugging on the rope, trying to separate himself from her. "Okay, how much do I make the check out for?" She flashed a somewhat shy smile at the receptionist. "I warn you, it might be slightly illegible."

Jonathan was tugging on his makeshift leash, desperately wanting to escape from the clinic—and in all likelihood, from her, as well. Legible writing under those circumstances went out the window.

Erika glanced at the paperwork that had just been sent to her computer monitor a moment ago. She looked up at the woman on the other side of her desk. "Nothing," she answered.

That couldn't be right. Could the vet really have been serious about not charging her? "For the visit," Lily prompted.

"Nothing," Erika repeated.

"But Dr. Whitman saw the dog," Lily protested.

Erika looked at the screen again.

"Well, he's not charging you for seeing the dog," Erika told her. "But now that I look, I see that he does have one thing written down here," the receptionist informed her, reading the column marked "special instructions."

Lily could feel her arm being elongated by the second. For a little guy, the Labrador was uncommonly strong in her opinion. She tugged him back. "What?" she asked the receptionist.

Instead of answering her immediately, Erika said, "Just a minute," and opened the large side drawer. She started rummaging through it. It took her a minute to locate what she was searching for.

"Dr. Whitman wants me to give you this."

"This" turned out to be not one thing but two things. One item was a small, bright blue braided collar made to fit the neck of a dog just about the puppy's size and the other was a matching bright blue braided leash.

Erika placed both on the counter in front of Jonathan's keeper.

"It's a collar and leash," Erika prompted when the woman with Jonathan continued just to look at the two items. "Dr. Whitman has a 'thing' against ropes. He's afraid that a pet might wind up choking itself," she confided.

Given the Labrador's propensity for dashing practically in two directions at the same time, getting a sturdy leash that wouldn't bite into his tender throat did make sense to her, Lily thought. She certainly wasn't about to refuse to accept the collar and leash.

"Okay, so what do I owe you for the collar and leash?" she asked.

The answer turned out to be the same. "Nothing," Erika replied.

She'd heard of nonprofit, but this was ridiculous. "They have to cost *something*," Lily insisted.

All of her life, she'd had to pay, and sometimes pay dearly, for everything she had ever needed or used. Taking something, whether it involved a service that was rendered or an item that was given to her, without the benefit of payment just didn't seem right to Lily. It also offended her sense of independence.

"Just pennies," Erika told her. When she looked at the young woman skeptically, the receptionist explained, "Dr. Whitman orders them practically by the crate full. He likes to give them out. Just think of it as a gesture of goodwill," Erika advised.

What she thought of it as was a gesture of charity placing her in debt, however minor the act seemed to the vet.

Lily tried one last time. "You're sure I can't pay you, make a contribution to your needy-dog fund, *something?*"

"I'm sure," Erika replied. She pointed to her monitor as if to drive the point home. "It says right here, 'no charge.'" The woman hit two keys and the printer on the stand behind her came to life, spitting out a hard copy of what was on her monitor. She handed what amounted to a nonreceipt to the puppy's keeper. "See?" Erika asked with a smile.

Lily took the single sheet of paper. Unable to pay for either the office visit or the two items now in her possession, all she could do was say thank you—which she did.

"No problem," Erika replied. She got up from her desk and came around to the other side, where the Labrador stood fiercely yanking against the rope.

"Why don't I put the collar on him while you try to hold him in place?" Erika suggested. "This way, he won't make a break for it."

"You're a godsend," Lily said with a relieved sigh. She'd been wondering just how to manage to exchange the rope for the collar and leash she'd just been given without having the puppy make a mad dash for freedom.

"No, just an animal clinic receptionist who's been at it for a while," Erika corrected modestly.

She had the collar on the puppy and the leash connected to it within a couple of minutes. Only at that point did she undo the rope. The next moment, the rope hung limp and useless in Lily's hand.

Lily was quick to leave it on the desk.

Standing up, Erika told her, "You're ready to go." The words were no sooner out of her mouth than Jonathan made an urgent, insistent beeline for the front door. "I think Jonathan agrees," Erika said with a laugh. "Here, I'll hold the door open for you," she offered, striding quickly over to it.

The instant the door was opened and no longer presented an obstacle, the dog made a break for the outside world and freedom. Lily was nearly thrown off balance as he took her with him.

"Bye!" she called out, tossing the words over her shoulder as she trotted quickly in the dog's wake, trying hard to keep up and even harder to keep from falling. Jonathan seemed oblivious to any and all attempts to rein him in.

Erika shook her head as she closed the door and went

back to her desk. "I give them two weeks. A month, tops," she murmured to herself.

The second she and her energetic, furry companion returned to Theresa's catering shop, Lily found herself surrounded by everyone she worked with. They were all firing questions at her regarding Jonathan's visit to the new animal hospital. He was the center of attention and appeared to be enjoying himself, barking and licking the hands that were reaching out to pet him.

To her amazement, Lily discovered that of the small band of people who worked for Theresa's catering company, she was the only one who had never had a pet—if she discounted the two-day period, twenty years ago, during which time she had a live goldfish.

Consequently, while keeping Jonathan out of the kitchen area for practical reasons that in no small way involved the Board of Health's regulations, the puppy was allowed to roam freely about the rest of the storefront office. As a result, Jonathan was petted, played with, cooed over and fed unsparingly by everyone, including Theresa. He became the company's mascot in a matter of minutes.

Because their next catering event wasn't until the next evening, the atmosphere within the shop wasn't as hectic and tense as it could sometimes get. Alfredo and his crew were still in the planning and preparation stages for the next day's main menu. Zack Collins, Theresa's resident bartender, was out purchasing the wines and alcoholic beverages that were to be served at the celebration, and Lily was in the semifinal preparation stage, planning just what desserts to create for the occasion.

Checking on everyone's progress, Theresa observed that Lily was doing more than just planning. She was also baking a tray of what appeared to be lighter-than-air crème-filled pastries.

"Did you decide to do a dry run?" Theresa asked, coming up to the young woman.

"In a manner of speaking," Lily replied. Then, because Theresa was more like a mother to her than a boss, Lily paused for a moment and told the woman what was on her mind. "You know that vet you had me bring Jonathan to?"

Theresa's expression gave nothing away, even as her mind raced around, bracing for a problem or some sort of a hiccup in Maizie's plan.

"Yes?"

"He wouldn't let me pay him for the visit," Lily concluded with a perturbed frown.

"Really?" Theresa did her best to infuse the single word with surprise and wonder—rather than the triumphant pleasure, laced with hope, she was experiencing.

"Really," Lily repeated. "I don't like owing people," she continued.

"Honey, sometimes you just have to graciously accept things from other people," Theresa began. But Lily interrupted her.

"I know. That's why I'm doing this," she told Theresa, gesturing at the tray she'd just taken out of the oven. "I thought that since he was nice enough to 'gift' me with his knowledge by checking out Jonathan, I should return the favor and 'gift' him with what I do best."

By now, Theresa was all but beaming. Maizie had gotten it right again, she couldn't help thinking.

"Sounds perfectly reasonable to me," Theresa agreed. She glanced at her watch. It was getting to be close to four o'clock. Maizie had mentioned that Christopher closed the doors to the animal clinic at six. She didn't want Lily to miss encountering the vet. "Since we're not actively catering anything today, why don't you take a run back to the animal clinic and bring that vet your pastries while they're still warm from the oven?" Theresa suggested.

Lily flashed her boss a grateful smile since she was perfectly willing to do just that. But first she had to take care of a more-than-minor detail.

Lily looked around. "Where's Jonathan?"

"Meghan's keeping him occupied," Theresa assured her, referring to one of the servers she had in her permanent employ. In a pinch, the young, resourceful blonde also substituted as a bartender when Zack was otherwise occupied or unavailable. "Why?" She smiled broadly. "Are you worried about him?"

"I just didn't want to leave the puppy here on his own while I make a run to the vet's office." She didn't want to even *begin* to tally the amount of damage the little puppy could do in a very short amount of time.

"He's not on his own," Theresa contradicted. "There are approximately eight sets of eyes on that dog at all times. If anything, he might become paranoid. Go, bring your thank-you pastries to the vet. Sounds as if he might just have earned them," the older woman speculated.

At the last moment, Lily looked at her hesitantly. "If you don't mind," Lily qualified.

"I wouldn't be pushing you out the door if I minded," Theresa pointed out. "Now shoo!" she ordered, gesturing the pastry chef out the door.

She was gone before Theresa could finish saying the last word.

When the bell announced the arrival of yet another patient, Christopher had to consciously refrain from releasing a loud sigh. It wasn't that he minded seeing patients, because he didn't. He enjoyed it, even when he was being challenged or confounded by a pet's condition. Plus, his new practice took all his time, which he didn't mind. It was paperwork that he hated. Paperwork of any kind was tedious, even though he readily admitted that it needed to be done.

Which was why he had two different receptionists, one in the morning, one in the afternoon, to do the inputting and to keep track of things.

However, on occasion, when one or the other was away for longer than ten minutes, he took over and manned the desk, so to speak.

That was what he was currently doing because Erika had taken a quick run to the local take-out place in order to buy and bring back dinner for the office. He looked up from the keyboard to see just who had entered.

"You're back," Christopher said with surprise when he saw Lily coming in. The moment she stepped inside, she filled the waiting area with her unconscious, natural sexiness. Before he knew it, he found himself under her spell. "Is something wrong with Jonathan?" It was the first thing that occurred to him.

And then he noticed that she was carrying a rectangular pink cardboard box. Another animal to examine? No, that couldn't be it. There were no air holes punched into the box, which would mean, under normal circumstances, that it wasn't some stray white mouse or rat she was bringing to him.

"You brought me another patient?" he asked a little warily.

"What?" She saw that he was eyeing the box in her hand and realized belatedly what he had to be thinking. "Oh, this isn't anything to examine," she told him. "At least, not the way you mean."

He had no idea what that meant.

By now, the savory aroma wafting out of the box had reached him and he could feel his taste buds coming to attention.

"What *is* that?" he asked her, leaving the shelter of the reception desk and coming closer. He thought he detected the scent of cinnamon, among other things. "That aroma is nothing short of fantastic."

Lily smiled broadly. "Thank you."

He looked at her in confused surprise. "Is that you?" he asked, slightly bemused.

Was that some sort of new cologne, meant to arouse a man's appetites, the noncarnal variety? He could almost *feel* his mouth watering.

"Only in a manner of speaking," Lily replied with a laugh. When Christopher looked even further confused, she took pity on him and thrust the rectangular box at him. "These are for you—and your staff," she added in case he thought she was singling him out and trying to flirt with him—although she was certain he probably had to endure the latter on a regular basis. Men as good-looking as Christopher Whitman *never* went unnoticed. From his thick, straight dirty-blond hair, to his tall, lean body, to his magnetic blue eyes that seemed to look right *into* her, the man stood out in any crowd.

"It's just my small way of saying thank you," she added.

"You bought these for us?" Christopher asked, taking the box from her.

"No," Lily corrected, "I *made* these for you. I'm a pastry chef," she explained quickly, in case he thought she was just someone who had slapped together the first dessert recipe she came across on the internet. She wasn't altogether sure what prompted her, but she wanted him to know that in her own way she was a professional, too. "I work for a catering company," she added, then thought that she was probably blurting out more details than the man wanted to hear. "Anyway, since you wouldn't let me pay you, I wanted to do something nice for you. It's all-natural," she told him. "No artificial additives, no gluten, no nuts," she added, in case he was allergic to them the way her childhood best friend had been. "It's all perfectly safe," she assured him.

"Well, it smells absolutely terrific." He opened the

box and the aroma seemed to literally swirl all around him. "If I didn't know any better, I would have thought I'd died and gone to heaven," he told her.

"I'm told it tastes even better than it smells," she said rather shyly.

"Let's see if they're right." Christopher took out a pastry and slowly bit into it, as if afraid to disturb its delicate composition. His eyes widened and filled with pleasure. "Heaven has been confirmed," he told her before giving in and taking a second bite.

And then a third.

Chapter 4

Despite the fact that she really was enjoying watching the veterinarian consume the pastry she'd made, Lily did feel a little awkward just standing there. Any second now, someone would either come in with a pet that needed attention, or one of the doctor's assistants would emerge and the moment she was experiencing, watching him, would vanish.

It would be better all around if she left right now.

"Well, I just wanted to drop those off with you," Lily said, waving a hand toward the contents of the opened pink box. With that, she began to walk out of the clinic.

Christopher's mouth was presently occupied, involved in a love affair with the last bite of the pastry that he'd selected. Not wanting to rush the process, he also didn't want Lily to leave just yet. He held up his hand, mutely indicating that he wanted her to stay a moment longer.

"Wait." He managed to voice the urgent request just before he swallowed the last bite he'd taken.

Lily stopped just short of the front door. She shifted slightly as she waited for the vet to be able to speak, all the while wondering just why he would ask her to remain. Was he going to tell her that he'd changed his mind about charging her for today? Or had the man had second thoughts about his offer to meet her in the dog park on Sunday?

And why was she suddenly experiencing this feeling of dread if it was the latter?

"You really made these?" Christopher asked once he'd regained the use of his mouth.

"Yes," she answered slowly, her eyes on his as she tried to fathom why he would think that she would make something like that up.

Unable to resist, Christopher popped the last piece into his mouth. It was gone in the blink of an eye. Gone, but definitely not forgotten.

"They're fantastic," he told her with feeling. Executing magnificent restraint, he forced himself to close the rectangular box. "Do you do this professionally?" he asked. "Like at a restaurant? Do you work for a restaurant?" he rephrased, realizing that his momentary bout of sheer ecstasy had temporarily robbed him of the ability to form coherent questions.

"I work for a caterer," Lily corrected. "But someday, I'd like to open up a bakery of my own," she added before she could think better of it. The man was only making conversation. He didn't want her to launch into a long monologue, citing her future plans.

Christopher nodded and smiled warmly as he lifted the lid on the box just a crack again. There was a little dab of cream on one side. He scraped it off with his fingertip which in turn disappeared between his lips as he savored this last tiny bit.

He looked like a man who had reached Nirvana, Lily couldn't help thinking. A warm, pleased feeling began to spread all through her. Lily forgot to be nervous or uncomfortable.

"You'd have standing room only," Christopher assured her. "What do you call these?" he asked, indicating the pastries that were still in the box.

She hadn't given the matter all that much thought. She recalled what Theresa had called them the first time she'd sampled one. "Bits of Heaven."

Christopher's smile deepened as he nodded his approval. He turned to face her completely as he said, "Good name."

That was when she saw it. The tiny dot of white cream just on the inside corner of his lips. Obviously not all of the dessert had made it *into* his mouth. She thought of ignoring it, certain that the more he spoke, the more likely that the cream would eventually disappear one way or another.

But she didn't want him to be embarrassed by having one of his patients' owners point out that his appearance was less than perfect.

"Um, Dr. Whitman," she began, completely at a loss as to how to proceed. She'd always felt out of sync pointing out someone else's flaws or shortcomings. But this was because she'd brought in the pastries so technically the remnants of cream on his face was her fault.

"Your pastry just made love to my mouth, I think you can call me Chris," Christopher told her, hoping to dismantle some of the barriers that this woman seemed to have constructed around herself.

"Chris," Lily repeated as she tried to begin again.

He liked the sound of his name on Lily's tongue. His smile reflected it. "Yes?"

"You have a little cream on your lip. Well, just below your lip," she amended. Rather than point to the exact location on his face, she pointed to it on hers. "No, the other side," she coached when he'd reversed sides to start with. When Christopher managed to find the spot on his second try, she nodded, relieved. "You got it."

Amused, Christopher was about to say something to her, but he was stopped by the bell over the door. It rang, announcing the arrival of his next patient: a Himalayan cat who looked none too happy about being in a carrier, or about her forced visit to the animal hospital for that matter.

The cat's mistress, a rather matronly-looking brunette with a sunny smile, sighed with relief as she set the carrier down on the floor next to the front desk. "Cedrick is *not* a happy camper today," she said, stating the obvious. Then, before Christopher could turn to the cat's file, the woman prompted, "Cedrick's here for his shots."

That was definitely her cue to leave, Lily thought. She'd stayed too long as it was. Theresa's people were watching Jonathan, but she had a feeling that she was on borrowed time as far as that was concerned.

"Well, bye," she called out to Christopher as she opened the door for herself.

She was surprised to hear his voice following her out of the office as he called, "Don't forget Sunday."

The butterflies she'd just become aware of turned into full-size Rodans in a blink of an eye.

Lily darted out of the office and hurried to her vehicle.

"You look like someone's chasing you," Theresa observed when she all but burst through the front door of the catering shop. "Is everything all right?" the older woman asked.

"Fine. It's fine," Lily answered a little too quickly.

Theresa opted to leave her answer unchallenged, asking instead, "How did he like your pastries?" When Lily looked at her blankly, her expression not unlike that of a deer caught in the headlights, Theresa prompted helpfully, "The vet, how did he like the pastries that you made for him?"

"Oh, that. He liked them," Lily answered. "Sorry, I'm a little preoccupied," she apologized. "I'm thinking about the desserts for tomorrow night's event," she explained. Because she always wanted everything to be perfect—her way of showing Theresa how grateful she was to the woman for taking such an interest in her—she was constantly reviewing what she planned on creating for any given event.

This time it was Theresa who waved a hand, waving away Lily's apology. She was far more interested in the topic she had raised.

"Well, what did he say?" she asked. "Honestly, child, sometimes getting information out of you is just like pulling teeth." Drawing her over to the side, she repeated her request. "Tell me what he said."

She could feel her eyes crinkling as she smiled, recalling the exact words. "That he thought he'd died and gone to heaven."

Theresa nodded in approval. "At least he has taste," she said more to herself than to Lily. Maizie had come up with a good candidate, she couldn't help thinking. "It's an omen," she decided, giving Lily's hand a squeeze. "We'll go with Bits of Heaven for the celebration tomorrow night." And then, because Lily didn't seem to be inclined to say anything further about Christopher for now, she changed topics. "By the way, if you're wondering where Jonathan is, Meghan took him out for a walk. Until he gets housebroken, one of us is going to have to take him out every hour until he finally goes," Theresa advised.

Utterly unaccustomed to anything that had to do with having a pet, Lily looked at her, momentarily confused. "Goes? Goes where? You mean with his owner?" she guessed.

Theresa suppressed a laugh. "No, I meant as in him relieving himself. Unless made to understand otherwise, that puppy is going to think the whole world is his bathroom."

Lily looked at her in complete horror. "Oh, God, I didn't think of that."

"Don't beat yourself up, Lily," Theresa told her kindly, putting her arm around her protégé's shoulders. "You've never had a pet before." Then, to further ease the young woman's discomfort, Theresa told her, "There were always dogs around when I was growing up. This is all like second nature to me."

If she felt that way, maybe there was a chance that she could convince her boss to take the puppy if no one came forward to claim him. Lily gave it one more try. "Are you sure that you don't want to—"

Immediately aware where this was going, Theresa deftly headed it off. "Not a chance. My Siamese would take one look at Jonathan and scratch his eyes out, then go on strike and not eat her food for a week just to make me suffer. As long as that prima donna resides with me, I can't have any other four-footed creatures coming within a yard of the house." Theresa gave her a sympathetic smile. "I'm afraid that until you find his owner, you and Jonathan are going to be roomies."

Lily nodded, resigned—for the moment. "Then I'd better get started trying to find his owner," she told Theresa.

With that, Lily retreated into the glass-enclosed cubbyhole where she came up with her recipes. It was a tiny office at best, with just enough space to fit an undersize desk and chair. She couldn't complain. It suited her needs. There was enough space on the desk for her laptop, which was all she required. That and the wireless portable printer she had set up on a folding table.

Lily got to work the second she sat down.

Deciding that an actual picture would do a better job

than a drawing, she'd taken a picture of Jonathan earlier with the camera on her cell phone. After attaching her phone to the laptop, she proceeded to upload the photograph—adorable in her opinion—onto her laptop.

"Why would anyone not realize you were missing?" she murmured to the photograph. "Okay, enough of that, back to work," she ordered herself.

Centering the photograph and cropping it to focus on his face, she wrote in a few pertinent words about the puppy—where and when he was found—then put down her phone number.

Reviewing everything on the screen, Lily went ahead and printed one copy as a test run. Except for the fact that she needed to tweak the color a little to get it just right, the results looked fine to her. She adjusted the color and changed a couple of the words she'd initially used, then saved this copy over the first one. She printed a copy of this version.

She reviewed the poster one final time, decided she was satisfied with both the message and Jonathan's photograph and saved *this* version for posterity. Then she ran off an initial twenty-five posters. She intended to put them up on trees and poles throughout her entire residential development.

Hopefully, that would do it. If she received no response to the flyers, she'd be forced to widen her circle and take in the adjacent development, but for the moment, she was hoping that it wouldn't have to come to that.

If Jonathan *had* been her puppy, she'd be frantically

searching for him by now. It only seemed right to her that his real owner would feel the same.

Once she and Jonathan left the catering shop for the day, Lily put her plan in motion. With the rear window cracked just far enough to let him have air, but not enough to allow the puppy to make an escape, she would drive from location to location within her development. She'd then get out—leaving the Labrador sitting in the backseat of her car—and put the flyers up on two to three trees.

Because she was trying to blanket the entire development, it took Lily more than an extra hour to get home. Jonathan barked louder and louder each time she got out, registering his growing displeasure at this game that seemed to be excluding him.

"You'll thank me when your owner turns up," Lily told the dog, getting in behind the wheel again. She had just tacked up the last of the posters.

Weary, she pulled up to her driveway. Jonathan began to bark again, as if anticipating that she was going to leave him behind.

"I'm coming," Lily assured him.

She rounded the hood of her vehicle to get to the rear passenger side. When she opened the rear door, she did her best to grab the leash the vet had given her but Jonathan was just too fast for her. He eluded her attempts and dove right between her legs as he made his break for freedom.

With a sigh, Lily gave up and let him go. She wasn't about to chase the animal down. With her luck, she'd fall flat on her face. Instead, she went to her trunk and unlocked it.

Theresa had insisted on making her a home-cooked meal—if home was a catering company—so that she'd have something substantial to eat for dinner.

"I know how you get all caught up in things and forget to eat, especially if you have to prepare something. Well, this time, you have no excuse," Theresa had told her as she thrust the large paper bag at her. The bottom had been warm to the touch.

It still was, Lily thought as she took the carefully packed, large paper bag out of the trunk.

Armed with her dinner, she walked up the driveway to the front door and then came perilously close to dropping the bag.

Jonathan was sitting on her front step. By all appearances, the puppy looked as if he was waiting for her.

"What are you doing here?" she cried, stunned. "I thought you'd be long gone by now."

Jonathan's expression was mournful as he glanced up at her. His tongue was hanging out and he was drooling onto her front step. The moment she inserted her key into the lock, the Labrador shot to his feet. His tail was thudding rhythmically on the step.

"I suppose you're going to want to come in," she said. As if he understood her—or perhaps he just wanted to be annoying, she speculated—Jonathan responded by barking at her. Barking even more loudly than he had before. The sound made her absolutely cringe as it echoed in her head. "House rule," she told the puppy as she pushed the door open with her shoulder. Jonathan was inside the house like a shot. She had to be careful not to trip on him—this was getting to be a habit. The puppy seemed to be everywhere at once. "Use your inside voice," she said firmly.

He chose to ignore her.

Jonathan barked again, just as loudly as before. Temporarily surrendering, Lily sighed as she closed the door and then made her way into the kitchen.

"Maybe you don't have an inside voice. I'm beginning to think that you didn't run off, someone *dropped* you off. Someone who didn't want to spend the rest of their life living on headache medication."

Jonathan ran around her in a circle then, suddenly and inexplicably, he apparently opted to become her shadow. He started to follow her every move, staying within a couple of steps from her at all times.

"It's just going to be a matter of time before you make me fall, isn't it?" she predicted, putting down both the bag Theresa had prepared for her and the one Alfredo had given her earlier in the day. The chef had sent his assistant out to the pet store to buy some cans of dog food for Jonathan.

She might not have adopted the Labrador yet, but it seemed as if everyone else had, Lily thought as she unpacked the cans and set them on the counter. There were ten cans in all, each one for a different kind of meal.

"Boy, dogs eat better than most people, don't they?" she marveled. Jonathan was now running back and forth, eagerly anticipating being fed. "Can you smell this through the can?" she asked incredulously. Jonathan just continued pacing.

She took a moment to choose a can for her house-guest, decided that she couldn't make up her mind and finally made her selection by closing her eyes and plucking a can out of the group. One was as good as another, she reasoned. She had a feeling the puppy would have made short work of cardboard had she decided to serve him that.

The can conveniently had a pop-top. "At least I won't have to look for the can opener."

Lily pulled the top off and emptied the contents of the can into a soup bowl. Placing the bowl gingerly before the Labrador, she managed to take a couple of steps back, out of his way. That took a total of three seconds, possibly less.

Jonathan was finished eating in six.

Lily stared at the empty bowl. "Don't you even *chew?*" she asked in amazement. The puppy followed her when she picked up the bowl to wash it out. As before he seemed to be watching her every move intently. "If you think I'm going to give you any more food, you're going to be sadly disappointed. Your kitchen is closed for the night, mister. Water is all you're going to be getting until tomorrow."

Drying the bowl, she then filled it with cold water and placed it back on the floor where it had stood before. The dog taken care of, she turned to her own dinner. Lily opened up the containers of food that Theresa had sent home with her.

The woman had made her favorite, she realized. Beef stroganoff. One whiff of the aroma had her appetite waking up, reminding her that she hadn't eaten very much today.

"God bless Theresa," she murmured.

Putting together a serving, Lily sat down at the table. Jonathan placed himself directly by her feet. The Labrador watched every forkful of food she placed between her lips, seemingly mesmerized.

Lily did her very best to ignore the puppy and the soft brown eyes that were watching her so very closely. She held out against feeding Jonathan for as long as she could—nearly seven minutes—then finally capitulated with a heartfelt sigh.

"Here, finish it," she declared as she put her plate down on the floor.

She barely had enough time to pull her hand away. Even so, her thumb was almost a casualty. Jonathan's sharp little teeth just grazed the skin on her thumb as he proceeded to make the last of the stroganoff disappear from her plate.

"You know," she told the animal, "if we're going to get along for the duration of the time that you're here, we're going to need some boundaries. Boundaries that you're going to have to abide by or it's 'hit the street' for you, buddy. Am I making myself clear?" she asked the puppy.

Getting up from the table, she deposited the nearly immaculate plate in the sink and made her way to the family room. Her shadow followed. Jonathan's tongue was hanging out and he had started to drool again. This time he left an erratic, wet trail that led from the kitchen to the family room.

Turning around, Lily saw the newly forged trail. With a sigh, she took her sponge mop out of the closet and quickly went over the drool marks, cleaning them up. Finished, she left the mop leaning against the kitchen wall—confident she would need it again soon—and looked down at the puppy.

Now what? "Hey, Jonathan, are you up for a hot game of bridge?"

The puppy looked up at her and then began to bark. This time, the sound also rattled her teeth, not just her head.

"Didn't think so. Maybe I'll teach you the game someday." Her words played back to her. "Hey, what am I saying? You're not going to be here 'someday.' By the time 'someday' comes, you, my fine furry friend, will be long gone, eating someone else out of house and home and turning their home into a pile of rubble. Am I right?"

In response, Jonathan began to lick her toes.

She sank down on the sofa and began petting Jonathan's head. "You don't fight fair, Jonathan."

The puppy barked at her, as if to tell her that he already knew that.

Lily had a feeling it was going to be a very long night.

Chapter 5

Christopher glanced at his watch and frowned. It was five minutes later—four and a half, actually—since he'd last looked at it.

He was standing in the dog park, where he'd been standing for the past fifty minutes. From his vantage point, he had a clear view of the park's entrance. No one could enter—or leave—without his seeing it. It was another "typical day in paradise" as someone had once referred to the weather here in Bedford, the Southern California city where he'd grown up, but he wasn't thinking about the weather.

The frown had emerged, albeit slowly, because Lily and her Labrador puppy were now almost an hour late.

She didn't strike him as someone who would just not show up without at least calling, but then, he wasn't exactly the world's greatest judge of character, he reminded himself. Look how wrong he'd turned out to be about Irene.

He laughed shortly as the memory insisted on replaying itself in his mind. He would have bet money—and despite his outgoing nature, he didn't believe in gambling—that he and Irene were going to be together forever.

Idiot, he upbraided himself.

They'd met the first week at college. Helping each other acclimate to living away from home, they discovered that they had the same interests, the same goals—or so he'd thought. But while he went on to attend Cornell University to become a veterinarian, Irene's career path had her turning to the same New York University they'd gone to as undergraduates to get an advanced degree in investment banking.

The latter, he came to learn, was the career of choice in her family. She had her sights set on Wall Street. That was when their very serious first major conflict occurred. She wanted to remain in New York while he had always planned on eventually returning back "home" to set up his practice.

When he discovered that his mother was not only ill, but dying, he felt it was a sign that he really *needed* to return to Bedford. It was then that things between him and Irene began to unravel and he found that he really didn't know the woman the way he thought he did. Irene had made a halfhearted attempt to be understanding. She even said she was willing to take a short hiatus—

she was already working at her father's firm—to accompany him to Bedford for one last visit to his mother.

The tension between them grew and he wound up going back home to see his mother without her. Irene required "maintenance" and while that didn't bother him too often, he knew it would interfere with the time he wanted to sped with his mother.

As it was, that time turned out to be shorter than he'd anticipated. One month to the day after he had arrived back in Bedford, his mother lost her fight to stay alive. He was heartsick that she hadn't told him about her illness sooner, but grateful that at least he'd had those precious few weeks to spend with her.

When he returned to New York and Irene, things went from bad to worse. Their relationship continued to come apart. The night that he saw things clearly for the first time, Irene had told him that she wanted him to seriously consider turning his attention to doing something a little more "prestigious" than dealing with sickly animals.

She went on to say that in her opinion, as well as the opinions of her father and uncles, being a veterinarian didn't fit in with the upwardly mobile image that she was going for.

Irene had stunned him by handing him a list of "alternative careers" he could look into. "I kept hoping you'd come to this conclusion on your own, but if I have to prod you, I will. After all, what's a future wife for if not to get her man on the right path where he belongs?"

She'd actually meant that.

He knew then that "forever" had a very limited life

expectancy in their particular case. He broke off the engagement as civilly as he could, being honest with Irene and telling her that much as he wanted to be with her, this wasn't the way he envisioned them spending their lives together: rubbing elbows with people more interested in profit than in doing some good.

Enraged, Irene had thrown her engagement ring at him. He left it where it fell, telling her she could keep it, that he didn't want it. Two days later, it showed up in his mailbox. He decided that he could always hock the diamond ring if he needed money for a piece of medical equipment.

He left New York for good the day after that.

In an incredibly short spate of time, he had lost his mother and the woman he had thought he loved.

It had taken him a while to get back into the swing of things. A while to stop thinking of himself as one half of a couple and to face life as a single person again. But then, he would remind himself when times were particularly tough emotionally, his mother had done it practically all of his life. His father, a policeman, had been off duty picking up a carton of milk at the local 7-Eleven when a desperate-looking gunman had rushed into the convenience store, waving his weapon around and demanding money. His father, according to the convenience store owner, tried to talk the gunman down.

The latter, jittery and, it turned out, high on drugs, shot him in the chest at point-blank range. The gunman got off three rounds before fleeing. He was caught less than a block away by the responding policemen. But they had arrived too late to save his father.

His mother had been devastated, but because he was only two years old at the time and they had no other family, she forced herself to rally, to give him as good a life as she could.

When he was about to go off to Cornell, he'd felt guilty about leaving her alone. He remembered asking her why she'd never even dated anyone while he was growing up. She'd told him that she'd had one really great love in her life and she felt that it would have been greedy of her to try to get lightning to strike again.

"Your dad," she'd told him, "was a one-of-a-kind man and I was very lucky to have had him in my life, even for a little while. I don't want to spoil that by looking for someone to fill his shoes when I already know it can't be done."

However, he thought now with a smile, his mother would have told him that just because Irene hadn't turned out to be "the woman of his dreams," that didn't mean that there wasn't someone he was meant to be with out there, waiting for him to find her.

And then again, maybe not, he concluded with a sigh.

It wasn't that he was looking for a relationship. It was still too soon to be contemplating something like that. But nonetheless, he did find himself wanting to spend time with Lily.

Christopher looked at his watch again. Five more minutes had gone by.

Okay, he'd been at this long enough, he decided with a vague shrug. For whatever reason, Lily and her overenergetic puppy weren't coming and the woman hadn't seen fit to call him and let him know.

The possibility that the Lab's owner had turned up and claimed "Jonathan" did occur to him, but even in that event, Lily would have called to cancel, wouldn't she?

Unless, maybe, she'd lost his card.

You can stand here all day and come up with a dozen excuses for her, but the fact is that she's not here and you are. It's time to go home, buddy, he silently ordered himself.

With that, Christopher straightened up away from the lamppost he'd been leaning against and began to head for where he had parked his car, a late-model, light gray four-door Toyota.

That was when he heard it.

A loud, high-pitched whistle literally seemed to *pierce* the air. It was an irritating sound, but he dismissed it—until he heard it again. His curiosity aroused, he looked around to see where the sound was coming from.

Before he could zero in on the source, a puppy was excitedly running circles around him.

The puppy.

There was a leash flying behind him like a light green streamer. For the moment, the puppy was a free canine.

With a laugh, Christopher stooped down to the puppy's level, petting him and ruffling the fur on his head. The animal responded like a long-lost friend who had finally made a connection with him against all odds.

"Hi, boy. Where's your mistress? Did you make a break for it?"

Christopher looked over his shoulder and this time he saw her. Lily. Her chestnut hair flying behind her, she was running toward him. Lily was wearing a striking green T-shirt that was molding itself to her upper torso and faded denim shorts, frayed at the cuff, which only seemed to accentuate her long legs.

Lily was covering a lot of ground, trying to catch up to the dog that had obviously managed to get away from her.

Seeing that Jonathan had found the man they were both coming to meet, Lily slowed down just a tad, allowing herself time to catch her breath so that she could speak without gasping.

"Hi," Christopher greeted her warmly, the fifty-five-plus minutes he'd been waiting conveniently vanishing into an abyss. "I was beginning to think you weren't coming."

"I'm sorry about that," she apologized. "I'm usually very punctual." Since Christopher was still crouching next to the puppy, she dropped down to the ground beside him. It seemed easier to talk that way. "Jonathan decided he wanted to give me attitude instead of cooperation." She wasn't trying to get sympathy from the vet, she just wanted the man to know what had kept her from being here on time. "I had a terrible time getting him into the car. It was like he was just all paws, spread out in all directions. And then, when I finally got to the park and opened the rear door, he raced out of the car before I could get hold of his leash. I tried to grab it, but Jonathan was just too fast for me." She shook her head. "He obviously has a mind all his own."

It was hard to believe that the whirlwind of stubbornness she was describing was the same dog that now appeared to be all obliging sweetness and light. Not only that, but the Labrador had just flipped onto his back, paws resting in the begging position because he wanted to have his belly rubbed.

Christopher obliged. The puppy looked as if he was in heaven. "Was that you I heard, whistling just now?" Christopher asked her incredulously.

He was wording his question politely, she noted. Embarrassed, Lily nodded.

"I know the whistle was kind of loud." The truth of it was that she didn't know *how* to whistle quietly. "But I was desperate to get him to at least stop running away even if he wasn't coming back to me."

Christopher found it rather amusing that someone as petite and graceful as Lily whistled like a sailor on shore leave gathering his buddies together. But he decided that was an observation best kept to himself, at least for now. He had a feeling that if he mentioned his impression to her, Lily would take it as criticism and it would undoubtedly cause her to feel self-conscious around him. That was the *last* thing he wanted to do. If nothing else, it would get in the way of her being able to adequately relate to the puppy she was so obviously meant to bond with.

So instead, Christopher aimed his attention—as well as his words—at the black furry creature that all but had his head squarely in his lap, still silently begging for attention and to be petted.

This, Christopher decided, was a dog that thrived on

positive reinforcement. That should ultimately make it easier for Lily.

"Have you been giving your mistress a hard time, Jonny-boy?" Christopher laughed, continuing to stroke the puppy. "Well, that's going to stop as of right now, do I make myself clear?" he asked in a pseudostern voice.

Eager-to-please brown eyes stared up at him, and then Jonathan's pink tongue darted out to quickly lick his hand. The same hand that had just been petting the animal.

Christopher pulled his hand out of the dog's reach. "No more of that for a while. You're not fooling anyone. We're here to work," he told the dog as he got up off the ground. The next moment, the leash in one hand, he offered his other hand to Lily. "C'mon, it's time to start both your training lessons."

Taking his hand, Lily had the momentary sensation of being enveloped and taken care of. The man had strong hands. He also wasn't as quick to let her hand go as she would have thought. It was just an extra second or so, but it registered.

Feeling herself start to flush, Lily quickly changed the subject. "You made it sound as if you're going to be training me, as well," she said with a nervous laugh.

The laugh dissipated in her throat when he looked at her with a wide smile and replied good-naturedly, "That's because I am."

Lily was so stunned by his answer that for a couple of minutes, she had no reply to render, snappy or otherwise. And then her brain finally kicked in.

"I'm happy to say that I'm housebroken," she told Christopher.

She watched, nearly mesmerized, as the corners of his mouth slowly curved. She found herself being drawn into his smile. The line "resistance is futile" flashed through her brain.

"Good to know," Christopher told her, "but that isn't exactly what I have in mind for you."

"Oh?"

She looked at him warily, unaccountably relieved that they were out in the open, in a fairly crowded area. For the life of her, she wouldn't have been able to explain why the thought of being alone with the man made her fingertips tingle and the rest of her feel nervous. She did her best not to let him see the effect he was having on her.

"And what is it that you have in mind for me?" she asked, brazening it out. It was a loaded question and had they been friends for some length of time, or at least at a stage where they knew one another a little better, the answer that flashed through her brain might have been obvious.

"I intend to train you on how to train Jonny here," he told Lily. "There's a right way and a wrong way to do just about everything. With a dog, the wrong way won't get you the results you want and it could get you in trouble. Remember, it's important to maintain positive reinforcement. I don't care if it's a treat—a small one," he emphasized, warning, "or you'll wind up with a severely overweight dog—or lavish praise, as long as it's positive. Remember, kindness works far better than fear," he told her as they began to walk to the heart of the park.

"Fear?" she repeated uncertainly. The word conjured up vivid memories of her own reaction to Jonathan and his nipping teeth.

Christopher nodded. "I've seen people scream at their pets, hit them with a rolled-up newspaper or anything else that happened to be handy. The pet was always the worse for it. You don't want your pet to be obedient out of fear but out of love. I can't stress that enough," he told her. And then he curtailed the rest of his lecture, as if not wanting to get carried away. "Although I have to admit that you don't look like the type who would take a stick to a dog."

Lily shivered at the very thought of someone actually beating their pet. Why would anyone get a pet if they had no patience? Every relationship, whether strictly involving humans, or extending to pets, required a large dose of patience unless it happened to be unfolding on the big screen in the guise of a popular studio's full-length cartoon feature.

"Also," he continued as they made their way to a more open section of the park, "regarding housebreaking—there will be occasional setbacks," he warned her. "I don't recommend dragging Jonny back and sticking his nose into what just came out his other end while sternly denouncing him, saying, 'No, no!' Best-case scenario," Christopher explained patiently, "all that teaches him is to do it somewhere a little more out of the way so he won't get reprimanded for it."

"And worst-case scenario?" she asked, curious what

he thought that was since what he'd just described *was* worst-case scenario as far as she was concerned.

Christopher laughed softly. "Your puppy just might find he has a taste for it. I've heard of more than one dog who believed in recycling his or her own waste products." He stopped walking, taking a closer look at Lily's face. "You look a little pale," he noted. "Are you all right?"

She put her hand over her stomach, as if that would keep her hastily consumed breakfast from rising up in her throat and purging itself from her stomach. Opening her door to this puppy had consequently left her open to more things than she'd ever dreamed of, no pun intended she added silently.

"I just didn't realize all the things that were involved in taking in a stray—even temporarily. The only dogs I ever knew were up on a movie screen," she confessed. Admittedly it had been a very antiseptic way of obtaining her knowledge. "They didn't smell, didn't go to the bathroom and had an IQ just a tad lower than Einstein's." She smiled ruefully as she elaborated a little more, realizing while she was at it that she was underscoring her naïveté. "The kind that when their owner said, 'I need a screw driver' would wait until he specified whether it was a flathead or Phillips head that he wanted."

Christopher grinned. He liked that she could laugh at herself. The fact that Lily had a sense of humor was a very good sign, as far as he was concerned.

"In the real world, if you don't bathe them, dogs smell, and they don't do long division in their heads."

And then he went on to list just a few of the positive reasons to own a dog. "But they *do* respond to the sound of your voice, are highly trainable and will come to an understanding with you, given the time and the training—coupled with a lot of patience. Always remember, anything worth doing is worth doing well. You let a dog into your life, remember to show him that while you love him, you're the one in charge, and you will never regret it."

Christopher paused for a moment. He caught himself looking into her eyes and thinking how easily he could get lost in them if he wasn't careful.

Taking a breath, he told himself that he needed to get down to business before she got the wrong idea about him and why he was here.

"Now then, are you ready to get started?" he asked Lily.

"Ready," she answered with a smart nod, eager to begin.

"All right," he said, stooping down to the dog's level again to remove the leash he'd given her. He replaced it with a long line, a leash that was three times as long as the initial one. Getting back up to his feet, Christopher told her, "The first thing we want to teach Jonny here is to come when you call."

She watched as he slowly backed up, away from Jonathan. "Um, how about housebreaking?" she asked hesitantly.

She would have thought that would be the very first thing the dog would be taught. She'd had to clean up several rather untidy messes already and couldn't see herself doing that indefinitely. To be honest, she'd rather hoped that the vet had some sort of magic solution regarding housebreaking that he was willing to pass on to her.

The sympathetic expression on his handsome, chiseled face told her that she'd thought wrong.

"That's going to take a little longer for him to learn, I'm afraid. I can—and will—show you the basics and what to say, but for the most part, that's going to require dedication and patience on your part. A *lot* of dedication and patience," he emphasized. "Because you're going to have to take Jonny here out every hour on the hour until he goes—as well as watch for signs that he's about to go."

This was completely new territory for her and something she had never given any attention to before now. "How will I know what signs to look for?"

"That," he replied with a smile that would have curled her toes had she allowed it, "is a very good question." Leaning in to her as if to confide a secret, he lowered his voice and said, "This would be the part where *you* get trained."

Drawing his head back again, he gave her a wink that seemed to flutter through layers of skin tissue and embed itself smack in the middle of her stomach.

"Okay, back to getting him to come when you call," he said, taking a firm hold on the long line. With that, he proceeded to go through the basics for her slowly and clearly before he went on to demonstrate what he'd just said, allowing her to see it in action.

Chapter 6

"Okay, now you try," Christopher said after successfully getting Jonathan to come to him when he called the puppy. The vet held out the long line to her.

Instead of taking it from him, Lily looked at the elongated leash uncomfortably. "Me?"

If there was one thing she really hated, it was appearing inept in front of people, even someone who seemed as nice as this man. Doing so only seemed to underscore her feelings of insecurity, not to mention that it reinforced the shyness that she grappled with every day.

Christopher instinctively knew when a situation required an extra dose of patience. Usually, it involved the animals he treated, but occasionally, he could sense the need to tap into his almost endless supply when dealing with a person. He could see that Lily's reluctance had nothing to do with being stubborn or reticent. From her stance, she was far from confident.

That had to change. If he could sense it, the dog definitely could. While he had a soft spot in his heart for all things canine, he also knew that dominance had to be established. If it wasn't, this cute little black ball of fur and paws was going to walk all over the woman beside him and most likely make her life a living hell—or at least turn her home into a shambles.

"Well, yes," Christopher told her. "Unless you intend to have me come home with you and take over raising Jonny here, you're going to have to learn how to make him obey you. Emphasis on the word *obey*," he said, still holding the end of the long line before her.

Lily pressed her lips together. The only thing she hated more than looking like a fool was looking like a coward. She took a deep breath and wrapped her fingers around the end of the long line.

Glaring at the puppy, she said as authoritatively as she could, "Come!" When Jonathan remained where he was, she repeated the command even more forcefully. "Come!" At which point Jonathan cocked his head and stared at her, but made no attempt to comply.

Taking pity on her, Christopher bent close to her ear and said in a low voice, "Remember to preface each command with his name and give the long line a little tug the way I did. He'll get the hang of it eventually."

Christopher's breath along the side of her face and neck would have caused an involuntary shiver to shimmy down her spine had she not steeled herself at the last moment.

Lily felt her cheeks growing pink. Use the puppy's name. How could she have forgotten something so simple so quickly?

"Right. Jonathan, come!" she ordered, simultaneously giving the elongated leash a little tug.

Despite its length, the impact of the play on the line telegraphed itself to the Labrador. Then, to her surprised relief, Jonathan trotted toward her, coming to a halt almost on top of her feet.

"He did it," she cried excitedly, stunned and thrilled at the same time. "He came!"

Christopher wasn't sure which was more heartening to him, seeing the animal respond to Lily's command or seeing Lily's joy *because* the animal had responded to her command.

"Yes, he did," Christopher acknowledged with a pleased smile. "Now give him that scrap of doggie sausage as a reward and play out the long line so you can do it again."

Jonathan appeared to be in sheer ecstasy as he swallowed his "reward" without so much as pausing a second to chew it.

It was a toss-up as to which appeared to be more eager for a repeat of what had just happened, Christopher mused: Jonathan or his mistress.

The brief exercise played out more smoothly this time.

"Again," Christopher instructed her after Lily tossed the treat to the eager puppy.

Lily and Jonathan repeated the training exercise a

total of five times before Christopher decided it was
time to move on to the next command.

"This is the exact opposite of what you've just taught
him," Christopher told her. He noticed that instead of
the reluctance she had initially exhibited, Lily seemed
to be almost as eager as the puppy to undertake the
next "lesson." "You're going to train him to stay where
he is. Now, not moving might seem like it's an easy
thing to get across, but for an antsy puppy that's approximately six to seven weeks old, staying put is not
part of their normal behavior—unless they're asleep,"
he told her. "Okay, instead of tugging on the long line,
you're going to use a hand gesture—holding your hand
out to him as if you were a cop stopping traffic—plus
a calm voice and patience. Lots of patience," Christopher emphasized.

"Okay," she said, nodding her head.

In a way, he couldn't help thinking that she reminded
him of the puppy—all eagerness and enthusiasm. Without fully realizing it, she'd gone a step up in his estimation of her.

"You tell him to stay and then slowly back away from
him," Christopher instructed, standing directly behind
her and ready to match her step for step as she backed
up. "Until he responds for the first time and stays in
place for as long as you've designated, you don't take
your eyes off him. *Make* him obey you. Your goal ultimately is to get Jonny to obey the sound of your voice
without being bribed to do it or being watched intently.
And that," he told her firmly, "is going to take doing the

same thing over and over again until he gets it, until he associates what he does with the key words you use."

"I was never very good at being authoritative," Lily admitted ruefully. But even so, her enthusiasm was still high.

"Then you're going to have to keep that little secret to yourself. As far as Jonny here is concerned, you are the lord and master of his world—or mistress of it if you prefer," he amended.

She didn't seem like the type to take offense over words where none was intended, Christopher thought, but since they were still in the getting-to-know-each-other stage, he wasn't about to take anything for granted.

Lily smiled at him. There was something about the way she looked at him that made him feel connected to her. It was as if, without his exactly knowing why, they were in sync to one another. "Either way is fine with me," she told him.

In all honesty, she'd never thought of herself in those sort of lofty terms. She was neither a mistress *nor* a master. Or at least she hadn't been until now, she thought with a smile.

"Okay." Christopher nodded toward their subject. "Let's see you make him stay."

"You're not going to do it first?" she asked Christopher.

"You mean warm him up for you?" he asked, amused. "He's your dog," he told her, wanting to subtly build up her confidence. "You should be the main authority figure he listens to."

"But he's not my dog," she protested. "I have these

flyers out in my development. His owner might still come looking for him." Although, she had to admit, she was now just a tad less eager for that to happen than she had been just a little while ago.

He looked at Lily for a long moment, seeing through the veneer she'd put up. "Then tell me again why you're going to all this trouble for an animal you might not get to keep?"

There was a struggle going on inside of her, a struggle between logic and emotions. At any given moment, she wasn't quite sure just which way she was leaning.

But for the sake of appearances and the role she was trying to maintain, Lily replied, "I'm trying to train Jonathan so that I can survive with him until his owner *does* turn up." She did her best to sound cool and removed as she added, "I don't want to get attached to him and then have to give him up."

"I hate to break this to you, Lily, but watching the two of you, in my opinion, you already *are* attached to him—and it looks to me as if he's attached to you as well, as much as an overenergized puppy can be attached to one person," he qualified with a laugh. "Don't get me wrong," he was quick to explain. "Dogs are extremely loyal creatures, but puppies tend to sell their souls for a belly rub and have been known to walk off with almost anyone—unless they've been given a better reason to stay where they are."

Christopher searched her eyes. He could readily see that Lily was grappling with the problem of wanting to keep the dog at an arm's length emotionally—while wanting to throw caution to the wind and enjoy the unconditional love that the puppy offered.

"And if I could add two more cents." Christopher paused, waiting for her to nod her head.

Surprised, she told him, "Go ahead."

"Personally, I don't think anyone is going to come looking for Jonny here," he told her. "The way I see it, his mom probably had a litter recently and this one made a break for it when he was old enough to explore the world and no one was watching him. Most likely, his mom's owner was busy trying to find a good home for him and his brothers and sisters. When Jonny took off, the owner probably took it to be a blessing—one less puppy for him to place.

"*Or* he might have been so overwhelmed that he didn't even notice Jonny was missing—especially if his dog had had an unusually large litter." A fond smile curved his lips as he gazed down at the Labrador that had taken to momentarily sunning himself and was stretched out in the grass. "These little guys move around so fast, it's hard to get a proper head count."

She couldn't quite explain the happy feeling growing inside of her, especially since she was trying so hard to maintain her barriers, so hard to not get attached and thereby leave herself open to another onslaught of pain.

Attempting to sound removed—and not quite succeeding—she said, "So what you're telling me is that I'd better get used to the idea of vacuuming up fur several times a week."

For the sake of her charade, Christopher inclined his

head—even though he saw right through her performance. "That's another way of putting it."

She was on shaky ground and she had a feeling that she wasn't fooling him—or herself. "What if I don't like the idea of having to vacuum that often?" she posed.

Rather than tell her that he would take the dog—which he actually would do if he believed she was serious—Christopher decided to play on her sympathies and create a heart-tugging scenario.

"Well, in that case, you could always bring Jonny to the animal shelter and leave him there. Bedford outlawed euthanizing animals after a certain period of time the way they do in some other cities, so there's no chance of his being put to sleep. Of course, he might not get all the love and attention he needs, getting lost in the shuffle because there are a large number of animals at the shelter. The city had to cut back on employees even though the animals all need care and attention.

"Not to mention the fact that lately the number of volunteers who come by to walk, feed and play with the animals has dropped off, too, but at least the little guy would still be alive—just not as happy as he would be here with you."

Beneath the steel exterior she was trying to maintain was a heart made of marshmallow. But even if there wasn't, Lily would have seen what the veterinarian was trying to do.

Shaking her head, she told him, "You left out the violins."

The comment, seemingly coming out of the blue, caught him by surprise. "What?"

"Violins," she repeated, then elaborated. "As background music. You left them out. They should have been playing while you painted that scene for me. They could have swelled to a crescendo right toward the end. But other than that, you just created a scenario that's bordering on being a tearjerker."

"Just wanted you to know what these little critters are up against," he told her with a very straight face. "Now, let's see if you can get Jonny to stay. In place," he added with emphasis in case she thought he was still referring to the dog staying with her. And then he winked at her.

Again.

Her reaction was exactly the same as it had been the first time he'd winked at her. Her breath caught in her throat and butterflies fluttered in her stomach. The only difference was that it seemed to her that there were even more now than there had been the first time he'd winked at her.

How could something that could technically be described as a twitch create such pure havoc inside of her? Was she really *that* starved for attention that any hint of it had her practically melting into tiny little puddles and reminding herself to breathe?

Lily had no idea how to begin to make any sense of that.

For the moment, she blocked it all out and turned her attention to what Christopher had just said, not how she'd reacted to how he'd looked as he said it.

"Okay, let's see if I can get him to listen."

"Oh, he'll listen," Christopher assured her. "That's not the issue. Whether he'll obey is a totally other story."

* * *

This particular story turned out to have a good ending some ninety minutes later.

With Christopher urging her on, she had managed to get the Labrador puppy to stay in place for a total of ten seconds as she backed away from him. This happened several times, building up her confidence both in herself and in her relationship with the eager Labrador. She'd still had to maintain eye contact with Jonathan, but Christopher promised her that that would change and the next time they got together, they'd work on her just turning her back on the Labrador and *still* getting the animal to remain in place.

"Next time?" Lily repeated. It wasn't exactly a question so much as she wanted to make sure that she'd heard him correctly.

"Yes, next weekend," Christopher answered.

He slanted a glance at her, wondering if he'd pushed a little too hard too fast. Normally, he wouldn't have given it a second thought, but this woman needed a little more delicate care in his estimation. He also felt certain she was worth it. Something about her aroused both his protective nature as well as an inherent response from him as a man. Though a little soured on the idea of relationships, he still genuinely *liked* this woman.

"I thought since you were having such success at this, you might want to push on, get a few more commands under your belt, so to speak. Unless you don't want to," Christopher said, giving her a way out if she really wanted one.

"Oh, I want to." She'd said that a little too eagerly,

Lily realized and dialed back her enthusiasm a notch as she continued. "But what I'm really interested in is getting him housebroken," she confessed, wondering if she was putting the veterinarian out too much, taking advantage of his generosity.

"For that to get underway, we can't be out here," he told her. "We'd have to work with him at your home. Jonny can't be taught to observe his boundaries if one of those boundaries is missing," he pointed out.

"Can't argue with that," she agreed. And then she glanced at her watch.

Christopher saw something that resembled an apologetic expression on her face. Had he missed something? "What's the matter?"

"I feel guilty that you're spending all this time helping me train Jonathan when you could be doing something else with your time. I wouldn't feel so bad if you were letting me pay you for your time, but you're not."

"I'm not about to charge you for something I volunteered to do." He could see that wasn't going to assuage her guilt. He thought of the other day—and went with that. "However, if you feel compelled to make some more pastries anytime soon, well, I couldn't very well refuse those, now could I?"

"How about dinner?" She was as surprised as he was to hear her make the suggestion. It seemed to have come out all on its own. For a second, she lapsed into stunned silence.

The sentence was just hanging there between them, so he took a guess at what she was saying. "You mean like going out to dinner first?"

You put it out there, now follow up on it before the man thinks he's spending time with a crazy woman.

"No, I mean how about if I make you dinner before the dessert? Like a package deal," she concluded with a bright, albeit somewhat nervous smile.

For just a heartbeat, he found himself mesmerized by her smile. Some people had smiles that seemed to radiate sunshine and make a person feel the better for being in its presence. Lily had such a smile.

"I wouldn't want you to go to all that trouble," he finally said when he recovered his ability to make coherent sentences. But he uttered it without very much conviction.

"Not that it's any actual trouble," she countered, "but why not? It seems to me like you're going through a lot of trouble helping me train Jonathan."

There were two people running around the perimeter of the park with their whippets. Moving out of their way, Christopher waited until they were out of earshot before continuing their verbal dueling match.

"I don't consider working with a dog as any sort of 'trouble.' To be honest, I can't remember a time when I didn't want to be a veterinarian," he told her. "My dad died when I was very young and my mother thought that having a dog—or two—around the house would somehow help fill the void in my life that his death left. Without knowing it, she inadvertently set me on a career path that shaped the rest of my life. I really appreciated what she tried to do, but to be honest, you can't miss what you don't remember ever having, can you?"

"Actually, you *could* miss it if you find yourself

imagining what it would have been like to have a father and then realize that no matter what you do, it was never going to be that way."

There was a sadness in her voice that caught his attention. "You sound like someone who's had firsthand experience with that."

Ordinarily, she would have just glossed over his observation, shrugging it off and simply saying no, she didn't. But lying—which was what it amounted to from her point of view—just didn't seem to be right in this situation. Even a little white one would have troubled her.

"I do," she admitted. For a moment, as she brought her childhood into focus, she avoided his eyes. "I never knew my dad. He took off before I was born. The story went that he told my mother he wasn't cut out to be a father and that then he proved it by just taking off," she concluded with a shrug that was way too careless to be what it portrayed.

He wanted to put his arms around her, to not just comfort her but to silently offer her protection against the world, as well. Until this moment, those reactions in him had been strictly confined to dealing with creatures in the animal kingdom. This was a whole new turn of events. But even so, he kept his hands at his sides, sensing that he might just scare her off if he did something so personal so early in their acquaintance.

So he restricted his response to a verbal one. "I'm sorry."

"Yes, I was, too—for my mother." Her father had abandoned the person she had loved the most in life—

her mother. And for that, she could never forgive the man. "She could have used a little help juggling raising me and paying the bills. Life was a constant struggle for her."

"That's the way I felt, too," he admitted. "But my mother never complained. I don't think I *ever* heard her even say a cross word against anyone. She just plowed through life, doing what she had to do."

"Mine held down two jobs trying to do the same thing." It felt almost eerie the way their lives seemed to mirror each other when it came to family life. She didn't normally seek details, but she did this time. "You have any siblings?"

Christopher shook his head. It was the one area that he wished had been different. "None. You?"

"Same," she answered. "None."

It should have felt eerie to her—but it didn't. Instead, she realized that it made her feel closer to this outgoing man. She knew the danger in that, but for now, she just allowed it to be, taking comfort in the warm feeling that was being generated inside of her.

Chapter 7

He walked Lily to her car, which was parked not that far from his own.

As he stood to the side and waited for her to coax the Labrador into the backseat, Christopher realized that he wasn't quite ready for their afternoon to come to an end.

His reaction surprised him. He hadn't felt any real interest in maintaining any sort of female companionship since his less-than-amicable breakup with Irene a few months ago. Maybe he was finally ready to move on with his life in every sense.

Watching Lily now, Christopher decided he had nothing to lose by suggesting that perhaps they could just continue with Jonathan's training session in a different setting.

As she turned away from the dog and closed the

rear passenger door, Christopher pretended to glance at his watch.

Looking up again, he said to her, "Listen, I have nothing scheduled for the rest of the day. Why don't I just follow you to your place and we'll get a head start in housebreaking your houseguest?"

"Really?"

"Really," Christopher answered. He didn't, however, want her having any unrealistic expectations about what they were going to accomplish this afternoon. "Remember, though, I did say 'get a head start.' This isn't a relatively quick process, like getting Jonny to come or stay. Or even getting him to do something trickier like rolling over or sitting up and begging. This," he warned her, "is going to take a while. With some luck and a lot of vigilance, best-case scenario, you might be able to get him completely housebroken in two weeks."

"But I work and the hours aren't always regular," she told Christopher. Looking at Jonathan in the backseat, she lamented, "How can I keep up a regular schedule with him?"

"That is a problem," Christopher conceded. "But it's not impossible."

She found herself clinging to those words like a drowning woman to a life preserver. If she was going to wind up actually keeping Jonathan, she would be eternally grateful that Theresa had sent her to this veterinarian. He was a godsend.

"Okay, I'm listening."

"You take him out every hour on the hour when you

are home. When you're not, you can leave him in a puppy crate."

"A puppy crate?" she repeated, not knowing if she was just stunned or actually horrified by the suggestion. She had to have misunderstood him. "You're telling me to stick Jonathan in a crate?" she asked in disbelief. "That's cruel."

"No, actually, it's not cruel at all. Puppy crates come in different sizes to accommodate the different breeds. They're airy and specifically designed to make the puppy feel safe. Puppies are placed in puppy crates for the same reason that they tightly bundle up newborn babies in a hospital. They actually like small spaces. An added bonus is if they only spend part of their time there each day—such as when you're away at work— they won't mess the crate up because they won't go to the bathroom where they sleep."

"What about in the pet stores?" she countered. She'd seen more than one employee in a pet store having to clean out the cages that the animals were kept in.

"That's because the animals are kept in their cages all the time. They have no choice but to relieve themselves in the same place that they sleep. Those conditions make it harder to train an animal, but not in the case I'm suggesting," he pointed out.

She could tell by his tone when he described conditions in a pet store that the veterinarian didn't really approve of them. Still, the idea of forcing Jonathan to spend part of his time in a crate didn't exactly sit well with her.

"Not that I'm doubting what you just said about puppy crates, but isn't there any other way to housebreak him? I

really don't like the idea of sticking Jonathan in a cage—
or crate—unless I have no other choice." She looked
at the dog, sympathy welling up inside of her. "It just
seems too much like making him spend time in prison
to me," she confessed.

He liked the fact that despite her attempts at project-
ing bravado, Lily was a pushover when it came to animals. "Well, there is one other alternative," he told her.

Lily second-guessed him. "Taking him to work with
me, the way I did the first day."

"Or you could drop him off at my animal hospital
when you go to work and then I could drop him off with
you in the evening. Unless you were leaving earlier than
I was, and then you could just come and get Jonny. And
in between, I can have one of the animal techs make sure
our boy here doesn't have any embarrassing 'accidents.'"

That really sounded as if it was the far better choice
in her opinion, but again, she felt as if it would definitely
be putting him out.

"Wouldn't they mind?" she asked, adding, "Wouldn't
you mind?"

"No and no," Christopher answered. He leaned
against the side of her vehicle as he laid out his new
plan for her. "I passed around those pastries you dropped
off the other day and if you're willing to supply the staff
with them, say once a week or so, I *know* that they'd be
more than happy to pitch in and get Jonny here potty
trained," he guaranteed.

Since they were still talking, he opened the front passenger door to allow air to circulate through the vehicle
for the Labrador. At the same time, he placed his body

in the way so that the puppy couldn't come bounding out and escape.

"You're serious?" Lily asked.

She could feel herself growing hopeful again. This last idea was infinitely appealing—and it meant she wouldn't have to feel guilty about putting the puppy into a cage just to keep her house from turning into one giant puppy latrine.

"Completely," Christopher replied with no reservations.

"Then it's a deal," she declared.

"Great. I'll alert the staff to start looking for new clothes one size larger than they're wearing right now," he said with a straight face. Only his eyes gave him away.

"You don't have to do that," Lily told him, waving away the suggestion.

To which he asked, "You've changed your mind about baking?"

There was no way that was about to happen. She absolutely loved baking, especially for an appreciative audience.

"Oh, no, it's not that," she said, dismissing his suggestion. "But I can duplicate the recipe and make a low-fat version—they'll never notice the difference—and nobody will need bigger clothing."

He appreciated what she was trying to do, but in his opinion, "lighter" was never "better." For that matter, it wasn't even as good as what it was supposed to be substituting.

"You say that now, but I can always tell the 'light' version of anything," he told her. "It never tastes the same."

Lily studied him for a long moment. Her expression was unreadable. And then he saw humor overtaking the corners of her mouth, curving it. "Are you challenging me?"

Christopher took measure of her. She meant well, but as an opponent, she was a lightweight.

"Not in so many words but, well, yes, maybe I am," he conceded.

Lily squared her shoulders. For the first time since she had come into his animal hospital, she looked formidable. It surprised him.

"Okay," Lily said with a nod of her head, "you're on. I'll bake my usual way, and then arbitrarily I'll make a batch of substitutes, and I defy you to definitively say which is which."

"You have a deal," he readily agreed, confident he'd win. He took her hand and shook it.

It was done as a matter of course, without any sort of separate, independent thought devoted to it. But the moment his strong fingers enveloped hers, she could have sworn she felt some sort of current registering, a shot akin to electricity suddenly coursing through her veins from the point of contact.

Her breath caught in her throat for the second time that day.

Out of nowhere, she suddenly caught herself wondering if he was going to kiss her.

The next second, she hastily dismissed the thought, silently asking herself if she was crazy. People didn't kiss after making what amounted to day boarding arrangements for their pet. That wasn't how these situations played themselves out.

Was it?

Clearing her throat, as if that somehow helped her shake off the thoughts swarming through her brain and turning up her body temperature to an almost alarming degree, Lily dropped the veterinarian's hand. She took a step back. She would have taken a few more, but her car was at her back, blocking any further retreat on her part.

"Do you still want to come over?" she heard herself asking in an almost stilted voice. "To start housebreaking him?"

Her mouth had gone completely dry by the end of the sentence.

"Unless you've changed your mind," Christopher qualified. He'd felt it, too, felt the crackle of electricity between them, felt a sudden longing in its wake that had left him a little shaken and unsteady. He was definitely attracted to this woman, but it was more than that. Just what, he wasn't sure.

Yet.

"No, I haven't," Lily heard herself saying.

Her own voice echoed in her head as if it belonged to someone else. Part of her, the part that feared what might be ahead of her, wanted to run and hide, to quickly thank him for his trouble and then jump into her car in order to make a hasty retreat.

But again, that would be the coward's way out.

What was she afraid of? Lily demanded silently. She was a grown woman who had been on her own for a while now, a grown woman who knew how to take care of herself. There was no one else to step up, no one else to take up her cause or fight any of her battles for her, so she had to stick up for herself. She was all she had to rely on and so far, she'd managed just fine—with a little help from Theresa.

Making up her mind, she decided that yes, she did want him to come over. She wanted his help—and if anything else developed along the way, well, she'd face it then and handle it.

"Let me give you my address in case we get separated," Lily said to him, taking a very small notepad out of her purse. Finding a pen took a couple of minutes longer, but she did and then she began to write down her address.

"Separated?" he questioned. "How fast do you intend to be driving?" he couldn't help asking.

"Not that fast," Lily assured him. "But there are always traffic lights turning red at the most inopportune time, impeding progress. I might make it through a light, but you might not, that sort of thing." Finished, she handed the small piece of paper to him. "Can you read it?" she asked. "My handwriting is pretty awful."

He looked down at the paper—and laughed. "You think this is bad? You should see the way some of my friends write—it's enough to make a pharmacist weep," Christopher told her with another laugh.

Glancing one last time at the address she'd written down for him, he folded the paper and put it in his pocket. "Just let me get to my car before you start yours," he told her. "I'll take it from there."

"Okay," Lily answered gamely.

She rounded the back of the vehicle—Jonathan eyeing her every move—and got in behind the steering wheel. Buckling up, she not only remained where she was until Christopher got to his car but waited until he started the vehicle and pulled out of the row where he had been parked, as well.

Only then did she turn her key in the ignition, back out and head for the exit. Within less than a minute, she was on the thoroughfare leading away from the dog park.

Lily glanced in her rearview mirror to make sure that Christopher was following her.

He was.

Meanwhile, Jonathan had taken to pacing back and forth on the seat behind her as she drove them home. Each time she came to a stop at an intersection light, even when she rolled into that stop, Jonathan would suddenly and dramatically pitch forward.

After emitting a high-pitched yelp that sounded like it could have easily doubled for a cry for help, the puppy apparently decided it was safer for him to lie low, which he did. He spread himself out as far as he could on the backseat and seemed to all but make himself one with the cushion.

"It's not far now," Lily promised the Labrador, hoping that if he didn't understand the words, at least the sound of her calm voice would somehow help soothe him.

If it did—and she had her suspicions that it might have because he'd stopped making those strange, whiny noises—the effect only lasted until she pulled up in her driveway some fifteen minutes later.

The second she put the vehicle into Park and got out, Jonathan was up on all fours again, pacing along the backseat—when he wasn't sliding down because of a misstep that sent his paws to the floor.

Since she had kept the windows in the back partially open, she didn't immediately open the rear door to let him out. Instead, she waited for Christopher to pull up alongside of her vehicle. She felt that he could handle the Labrador far better than she could. For one thing, the man was a lot stronger.

The minutes began to slip away, banding together to form a significant block of time.

When Christopher still didn't show up, she began to wonder if he had somehow lost sight of her. She'd stopped looking in the rearview mirror around the time when Jonathan's head was in her direct line of vision, blocking out everything else.

And then she realized that it didn't really matter if Christopher had lost sight of her car or not. She'd given him her address, so even if he had lost sight of her vehicle he still should have been pulling up in her driveway by now.

Since he wasn't, she took it as a sign that he'd changed his mind about coming over.

The more the minutes ticked away, the more certain she became that she was right. Somewhere along the route, he had obviously decided that he had given her enough of his time.

She felt a strange sensation in her stomach, as if it was puckering and twisting.

Why his sudden change of heart left her feeling let

down, she didn't know. After all, it wasn't as if this was a date or anything. The man had already been extremely helpful, getting her started on the proper way to train her dog, and she was very grateful for that. No reason to be greedy, Lily silently insisted. The man had already gone over and above the call of duty.

Jonathan began to whine, bringing her back to her driveway and the immediate situation. She was allowing her disappointment to hijack her common sense.

Lily quickly shut down any stray emotions that threatened to overwhelm her.

"Sorry," she apologized to the puppy. She opened the rear passenger door a crack—just wide enough to allow her to grab his leash. She was learning. "I didn't mean to forget about you," she told the dog.

Getting a firm hold of the leash, Lily opened the door all the way.

Jonathan needed no further encouragement. He came bounding out, savoring his freedom like a newly released prisoner after a lengthy incarceration.

"Easy," she cautioned. "Easy now!"

The words had absolutely no effect on Jonathan, a fact that only managed to frustrate her. And then she remembered what Christopher had taught the dog—and relatedly, what he had taught her.

Grabbing a firmer hold on the leash, she said in the most authoritative-sounding voice she could summon, "Jonathan, stay!"

The dog abruptly stopped trotting toward the house and stood as still as a statue, waiting for her to "release" him from her verbal hold with the single word Christopher had told her to use.

Getting her bearings, Lily turned toward the front of the house so that the dog wouldn't catch her off guard when he resumed running. Only then did she say, "Okay," in the same authoritative voice.

Just as she'd expected, the very next moment Jonathan was back to bounding toward the front door.

Lily was right on his heels. "Someday, dog, you are just going to have to get a grip on that enthusiasm of yours. But I guess that day isn't going to be today," she said, resigned to having a barely harnessed tiger by the tail—at least for a few more weeks.

The veterinarian's idea of having her drop the dog off at his animal hospital each morning was beginning to sound better and better, she thought as she unlocked her front door.

Once Jonathan had passed over the threshold, she let the leash go and entered the house herself. She locked her front door a moment later. There had been several break-ins in the development in the past couple of months and she was determined that her house was not going to be part of those statistics.

Turning from the door, Lily looked down at the dog. "Looks like we're on our own tonight, Jonathan. But that's okay, we don't need Christopher around. We'll do just fine without him."

The dog whined in response.

Lily sighed, sinking down on the couch. "I know, I know, who am I kidding? We're not really fine on our own, but we just have to make the best of it, right? Glad to hear you agree," she told the dog, pretending to take his silence as agreement.

She thought of the housebreaking lessons that lay ahead of her. No time like the present, right?

"What do you say to having some superearly dinner. We'll fill that tummy of yours and then spend the rest of the evening trying to empty it. Sound like fun to you?" she asked, looking at the puppy. "Me, neither," she agreed. "But what has to be done, has to be done, so we might as well get started. The sooner this sinks in for you, the happier both of us are going to be."

Just then, she heard her cell phone ringing. Her first thought was that Theresa had gotten another booking and wanted to run a few desserts past her to see what she thought of them.

Grabbing her purse, she began to dig through the chaotic interior to locate her phone.

"Why is it always on the bottom?" she asked the dog, who just looked at her as if she was speaking in some foreign language. "You're no help," she murmured. "Ah, here it is." Triumphantly, she pulled the phone out of the depths of her purse.

Just before she pressed "accept" she automatically looked at the caller ID.

The caller's name jumped out at her: Christopher Whitman.

Chapter 8

Lily pressed the green band labeled "accept" on her cell. "Hello?"

"Lily, hi, it's Chris." The deep voice on the other end of the line seemed to fill the very air around her the moment he began to speak. "I'm afraid there's been a change of plans. I'm not going to be able to make it over to your place."

"I kind of figured that part out already," she told him, trying very hard to sound casual about the whole thing, rather than disappointed, which she was. While she had more or less assumed that he wasn't going to come over, she had to admit that there was still a small part of her that had held out hope when she saw that the incoming call was from him.

Ordinarily, Christopher would have just left it at that,

ending the call by saying goodbye with no further explanation.

But he didn't want to, not this time.

He'd always been nothing if not honest with himself and he had to admit that this was *not* an ordinary, run-of-the-mill situation. Not for him. He wasn't sure just what it actually was at this point, but he did know that he wanted to be able to keep all his options open—just in case.

"Rhonda was hit by a car," he told Lily.

"Oh, my God, how awful." Lily's sympathies instantly rushed to the foreground, completely wiping out every other emotion in its path, even though the person's name meant nothing to her. He hadn't mentioned the woman before, but she obviously meant a great deal to him. "Is there anything at all that I can do to help?"

"No, I've got it covered," he told her. "But I'd like to take a rain check on that home training session if it's okay with you."

"Sure, absolutely." Her words came out in a rush. The thought of car accidents always ran a cold chill down her spine. She could relate to loss easily. At times she felt *too* easily. "Don't give it another thought. Go be with Rhonda."

Whoever that was, she added silently.

It occurred to her that she had no idea if Christopher was talking about a friend, a relative, or possibly a girlfriend, or someone more significant to him than that. What she did know was that the event itself sounded absolutely terrible and she really felt for him.

It did cause her to wonder how he could have even

spared a single thought about helping her to start house-breaking Jonathan at a time like this. The man either had an exceedingly big heart, or she was missing something here.

"I really hope she pulls through, Christopher," Lily told him in all sincerity.

She heard silence on the other end. Just when she'd decided that the connection had been lost or terminated, she heard Christopher respond.

"Yeah, me, too."

"Let me know how she's doing—if you get a chance," Lily added hastily. The last thing she wanted was for him to think she was being clingy or pushy at a time like this.

It might have been her imagination, but she thought he sounded a little strange, or possibly slightly confused, as he said, "Yeah, sure." And then his voice became more urgent and almost gruff as she heard him tell her, "I have to go."

The line went dead.

She stood looking at her cell phone for a long moment, even though there was no one on the other end anymore.

"Guess it really is just the two of us, Jonathan." The Labrador made a yipping sound, as if in agreement.

Putting her cell phone down on the coffee table, Lily went to the kitchen to see if her landline's answering machine had any incoming calls on it. She hadn't had a chance to check today's messages and wondered if there were any messages on it from a frantic dog owner who had seen one of her posters.

She had a total of three calls waiting to be heard. For a moment, she stood looking at the blinking light, considering erasing the calls without playing them. Lily reasoned that if she didn't hear the message, she wouldn't be responsible for not returning the call.

C'mon, Lil, since when is ignorance the kind of excuse you want to hide behind? You were eager enough to get rid of Mr. Ball of Fur when you first found him, remember? You wouldn't have posted all those flyers everywhere if you weren't.

While that was true enough then, she'd had a change of heart in these past few hours. Actually, now that she thought of it, her change of heart had been ongoing and gradual.

With all the problems that having this puppy in her life generated, she still found herself reluctant to just hand him over to some stranger, to in effect close her eyes and banish him from her life.

Lily shook her head, looking at the puppy again. It was amazing to her how quickly she could get used to another creature roaming around in her space.

"You're getting attached again, Lil," she reprimanded herself sternly. "You know that was something you didn't want happening."

Well, whether or not she wanted it, Lily thought, looking down at the dog again, it was now official. She *liked* this moving repository of continually falling fur. *Really* liked him.

"So, what do you want to do first?" she asked Jonathan.

And then her eyes widened as she saw his tail go up

in that peculiar way he had of making it look like one half of a squared parenthesis. The next moment, she remembered the only time he did that was when he wanted to eliminate wastes from his body.

"Oh, no, no, no, you don't," she insisted.

Grabbing him by his collar—his leash was temporarily missing in action—keeping her fingers as loose as she could within the confining space, she quickly pulled the dog to the rear of the house and ultimately, to the sliding glass back door.

All the while she kept repeating only one order: "Hold it, hold it, hold it!"

She finally stopped saying that the moment she got Jonathan into the backyard. And that was when the energetic puppy let loose. She would have preferred he hadn't made his deposit on the cement patio instead of in the grass just beyond that strip, but in her opinion that was still a whole lot better than having that same thing transpire on the rug or—heaven forbid—the travertine in the kitchen. The latter would become permanently stained if she wasn't extremely quick about cleaning up every last trace of Jonathan's evacuation process.

"You finished?" she asked the dog. As if in response, he trotted back to the sliding glass door, wanting readmittance to the house. "Okay, I'll take that as a yes," she told the animal gamely. "But I want to hear the moment you think you have another overwhelming urge to part company with your breakfast or any of those treats you all but mugged me for in the park."

Acting as if his mistress had lapsed into silence rather than putting him on notice, Jonathan immediately began sniffing around the corners of the room, making no secret of the fact that he was foraging.

He was able to stick his nose in and under all the tight spots, where the cabinets just fell short of meeting the floor. Crumbs had a habit of residing there and Jonathan was hunting crumbs in lieu of snaring any bigger game.

Lily observed his progress. "You're not going to find anything," she warned the animal. "I keep a very clean house—which means that if you have any further ideas about parting ways with your fur—*don't*. I've got better things to do than vacuum twice a day because you shed 24/7." She turned toward the pantry. "C'mon, I'll give you your dinner—and then I'd appreciate it if you just stretched out over there on the floor by the sofa and went to sleep."

She put Jonathan's food out first, then went to fix something for herself.

The puppy, she noticed out of the corner of her eye, instantly vacuumed up what she'd put into his bowl. Finished, he came over to sit at her feet in the kitchen, waiting for her to either drop something on the floor or pity him enough to share her dinner with him.

"Eye me all you want with those big, sad, puppy eyes of yours," she told him firmly. "It's not happening. While I'm in charge of taking care of you, you're not about to turn into some huge treat-based blimp."

If he understood her—or appreciated her looking out for his health—Jonathan gave her no indication of it. Instead, he seemed to turn into just a massive, needy, walking stomach, ready to desperately sell his little doggie soul for a morsel of food.

Lily had every intention of remaining firm. She held out for as long as she could, looking everywhere but down as she ate. But he got to her. She could *feel* Jonathan pathetically staring at her. And while she knew she was partially responsible inasmuch as she was reading into that expression, she found she couldn't hold out against the canine indefinitely.

With a sigh, she broke off a piece of the sandwich she settled on having and put it on the floor in front of Jonathan. It was gone, disappearing behind his lips faster than she could have executed a double take. She'd barely sat up straight in the chair again.

Looking at the animal, Lily could only shake her head incredulously. "Certainly wouldn't want to be marooned on a deserted island with the likes of you. Two days into it and you'd be eyeing me like I was a pile of raw pork chops—center cut," she added for good measure.

Jonathan barked and she was sure that he was voicing his agreement.

After clearing away the two d' ;hes and the bowl that she had used, Lily found herself way too wound up as well as just too restless to go to bed or even to watch some mundane television program with the hopes that *it* would put her to sleep.

It was Sunday night and as a rule, there was simply nothing worthwhile watching on any of the countless cable channels that she received at that time.

Still, it was far too quiet without the TV, so she switched it on as she washed off the dishes. She kept

it on as soothing background noise, glancing at it occasionally just to see if anything interesting turned up.

It never did.

Without anything to watch and with her new four-
footed companion sleeping in the corner, Lily did what
she always did when she needed to unwind.

She baked.

She started by taking out everything that might lend
itself to baking pastries and lining up the various containers, boxes and jars, large and small, on the far side
of the kitchen counter. Seeing what she had to work
with, Lily decided what to make.

She was on her third batch of Bavarian-style pastries—
low-fat just to prove her point that baking didn't necessarily mean fattening—when she heard the doorbell ring.

The dog's head, she noticed, instantly went up. The
dog had gone from zero to sixty in half a second. Jonathan was wide-awake and completely alert.

"Hold that pose, I might need you," she told Jonathan.

Wiping her hands, she went to the front door. Her
furry shadow came with her. She didn't bother wasting
time by telling him to stay. Having him there beside her
generated an aura of safety that had been missing from
her life for a while now. Mentally, she crossed her fingers and hoped it wasn't anyone in response to the flyer.

Instead of looking through the peephole, which she
found usually distorted the person on the other side of
the door, she called out, "Who is it and what are you
doing here?"

"Dr. Chris Whitman and I've come to apologize."

Lily's heart ramped up its pace. She fumbled with the lock as she flipped it.

"You already apologized. Don't you remember?" she asked as she opened the door for him. "When you called to tell me you weren't coming, you apologized over the phone."

He remembered, but it hadn't seemed nearly adequate enough to him. And besides, after what he'd just been through, he didn't want to immediately go home to his empty house. He wanted to see a friendly face, talk to a friendly person—and relax in her company. The very fact that he did was a surprise to him since toward the end, he felt nothing but relief to get out of his relationship with Irene.

But then, Lily wasn't Irene. "Then I've come to apologize again," he amended. "And I'm still Dr. Chris Whitman," he added cheerfully, referring to her initial inquiry through the door.

"You didn't have to apologize the first time," she told him. "I mean, it was nice that you thought you had to, but I understand. You had a crisis to handle. By the way, how is she doing?"

He nodded, as if to preface what he was about to say with a visual confirmation. "She's actually doing better than I expected. It looks like she's going to pull through."

It had been touch and go for a while there. It wasn't as if this was the first operation he'd ever performed but it was by far the most demanding and he had done extensive volunteer work at several animal shelters.

The five-year-old Irish setter had required a great deal of delicate work.

"That's wonderful news," Lily said, genuinely pleased. She had to raise her voice because Jonathan had decided to become vocal. The animal obviously felt that he was being ignored by the two people in the room, most especially by the man he had taken such a shine to. "But what are you doing here? Shouldn't you be back at the hospital with her?"

Christopher crouched down to scratch the puppy behind his ears. Jonathan fell over on the floor, clearly in ecstasy.

"Under normal circumstances," Christopher agreed, "I might have stayed the night, but Lara's there. She volunteered to take over this shift. And my number's on speed dial if anything comes up."

That was rather an odd way to put it, Lily thought. Out loud she repeated, "Lara?" Another woman? Just how many women were part of this man's life?

"Yes." He realized that he probably hadn't properly introduced Lily to everyone by name the one time she'd been at his animal hospital. "She's one of the animal techs. You met her the other day when you brought Jonny in to see me."

Lily came to a skidding halt mentally. She put up her hand to stop the flow of his words for a minute. She needed to get her head—not to mention facts—straight.

"You have one of your animal techs watching over Rhonda?" Lily asked incredulously, trying her best to unscramble what Christopher was telling her.

"Yes. Why? What's wrong?" he asked, mystified by

the very strange expression that Lily had on her face right now. "It's not like this is her first time."

Well, the only way she was going to clear this up was by asking some very basic questions, Lily decided. "What relation is Rhonda to you? I know it's none of my business, but I'm getting a very strong feeling that we're not on the same page here—"

He'd drink to that, Christopher thought.

"Hold it," he ordered out loud. "Back up." He really wasn't sure he'd heard her correctly. Or had he? "What did you just ask me?"

He was angry because she was prying, Lily thought. She didn't want to jeopardize her relationship with Christopher. She needed him to help her with the puppy. She just wasn't good at these sorts of things, despite her best intentions.

"Sorry, I stepped over the line, I guess," she told him. "I was just trying to get things straight, but if you don't want to tell me about Lara, or Rhonda, that's your right and I—"

This misunderstanding was getting way out of hand, Christopher realized. The only way to stop this rolling snowflake from becoming a giant, insurmountable snowball to end all snowballs was just to blurt out the truth to Lily, which he did—as fast as possible.

"Rhonda's my neighbor's Irish setter," he explained in as few words as he could. "Josh called me in a panic just as I was driving to your place, said someone driving erratically had hit Rhonda and then just kept on going. She was alive, but had lost a lot of blood. I couldn't turn him down."

Rhonda was a dog? The thought presented itself to her in huge capital letters. The rush of relief that ushered those words in was almost overwhelming. She did her best to refrain from analyzing it. She wasn't equipped for that right now.

"Of course you couldn't." She said the words so fiercely, at first he thought that Lily was putting him on.

But one look into her eyes and he knew she was being completely serious.

And completely lovable while she was at it, he couldn't help thinking.

Christopher only realized much later that his real undoing began at that very minute.

Just as hers did for her.

For Lily, it was realizing that the man who was helping her discover the right way to train Jonathan wasn't just someone who was kind when it was convenient for him to be that way, or because he was trying to score points with a woman he'd just met and appeared to be moderately attracted to. The turning point for her, the moment she discovered that she had absolutely no say when it came to being able to properly shield her heart from being breeched, was in finding out that Christopher was selfless across the board, especially when it came to animals who needed him.

Her heart went up for sale and was simultaneously taken off the market by that same man in that very small instant of time.

Instantly distracted, Christopher stopped talking and took a deep breath. His question was fairly rhetorical because he had a hunch that he knew the answer to it. "What is that fantastic smell?"

It was very hard to keep her face from splitting in half; her smile was that wide and it just continued to widen. It had swiftly reached her eyes when she suggested, "Why don't you come into the kitchen and see for yourself?"

Turning on her heel, she led the way into her small kitchen. She didn't realize at the time that there was a bounce to her step.

But Christopher did.

In keeping with the kitchen's compact size, there was an island in the middle, but a small one, just large enough to accommodate two of the three trays she'd placed in the oven earlier. She had taken the two trays out while the third one was still baking.

The closer he came, the stronger the aroma seemed to be. His appetite was firmly aroused and Christopher immediately transformed into a kid walking into his favorite candy shop. "Are those the same pastries you made the other day?"

"Some are, some aren't. I like to mix it up," she confessed.

The pastries on the trays were still warm and were most definitely emitting a siren song as he stared at them.

"Are these all for work?" he asked, circling the trays on the island slowly.

"No, they're for me," she corrected. "Not to eat," she explained quickly. "Baking relaxes me. I usually give them away after I finish." Gesturing toward the trays, she asked, "Would you like to sample one?"

She got as far as gesturing before he took her up on the offer he'd assumed she'd been about to make.

Chapter 9

"You are, without a doubt, an amazingly gifted young woman."

Christopher uttered the unabashed praise the minute he had finished savoring his very first bite of the pastry he had randomly chosen off the nearest tray. The pastry was filled with cream whipped into fluffy peaks and laced with just enough Amaretto to leave a very pleasant impression. It was practically light enough to levitate off the tray.

"I bake," she said, shrugging carelessly. Lily was warmed by his praise, but she didn't want to make it seem as if she was letting his compliment go to her head.

"No," Christopher corrected her. "My late mother, God bless her, 'baked.' Her desserts, when she made them, always tasted of love, but they were predictable, and while good, they weren't 'special.' Yours are definitely special. You don't just 'bake,' you *create*. There's a big difference."

Christopher paused as he indulged himself a little more, managing to eat almost three quarters of the small pastry before he went on.

"You know, I'm usually one of those people who eat to live, not live to eat. Nobody could *ever* accuse me of being a foodie or whatever those people who love to regale other people with their so-called 'food adventures' like to call themselves. But if I had access to something like this whenever I felt like indulging in a religious experience, I'd definitely change my affiliation—not to mention that I'd probably become grossly overweight. Speaking of which," Christopher went on, switching subjects as he eyed her, "why aren't you fat?" he asked.

"I already told you, I don't eat what I make." Then, before he could say that he had a hard time believing that, she admitted, "Oh, I sample a little here, a dab there, to make sure I'm not going to make someone throw up, but I've just never felt the inclination to polish off a tray of pastries."

Christopher's expression told her that he was having a hard time reconciling that with his own reaction to the end product of her culinary efforts.

"If I were you," he told her, "I'd have a serious talk with myself, because your stubborn half is keeping you from having nothing short of a love affair with your taste buds." He licked the last of the whipped cream from his fingertips, discovering he craved more. "How *did* you come up with these?" he asked, waving his hand at the less-than-full tray of pastries that was closest to him on the counter.

Her method was no big secret, either. It was based on a practical approach.

"It's a very simple process, really. I just gather together a bunch of ingredients and see where they'll take me," she told him.

As if to back up her explanation, Lily indicated the containers, bottles and boxes that had been pressed into service and were now all huddled together on the far side of the counter.

He thought that was rather a strange way to phrase it. But creative people had a very different thought process.

"That means what?" he asked her, curious about her process. "You stare at them until they suddenly speak to you?"

"Not in so many words, but yes, maybe. Why?"

He shook his head, still marveling at her stripped-down approach to creating something so heavenly. With very little effort, he could have easily consumed half a dozen pastries until he exploded.

"Just trying to familiarize myself with your creative process," he answered, then added, "I've never been in the presence of a magician before."

"And you aren't now. It's not magic, it's baking. And that, by the way," she said, indicating the pastry he'd just had, "was one of my low-fat pastries."

He stared at her, undecided if she was telling him the truth or putting him on. "You're kidding."

"Not when it comes to calories," she answered with solemnity.

"Low-fat?" he asked again, looking at the rest of the pastries.

"Low-fat," she confirmed. "Told you you couldn't tell the difference."

Christopher shook his head, clearly impressed. "Now that's really *inspired* baking," he told her with just a hint of wonder.

If he wanted to flatter her, who was she to fight it? Lily thought.

"Okay, I'll go with that." She carefully moved around Jonathan, who appeared to be hanging on his hero's every word. "Now, can I fix you some dinner to go with your 'magical' dessert?" she asked.

He shook his head. "I'm good," he told her. When she raised an eyebrow, waiting for him to explain, he said, "I grabbed a burger on the way over here. I didn't want to put you out."

"Did you eat the burger you grabbed?" she asked. "Because I can still make you something a little more edible than a fast-food hamburger."

He liked the way she crinkled her nose in what appeared to be unconscious disdain of the entire fast-food industry. "I'm sure you can, but the burger filled the hole in my stomach for the time being. Besides, that rain check I mentioned earlier was supposed to be for dinner, too. Dinner out," he emphasized.

"You don't have to wait to be seated if we have dinner in," she pointed out gently. Lily viewed all cooking as an outlet for her and she thoroughly enjoyed doing it.

She wanted to convince him that this definitely wasn't "putting her out."

"Don't you like being waited on?" he asked Lily.

"Not particularly," she admitted. Then, not wanting to sound like some sort of a weirdo, she told him, "Although I'm not overly fond of washing dishes."

"Do you?" he asked in surprise. "Wash dishes," he elaborated when he didn't get a response.

"Yes." Why was he asking? She thought she'd just said as much.

He glanced over toward the appliance next to her stove. "Is your dishwasher broken?"

She automatically glanced at it because he had, even though she didn't need to in order to answer his question. "I don't know, I've never used it. There's just me and it doesn't seem right to run all that water just for a few plates."

There was a solution to that. "Then wait until you have enough dishes to fill up the dishwasher," he suggested.

"That seems even less right." Lily suppressed a shiver as she envisioned stacking dirty plates on top of one another.

"Leaving a bunch of dirty dishes lying around until there's enough for a full load sounds awful. Either way is offensive," she said with feeling. "It's a lot easier if I just wash as I go. My mom taught me that," she told him out of the blue. "This was her house—*our* house, as she liked to put it even though I never paid a dime toward its purchase. My mom handled everything," she recalled fondly. "Held down two, sometimes three jobs, just to pay the bills.

"If there was anything extra, she proudly put it toward my college fund. By the time I was set to go to college, there was a lot of money in that little slush fund of hers. Enough to set me on the road to any college I wanted."

Caught up in her reminiscing, Christopher asked, "So where did you go?"

He watched as her smile faded. Sorrow all but radiated from her. "I didn't. That was the year my mother got sick. Really sick. At first, the doctors she went to see all told her it was in her head, that she was just imagining it. And then one doctor decided to run a series of more complex tests on her—which was when Mom found out that she wasn't imagining it. She had brain cancer." She said the diagnosis so quietly, Christopher wouldn't have heard her if he wasn't standing so close to her.

"By the time they found it, it had metastasized to such a degree that it was too hard to cut out and get it all. They went in, did what they could, and then Mom said, 'No more.' She told them that she wanted to die at home, in one piece. And she did," Lily concluded proudly, her voice wavering slightly as she fought back the tears that always insisted on coming whenever she talked about her mother at any length.

"I used the money she had set aside for my college fund to pay off her medical bills." Lily shrugged helplessly, as if paying off the bills had somehow ultimately helped her cope with her loss. "It seemed only right to me."

Lily stopped talking for a second to wipe away the tears that insisted on seeping out from the corners of her eyes.

"Sorry, I get pretty emotional if I talk about my mother for more than two minutes." She attempted to smile and was only partially successful. "I didn't mean to get all dark and somber on you."

"That's okay," he assured her. "I know what it feels like to lose a mother who's sacrificed everything for you." She looked up at him. "You'd trade every last dime you had just to spend one more day with her. But you can't, so you do the next best thing. You prove to the world that she was right about you. That you *can* do something that counts, to make some sort of a difference. And I have no doubt that somewhere, tucked just out of sight, my mom and yours are watching over us and are pretty satisfied with the people they single-handedly raised," he told her with a comforting smile.

She took in a deep breath, doing her best to get her emotions under control. His words were tremendously comforting to her.

"You think?" she asked.

"I know," he countered. Looking at her, he saw the telltale trail forged by a stray teardrop. "You missed one."

With that, he lifted her chin with the tip of his finger, tilting it slightly. Using just his thumb, Christopher very gently wiped the stray tear away from the corner of her eye.

Their eyes met for one very long moment and her breath felt as if it had become solid in her throat as she held it.

Waiting.

Hoping.

Trying not to.

And then everything else, her surroundings, the kitchen, the pastries, even the overenergized puppy that was responsible for bringing them together in the first place, it just faded into the background like so much inconsequential scenery.

She was acutely aware of her heart and the ramped-up rhythm it had attained.

Christopher lowered his mouth to hers and ever so lightly, like a sunbeam barely touching her skin, he kissed her.

The next moment, he drew back and she thought for a second that the sound of her heart, beating wildly, had driven him back.

"Sorry, I didn't mean to take advantage of you like that," he told her, still cupping her cheek with the palm of his hand.

Her voice felt as if it was going to crack at any second as she told him, "You didn't. And there's nothing to be sorry about, except…"

"Except?" he prodded.

Lily shook her head, not wanting to continue. She was only going to embarrass herself—and him—if she said anything further. "I've said too much."

"No," he contradicted, "you've said too little. 'Except' what?" he coaxed.

Lily wavered. Maybe he did deserve to know. So she told him.

"Except maybe it didn't last long enough," she said, her voice hardly above a whisper, her cheeks burning and threatening to turn a deep pink.

"Maybe it didn't," he agreed. "Let's see if I get it right this time," he murmured just before his mouth came down on hers for a second time.

This time nothing happened in slow motion. This time, she could feel the heat travel through her as if its path had been preset with a thin line of accelerant, a line that ran between the two of them as well as over the length of her.

They'd been sitting at the counter on stools that swiveled and were now turned toward one another. Lily caught herself sliding from the stool, her arms entwined around the back of Christopher's neck.

He stood up at the same moment that she had gotten off the stool.

The length of her body slid against his. His ridges and contours registered with acute details. All the electricity between them crackled with a fierceness that was all but staggering.

He savored the sweetness of her mouth in a far more profound way than he had savored the flour-and-cream creations she'd made. The Amaretto in the pastry had been just the tiniest bit heady. The taste of her lips was far more intoxicating.

So much so that it sent out alarms all throughout his body, warning him that he was walking into something he might not be prepared for. Something he might not be equipped to handle at this juncture of his life, all things considered.

The magnitude of his feelings right at this moment was enough to make Christopher back away, concerned about the consequences that waited for him if he wasn't careful.

It wasn't easy, but he forced himself to draw back again.

"Maybe I better go," he told her, the words that emerged sounding low and almost gravelly.

She needed time to pull herself together. Time to try to understand just what it was that was going on here— aside from her complete undoing. Time to fix the shield around her heart because it had seriously cracked.

"Maybe you'd better," she agreed.

He tried to remember what had brought him here in the first place. It was difficult to get a fix on his thoughts; they were scattered and unfocused. All he was aware of was how much he wanted her.

"I just wanted to tell you in person why I backed out this afternoon," he finally managed to say.

"I appreciate that," she told him, then added belatedly, "I appreciate everything you've done."

Her wits managed to finally come together. The relief she experienced at being able to think again was incredible. She almost felt as if she was in full possession of her mental faculties again. Or at least enough to be able to carry on a normal conversation. Even so, she didn't want to push herself and have it all fall apart on her again.

Something about this man threatened her carefully

constructed world and if she wasn't on her guard, all
the work she had put in to keeping her heart out of danger's reach would go up in smoke.

"Why don't you take one or two for the road? Or
more if you like," Lily suggested, doing her very best
to sound casual. It wasn't easy talking with one's heart
in one's throat.

"One or two for the road?" he echoed. They'd just
been locked in a kiss, so was she talking about those?
he wondered, looking at her uncertainly.

"Or more," she repeated again. "I can wrap up as
many pastries as you'd like to take home with you.
Maybe even give a couple to your poor neighbor for
what he's just gone through."

And then it all clicked into place. She was talking
about the pastries, not about kissing him again. Christopher laughed—more at himself and at what he had
thought she was saying than at what Lily was actually
telling him.

"You're being too generous," he said.

She didn't quite see it that way. "I like to spread
smiles around and these pastries make people smile."

"That they do," he wholeheartedly agreed. He looked
over toward the remaining two and a half trays. "I can
completely attest to that."

"Then let me give you some." It was no longer a suggestion but a statement of intent.

She had a total of eight pastries wrapped, placed in
a cardboard container and ready to go within a couple
of minutes.

"You sure you don't want more?" she asked. He'd

stopped her when she had reached for the ninth pastry, saying eight was already too much.

"I want them all," he told her honestly. *And more than just pastries right now,* he added silently. He concentrated, determined to keep even a hint of the latter thought from registering on his face. "But in the spirit of sharing, what you just packed up for me to take with me is more than enough." Not wanting to leave it just at that, he told her, "I can come by tomorrow afternoon if you like—and we can pick up where we left off."

Belatedly, Christopher realized he had worded that last line rather poorly, allowing her to misunderstand his meaning. "Left off training Jonny," he tacked on awkwardly.

He had never been a smooth talker—the type who was able to sell ice cubes to polar bears—but he had never had this much trouble saying what he meant. This woman had definitely scrambled his ability to communicate. Why was that?

He had no hard-and-fast answer—and the one that did suggest itself made him nervous.

"That would be very nice of you," Lily was saying as she walked him to the front door. Jonathan came along, prancing around, all but tripping both of them as he wove in and out between them. "I'll bake you something else next time," she promised with a smile that completely seeped under his skin.

Christopher laughed, shaking his head as he opened the front door. "You do that and I'm going to have to start shopping in the husky-men section of the local department store."

Her eyes swept over him, as if to verify what she already knew. "You have a long way to go before that happens," she assured him.

"Not as long as you think," he replied just before he turned and walked out. He didn't trust himself to stand on the doorstep one second longer.

She made him want things he had no business wanting. Things that, if he recalled correctly—and he did— would only ultimately promise to lead to an unhappy ending sometime in the near future.

Been there, done that, he thought as he got into his car and drove away.

As if to contradict him, the warm scent coming from the pastries seemed to rise up and intensify, filling his car. It made him think of Lily all the way home.

Chapter 10

There wasn't a single position on her bed that felt comfortable enough for her to fall asleep for more than a few minutes at a time. And when she actually *did* manage to fall asleep, she wound up dreaming about what was keeping her awake, perpetuating her dilemma.

She dreamed about a magnetic pair of blue eyes that pulled her in and thick, dirty-blond hair that curled just enough to make her fingers itchy to run through it.

And at the end of each and every one of these mini-dreams Lily would experience a deep, dark feeling of bereavement, of being suddenly, irreversibly left behind, to continue on alone.

She felt as if her insides had been hollowed out by a sharp, serrated carving knife. Then she'd bolt upright, awake and damp with perspiration despite the fact that the night air was cool tonight.

Alone in her bedroom, her knees drawn up against her chest as if her body was forming an impenetrable circle, Lily recognized her nightmares for what they were, what they signified: fear. Fear of caring, fear of experiencing the consequences that came from allowing herself to care about someone.

Was she crazy to even *think* that she could have some sort of a relationship without paying the ultimate terrible price that relationship demanded? If you danced, then you were required to pay the piper. She knew that and she desperately didn't want to have anything at all to do with the piper.

Not ever again.

The best thing was just to remain strangers, the way they were now.

Finally, at six in the morning, Lily gave up all attempts of trying to get even a solid hour of uninterrupted sleep.

With a deep sigh, she threw off her covers and got out of her extremely rumpled bed. Glancing at the tangled sheets and bunched-up comforter, it occurred to her that her bed looked as if it had been declared a war zone.

Maybe it had been, she thought ruefully. Except that there had been no winner declared.

She normally never left her bedroom in the morning without first making her bed, but this morning, she abandoned the bed entirely. She just wanted to get out of the house.

Maybe some fresh air would do her some good.

Putting on a pair of jeans and donning a light sweater, she announced to the puppy that had insisted on sleeping on her bedroom floor, "We're going out for a walk, Jonathan."

Fully awake in less than an instant, the Labrador half ran, half slid down the stairs and then darted around until she reached the landing to join him. Picking the leash up where she'd dropped it by the staircase, Lily hooked it onto the dog's collar. At the last minute she remembered to take a bag with her just in case she got lucky and the dog actually relieved himself while they were out.

Taking Jonathan for a walk was yet another exercise in patience. It consisted of all but dashing down one residential street after another, followed by periods of intense sniffing that lasted so long Lily finally had to literally drag the puppy away—at which point he would abruptly dash again.

This theme and variation of extremes went on for close to an hour before Lily finally decided that she'd had enough and wanted to head back to the house.

Just before they reached their destination, Jonathan abruptly stopped dead, nearly causing her to collide with him because of the shift in momentum. When she turned toward the dog to upbraid him for almost tripping her, she saw that the puppy was relieving himself.

She realized that meant she didn't need to be so vigilant for the next few hours. "I guess I'm home free for half the day, right?"

The Labrador had no opinion one way or the other.

He was far too busy investigating what he had just parted with. Lily pulled him back before he managed to get too close to it.

This having a dog was going to take some getting used to, she thought, elbowing the puppy out of the way in order to clean up after him.

A *lot* of getting used to, she amended after she finished with her task.

Lily got back to her house just in time to hear her landline ring. Unlocking the door and hurrying inside, she managed to get to the telephone a scarce heartbeat before it went to voice mail.

Dropping Jonathan's leash, she picked up the receiver. "Hello?"

There was about a second or so delay before someone answered her. She reacted the moment that she heard his voice.

"Lily, hi. I was just getting ready to leave a message on your machine," the deep voice on the other end told her.

She could feel goose bumps forming on her skin. There was something incredibly intimate and, okay, *arousing* about Christopher's voice on the phone. But that still didn't change her resolve about keeping the man at arm's length. If anything, it strengthened it.

"Now you can leave a message with me," she said, forcing herself to sound as cheerful as she possibly could.

When she heard him draw in a long breath, she knew

it couldn't be good. "I'm afraid I'm going to have to cancel today."

She had a feeling, a split second before he said the words, that he was going to bow out. Which was fine, because that was what she wanted.

But if that was the case, why was there this vast, hard lump of disappointment doing a nosedive in the pit of her stomach?

"I didn't know you had the power to do that," she said, still doing her best to sound light and upbeat. "To cancel an entire day." The silence on the other end made her feel like squirming. "Sorry, that was me just trying to be funny. I didn't mean to interrupt you while you were talking."

He did the worst thing he could have done, Lily thought. He was understanding. "You weren't interrupting, you were being humorous."

Maybe he was canceling because he had another emergency, and she was making wisecracks. Lily felt terrible.

"And you're being nice." She apologized in the best way she knew how. She absolved him of any obligation. "It's okay, about canceling," she added since she knew her words sounded vague. "I understand."

"How can you understand?" Christopher asked. "I haven't told you why I'm canceling yet."

He had a point. Her nerves were making her jump to conclusions. She searched for something plausible to use as an excuse, but came up empty. She went with vague. "I'm sure it's for a good reason."

"I wish it wasn't," he told her honestly. Something

had made him go in very early this morning, to check on his neighbor's dog. Rhonda hadn't been as responsive as he would have liked. Further investigation had brought him to this conclusion. "Rhonda had some internal bleeding suddenly start up. I have to go back in and cauterize the wound, then sew her up again. When I finish, I want to watch her for a few hours, just to be sure she's on the mend this time. That means I won't be coming over today to work with Jonathan."

That he could even think about that when he had an emergency on his hands made her feel that he was a very exceptional person. She didn't want him to feel as if he was letting her down in any way.

"Well, as it turns out, Jonathan and I went out for a long walk this morning and he decided he couldn't hold it long enough to come back to the house to make a mess, so he went outside."

Tickled at the way she'd narrated her latest adventure with the dog, Christopher laughed. "Congratulations. But you do realize you're not out of the woods yet, right? The process has to be repeated—a lot—before it becomes ingrained. Did you remember to praise him after he finished going?"

Lily pressed her lips together. She *knew* she'd forgotten something. "Is praising him important?" she asked, hoping he'd tell her that it was just a minor detail.

"It is—and I'll take that as a no. Next time Jonny goes, praise him to the hilt and tell him what a wonderful puppy he is. Trust me," he assured her, "it works wonders."

She sighed, glancing at the dog who had plopped

down at her feet, apparently content to lie there, at least for the moment. "I'll remember next time."

"Listen, I need to go, but you can still drop Jonny off here on your way to work tomorrow—unless you feel confident enough to leave him alone at your house," he added, not wanting her to think he was talking her into leaving the dog at his clinic for the day.

"I'll drop him off," she said quickly, relieved that he hadn't taken back his offer. She wasn't naive enough to think that one success meant that the puppy's behavior was permanently altered. "And thank you."

"Don't mention it. Now I've really got to go," he told her again.

Christopher hung up before she had a chance to say goodbye.

Mixed feelings scrambled through her as Lily hung up the receiver. She didn't know whether to be relieved that Christopher wasn't coming over—relieved that she wouldn't find herself alone with him—or upset for the very same exact reason.

Jonathan barked and she realized that he was no longer lying down at her feet. The bark sounded rather urgent. She had a feeling that he was asking for his breakfast. Christopher—and her present ambivalent dilemma—wouldn't have been part of her life if Jonathan hadn't been on her doorstep that fateful morning.

"Life was a lot simpler before you came into it, Jonathan," she told the puppy.

Jonathan just went on barking at her until she began walking to the kitchen. Following her, his barking took on a different, almost triumphant intensity.

Lily laughed to herself. Exactly who was training whom here?

She had a sneaking suspicion she knew. Right now, the score was Jonathan one, Lily zero. She took out a can of dog food and popped the top.

The following morning, Lily nearly drove right past the turn she was supposed to make to get to the animal hospital. At the last minute, she slowed down and deliberately made the right-hand turn.

Less than a mile later, she was driving into the rather busy upscale strip mall where Christopher's animal hospital was located.

Lily had come close to driving past the initial right-hand turn not because she had a poor sense of direction, but because she had a strong sense of survival. The more she interacted with the handsome, sexy veterinarian, the more she was going to *want* to interact with him—and that sort of thing would lead to an attachment she told herself that she ultimately didn't want.

But, as always, stronger still was her utter disdain for behaving like a coward. It didn't matter whether no one knew or not. *She* would know and that was all that really counted. Once she began going off in that direction, there would be no end to the things she would find excuses to run from.

She didn't want to live like that, didn't want fear to get the upper hand over her or to govern any aspect of her life.

If she allowed it to happen once, then it would be sure to happen again. And next time, it would be easier to just back away from something. Before she'd know it, her individuality would be forfeited, buried beneath an ever-growing mountain of things for her to fear and to avoid *because* of that fear.

At that point, she wouldn't be living, merely existing. Life, her mother had always told her, had to be relished and held on to with both hands. It wasn't easy, but it was definitely worth it.

Conquering this fear of involvement because she feared being left alone had to be on the top of her to-do list. Otherwise, she was doomed to be lonely right from the beginning.

The receptionist, Erika, looked up, a prepasted smile on her lips as she said, "Hello." And then recognition set in. Once it did, the woman's smile became genuine.

"Hi, Dr. Whitman said you might stop by." Coming out from behind the desk, Erika turned her attention to Jonathan. "Hi, boy. Have you come to spend the day with us?"

"I guess I'm boarding him," Lily said, handing over the leash to the receptionist.

"Not technically," Erika told her. "If you were boarding him, there'd be a charge. Dr. Whitman said there'd be no charge, so Jonathan's just visiting," she concluded with a warm smile.

While she was grateful, that didn't sound quite right to Lily. "Do you often have pets come by who are just visiting?"

"Jonathan's our first," the receptionist answered honestly. Then, sensing that the Labrador's owner might be having second thoughts about leaving him for the day, Erika told her, "Don't worry, Jonathan will be just fine here. We could stand to have a mascot hanging around the place. Right, Jonathan?"

The dog responded by wagging his tail so hard it thumped on the floor.

"I'm not worried."

Truthfully, Lily wasn't having second thoughts about leaving Jonathan. The second thoughts involved her running into Christopher. She wondered if he was already here, and if he was, why hadn't he come out?

Maybe it was better if he didn't, she decided in the next moment.

Right, like that's going to change anything about your reaction to the man.

She pressed her lips together and blocked out the little voice in her head that insisted on being logical. It was time for her to say goodbye to the puppy and get going.

Yet for some reason, her feet weren't getting the message. They remained planted exactly where they were, as if they were glued to the spot.

She allowed herself just one question—and then she was going to leave, she insisted. Really.

"How's Rhonda?"

Holding on to Jonathan's leash, Erika looked at her in surprise. "You know Rhonda?"

Serves you right for saying anything.

"Not exactly," Lily admitted. "But Chris—Dr. Whitman," she amended quickly, "mentioned that she was his neighbor's dog and that she'd been hit by a car the other day. I was just wondering if she was doing any better now."

Erika actually beamed.

"Oh, she's doing *much* better. Would you like to see her?"

The response, followed by the question, didn't come from Erika. It came from the veterinarian who had come out of the back of the clinic and was now standing directly behind her.

Lily turned around to face him, trying to act as if her heart hadn't just given up an extra beat—or maybe three.

"Oh, I don't want to put you out any more than I already have—" She saw the puzzled expression on Christopher's face, so she explained, "By leaving Jonathan here."

"You're not putting anyone out leaving Jonny here," he assured her. He ruffled the dog's head before pushing open the swinging door that led to the back of the clinic. "Rhonda's back here," Christopher told her.

He stood, holding the rear door open with his back, waiting for her to cross the threshold and come follow him.

Lily had no choice but to do as he asked. To do otherwise would have been rude.

Christopher led the way to where the Irish setter was recuperating from her second surgery. The dog was dozing and looked almost peaceful—except for the bandages wrapped around part of her hindquarters. The dog was in a large cage.

"Isn't she cramped, staying in there?" Lily asked, looking at him. Her voice was filled with sympathy.

"Right now, I don't want her moving around too much," he explained. "If I think she's responding properly to the surgery and her stitches are healing well, I'll have her transferred to the run before I have my neighbor take her home with him."

"The run?" Lily echoed.

Rather than explain verbally, Christopher quietly took her by the hand and drew her over to another area of the hospital.

There were three wide enclosures all next to one another. All three were sufficiently wide for a large animal to not just stretch out, but to literally run around if it so chose.

Christopher stood by silently, letting her absorb it all, then waved his hand at the enclosures. "Hence the term," he explained.

It began making a little more sense, she thought, taking everything in. And then she looked at Christopher again.

"You sure you don't mind my leaving Jonathan here all day?" she asked again.

"I'm sure," he answered. And then he smiled. "Besides, it'll give you a reason to come back."

Why was it that the man could instantly make her heart flutter with just a glance. After all, she wasn't some freshly minted teenager with stars in her eyes. She was an adult who'd endured death and lived life on her own. Heart palpitations over a good-looking man were definitely *not* in keeping with the way she envisioned herself.

There was no one to give her any answers.

Just then, the receptionist popped her head in. Lily noticed that Jonathan was no longer with the woman. "Doctor, Penelope is here for her shots. I put her in Room 3."

"Tell Mrs. Olsen I'll be right in, Erika," he told his receptionist. And then he turned to Lily. "Penelope is a Chihuahua. Giving her injections is a challenge. The needle is almost bigger than she is. Poor thing shakes uncontrollably the minute I walk into the room and she sees me. I hate having any animal afraid of me," he confided as they left the area.

He paused by the swinging door that led to the reception desk. "We're open until six," he told her. "If you need to leave Jonny here longer than that, I'll just take him home with me," he offered.

"Thank you, but that really won't be necessary. I've got a very understanding boss and she'll let me take off to pick up Jonathan," she told him. "I'll see you before six," she promised.

And with that, Lily hurried out of the animal hospital, moving just a little faster than she might have under normal circumstances.

But even as she reached her vehicle and slid in behind the steering wheel, she had to come to terms with the very basic fact that no matter how quickly she moved, there was no way she was going to come close to outrunning her own thoughts.

Chapter 11

Lily felt as if she had never been busier.

Theresa's catering company had not one but two catering events going on, with both taking place that evening.

One event was a fund-raiser for a local charity. It entailed a full seven-course meal and the guest list was for a hundred and fifty-eight people. The other was a celebration on a smaller scale. It was a bridal shower and the only things that were required were champagne and a cake that could feed a group of thirty guests, give or take a few.

Lily worked almost nonstop from the moment she entered the shop until the last dessert was carefully boxed up and sent off on its way.

Without being fully aware of it, she breathed a long

sigh of relief. It felt as if she'd been on her feet for at least eighteen hours straight and, although she loved to bake, it was really good to be finished,

"You outdid yourself today," Theresa told her as she oversaw the last of the food being placed in the catering van. Turning from the vehicle, she took a closer look at her pastry chef. "You look really tired, Lily."

Concern elbowed its way to the surface. No matter what else she did or accomplished with her life, Theresa was first and foremost a mother with a mother's sense of priorities. "Do you need someone to drive you home, dear? I don't want you falling asleep behind the wheel. I'd drive you myself but I already have to figure out how to be in two places at once. Three is completely beyond my limit—for now," the older woman added with a twinkle in her eye.

"I'm fine, Theresa," Lily assured the older woman. She didn't want Theresa worrying about her. "Besides, I'm not going straight home."

Halfway out the front door, ready to drive over to the fund-raiser first to make sure that all would go well there, Theresa turned back to her. It was obvious that her interest was piqued.

"Oh?" Her bright eyes pinned Lily in place. "Do you have a date?"

"With the dog," Lily quickly informed her boss with a laugh. "I left Jonathan at the animal hospital before coming here this morning."

"Oh, is he sick?" Since this was partially her idea, to unite Lily with the puppy, she couldn't help feeling responsible for this turn of events.

Lily immediately set her straight. "Oh, no, nothing like that. Christopher, um, Dr. Whitman," she quickly amended, "said I could drop Jonathan off at his office so that he'd be properly looked after while I was gone. Otherwise, he might cause havoc in the house and I really didn't have the heart to stick him into one of those crates."

Theresa cocked her head, still regarding her intently. "You *are* talking about the dog and not the veterinarian, right?" the catering company owner wanted to verify.

Lily couldn't help laughing. Thanks to that, she felt close to rejuvenated as she answered, "Yes, but just for the record, I wouldn't want to put Dr. Whitman into a crate, either."

Theresa inclined her head, agreeing. "I'm sure that he'll be happy to hear that. And now," she announced as the catering van's driver honked to remind her that she had to get going, "I'm overdue getting out of here and have to fly. Enjoy yourself."

Lily felt the instruction was completely misplaced. "I'm only picking up my dog."

A rather ambiguous, mysterious smile graced Theresa's lips. "No reason you can't enjoy that," the older woman tossed over her shoulder just before she finally hurried out the door.

That was definitely a very odd thing to say, Lily thought, staring at the closed door.

But she didn't have any time to puzzle it out. She had a dog to pick up and—Lily glanced at her watch—only half an hour to do it in. The animal hospital closed at six o'clock.

She could make it there in twenty, Lily thought confidently.

She didn't.

Under ordinary circumstances, she could have easily made it to the animal hospital in the allotted amount of time left. However, ordinary circumstances did *not* involve a three-car collision that caused several blocks to be shut down to through traffic as two ambulances and three tow trucks were dispatched and made their way through the completely clogged area.

Utterly stressed out, the last of her patience all but stripped from her, Lily finally arrived at the Bedford Animal Hospital sixteen minutes after its doors had closed for the evening.

Even so, ever hopeful, Lily parked in the first space she could find, jumped out of her vehicle and ran to the animal hospital's front door. Lily tried turning the knob, but it was securely locked and the lights inside the office were turned off.

Everything was dark.

Now what? Christopher was going to think that she deliberately left the dog with him and wasn't coming back for Jonathan.

That was when she finally saw it.

There was a business envelope with the hospital's return address in the corner taped to the side of the doorjamb. Her name was written across the front in bold block letters.

She lost no time in pulling off the tape and opening the envelope. Inside was a single sheet of paper.

It read: "Lily, had to close up. Couldn't reach you by phone so I'm taking Jonny home with me. If you want to pick him up tonight, here's the address."

Just like the rest of the note, the address on the bottom was printed in block letters, but even bigger than the previous part so that there was no chance that she would have trouble reading it.

Staring at it, she realized that the address was close to her own house. If she wasn't mistaken, the veterinarian's house was just two developments away.

It really was a small world.

With her GPS turned on and engaged to make sure she didn't accidentally go off in the wrong direction, Lily lost no time in driving over to the address in Christopher's note.

She didn't know why, maybe because of his practice, but she had just naturally assumed that Christopher would be living in one of the newer homes that had recently gone up in the area. Once a homey small town built around a state university, Bedford had grown and was still continuing to grow. A thriving city now, it still managed to maintain its small-town feel.

Her GPS brought her to one of the older, more mature neighborhoods. Looking at the address that matched the one in the note, she judged that the house had to be around the same age as the one she lived in. That made the building approximately thirty years old.

After her mother had died, Lily found that she couldn't bear to sell the house. The thought of having another family move in and change everything around had just been too hard for her to cope with at the time. There were just too many memories there for her to part with so easily.

As she slowed down and approached the house, she saw Christopher's car in the driveway. Parking at the curb, Lily got out and made her way to the massive double front doors. The moment she rang the doorbell, she heard barking.

Jonathan.

But the very next moment Lily thought she made out two distinct barks—or was that three? There was definitely another dog there besides Jonathan. Had her dog learned to play with other dogs? The thought raised other questions in her mind, all having to do with the energetic puppy's safety.

Worried, Lily was about to ring the doorbell a second time when the door suddenly swung open. Christopher was standing inside, one hand on the door, the other holding off not one dog, but three.

The second he realized it was her, he grinned. "So you made it." The way he said it sounded as though congratulations were implied. "I wasn't sure if you'd see the note."

He shouldn't have had to post the note, Lily thought, feeling guilty that he'd had to go to extra trouble on her account. She should have been at the hospital to collect her pet before he'd ever left the place.

Her apology came out in a rush. "I'm sorry. We had two big events going on at the same time then there was a three-car collision and—"

Somewhat overwhelmed by the words and her speed in offering them, Christopher held his hand up as if to physically stop the flow of explanation.

"That's okay, no harm. I would have kept him here overnight if you couldn't come to pick him up for some reason. I did try reaching you before we closed up," he told her. All three attempts went directly to voice mail. Usually there was only one reason for that. "Is your phone off?"

She would have been the first to admit that this had not been her best day. "My cell phone battery died," she said, chagrinned but owning up to her oversight. "I left it on overnight and forgot to charge it."

Christopher looked amused rather than fazed. "I do the same thing," he told her.

Lily doubted it. She had a feeling the man was only saying that to make her feel better, and he had a tiny bit.

"Jonathan's been making friends with Leopold and Max," he told her, gesturing toward the two Great Danes that were on either side of her puppy like two huge, somewhat messy bookends. "I think they think he's a toy I brought home for them."

"As long as they don't think he's a chew toy or try to bury him in the backyard," Lily quipped, then became serious. "I don't know how to thank you," she began. "Except to just grab his leash and get out of your way."

"No need to hurry off," he countered. His eyes swept over her, backing up his statement. "I'm having pizza delivered. You can stay and have some if you like. There's more than enough to share."

"Pizza?" Lily repeated.

He wasn't quite sure why she looked at him uncertainly. "Yes. You know, that round thing with sauce and cheese. People usually have more things put on top of it."

"I know what pizza is." She looked around at the towering boxes that seemed to be just about everywhere. "Are you having that for dinner because you're busy packing up to move?"

"I'm not packing up," he told her, then asked, "What makes you think I'm moving?"

"There are boxes stacked up all over the place," she said, gesturing toward the nearest cardboard tower. "You're not moving?" she questioned. Then why were all these boxes here?

"I'm not moving *out*," he corrected. "I'm moving *in*. This is—was," he amended, "my mother's house. I thought I'd stay here instead of renting an apartment until I decide if I want to sell the place or not."

She could more than understand how he felt. "So you lost your mother recently." It wasn't a question so much as a conclusion, one voiced with all due sympathy since she vividly recalled how she had felt at the time of her mother's death.

"Feels like it," he admitted. Still, he didn't want the facts getting lost. "But it's been close to five months."

Her eyes swept around the area. The boxes almost made her claustrophobic. In his place, she didn't think she could rest until she got everything put away and the boxes stashed in some recycling bin.

"When did you move in?" she asked him, curious.

"Close to three months," he answered.

He was kidding, she thought. But one look at his chiseled face told her that he was being serious. How could he *stand* it like this?

"Three months? And you haven't unpacked?" she questioned, staring at him.

"Not all of it," he answered vaguely, hoping she didn't want any more details than that.

The truth was, except for some of his clothes, he hadn't unpacked at all. A reluctance had taken hold of him. If he didn't actually unpack his things, he could pretend that somewhere, on some plane, his old life was still intact, maybe also that his mother was still alive. He knew that was far-fetched but the mind didn't always work in a logical, linear fashion.

"I'm doing it slowly. I'm really not much on unpacking," he admitted.

Lily ventured into the next room, which looked a great deal like the room she had initially entered.

"Really? I would have never guessed," she told him, raising her voice so that he could hear her. Coming out again, she made him an offer. "How would you like some help? It goes faster if there're two people unpacking instead of one."

He didn't want to put her out and, if he read that look in her eyes correctly, he definitely didn't want her pity.

"Thanks, but I can handle it."

"No offense, Christopher, but I don't think you can. Besides, it would make me feel that in a way, I'm paying you back for taking care of Jonathan."

The doorbell rang. "Hold that thought," he instructed as he went to answer the door. "Does that mean you'll have some pizza with me?" he asked as he reached for the doorknob.

"Okay, if that's the package deal, then yes, I'll have a slice of pizza—and then get to work," she specified.

Christopher paid the delivery boy, handing him a twenty and telling him to keep the change. Closing the door with his back, he held on to the oversize box with both hands. The pizza inside was still very warm and the aroma that wafted out was mouthwatering.

Lily couldn't take her eyes off the box he was holding.

"That box is huge," she couldn't help commenting.

He glanced down as if seeing it for the first time. It *was* rather large at that. "I thought while I was at it, I might as well get enough to last until tomorrow night, too."

Lily shook her head. "Oh, no, tomorrow night you're having a hot meal," she contradicted.

"This is hot," he told her.

"A *real* hot meal," she emphasized. Since he seemed to be resisting her suggestion, one she was making for the purest of reasons, she further said, "You don't even have to go out of your way to get it. I'll bring it here to you." Once out of her mouth, she found she liked what she'd just come up with. "That way, we can eat as we unpack."

He didn't remember this becoming a two-day joint project. And while he liked the idea of having her come over and sharing another meal with him, he didn't want her to feel that this was some sort of a two-for-one deal. "You don't have to do that," he insisted.

"You didn't have to offer to watch Jonathan for me, or teach him—and me—a few of the basic commands," she countered.

Christopher could see that arguing with her was futile. She certainly didn't look stubborn, but she obviously was.

"Point taken," he allowed, "but this—" he gestured around "—is a lot more than just having a pet take up a little space."

"Potato, po*ta*to." She sniffed. "Those are my terms, take them or leave them."

He didn't quite comprehend the connection and said as much. "Not quite sure what you're getting at, but all right," he agreed, knowing when to surrender and when to dig in and fight. This was not the time for the latter. "I guess I could stand the help."

Lily smiled her approval at him. "Good, because I was going to help you whether you wanted me to or not," she told him.

"And just how were you going to do that?" Christopher asked, curious. "You don't know where anything goes."

"Granted," she allowed. "But I'm good at making educated guesses, and besides, I'm pretty sure you'd break down eventually and tell me."

"Can we eat first?" Christopher suggested, nodding at the pizza box, which was now on the coffee table, awaiting their pleasure. "After all, the boxes aren't going anywhere."

"True, but they also aren't going to unpack themselves," Lily countered.

"How about a compromise?" he asked.

Lily had always believed in compromise. And, in any event, she didn't want the man thinking she was some sort of a fanatic who picked up all the marbles and went home if she couldn't have her way.

"Go ahead," she urged, "I'm listening."

"We each have a slice first, *then* we get started," he suggested, shifting the box so that it seemed closer to her. "I don't know about you, but I had a nonstop day and I'm starving. If I don't eat something soon, I'm not going to have enough energy to *open* a box, much less put whatever's in the box away."

That just about described her day as well, she thought. But before she could say as much, or agree with him, her stomach rumbled, as if to remind her that it was running on empty. She'd worked through lunch, grabbing a handful of cherry tomatoes to try to appease her hunger. Cherry tomatoes only went so far.

"I'll take that as a yes," Christopher concluded with a satisfied grin. To cinch his argument, he raised the lid on the pizza box and inhaled deeply. The aroma was damn near seductive. "Right now, that smells almost as good to me as your pastries did the other day."

"Okay, one slice apiece and then we work. If you point me in the right direction, I'll get a couple of plates and napkins," she offered.

Christopher laughed. "Thanks, but it would probably take me more time to explain where to find them than it would take for me to get them myself." He began to cross to the kitchen, then abruptly stopped as one of the dogs sashayed around him. "Guard the pizza," he told

Lily. "And look fierce," he added. "If either Leopold or Max detect the slightest weakness, they'll tag team you and get that box away from you before you even know what's going on."

She looked at him, utterly stunned. "Tag team?" Lily repeated. "You mean like in wrestling?"

That seemed rather unbelievable to her. After all, Christopher was talking about dogs, and while this was still pretty unfamiliar territory to her, she wasn't about to endow four-footed animals with a humanlike thought process.

He had to be pulling her leg.

But Christopher seemed dead serious. "Exactly like in wrestling." He looked rather surprised and then pleased that she was familiar with the term he'd used. "Don't let those faces fool you. They're a cunning duo."

"Apparently," she murmured.

She wasn't sure if she believed Christopher, but she focused her attention on the two Great Danes just to be on the safe side.

Meanwhile, Jonathan had gotten tired trying to get the best of the two older, larger dogs and had fallen back on the familiar. He had plopped down at her feet where he remained, lying there like a panting rug. He continued to stay there even after Christopher returned with a handful of napkins as well as a couple of plates.

The second Christopher offered her the first slice, Leopold and Max both raised their heads, their interests completely engaged.

"Down, boys," Christopher ordered. "You're not being polite to our guest." When the two dogs continued to stare at Lily's plate and drool, he said the command a second time, this time with more force.

Moving as one, the two Great Danes dropped their heads, sank down on the floor simultaneously and stretched out. Within seconds, their eyelids had drooped—along with their heads.

She could have sworn the two dogs had instantaneously fallen asleep.

Chapter 12

She stared at the two Great Danes for another few seconds. The sound of even breathing was evident. They really *were* asleep, she marveled.

"Nice trick," she said to Christopher, greatly impressed by the way his pets had responded to him. He had a gift, no two ways about it, she thought.

"Training," he corrected.

Lily supposed it was all in the way someone looked at it. But he did have a point. She could see how there would be no living with animals as large as these two dogs were if he hadn't succeeded in rigorously training them to respond to his commands.

"That, too," she allowed.

"Want another one?" he asked her.

Lily turned around to face him. She wasn't sure what

the veterinarian was referring to. "Training trick?" she asked uncertainly.

He laughed. "No, pizza slice." He moved the opened box closer to her side of the coffee table. "You finished the slice I gave you, but there's still three quarters of a box to go."

"No, thank you, not right now." She had more than enough room for another slice, but she really wanted to make at least a slight dent in this box city that was invading his house. The aroma from the pizza teased her senses. She would have given in if she'd been less disciplined. "Although I can see the attraction," she admitted.

Christopher's eyes skimmed over her a little slower than they might have. "Yes, me, too."

Her mouth curved, silently accepting the compliment he was giving her. "I'm talking about the pizza," she told him pointedly.

"I know. Me, too," he replied whimsically. He still wasn't looking at the slices inside the pizza box.

Lily felt herself growing warmer, her mind filling with thoughts that had nothing to do with restoring order to his house, or eating pizza, or training unruly puppies. The way he watched her made her feel desirable; moreover, it made her imagination take flight.

Right, because you're so irresistible, just like veritable catnip to the man, the little voice in her head mocked.

Straighten up and fly right, she silently lectured. Out loud, she laid out terms that she felt would satisfy both of them.

"We can both have another slice after we each un-pack two boxes," she told him. When he gave her a rather amused, dubious look, she amended her terms. "Okay, one box for you, two for me." Then, in case he thought she was saying she was faster than he was, she explained, "I've had practice at packing and un-packing."

He got started opening the large box next to the sofa. "You moved around often?"

She laughed softly, shaking her head. The house she lived in was the house she'd been born in. "Not even once."

For a second, he seemed slightly lost. "Then why—?"

"—did I say I've had practice?" She filled in the rest of his question and continued, "Because I have. I pack pastries before they're transported to their destination and once they get there, I have to unpack them, making sure that they make it to the table in perfect condition, the way the customer expected when they paid the cater-ing bill. Making sure the pastries are displayed to their best advantage requires a delicate touch," she pointed out. "There's nothing worse-looking than a squashed or lopsided pastry or cake at a party."

"If they taste anywhere near as good as what I've sampled from your oven so far, I'd be willing to scrape them off the inside of a cardboard box just to be able to eat them."

She laughed. "That's very nice of you, but it doesn't change my point, which is that I can unpack things quickly, whereupon it looks as if you're willing to latch on to any excuse, any port in a storm no matter how flimsy it might be, just as long as you don't have to tackle what's inside those boxes."

"Busted," Christopher freely admitted, then in his defense, he added, "I'm pretty much the same way about groceries, which is why I don't have any and I'm on a first-name basis with a lot of take-out places around here."

Pushing up her sleeves, Lily turned her attention to the closest large carton. "I wouldn't have pegged you as a procrastinator."

On the contrary, she would have said that he seemed like the type that tackled whatever was in front of him rather than putting it off till another time. Looks could be deceptive.

His were also very distracting, she couldn't help noticing.

"I guess that makes me a man of mystery—someone you *can't* read like an open book," he said, amusement highlighting his face.

"What that makes you," she corrected, "is a man who needs to be prodded. Now, do you have a utility knife—or if you don't, just a plain knife will do," she told him. She'd tried pulling the carton apart and the top just wouldn't give. "I just need something I can open the boxes with. If I keep trying to do it with my bare hands, I'm going to wind up breaking off all my nails in the process."

"I wouldn't want you to do that," he told her, going back to the kitchen to get a knife out of one of the drawers.

When he gave it to her, hilt first, she nodded toward

the utensils that were in the drawer. "So you did put some things away."

He glanced over his shoulder, back at the drawer, which hadn't closed properly and had subsequently rolled back open again. He crossed to it to reclose it.

"Much as I'd like to take the credit," he answered, "no, I didn't."

"The drawer's full, and from what I could see those were all utensils in it. In other words, it's not just a junk drawer that you tossed things into as you came cross them. That's organization."

"No," he corrected, "that's my mother. Those were her utensils. After she died, I just couldn't get myself to throw any of her things away."

Not to mention the fact that hers had been a better quality than the ones he'd picked up when he'd lived off campus while attending school back East. When things had blown up on him so suddenly with Irene, he'd just told the movers to throw everything into boxes and move the lot to his mother's house in California.

She understood where he was coming from. But right now, the issue was a practical one of two things not being able to occupy the same space.

"There are always charities you can donate things to," she told him gently.

Christopher nodded. He knew she was right. "Soon—but not yet."

Lily didn't want him to think she was being insensitive—or pushy, especially not in this instance. "Actually, I understand exactly how you feel. When my mother passed away, I couldn't get myself to give anything of hers away, either. But after a while, I decided I was being selfish. My mother had a lot of nice things that still had a lot of life left in them. There were women out there who were—and are—needy, who could use one nice pair of shoes, or one nice dress, to lift their spirits, to maybe even turn them around and start them back toward a positive feeling of self-worth."

Lily went on talking as she methodically emptied the first box, arranging its contents on the coffee table and the floor next to it.

"My mother was the type that liked helping people, even when she barely had anything herself. I know she would have wanted me to give her things away, so I picked a few special things to keep, things that really reminded me of her, and then I distributed the rest between a handful of charities. But it took me a long time before I could do that," she emphasized. "So I really do understand exactly what you're feeling."

Lily was coming to the bottom of the box and she felt that she had to comment on what she'd found while unpacking.

"You know, for a man who doesn't like to unpack, you certainly pack well."

Christopher thought of letting her comment go and just accepting it as a compliment. But not saying anything was practically like lying—or at least allowing a lie to be established. He couldn't do that, seeing as how she was really putting herself out for him—as well as the fact that he was giving serious thought to having a relationship with this unique woman.

"Not me," he told her. She looked at him in surprise. "It was the movers I hired, they did the packing for me. Unfortunately, while they obviously could pack extremely efficiently, they couldn't be bribed to unpack once they reached their destination."

"You actually tried to bribe them?" she asked, trying not to laugh at him.

"No," he admitted, "but looking back, I should have. I honestly didn't think that I would be putting it off as long as I have. But each day I found a reason not to get started—and Leopold and Max didn't seem to mind," he added, spreading the blame around. "I actually think they kind of like having all these boxes scattered throughout the house. For them it's like having their own private jungle gym."

This time she did laugh. "No offense, but I don't think dogs care about a jungle gym. In any case, even if they do, they're going to have to adjust," she informed him.

For the time being, she set the now-empty box to one side. She intended to break the carton down for easier transport and recycling later.

Christopher looked at her a little uncertainly. "Are you telling me that you intend to stay here until all these boxes are unpacked and taken apart?"

She couldn't tell if he was just surprised—or if the idea of her being here like that put him off. "No—but I do intend to keep coming back until they are."

Curiosity got the better of him. None of his old friends from high school had ever volunteered to help him conquer this cardboard kingdom of his. "Why would you do that?"

There was no hesitation on her part. "Call it repaying one favor with another—besides, my mother taught me to never leave something half-done. The job's done when the job's done," she told the veterinarian, reciting an old axiom.

She'd amused him—again. "That sounds like something out of Yogi Berra's playbook," he said, referring to the famous Yankees catcher.

The smile she gave him told Christopher that she was familiar with baseball history. Something else they had in common, he couldn't help thinking.

"Wise man, Yogi Berra," Lily commented with a smile as she went back to work.

By the end of the evening, they had managed to unpack a total of five boxes and they had put away the contents of three of them—not to mention all but polishing off the pizza he had ordered. There were only two slices left, which Christopher earmarked for his breakfast for the following morning.

Tired, Lily rotated her shoulders to loosen them a little.

"Well, I've got an early day tomorrow," she told Christopher, "so I'd better be going home."

He wanted to ask her to stay a little longer. Not to unpack, but just to talk.

Just to *be*.

He found that he liked Lily's company, liked her sense of humor and her determination, as well. Liked, too, the way her presence seemed to fill up his house far more than the towering boxes she had them tackling ever had.

But asking her to stay when she had to be up early would be selfish of him. So he let the moment pass—except to voice his thanks for her help as he walked her and Jonathan to the door.

"You know, this has to be one of the most unique evenings I've ever spent," he confessed, then added, "I enjoyed it."

The dimpled smile on his face seemed to work its way into every single nook and corner of her being. Lily returned his smile and replied, "So did I."

He wanted to be sure that, despite what she'd said, having her work like this, putting his things away, wasn't going to ultimately scare her off. So he asked, "And you'll be dropping Jonny off at the animal hospital tomorrow?"

She wanted to, but there was a problem. "I've got to be at work at seven," she told him, knowing the clinic opened at eight.

If she needed to leave the dog at seven, then he was going to be there at seven. He found himself *wanting* to be there for her. "Funny, so do I."

"No, you don't," she countered, seeing through his lie. She didn't want to put him out and he'd already been so helpful to her.

He pretended to narrow his eyes, giving her a reproving look. "It's not nice to call your pet's doctor a liar."

Her heart felt as if it was under assault. Her mouth curved again as she shook her head. "I'm not calling you a liar—" Then, whimsically, she made a suggestion. "How about a stretcher of truth?"

"I'll take that under consideration," he told her. His tone changed as he told her fondly, "Now go home and get some sleep."

That was the plan. Whether or not it worked was going to be another story, she thought, looking at Christopher. "Thanks for the pizza."

"Thanks for the help," he countered. "And for the kick in the pants."

That sounded so callous when he said it that way. "I didn't kick, I prodded," she amended politely.

He laughed as he inclined his head, playing along. "I stand corrected." Reaching the door, he paused, his brain engaged in a verbal tennis match. He decided to leave the decision up to her—sort of.

"Lily—"

There was something in his voice that put her on alert. "Yes?"

His eyes held hers for a full moment before Christopher put his question to her. "Would you mind if I kissed you?"

This time, the smile she offered began in her eyes. "Actually," Lily admitted, "I think I'd mind if you didn't."

"I definitely wouldn't want that," Christopher confessed as he framed her face with his hands. The next moment he brought his lips down to hers.

It began lightly, politely, but almost instantly took on a life and breadth of its own, escalating quickly.

Along with that escalation, it brought with it a whole host of emotions.

She didn't quite recall wrapping her arms around Christopher's neck, didn't remember, once anchored to him this way, tilting her body into his. What she did remember was the wild burst of energy that seemed to spring out of nowhere and wrapped itself around her tightly for the duration of that intense kiss.

Lily's mouth tasted of every forbidden fruit he'd ever fantasized about. It made him want more.

Made him want her.

He struggled to hold himself in check, to only go so far and no further. It was far from easy, but he was not about to pay this woman back for her help, for her providing him with his first decent evening since his breakup with Irene, for giving him his first shot at feeling *human* since Irene had taken a two-by-four to his life—and his pride—he was not going to pay her back for all that by overpowering Lily and forcing himself on her.

So, with a wave of what he felt was close to superhuman control, Christopher forced himself to back away from what could have easily become his with just the right moves.

He wasn't about "moves," he reminded himself, he was about sincerity, no matter *what* his body was attempting to dictate to him.

Drawing back, he paused to take a couple of discreet, very deep breaths, doing his best to regulate the timbre of his voice.

"Thank you again," he murmured.

She knew he wasn't thanking her for helping him to unpack those few boxes. She struggled to stifle the blush that wanted so badly to take root. But she didn't seem to have a say in that. Her body seemed to be on its own timetable, one that had little to do with anything she might have dictated.

After a beat, Lily cleared her throat, managed to murmur something that sounded like "Don't mention it," and then left quickly with her puppy.

She wasn't sure just how long it had taken for her heartbeat to settle down and return to normal. All she was aware of was that it had remained rather erratic for the entire trip home, and even for a few minutes after she'd walked into her house.

She was also aware of the happy glow that had taken hold of her.

This, she felt rather certain, was the very first leg of the journey that ultimately led to genuine affection. Lily stubbornly refused to use the *L* word to describe what she might wind up achieving since she felt if she did, she might just jinx what was happening.

Deep down, though she wasn't a superstitious person by nature, she was afraid that thinking about falling in love with this man would almost assuredly guarantee that there would be no happily ever after waiting for her at the finish line.

Besides, she hardy knew anything about the man except that he hated unpacking—and he had a killer smile. The really safe, smart thing to do, Lily told herself as she unlocked the front door and Jonathan pushed the door opened with his shoulder, walking right in, would be for her to find Jonathan another veterinarian.

If she went that route, it would guarantee that she would have no entanglements with the man whose house she'd just left, no further temptation to wander down the wrong road someday soon.

Oh, who are you kidding? she scolded herself.

She had never been one to automatically opt for doing things the "smart way," especially if that "smart way" promised just more of the same.

More dullness, more playing it safe.

And that in turn meant that there wouldn't be anything to light up her life. Nothing would cause her fingertips to tingle and her imagination to take flight, going to places she would have never admitted to yearning for, at least not out loud.

"You continue torturing yourself like this and you are not going to get any sleep no matter what you try. Turn off your brain, change into your pj's and for God's sake, get some rest before you wind up dropping from exhaustion."

Easier said than done.

Oh, she could certainly change into her pajamas and crawl into bed. The next-to-impossible part of the equation was the part about turning off her brain.

Her brain, it seemed, wanted only to vividly relive that last kiss and play it over and over again in her mind's eye, heightening every last nuance to its uppermost limit.

She was doomed and she knew it.

Resigned, Lily went up the stairs to her bedroom, her four-footed black shadow following right behind her, barking happily.

Chapter 13

Christopher knew it would make a difference, but until the job was almost completed, he hadn't realized just how *much* of a difference the undertaking would actually make.

Each time he looked around, the amount of space surprised him all over again. Without fully being conscious of it, he'd gotten accustomed to weaving his way in and out between the boxes, accepting the clutter that existed as a given. With Lily insisting on helping him unpack the countless boxes, large and small, that had been here for months, the house gradually returned to looking like the place he'd known during his childhood, growing up with a single mom. Lily had not only gotten him to organize and clear away the physical clutter, but through doing that he had also wound up clearing away some emotional clutter, as well.

Without boxes being everywhere he turned, Christopher felt as if his ability to think clearly had vastly improved, allowing him to finally move forward in his private life.

It was almost as if his brain was like a hard drive that had been defragmented. The analogy wasn't his. Lily had tossed the comparison his way when he'd commented that he felt less oppressed, more able to think these past few days. He thought her analogy seemed to hit the nail right on the head.

As they worked together, he discovered that Lily had an uncanny ability to simplify things. She seemed to see into his very soul.

Without discussing it or even being fully conscious of it, he and Lily had settled into a routine that was beneficial to both of them. Weekday mornings she would swing by with Jonathan, dropping the Labrador off at the animal hospital, and then in the evenings she would collect her pet and then follow Christopher to his home. Once there they would both tackle emptying out and breaking down at least one of the boxes, if not more.

They also ate dinner together, usually one she had prepared in his kitchen. It was just something she had gotten into the habit of doing. While he continued to tell her that she really didn't have to go out of her way like this, Christopher made no secret of his enjoyment of each and every meal she prepared.

As much as he appreciated her help de-cluttering his house and looked forward to exhibits of her stellar culinary abilities, what he looked forward to most of all were the conversations they had. Each evening while they worked and ate, they talked and got to know one another a little better than before.

It definitely made Christopher anticipate each evening.

Oh, he loved being a veterinarian, loved being able to improve the lives of almost all the animals who were brought to his hospital.

He was lucky enough to treat a larger variety of pets than most, everything from mice, hamsters and rabbits to dogs and cats and birds, as well as several other types of pets who fell somewhere in between. He couldn't remember a time when he hadn't wanted to be a veterinarian, and if he hadn't become one he honestly didn't know what he would be doing these days.

But Lily, well, she represented a completely different path in his life, a path he was both familiar with in a distant, cursory fashion, and one different enough for him to feel that he hadn't actually traveled it before.

She very quickly had become an integral part of his life. Being around her made him feel alive, with an endless font of possibilities before him. It was akin to being brought back from the dead after having attended his own funeral. He'd never thought he could feel like this again—and it was all because of Lily.

"We're almost done, you know," Lily said one evening, pointing out what she knew was the obvious. But it felt good to say it nonetheless. "There are just a few boxes left. When they're gone, I really won't have a reason to stop by here after work each night." She held her breath, waiting to see if Christopher would express regret or relief over what she'd just said.

His answer more than pleased her—and put her mind at ease. "I could try rustling up some more boxes, maybe steal some from the local UPS office or from FedEx, or the post office on Murphy if all else fails."

She laughed at the very thought of his contemplating hijacking boxes. He was nothing if not exceedingly upstanding. "It's not the same thing."

He stopped working and looked at Lily seriously. She had become part of his life so quickly that it all but took his breath away.

Just like she did.

"I'd still do it if it meant that it would keep you coming over every evening. Besides, as selfish as this might sound, you've gotten me hooked on your cooking. I find myself expecting it by the end of the day," he freely admitted. "You wouldn't want to deprive me of it, now, would you?"

She turned away from the box she'd almost finished emptying and gazed at him, a hint of a pleased smile playing on her lips. "Just so I'm clear on this, let me get this straight. You want me to keep coming over so I can continue unpacking your boxes and cooking your dinner, is that right?"

"What I want," he told her, crossing over to Lily and taking the book that she'd just removed from the last box out of her hands, "is to continue having *you* to look forward to each evening."

His eyes on hers, Christopher let the book he'd just taken out of her hands fall to the floor.

He realized that he was risking a great deal, crawling out on a limb that had no safety net beneath it. But if he didn't, if he didn't *say* something, he ran the very real risk of losing her, of having her just walk away from his life.

This, he knew, was a crossroads for them, for although they had shared an occasional heated moment, an occasional kiss, they had each always returned to their corners, respectful of the other's barriers and limits. They pushed no boundaries, leaving envelopes exactly where they lay.

Risk nothing, gain nothing.

Or, in this case, Christopher thought, risk nothing, lose everything.

He didn't want to lose everything.

"I'd still be stopping by the animal hospital to pick up Jonathan," Lily reminded him. "That is, if, once we're finished here, you'd still be willing to have me drop him off with you in the morning."

"Sure, that goes without saying," he assured her. Jonathan barked as if he knew he was being talked about, but Christopher continued focusing on her. "Everyone looks forward to having Jonny around during the day. But that still leaves a large chunk of my evening empty. I'm not sure I'd know how to deal with that," he told her in a voice that had become hardly louder than a whisper.

As she listened, giving him her undivided attention, that whisper seemed to feather along her lips, softly seducing her, causing havoc to every single nerve ending within her body.

"Why don't we talk about it later?" Christopher suggested in between light, arousing passes along her lips.

"I know what you're doing," she said. It was an effort for her to think straight. "You're just trying to get me to stop unpacking the last boxes."

She saw his mouth curve in amusement, *felt* his smile seeping into her soul.

"I always said you were a very smart lady," Christopher told her.

"And you are exceedingly tricky. Lucky I majored in seeing through tricky," she quipped.

"Maybe lucky for you, not so much me," he told her in a low, unsettling voice.

He was still playing his ace card, Lily thought. Still managing to reduce her to a pliable, warmed-over puddle. And she'd discovered something just now, in this moment of truth. Christopher wasn't just hard to resist. When he got going, moving full steam ahead, the man was damn near *impossible* to resist.

Even so, she did her best to try.

Her best wasn't good enough.

Gladly taking the excuse that Christopher had so willingly handed her, she completely abandoned the box she'd been emptying, leaving it to be tackled on some other day. She certainly wasn't up to doing that this evening.

Tonight had suddenly become earmarked for something else entirely. Tonight she was finally going to give in to all the demands that had been mounting within her, all the demands that were vibrating within her.

She had given herself endless pep talks against taking the step she was contemplating, mentally listing all the reasons she would regret crossing this final line in the sand. The line separating flirtation from something a great deal more serious.

And possibly a great deal more fulfilling.

Commitment and, yes, possibly even love were on the other side of that line.

But just because she was willing to cross that line, Lily reminded herself, that did not necessarily mean that he did or would.

Even if Christopher said it, said that he *wanted* to cross the line and made a show of embracing both concepts—commitment *and* love—that wouldn't really make it a reality. She wasn't naive enough to believe that just because someone said something meant that there had to be even an iota of truth to it.

That was the part where a leap of faith would need to come in.

She knew that. Logically, she knew that. But right now, logic had been left standing somewhere at a door far away. She would have to deal with this later, one way or another.

Right now, at this burning moment in time, Lily realized that what she wanted, what she *needed,* was to have him make her feel wanted, make her feel that she was special to him.

Never mind whether or not it was true. She would pretend it was true.

And maybe, just maybe, if wishing hard enough could make it so, it *would* be true. But again, that was a struggle, a battle to be undertaken later.

Right now, every fiber of her being wanted to be made love to—make love with—Christopher.

So rather than resist, or coyly move just out of his reach, gravitating toward another excuse, another road-block to get in the way of what she knew they both wanted, Lily remained in his arms, kissed him back the way he had kissed her and, just like that, effectively brought down every single barrier, every make-shift fence, every concrete wall they had each put up to protect the most frail thing they each possessed: their hearts.

This was different, Christopher realized. She wasn't kissing him back with feeling, she was kissing him back with fire. He could feel the passion igniting, could feel it being passed back and forth between them and grow-ing sharply in intensity by the nanosecond.

He kissed Lily over and over again and with each kiss he only craved more. He made love to her with his mouth, first to her lips, then to her throat, sliding down to the tender hollow between her breasts.

Her moan only served to inflame him more. It in-creased the tempo, inciting a riot right there within his veins.

Christopher was afraid of letting loose. And equally afraid not to.

To contain this amount of passion would bring about his own self-destruction. Not someday but before the evening's end.

Her hands passed over his chest, possessing him even before her fingertips dove beneath his shirt, sliding along the hard ridges of his pectorals, hardening him at the same time that she was reducing him to a mass of fluid flames and desires.

He had to hold back to keep from ripping off her clothes. But even as he tried to keep himself in check, he felt Lily's quick, urgent movements all but tearing away his shirt and slacks.

It was the proverbial straw, unleashing the passionate creature caged within.

His hands, sturdy and capable yet so gentle, were everywhere, touching, caressing, possessing.

Worshipping.

He just couldn't seem to get enough of her. He felt himself feeding on her softness; feeding on her frenzy as if it comprised the very substance of his existence.

As if Lily and only Lily could sustain his very life force.

Christopher was making her crazy, playing her body as if it was a highly tuned musical instrument that would only—*could* only—sing for him, because only he knew just how to unlock the melody that existed just beneath the surface.

Lily ached to feel his touch—to feel *him* along her body.

She arched her back, pressing herself against him as he made the fire inside of her rise to greater and greater heights.

There hadn't been all that many lovers and she knew she wasn't exactly all that experienced before tonight, but Lily honestly thought that she'd been to the table before. It was only now that she realized she had only had her nose pressed up against the glass window, aware of the existence of these sensations, but never really *feeling* any of them.

Certainly not like this.

She felt things now, responded to things now. Did things now, things that had never even crossed her mind to consider doing before tonight.

But suddenly, she wanted to pleasure this man who had utterly lit up her entire world. She wanted to give him back a little in kind of what he had so generously given her.

With the feel of his breath trailing along the more sensitive areas of her skin still incredibly, indelibly fresh along her body, Lily arched and wrapped her legs around his torso, teasing him, urging him to cross the final line.

To form the final union.

Her body urgently moving beneath his, Christopher discovered that he hadn't the strength to hold off any longer. His goal had been to bring her up and over to a climax a handful of times before he claimed the irresistible, but he was only so strong, could only hold out for so long and no more.

That time was now.

With a moan that echoed of surrender, Christopher proceeded to take what she so willingly offered him. Shifting seductively, Lily opened for him.

His mouth sealed to hers and, balancing his weight as best he could, he entered her.

Her sharp intake of breath almost drove him over the brink. At the last moment, he did his best to be gentle, to rein himself in before the ultimate ride took hold and control was all but yanked away from him, no matter how good his intentions.

The more she moved, the more he wanted her.

Wanting her became his only reality.

His heart pounding hard, Christopher stepped up his pace until the ride became dizzying for both of them.

By the end, just before the heat exploded, embracing them fiercely a beat before the inevitable descent began, he felt confident that he had been granted every wish he'd ever made in life.

The feeling was so intense, he tightened his arms around her to the point that he almost found himself merging with her very flesh.

Somehow, they remained two very distinct, if two very exhausted people. Two people clinging to one another, forming their own human life raft in the rough sea of reality as it gradually descended upon them and came back into focus.

When Christopher could finally draw enough air into his lungs to enable him to form a sentence, albeit a softly worded one, he kissed the top of her head and said, "I am definitely hijacking a moving van and having more boxes delivered."

She laughed and her warm breath both tickled him and somehow managed to begin to arouse him again. He didn't understand how that was possible, but there was a magic to this woman that seemed to make all things possible.

After all, he had been so sure, after what Irene had done to him, that he could never feel again, never *want* to feel again, and yet here he was, feeling and grateful to be doing it.

"I think," she said as she lay her head on his chest, "that we've gotten past that stage—needing boxes as an excuse."

Christopher managed to kiss the top of her head again before he fell back, almost exhausted by the effort as well as insanely happy.

"Can't argue with that," he said, the words straggling out one after the other in an erratic fashion. "Even if I wanted to," he added, "I can't argue. Not enough air in my lungs to argue and win."

He felt her smile against his chest. "Then I win by default."

They both laughed at the absurd way that sounded. And they laughed mainly because just hearing the sound of laughter felt so good and so satisfying, as well as oddly soothing at the same time.

Christopher's arms tightened around her.

Feeling Lily's heart beat against his felt as if it was the answer to everything that was important in his life.

He knew that he had never been happier than right at this very moment.

Chapter 14

Lily very quickly came to the conclusion that there really was no graceful way to go from making mind-blowing love with a man to getting dressed and slipping back into the everyday world that she had temporarily stepped away from.

It would have been a great deal easier to get dressed and make her getaway if Christopher had been asleep. But the man who had lit up her entire world, complete with skyrockets and fireworks, was lying right beside her and he was very much awake.

Even if he was asleep, there was still the small matter of actually making a soundless getaway with her Labrador in tow *and* getting by Christopher's two Great Danes, Leopold and Max. She'd made friends with them over the past few weeks so she was fairly confident that the dogs wouldn't immediately begin barking the moment she stirred. But she had a feeling that they wouldn't turn into two docile statues, silently watching her slip out of the house with Jonathan in her arms.

Any attempt to see if she was right went up in smoke the very next moment.

"Going somewhere?" Christopher asked as she tried to sit up on the sofa, ready to begin the taxing hunt for her clothes—*any* of her clothes.

He slipped his arm around her waist, firmly holding her in place as he waited for her to come up with an answer.

"I thought I'd finish tidying up the family room, break down the empty boxes we left behind, little things like that," she told him innocently.

"In the nude?" Christopher sounded both amused and intrigued. "Glad I didn't doze off like you did. This I have to see."

She looked at him over her shoulder and protested, "I didn't doze off."

"Yes, you did, but that's okay," he told her. "It was only for a few minutes." He drew her in a little closer, his arm still around her waist. "Besides, you look cute when you sleep. Your face gets all soft."

Lily turned her body toward him and gazed down at his face. "As opposed to what? Being rock hard when I'm awake?"

"Not rock hard, but let's just say…guarded," he concluded, finally deciding upon a word. Once he said it out loud, it seemed to fit perfectly. "You know, kind of like a night watchman at an art museum who's afraid someone's going to steal a painting the second he lets his guard down."

Lily frowned. "Not exactly a very romantic image," she commented.

"But an accurate one," he pointed out. His intention hadn't been to insult her or scare her away. He was just being observant. "You don't have to go, you know."

Oh, yes I do. I can't think around you, especially after this.

"I know," she said out loud. "But I'm thinking that a little space between us might not be a bad thing, so I can get my bearings."

He wasn't about to keep her against her will if it came down to that, but he wasn't going to just give up without a word, either.

"A GPS can give you the exact latitude and longitude, but it can't give you a secure feeling. That kind of thing only happens between people," he told Lily, lightly brushing her hair away from her face.

She felt herself tensing. Reacting. "Don't do that," she told him, moving her head back, away from him. "I can't think when you do that."

"Good, I was hoping you'd say that."

Lying back against the sofa again, Christopher pulled her down to him. Before she could make a halfhearted protest, his lips brushed hers.

In less than a moment, she lost the desire to speak, as well. He had relit her fire and they began making love all over again.

* * *

There were still a few boxes left scattered around his house. It was a definite improvement over the first time she'd walked into the older home, but the fact that there were any left at all bothered her.

But each time she thought they were going to spend a quiet evening going through the last of moving cartons, something came up. The first time he'd had another emergency surgery to perform, this time on a mixed-breed dog that had been left on the animal shelter's doorstep. The poor dog had been more dead than alive and, he'd explained to Lily, he was one of the vets who volunteered their services at the shelter. He couldn't find it in his heart to say no when they called. One look at the sad mutt—a photo had been sent to his smart phone—and neither could Lily.

She'd insisted on coming with him to help in any way she could. As sometimes happened, she had made extra pastries for the event that Theresa's company had been catering that day, and Lily brought some of the overage with her to share with Christopher and the other volunteers who were at the shelter.

In the end, the surgery had been a success—and so had her pastries.

"I think they want to permanently adopt you," he told Lily as they left the shelter several hours later. He smiled at her, lingering in the all-but-deserted parking lot. "Those pastries you brought with you were certainly a hit. Thanks."

She looked at him a bit uncertainly. "For what?"

"For coming along. For being so understanding. For

being you." He took her into his arms, something he had gotten very used to doing. "It's pretty late, but we can curl up in front of the TV and not pay attention to whatever's on cable. I can order in."

"You need your rest," she told him, amused.

He kissed the top of her head. "What makes you think I won't be resting?"

Amusement highlighted her face. "I'm beginning to know you."

"Damn, foiled again. I'll make it up to you tomorrow," he promised.

She paused for a moment, tilted her head back and, grabbing the front of his shirt, pulled him down slightly to her level. Lily pressed her lips against his, kissing him with feeling.

Before either of them could get carried away, she moved her head back and told him, "There's nothing to make up for. I like watching you come to the rescue like that. You're like a knight in shining armor, except that instead of a lance, you're wielding a scalpel." Stepping away from him, she unlocked her car. The second she opened up the rear passenger door, Jonathan bounded inside. "Now go home."

"Yes, ma'am," he answered obediently, then repeated, "Tomorrow."

"Tomorrow," she echoed.

Despite occasional detours like that, she had expected that they would be back on track the next evening, spending it at his place, unpacking the last of the boxes that were upstairs in his bedroom. Dinner would consist of something she'd prepared.

But when Christopher closed up the hospital for the evening, he informed her that he had a surprise for her.

"What kind of surprise?" she asked suspiciously.

"The kind you'll find out about when we get there," he said mysteriously.

"We're going somewhere?"

"Good deduction," he applauded.

"Shouldn't we drop Jonathan off first?"

"No. He's coming along with us."

"Then we're not going out to eat?" That would have been her first guess at the kind of surprise he was taking her to.

Instead of answering, he merely smiled at her and told her to follow him.

She was intrigued. He had succeeded in capturing her complete attention.

"This is a restaurant," she noted when, fifteen minutes later, she had pulled her vehicle up next to his in a semicrowded parking lot. She was standing beside her car, looking at the squat building that was obviously Christopher's intended destination.

"It is," he confirmed cheerfully.

"We can't leave Jonathan in the car while we eat."

"We're not going to," he informed her, taking the leash from her hand.

"But—"

"Ruff's is a restaurant where people can go to dine

out with their pets," he told her. "I thought you might get a kick out of it.

She didn't get a kick out of it, she *loved* it and told him as much over dinner, and continued to do so when they got back to his place.

"How did you find it?" she asked.

"One of my patients' owners opened it up not too long ago. I thought it was an idea whose time has come. I'm one of the investors," he confided to her.

"Really?" The idea excited her—just as the man did, she thought as she felt him trail his fingertips along the hollow of her throat.

"Really," he confirmed. "I'd never lie to a beautiful woman."

"But I'm the only one in the room."

He laughed. "Fishing for compliments, are we?"

She put her hand to her breast. "Me?"

"You," he said, nipping her lower lip.

That was the last of the conversation for quite a while.

"Who's this?" Lily asked, pulling a framed photograph out of the last carton that was still only semiunpacked in his bedroom.

Time had gotten away from her and she'd wound up spending the night. Which meant she needed to hurry getting dressed so she could swing by her place and get a fresh change of clothing before proceeding on to work.

They had already decided, sometime during the night, that Jonathan would remain here and Christopher would take the dog with him when he went in to the animal hospital.

The framed photograph—Christopher posing with an aristocratic-looking brunette, his arm around her waist in the exact same fashion that it had been around hers that first time she'd tried to slip out of his bed— had all but fallen at her feet when she'd bumped into the open box. It had fallen over, spilling out its contents. The framed photograph was the first thing she saw.

"Who's who?" Christopher asked, preoccupied.

He was searching the immediate area for his keys. He assumed they had fallen somewhere as he and Lily had made love last night. Rather than settling into a certain predictability, their lovemaking only seemed to get better each time.

Instead of answering, she turned toward Christopher holding up the framed photograph. "This woman you've got your arm around," she told him. Even as the words came out, she had a sinking feeling she wasn't going to like his answer.

Christopher's mind went temporarily blank as he saw the frame she had in her hands. "Where did you get that?" he asked, his throat drier than he could ever recall it being.

"It fell out of that box when I accidentally knocked it over," she told him, nodding her head toward the carton that was still on in its side. "Who is she, Chris?" Lily repeated. With each word, the deadness inside of her seemed to grow a little larger, a little more threatening. "She has to be someone because you wouldn't have packed up this photograph if she wasn't."

"I didn't do any of the packing," he reminded her. "The movers did."

The point was that it had been there, at his residence, for them to pack. The fact that he was being evasive right now just made her more anxious.

"Well, it has to be yours," she insisted. "The movers wouldn't have packed up a stranger's things and put them into your moving van—besides, you're *in* the picture and that's your arm around her waist." Each word tasted more bitter than the last. "Who *is* she, Chris?" Lily asked for a third time, growing impatient. It wasn't as if they didn't both have pasts, but she didn't like the idea of not knowing enough about him—and his having secrets.

"She's nobody," he told her, taking the frame out of her hand and tossing it facedown on his rumpled bed.

Lily squared her shoulders defiantly. "If she was nobody, you would have said that right away. You don't take a picture with nobody and then have it framed," she pointed out. "Why won't you tell me who she is?"

Christopher blew out a breath. He'd honestly thought he'd thrown that photograph—all the photographs of her—out. "Because she doesn't matter anymore."

Lily heard what wasn't being said. "But she did once, right?"

"Once," he admitted because to say otherwise would really be lying.

Lily's voice became very quiet. "How much did she matter?"

Because he knew he had to, Christopher gave her the briefest summary of the time he had spent with

Irene. "Her name was Irene Masterson and we were engaged—but we're not anymore," he emphasized. "We haven't been for three months."

Three months. The words echoed in her brain. She had him on the rebound. There was no other way to interpret this. She was a filler, a placeholder until he got his act together. How could she have been so stupid as to think this was going somewhere? Things didn't go anywhere except into some dark abyss.

For a moment, Lily stared at him, speechless. She felt her very fragile world shattering and crumbling. "And you didn't think that was important enough to tell me?"

He told her the only thing he could in his own defense. "The topic never came up."

Was he saying it was her fault because she hadn't interrogated him?

"Maybe it should have," she countered, feeling hurt beyond words. "Preferably before things got too hot and heavy between us." At the last moment, she had stopped herself from saying "serious between us" because it wasn't. How could it be if he had kept something so important from her? She'd been deluding herself about his feelings for her. It was painfully obvious now that she had read far too much into ther relationship. There wasn't a "relationship," it was just a matter of killing time for him, nothing more.

"I don't remember a single place where I could have segued into that. When was I supposed to say something?" he asked. "Just before we came together? 'Excuse me, Lily, but in the interest of full disclosure, I think you should know that I had a serious girlfriend for a few years and we were engaged for five months.'"

Five months. The woman in the photograph had had a claim on him for five months—longer than they had known each other. Plus, it had only ended recently, which made her presence in his life shaky at best. The very thought twisted in her stomach, stealing the air out of her lungs.

"Yes," she retorted. "You should have told me, should have said something."

Trying to get hold of herself, Lily took a deep breath.

This was her fault, not his. Her fault because she'd given in to the longing, the loneliness she'd felt, thinking that she'd finally found a steady, decent man, someone she could love and go through life with. But Christopher wasn't the guy. He couldn't be with what he'd just gone through. She didn't want to be the girl who picked up other people's messes, a placeholder while the injured party healed.

Her voice was emotionless as she said, "Why aren't you still engaged?"

Christopher lifted a shoulder and let it fall in a careless shrug. "We wanted different things. She wanted me to change, to be someone else, someone who fit into her blue-blooded world. I didn't want to change."

Lily was struggling to understand, to come to grips with what she'd just stumbled across. Trying to tell herself that it didn't matter when every fiber of her being told her that it did.

"Did the engagement just disintegrate on its own?" she asked.

What could he say to make this right? To fix what he seemed to have broken? "It probably would have in time."

Her eyes held his. "But?"

He had no choice. He had to tell her the truth and pray that he wasn't going to regret it. "But with everything going on, losing my mother, I just wanted to get away and be done with it."

Her expression gave him no indication what she was thinking. "So you broke it off?"

Christopher nodded. "Yes."

She needed to get this absolutely straight in her mind. "You made a commitment to someone you loved and then you broke it off?" she pressed.

He wanted to deny it, to deny that he had ever loved Irene. But he *had* loved her, and if he lied about it he knew it would backfire on him, if not now then someday. That damage would be irreparable.

"Yes."

The sadness that washed over her with that single word was almost overwhelming. She couldn't stay here any longer, not without breaking down. "I have to go," she said abruptly. "Jonathan!" she called, her voice growing edgy. "Jonathan, come!"

After a moment, the Labrador appeared at the bottom of the stairs, barking at her. Lily practically ran down the stairs. Not wanting to waste time looking for his leash, she grabbed the dog's collar and as quickly as possible guided him toward the front door.

Christopher flew down the stairs right behind her.

"Wait, I thought we agreed that I'd take him to the animal hospital for you this morning."

Lily didn't even turn around. "There's no need. He's coming with me."

"Lily—" Her name echoed of all the hurt, the concern that was ricocheting through him.

"I've change my mind, okay?" she snapped, afraid that she would start to cry at any second. She had to get out of there before it happened. "You changed yours, right? Why can't I change mine?"

Wanting to sweep her into his arms, to hold her against him until she calmed down, Christopher took a step back instead. His instincts told him not to press. "Sure, you can change your mind," he told her quietly. "Will I still see you tonight?"

"I don't think that's a good idea," she told him crisply.

Lily found she had to all but drag Jonathan away—the Labrador seemed reluctant to leave both his canine friends and the man who had treated him so nicely. When he resisted, Lily pulled his collar harder, said his name in a very authoritative voice followed by a command that Christopher had taught her. After a second, Jonathan followed her.

The training had worked out well, she thought, fighting back tears as she crossed the threshold. The trainer, however, had not.

"Lily," Christopher called after her. "I don't want you to leave."

It took a great deal for him to put himself out there like that after he had promised himself not to even think about having a relationship with a woman until he had gotten over his grieving period. Telling himself that his mother would have really liked Lily hadn't exactly tipped the scales in Lily's favor—but it hadn't hurt, either.

"Now," she said, aiming the words over her shoulder as she hurried to her car. "You don't want me to leave *now*. But you'll change your mind soon enough," she said between clenched teeth. She had to clench them or risk beginning to sob.

Served her right for allowing herself to connect with a man so quickly. Lily could feel tears aching in her throat.

Two weeks passed.

Two weeks that moved with the torturous pace of a crippled turtle. Every minute of every day seemed to register as time dragged itself from one end of the day to the other. He felt as if he was going crazy. His work, rather than being his haven, became his trial instead.

He had trouble concentrating.

He tried to move on, he really did. Following his breakup with Irene, after the initial hurt subsided and after he stopped feeling as if he'd been a colossal fool for missing all the signs that had been right there in front of him, Christopher had actually experienced a sense of relief. The kind of relief survivors experienced after learning that they had just narrowly managed to dodge a bullet. The young woman he had thought he had fallen in love with wouldn't have been the woman that he was supposed to end up marrying. Avoiding that was the part where the relief came in.

But in this case, with Lily, there was no sense of relief. There was only a sense of loss, a sense that something very special had somehow managed to slip right through his fingers and he was never going to be able to recover what he had lost.

Consequently, life had progressively become darker for him. It felt as if the light had gone out of his world and he had no way to turn it back on. Resigned to this new, grimmer view of life, he found his whole demeanor changing.

Theresa had alerted her that something was definitely up. She'd said that Lily had become very quiet and withdrawn these past two weeks and that the young woman had taken to bringing the puppy to work with her instead of leaving Jonathan with Christopher. But atypically, Theresa had added, Lily wasn't talking. The pastry chef had told her that everything was "fine" every time she'd asked if something was wrong.

Maizie decided to find out some things for herself.

Which was why she popped into the animal clinic the following Tuesday, when things had slowed down in her own real estate office.

She came armed with one of Cecilia's remaining puppies, telling the receptionist that she had recently acquired this pet and was going to give it to her granddaughter as a gift. Erika had managed to fit her in between scheduled appointments.

"Hi," Maizie said cheerfully, popping into the last

exam room where she'd been told she'd find the object of her visit. "Your receptionist—lovely girl, Erika," she commented before continuing, "said you were back here and that it was all right for me to bring Walter to you. I hope you don't mind my just dropping by. But Walter's going to be a gift for my granddaughter and I just want to be sure he's healthy before I give him to her," she said.

Christopher stared at the puppy. It looked almost exactly like Jonathan. But it couldn't be—could it?

"Where did you get him?" he asked Maizie.

"I know a breeder up north, around Santa Barbara," Maizie replied innocently. "Why do you ask?"

Christopher tried to sound casual as he explained, but just the thought of Lily put longing in his voice. "Someone I know has a dog just like that. She said he just turned up on her doorstep a couple of months ago."

Maizie pretended to take the story in stride. "I hear that Labradors are popular these days because they're so friendly. That's why I got one for my granddaughter." She looked closely at Christopher as he proceeded to examine the puppy. "Is something wrong, dear?"

"The puppy seems to be fine," he said as he continued with his exam.

"I was talking about you, Christopher," Maizie said gently.

He shrugged, wishing the woman would just focus on the puppy she'd brought in and not ask him any personal questions. He couldn't deal with them right now.

He'd left numerous messages on Lily's phone. She hadn't called back once. When he went by her house, there were never any lights on and she didn't answer the door when he rang the bell.

"I'm fine," he told Maizie again.

Maizie placed her hand on his shoulder—she had to reach up a little in order to do it. "You know, Christopher, I feel that I owe it to your mother to tell you that as an actor, you're not very convincing. What's bothering you?" she asked. "I might not be able to help, but I can certainly give you a sympathetic ear."

He didn't want to talk about it. Concluding his exam, he looked at her. "Walter's very healthy. And as for me... Mrs. Connors, I know you mean well—"

Maizie took the puppy off the exam table and placed him on the floor. "You can call me Maizie at this point and hell, yes, I mean well." Her eyes locked with the young veterinarian's. "When my daughter looked like you do right now, it was because something in her relationship with the man she eventually married—wonderful son-in-law, by the way—had gone wrong. Now, out with it. You need an impartial third party to tell you if you're overreacting or if you should give up—and since your mother's not here to listen, I'll be that party in her memory."

Crossing her arms before her, Maizie gave him a very penetrating look that all but declared she was *not* about to budge on this. "Now, you might as well talk to me because I'm not leaving until you do. If you plan on seeing any more patients today, you had better start talking, young man."

Chapter 15

He wound up telling her everything.

It was against his better judgment, against anything he'd ever done, but he gave Maizie a condensed version of what had transpired, right up to Lily discovering the photograph of Irene and him, the one he had since thrown out.

Christopher secretly hoped that, in saying the words out loud, it would somehow help him purge himself of this awful deadness he was experiencing and *had* been experiencing ever since Lily had walked out.

It didn't. It just made it feel worse, if that was possible.

Desperate, he tried to describe to Maizie what he was feeling.

"It's like someone just sucked the very life force

out of me." He shrugged, embarrassed. He was being weak and that just wasn't like him. "I'm sorry, I'm not explaining this very well and you didn't come here to hear me carry on like some twelve-year-old schoolboy, lamenting about his first crush." He sighed, resigned to his present state as he squatted down to the puppy's level to scratch the animal behind his ear. "I suppose you do remind me of my mother and I guess I just needed a sympathetic ear."

"Well, I'm very flattered to be compared to Frances, Christopher," Maizie assured him. "Your mother was a very warm, wonderful lady." Touching his arm, she coaxed him back up to his feet. "You know what she'd say to you if she were here?"

He doubted that the woman had the inside track on his late mother's thoughts, but since he'd unburdened himself to Maizie, he did owe her the courtesy of listening to what she had to say. Besides, he really did like the woman.

"What?"

"She'd ask you if you really cared about this Lily you just talked about and then, if your answer was yes, she'd tell you to not just stand there and grieve, but *do* something about it."

The laugh that Christopher blew out had no humor to it. "I think they call that stalking these days, Mrs. Connors."

In contrast, Maizie's laugh was light, airy and compassionate. "I'm not talking about standing beneath this young woman's bedroom window, reciting lines from *Romeo and Juliet* or *Cyrano*. I'm suggesting doing something creative that would allow your two paths to cross—initially in public," she added for good measure.

Maybe the woman did have something up her sleeve. At this point, he was willing to try anything. He felt he had nothing to lose and everything to gain.

"Go on," he urged.

"What does your young lady do for a living?" Maizie asked innocently as she stroked the Labrador. "Is she an accountant, or a lawyer, or—"

"She works for a catering company."

"A catering company," Maizie repeated, seeming very intrigued. "In what capacity?" she pressed, knowing very well that Lily was Theresa's pastry chef. "Cooking? Serving?"

"Lily bakes," he answered, although the word was hardly adequate to describe just what she could do. "Creating delicacies" was closer to the actual description, he thought.

Maizie made sure she appeared properly delighted. "Ah, perfect."

Christopher didn't understand. At his feet, the puppy who was Maizie's accomplice in this was beginning to chew the bottom of the exam table. Christopher took out a hard rubber bone and offered it to the teething puppy.

Walter took the bait.

"Perfect?" he asked Maizie.

"Yes, because I just thought of a plan. Every so often, the Bedford animal shelter has Adopt a Best Friend Day. The local businesses contribute donations or their time to help out."

Since he volunteered at the shelter, they had taken

to sending him their newsletters. "I'm aware of those events, but I don't see—"

He never knew what hit him as Maizie went into automatic high gear. "I could pull a few strings, make a few suggestions, get this event up and running in, say, a week—two, tops—but probably a week."

How was this supposed to get Lily back into his life? "I still don't see how this has anything to do—"

Maizie held up a finger, about to make a crucial point. "Think how many more people might be attracted to come see the animals in the shelter if they knew that there were pastries being offered, the proceeds all going to keep the shelter operational? 'Come sample the pastries and go home with a best friend,'" Maizie said, coming up with a slogan right on the spot.

Then she eyed Christopher thoughtfully. "Didn't you say that you sometimes volunteer at the shelter, check out the animals, make sure they're healthy?" She knew the answer to that, as well.

His face lit up as his mind filled in the blanks, padding out what his mother's friend was telling him. "You know, that's just crazy enough to work," he agreed. "And Lily makes the most exquisite pastries." Christopher stopped short. He looked at her, slightly puzzled. "How did you know that?" he asked. "How did you know that Lily makes pastries?"

That had been a slip, but one that Maizie was quick to remedy. "I didn't. It was just a lucky guess," she told him. "I have a weakness for pastries."

"Well, if this gets her talking to me, Mrs. Connors, I'll make sure you get a pastry every day for the rest of your life," he promised, getting into the spirit of the thing.

"Which is guaranteed to be short if I start indulging like that," she told him with a laugh. Bending down, she picked up the puppy she had brought as a prop. "So, you're sure that Walter here is healthy?"

"Absolutely in top condition," he assured her. Christopher paused and regarded the Labrador thoughtfully as he scratched the dog's head. "He really does look like Lily's puppy," he told her.

"Then this Lily's puppy must be a very fine-looking dog," Maizie speculated with a wink.

She was quick to turn away and walk out before Christopher had a chance to see how broad her smile had become.

When she first heard about it, Lily's first inclination was to beg off. She knew that if she gave Theresa some excuse as to why she couldn't go to the catering event to serve her pastries, the woman would believe her and say it was all right.

But that would mean lying to someone who had been like a second mother to her. Not only that, it would be putting Theresa in a bind since she already found herself shorthanded. At the last minute, two of her regular servers, Theresa told her, had both come down with really bad colds, making them unable to work.

Lily didn't mind working, didn't mind being in the middle of things and hearing people rave about her desserts. But this particular event had to do with an adoption fair for the city's animal shelter. And that meant that Christopher might be there.

She knew that he volunteered his services at the shelter, that he periodically treated some of the animals that were left there. Funny how the very same thing that had made her love him now just made her feel uneasy.

It had been over two weeks since she'd walked out. Two weeks she'd been functioning—more or less— without a heart. She hadn't taken any of his calls since that night.

The night that had been by turns one of the best and then worst nights of her life.

For a brief, shining moment, she had thought that she'd finally found the man she'd been looking for all her life. She and Christopher seemed to be of one mind when it came to so many things.

She had wound up running toward him when what she should have done was walked—slowly. Walked slowly and gotten to know the man.

But she hadn't, and then that bombshell had dropped, shattering her world.

Not only hadn't he told her that he'd been engaged, but he'd been the one to break off the engagement— and so recently. That meant he wasn't serious enough about his commitment. If he could break an engagement, walk out on a promise once, well, what was to keep him from doing it again? From bringing her up to the heights of joy only to let her fall onto the rocks of bitter disappointment somewhere down the line? Even if he could put all that behind him and change, that would take time for him to work out. He couldn't be ready for something so solid so soon after breaking off his engagement. He had to see that and once he did, he'd back away from her on his own.

She wasn't going to risk that, risk having her heart ripped out of her chest, risk tumbling down into the abyss of loneliness and despair. She just wasn't built like that. It was better not to dream than to have those dreams ripped up to pieces.

She hurt now, but she would hurt so much more later if she continued seeing Christopher—continued loving him—only to be abandoned in the end.

"You are a lifesaver," Theresa was saying to her, the woman's very words of praise sabotaging any hope of remaining behind. "I am so shorthanded for this event, I might just have to put out a call to my children to have them come and help. This Adoption Fair promises to be huge." Theresa slanted a look at her protégée. "You are all right with doing this, aren't you, Lily?"

Lily forced a smile to her lips. There was no way she was going to let Theresa down—even if she spent the whole time there looking over her shoulder.

"I'm fine."

"This is for a good cause," Theresa said by way of a reminder. "But I don't have to tell you that. Once you take a pet into your home and into your heart, you see the other homeless animals in a completely different light. You outdid yourself, by the way." Theresa looked over to the boxed-up pastries that were all set to be transported. "Everything smells just heavenly, even through the boxes." Theresa beamed, then asked, "Are you ready?"

Lily snapped out of her mental wanderings. "You mean to go? Sure," she answered a bit too cheerfully.

She was ready to transport the pastries she'd made, ready to do her job. But as far as being ready to see Christopher again, the answer to that was a resounding no.

The best she could hope for was that he didn't show up. After all, it wasn't as if there were going to be any sick animals at the event. The object of this fair was to get as many of the shelter's residents adopted as possible. That guaranteed that only the healthy ones would be on display.

He probably wouldn't be there.

Lily was still telling herself that more than an hour later.

The adoption fair had gotten underway and it seemed as if at least a quarter of Bedford's citizens had turned out to check on the available animals and, as an afterthought, the food, as well.

Her pastries were going fast. She could only hope that some of the people doing all that eating were also seriously considering going home with one of the cats, dogs, rabbits, hamsters and various other species the shelter had on display.

"Your pastries are certainly a major attraction," Theresa said as she passed by the table where Lily was set up. "I think that by the end of the day, your 'contribution' will have raised the biggest amount of money for the animal shelter," Theresa told her with warm approval. In keeping with it being a charitable event, Theresa had charged only half her regular fee. "You should be very proud of yourself."

Although Lily did like receiving compliments, they always made her feel somewhat uncomfortable. She never knew what to say, how to respond, so she usually said nothing, only smiled. This time was no different. After smiling her thanks, Lily pretended to look off toward a group of children who were having fun with a litter of half Siamese, half Burmese kittens that had been born at the shelter. The mother, she'd been told, had been left at the shelter already pregnant.

Patting her hand, Theresa murmured something about seeing how the others were doing and wove her way into the crowd.

No sooner had she left than Lily heard a voice behind her. "How much for that raspberry pastry?"

Lily stiffened. She would have recognized that voice anywhere. It was the voice that still infiltrated her dreams almost every night. The voice that made her ache and wake up close to tears almost every morning.

"Two dollars," she replied formally.

"Very reasonable." Christopher came around the table to face her. He handed her the two dollar bills and she pushed the paper plate with the aforementioned raspberry pastry toward him. Christopher raised his eyes to hers. "How much for five minutes of your time?"

"You haven't got that much money," she told him crisply.

More than anything, she wanted to flee the premises, to just take off and leave him far behind in her wake.

But there was no one to cover for her and she couldn't let Theresa down after she'd agreed to be here.

She was just going to have to tough it out, she thought, hoping that she could.

"I've called you every day, Lily," he told her in a low voice so that they wouldn't be overheard. "You haven't returned any of my calls."

She looked at him sharply. Ignoring each call had been agony for her, especially the ones that came while she was home. The sound of his voice, leaving a message on her answering machine, would fill her house. Fill her head. He made it so hard for her to maintain her stand.

"I didn't see the point, Christopher. It wasn't going to work anyway. Please just accept that," she told him as calmly as she could.

Now that he had her in front of him, he wasn't about to let this opportunity get away. "Lily, I'm sorry I didn't tell you about Irene, especially since it happened not too long ago. You have every right to be angry about that. I shouldn't have kept it from you."

"I'm not angry that you didn't tell me. I'm not denying that it didn't hurt, finding out that way, but that's not why I haven't returned your calls."

He looked at her, completely at a loss. "Then I don't understand," he confessed.

"*You're* the one who broke off the engagement. And how could you be ready to be with anyone yet?" she asked. "You made a commitment, Christopher. A *life-long* commitment," she stressed. "And then you backed out of it just like that. Suddenly I come along, and who's to say you wouldn't drop me, just like that, too?" She snapped her fingers to underscore her point.

Unable to remain in the same space as Christopher any longer, she threw up her hands in despair and started to walk away. But she couldn't outpace him and she had a feeling that if she began to run, he'd only catch up. She didn't want to cause a scene, so she stopped moving. Maybe if she heard him out, *then* he'd go away.

"It wasn't 'just like that,'" Christopher contradicted, angry and frustrated by the accusation. "You didn't give me a chance to explain what happened. I wasn't just engaged to Irene for a day or a week, it was for five months—and during that time, she began to change from the person I thought I was going to marry to a completely different woman. Not only that, but she made it clear that she expected me to change as well, to transform into what she, and her family, felt was a suitable match for her and her world.

"I realized that our marriage wasn't going to be a happy one. What I'd pictured was going to be our life together just wasn't going to happen. She wanted me to give up being a veterinarian and go to work for her father's investment firm. In essence, she wanted me to give up being me and I couldn't do that.

"So I broke off the engagement, hired a moving company to pack up all my things and I came back to a place I always considered to be my home."

His eyes on hers, Christopher took her hand in his, in part to make a connection, in part to keep her from running off until he was finished. He still wasn't sure just what she was capable of doing in the heat of the moment.

"After the breakup, I was certain that the last thing I wanted was to be involved in another relationship, but I hadn't counted on meeting someone as special as you. You brought out all the good things I was trying so hard to bury," he confessed. "You made me feel useful and whole and you made me want to protect you, as well.

"I honestly didn't think I could feel this alive again, but I did and it was all because of you. I know how I feel about you." He tried to make her understand, to see what was in his soul—and to see how much she mattered to him. "I don't want to go back into the darkness, Lily. Please don't make me." His hands tightened ever so slightly on hers and he was relieved when she didn't pull them away. "I haven't been able to concentrate, to think straight since you walked out that morning. And frankly," he confided, his expression even more solemn than before, "the animals are beginning to notice that something's very off with me."

He made her laugh. Lily realized that it was the first time she had laughed since before she'd run out of his house.

"Let's just say—for the sake of argument," she qualified, "that I believe you—"

He jumped the gun and asked, "So you'll let me have a second chance?"

"If you did have a second chance at this relationship, what would you do with it?"

There was absolutely no hesitation, no momentary

pause to think. He already knew what his answer would be. "I'd ask you to marry me."

She lifted her chin. He knew that meant she was preparing for a confrontation. "The way you asked Irene," she concluded.

"No, because I know now that the Irenes of this world are to be avoided if at all possible," he told her. "They don't want a husband, they want a do-it-yourself project. I want someone who loves me—who *likes* me for who I am and what I have to offer. More than that," he amended, looking into her eyes with a sincerity that almost made her ache inside, "I want you."

"For how long?" she challenged, even though she felt herself really weakening.

"I have no idea how long I have to live," he told Lily honestly, rather than resorting to fancy platitudes, "but for however long it is, I want to be able to open my eyes each morning and see you there beside me. These past two weeks without you have been pure hell and I will do anything, *anything*," Christopher stressed, "for a second chance."

"Anything?" she asked, cocking her head as she regarded him.

"Anything," he repeated with feeling.

"Well," she began philosophically, "you could start by kissing me."

He immediately swept her into his arms and cried, "Done!"

And it was.

Epilogue

"Well, ladies, I believe we can happily chalk up another successful venture," Maizie whispered to Theresa and Cecilia.

All three women were seated together in the third pew of St. Elizabeth Ann Seton Church. It was six months since the animal shelter adoption fair had taken place, resulting in more than one happy ending.

Maizie beamed with no small pride as she watched the young man standing up at the altar. He was facing the back of the church, anxiously waiting for the doors to open, and for the rest of his life to finally begin.

He looked very handsome in his tuxedo, Maizie couldn't help noticing.

Theresa dabbed at her eyes. No matter how many weddings she attended—and there had been many in the past few years—hearing the strains of "Here Comes the Bride" never failed to cause tears to spring to her eyes.

"Frances should be here," Theresa told her two friends wistfully.

Cecilia leaned in so that both Theresa and Maizie could hear her. "What makes you think she isn't?" she asked in all seriousness.

Neither of her two friends offered a rebuttal to her question. The thought of their friend looking down on her son with approval as the ceremony unfolded was a comforting one.

"Oh, isn't she just spectacularly beautiful?" Theresa said in awe as they watched Lily slowly make her way down the aisle, each step bringing her closer to the man she was going to spend forever with.

"Every bride is beautiful," Maizie whispered to her friend.

"But some are just more beautiful than others," Theresa maintained stubbornly. Lily had become very special to her in the past year.

"Do you think she ever figured out how Jonathan just 'happened' to appear on her doorstep that morning?" Cecilia asked the others.

"I'm pretty sure she didn't. But I think that Chris might have a few suspicions about that," Maizie whispered back, thinking back to her impromptu visit to his office. He was, after all, a very intelligent young man.

"I told you that you should have used a different dog than one of Jolene's puppies," Cecilia reminded her.

Maizie shrugged. "Water under the bridge," she answered carelessly. "Besides," she went on with a grin her friends had always referred to as mischievous, "it did the trick, didn't it?"

"Shh, it's about to start." Theresa waved a silencing hand at her friends as she nodded toward the priest, who was standing at the front of the altar.

"Not yet," Maizie pointed out as she glanced over her shoulder to the rear of the church. Just before the doors closed, one more wedding participant had to make his way through the narrow opening.

A buzz went up in the church as guests nudged one another, each turning to look at the last member of the wedding party.

"Well, would you look at that."

"Certainly isn't your everyday member of a wedding, is it?"

"Aren't they afraid he's going to swallow the rings?"

The last comment had come from the man in the pew directly in front of the trio.

Unable to hold her tongue any longer, Maizie tapped him on the shoulder. When he turned around to look at her quizzically, she said, "They're not worried about the rings because that's the bride's dog and the groom did an excellent job training him. Besides, if you look very closely, both the rings are secured to that satin pillow in his mouth."

"Why would they include a dog in their wedding?" someone else asked.

The person's companion explained in a voice that said he was the final authority on the subject, "The way I hear it, if it hadn't been for that dog, the two of them would have never met and gotten together."

"Imagine that," Maizie murmured.

She slanted a glance toward Theresa and Cecilia, her eyes shining with amusement. What the young man had just said was the way Lily and Christopher might have viewed how their meeting had come about, but she, Theresa and Cecilia knew the whole story.

Maizie sat back in the pew, paying close attention to what was being said by the couple at the altar. She never tired of hearing vows being exchanged, sealing two people's commitment to one another.

This one, Frances, is for you, Maizie declared silently.

And then, just as with her two friends, her eyes began to tear.

* * * * *

Nikki Logan lives on the edge of a string of wetlands in Western Australia with her partner and a menagerie of animals. She writes captivating nature-based stories full of romance in descriptive natural environments. She believes the danger and richness of wild places perfectly mirror the passion and risk of falling in love. Nikki loves to hear from readers via nikkilogan.com.au or through social media. Find her on Twitter, @readnikkilogan, and Facebook, nikkiloganauthor.

Books by Nikki Logan

Harlequin Romance

Their Miracle Twins
Mr. Right at the Wrong Time
Once a Rebel...
His Until Midnight
Awakened by His Touch
Her Knight in the Outback
Bodyguard...to Bridegroom?
Stranded with Her Rescuer

Harlequin KISS

How to Get Over Your Ex
My Boyfriend and Other Enemies
The Morning After the Night Before

Visit the Author Profile page
at Harlequin.com for more titles.

SLOW DANCE
WITH THE SHERIFF

Nikki Logan

For Lesley—because mothers are always mothers, birth or otherwise.

And for Cil—because so are sisters.

Chapter 1

Sheriff Jed Jackson eased down on the brake and slid one arm across to stop his deputy sliding off the front seat.

'Well,' he muttered to the grizzly bear of a dog who cocked an ear in response, 'there's something you don't see every day.'

A sea of loose steer spilled across the long, empty road out to the Double Bar C, their number swollen fence-to-fence to seal off the single lane accessway, all standing staring at one another, waiting for someone else to take the lead. That wasn't the unusual part; loose cattle were common in these parts.

He squinted out his windscreen. 'What do you reckon she's doing?'

Adrift right in the middle of the massing herd, stand-

ing out white in a sea of brown hide, was a luxury sedan,
and on its roof—standing out blue in a sea of white lac-
quer—was a lone female.

Jed's mouth twitched. Ten-fifty-fours weren't usually
this entertaining, or this sizeable. This road didn't see
much traffic, especially not with the Calhouns away, but
a herd of cattle really couldn't spend the night here. His
eyes lifted again to the damsel in distress, still standing
high and dry with her back to him, waving her hands
shouting uselessly at the cattle.

And clearly she couldn't.

He radioed dispatch and asked them to advise the
Calhoun ranch of a fence breach, then he eased his foot
off the brake and edged closer to the comical scene. The
steer that weren't staring at one another looked up at the
woman expectantly.

He pulled on the handbrake. 'Stay.'

Deputy looked disappointed but slouched back into
the passenger seat, his enormous tongue lolling. Jed
slid his hat on and slipped out the SUV's door, leaving
it gaping. The steer didn't even blink at his arrival they
were so fixated on the woman perched high above them.

Not entirely without reason.

That was a mighty fine pair of legs tucked into tight
denim and spread into a sturdy A-shape. Not baggy
denim, not the loose, hanging-low-enough-to-trip-on,
did-someone-outlaw-belts, de-feminising denim.

Fitted, faded, snug. As God intended jeans to be.

Down at ground level, the length of her legs and the
peach of a rear topping them wouldn't have been all that

gratuitous but, from his steer-eye view, her short blouse didn't do much to offset, either.

The moaning of the cattle had done a good job disguising his arrival but it was time to come clean. He pushed his hat back with a finger to the rim and raised his voice.

'Ma'am, you realise it's a state offence to hold a public assembly without a permit?'

She spun so fast she almost went over, but she steadied herself on bare feet, and then lifted her chin with grace.

Whoa. She was...

His synapses forgot how they worked as he stared and he had to will them to resume sending the signals his body needed to keep breathing. He'd never been so grateful for his county-issue sunglasses in his life; without them she'd see his eyes as round and glazed as the hypnotised steer.

'I hope there's a siege happening somewhere!' she called, sliding her hands up onto her middle. Her righteousness didn't make her any less attractive. Those little clenched fists only accentuated the oblique angle where her waist became her hips. Her continuing complaint drew his eyes back up to the perfectly even teeth she flashed as she growled at him with her non-Texan vowels.

'Because I've been on this rooftop for two hours. The cows have nearly trebled since I called for help.'

Cows. Definitely a tourist.

Guess an hour was a long time when you were stuck on a roof. Jed kept it light to give his thumping pulse time to settle and to give her temper nowhere to go. 'You're about the most interest these steer have had all day,' he said, keeping his voice easy, moving cautiously between the first two lumbering animals.

He leaned back against the cattle as hard as they leaned into him, slapping the occasional rump and cracking a whistle through his curled tongue. They made way enough for him to get through, but only just. 'What are you doing up there?'

Her perfectly manicured eyebrows shot up. 'I assume that's a rhetorical question?'

A tiny part of him died somewhere. Beautiful and sharp. Damn.

He chose his words carefully and worked hard not to smile. 'How did you come to be up there?'

'I stopped for...' Her unlined brow creased just slightly. 'There were about a dozen of them, coming out in front of me.'

He nudged the nearest steer with his hip and then shoved into it harder until it shuffled to its right. Then he stepped into the breach and was that much closer to the stranded tourist.

She followed his progress from on high. It kind of suited her.

'I got out to shoo them away.'

'Why not just nudge through them with your vehicle?'

'Because it's a rental. And because I didn't want to hurt them, just move them.'

Beautiful, sharp, but kind-hearted. His smile threatened again. 'So how did you end up on the roof?' He barely needed to even raise his voice now; he was that close to her car. Even the mob had stopped its keening to listen to the conversation.

'They closed in behind me. I couldn't get back round to my door. And then more came and I…just…'

Clambered up onto the hood and then the roof? Something caught his eye as he reached the front corner of the vehicle. He bent quickly and retrieved them. 'These yours?'

The dainty heels hung from one of his crooked fingers.

'Are they ruined? I kicked them off when I climbed up.'

'Hard to know, ma'am.'

'Oh.'

Her disappointment seemed genuine. 'Expensive?'

She waved away that concern. 'They were my lucky Louboutins.'

Get lucky more like it. He did his best not to imagine them on the end of those forever legs. 'Not so lucky for them.'

He edged along the side of the car to pass the shoes up to her and she folded herself down easily to retrieve them.

She stayed squatted. 'So…now what?'

'I suggest you get comfortable, ma'am. I'll start moving the steer back towards the fence.'

She glanced around them and frowned. 'They don't look so fierce from up here. I swear they were more aggressive before.'

'Maybe they smelled your fear?'

She studied him, curiosity at the front of her big blue-green eyes, trying to decide whether he was serious. 'Are you going to move them yourself?'

'I'll have Deputy help me until the men from the Double Bar C arrive.'

That got her attention. 'These are Calhoun cows?'

'Cattle.'

She pressed her lips together at his correction. 'That's where I was coming from. Calling on Jessica Calhoun. But she was out.'

He paused in his attempts at shoving through the steer and frowned. 'Jess expecting you?'

'What are you, their butler?'

Again with the sass. It wasn't her best feature, but it did excite his blood just a hint. Weird how your body could hate something and want it all at the same time. Maybe that was a carryover from his years in the city. 'I just figured I'd save you some time. Jess is more than out, she's on her honeymoon.'

That took the wind from her sails. She sagged, visibly.

'Sorry.' He shrugged and then couldn't help himself. He muttered before starting up on the steer-shoving again, 'Would you like to leave your card?'

She sighed. 'Okay, I'm sorry for the butler crack. You're a police officer—I guess it's your job to know everyone's business, technically speaking.'

A pat with one hand and a slap on the way back through. With no small amount of pleasure in enlightening her, he pointed at his shoulder. 'See these stars? That makes me county sheriff. Technically speaking.'

She blew at the loose strand of blond hair curling

down in front of her left eye and carefully tucked it back into the tight braid hiding the rest of it from him. Working out whether to risk more sarcasm, perhaps?

She settled on disdain.

Good call. Women in cattle-infested waters...

'Well, Sheriff, if your deputy could rouse himself to the task at hand maybe we can all get on with our day.'

That probably qualified as a peace offering where she came from.

He lifted his head and called loudly, 'Deputy!'

One hundred and twenty pounds of pure hair and loyalty bounded out of his service vehicle and lumbered towards them. The cattle paid immediate attention and, as a body, began to stir.

'Settle,' he murmured. Deputy slowed and sat.

She spun back to look at him. 'That's your deputy?'

'Yup.'

'A dog?'

'Dawg, actually.'

She stared. 'Because this is Texas?'

'Because it's his name. Deputy Dawg. It would be disrespectful to call him anything else.'

'And he's trained to herd cows?'

He hid his laugh in the grunt of pushing past yet another stubborn steer. 'Not really, but from where I'm standing beggars can't be choosers—' he made himself add some courtesy '—ma'am.'

She squatted onto her bottom and slid her feet down the back windscreen of the car. They easily made the trunk.

'You have a point,' she grudgingly agreed, then gestured to a particular spot in the fence hidden to him by the wall of steer. 'The hole's over there.'

But her concession wasn't an apology and it wasn't particularly gracious.

Just like that, he was thinking of New York again. And that sucked the humour plain out of him.

'Thank you,' he said, then turned and whistled for Deputy.

Every single cell in Ellie Patterson's body shrivelled with mortification. Awful enough to be found like this, so absurdly helpless, but she'd been nothing but rude since the officer—sheriff—stopped to help her. As though it was somehow his fault that her day had gone so badly wrong.

Her whole week.

She shuddered in a deep breath and shoved the regret down hard where she kept all her other distracting feelings. Between the two of them, the sheriff and his... Deputy...were making fairly good work of the cows. They'd got the one closest to the hole in the fence turned around and encouraged it back through, but the rest weren't exactly hurrying to follow. It wasn't like picking up one lost duckling in Central Park and having the whole flock come scrambling after it.

The massive tricolour dog weaved easily between the forest of legs, keeping the cows' attention firmly on it and away from her—a small blessing—but the sheriff was slapping the odd rump, whistling and cursing lightly at the animals in a way that was very...well... Texan.

He couldn't have been more cowboy if he tried.

But there was a certain unconcerned confidence in his actions that was very appealing. This was not a man that would be caught dead cowering on the roof of his car.

Another animal lumbered through to the paddock it had come from and casually wandered off to eat some grass. Thirty others still surrounded her.

This was going to take some time.

Ellie relaxed on her unconventional perch and channelled her inner Alex—her easygoing baby sister—scratching around for the positives in the moment. Actually, the Texan sun was pleasant once the drama of the past couple of hours had passed and once someone else was taking responsibility for the cows. And there were worse ways to pass the time than watching a good-looking man build up a sweat.

'Sure you don't want to come down here and help now that you've seen how docile they are?' the man in question called.

Docile? They'd nearly trampled her earlier. Sort of. Getting friendly with the wildlife was not the reason she drove all this way to Texas.

Not that she'd really thought through any part of this visit.

Two days ago she'd burst out of the building her family owned, fresh from the devil of all showdowns with her mother in which she'd hurled words like hypocrite and liar at the woman who'd given her life. In about as much emotional pain as she could ever remember being.

Two hours and a lot of hastily dropped gratuities later, she was on the I-78 in a little white rental heading south.

Destination: Texas.

'Very sure, thank you, Sheriff. You were clearly born for this.'

He seemed to stiffen but it was only momentary. If she got lucky, country cowboys—even ones in uniform—had dulled sarcasm receptors.

'So… Jess just got married?' she called to fill the suddenly awkward silence. Back home there was seldom any silence long enough to become awkward.

'Yep.' He slapped another rump and sent a cow forward. 'You said you know the Calhouns?'

I think I am one. Wouldn't that put a tilt in his hat and a heap more lines in his good ol' Texan brow.

'I… Yes. Sort of.'

He did as good a job of the head tilt as his giant dog. 'Didn't realise knowing someone or not was a matter of degrees.'

It really was poor on her part that two straight days on the road and she hadn't really thought about how she was going to answer these kinds of questions. But she hadn't worked the top parties of New York only to fall apart the moment a stranger asked a few pointed questions.

She pulled herself together. 'I'm expected, but I'm… early.' Cough. A couple of months early. 'I wasn't aware of Jessica's plans.'

They fell to silence again. Then he busied himself with more cows. They were starting to move more easily now that their volume had reduced on this side of the wire, inversely proportional to the effort the sheriff was putting in. His movements were slowing and his breath came faster. But every move spoke of strength and resilience.

'Your timing is off,' he puffed between heaving cows. 'Holt's away, too, right now and Meg's away at college. Nate's still on tour.'

Her chest squeezed. Two brothers and two sisters? Just like that, her family doubled. But she struggled to hide the impact his simple words had. 'Tour? Rock star or military?'

He slowly turned and stared right at her as if she'd insulted him. 'Military.'

Clipped and deep. Maybe she had offended him? His accent was there but nowhere near as pronounced as the young cowboy she'd met out at the Calhoun ranch who told her in his thick drawl that Jess wasn't home. Least that's what she'd thought he'd said. She wasn't fluent in deep Texan.

The animals seemed to realise there were now many more of them inside the field than outside it and they began to drift back through the fence to the safety of their numbers. It wasn't quick, but it was movement. And it was in the right direction.

The sheriff whistled and his dog immediately came back to his side. They both stood, panting, by her rental's tailpipe and watched the dawdling migration.

'He's well trained,' Ellie commented from her position above the sheriff's shoulder, searching for something to say.

'It was part of our deal,' he answered cryptically. Then he turned and thrust his hand up towards her. 'County Sheriff Jerry Jackson.'

Ellie made herself ignore how many cow rumps that hand had been slapping only moments before. They weren't vermin, just…living suede. His fingers were warm as they pressed into hers, his shake firm but not crippling. She tried hard not to stiffen.

'Jed,' he modified.

'Sheriff.' She smiled and nodded as though she was in a top-class restaurant and not perched on the back of a car surrounded by rogue livestock.

'And you are…?'

Trying not to tell you, she realised, not entirely sure why. For the first time it dawned on her that she'd be a nobody here. Not a socialite. Not a performer. Not a Patterson.

No responsibilities. No expectations.

Opportunity rolled out before her bright and shiny and warmed her from the inside. But then she remembered she'd never be able to escape who she was—even if she wasn't in fact who she'd thought she was for the past thirty years.

'Ellie.' She almost said Eleanor, the name she was known by in Manhattan, but at the last moment she used the name Alex called her. 'Ellie Patterson.'

'Where are you staying, Ellie?'

His body language was relaxed and he had the ultimate vouch pinned high on his chest—a big silver star. There was no reason in the world that she should be bristling at his courteous questions and yet…she was.

'Are you just making conversation or is that professional interest?'

His polite smile died before it formed fully. He turned

up to face her front-on. 'The Calhouns are friends of mine and you're a friend of theirs...' Though the speculation in his voice told her he really wasn't convinced of that yet. 'It would be wrong of me to send you on your way without extending you some country courtesy in their place.'

It was credible. This was Texas, after all. But trusting had never come easy to her. And neither had admitting she wasn't fully on top of everything. In New York, that was just assumed.

She was Eleanor.

And she'd assumed she'd be welcomed with open arms at the Calhoun ranch. 'I'm sure I'll find a place in town...'

'Ordinarily I'd agree with you,' he said. 'But the Tri-County Chamber of Commerce is having their annual convention in town this week so our motel and bed and breakfasts are pretty maxed out. You might have a bit of trouble.'

Embarrassed heat flooded up her back. Accommodation was a pretty basic thing to overlook. She called on her fundraising persona—the one that had served her so well in the ballrooms of New York—and brushed his warning off. 'I'm sure I'll find something.'

'You could try Nan's Bunk'n'Grill back on I-38, but it's a fair haul from here.' He paused, maybe regretting his hospitality in the face of her bland expression. 'Or the Alamo, right here in town, can accommodate a single. It's vacant right now but that could change any time.'

Having someone organise her didn't sit well, particularly since she'd failed abysmally to organise herself.

If she had to, she'd drive all the way to Austin to avoid having to accept the condescension of strangers.

'Thanks for the concern, Sheriff, but I'll be fine.' Her words practically crunched with stiffness.

He studied her from behind reflective sunglasses, until a throat gurgle from Deputy got his attention. He turned and looked back up the dirt road where a dust stream had appeared.

'That's Calhoun men,' he said simply. 'They'll deal with the rest of the steer and repair the fence.'

Instant panic hit her. If they were Calhoun employees, then they were her employees. She absolutely didn't want their first impression of her to be like this, cowering and ridiculous on the rooftop of her car. What if they remembered it when they found out who she was? She started to slide off.

Without asking, he stretched up over the trunk and caught her around the waist to help her dismount. Her bare feet touched softly down onto the cow-compacted earth and she stumbled against him harder than was polite.

Or bearable.

She used the moment of steadying herself as an excuse to push some urgent distance between them but he stayed close, towering over her and keeping the last curious cows back. A moment later, a truck pulled up and a handful of cowboys leapt off the tray and launched into immediate action. That gave her the time she needed to slip her heels back on and slide back into the rental.

She was Eleanor Patterson. Unflappable. Capable. Confident.

Once inside, she lowered her window and smiled her best New York dazzler out at him. 'Thank you, Sheriff—'

'Jed.'

'—for everything. I'll know better than to get out in the middle of a stampede next time.'

And just as she was feeling supremely on top of things again, he reached through her open window and brushed his fingers against her braided hair and retrieved a single piece of straw.

Her chest sucked in just as all the air in her body puffed out and she couldn't help the flinch from his large, tanned fingers.

No one touched her hair.

No one.

She faked fumbling for her keys and it effectively brushed his hand away. But it didn't do a thing to diminish the temporary warmth his brief touch had caused. Its lingering compounded her confusion.

But he didn't miss her knee-jerk reaction. His lips tightened and Ellie wished he'd take the sunglasses off so she could see his eyes. For just a moment. She swallowed past the lump in her throat and pushed away her hormones' sudden interest in Sheriff Jerry Jackson.

'Welcome to Larkville, Ms. Patterson,' he rumbled, deep and low.

Larkville. Really, shouldn't a town with a name like that have better news to offer? A town full of levity and pratfalls, not secrets and heartbreak.

But she had to find out.

Either Cedric Patterson was her father...or he wasn't.

And if he wasn't—her stomach curled in on itself—
what the hell was she going to do?

She cleared her throat. 'Thank you again, Sheriff.'

'Remember…the Alamo.'

The timing was too good. Despite all her exhaustion and uncertainty, despite everything that had torn
her world wide open this past week, laughter suddenly
wanted to tumble out into the midday air.

She resisted it, holding the unfamiliar sensation to
herself instead.

She started her rental.

She put it in gear.

Funny how she had to force herself to drive off.

Chapter 2

Larkville was lovely. Larkville was kind. Larkville was extremely interested in who she was and why she'd come and clearly disappointed by her not sharing. But no one in the small, old Texas town had been able to find a bed for her. Despite their honest best efforts.

Remember the Alamo...

Sheriff Jackson's voice had wafted uninvited through her head a few times in the afternoon since her sojourn with the cows but—for reasons she was still trying to figure out—she didn't want to take his advice. The Alamo might be a charming B & B run by the most delightful old Texan grandmother with handmade quilts, but she'd developed an almost pathological resistance to the idea of driving across town to check it out.

Although three others had suggested she try there.

Instead she'd steadfastly ignored the pressing nature of her lack of accommodation and she'd lost herself in Larkville's loveliest antique and craft shops as the sun crawled across the sky. She'd had half a nut-bread sandwich for a late lunch in the town's pretty monument square. She'd grabbed a few pictures on her phone.

None of which would help her when the sun set and she had nowhere to go but back to New York.

No. Not going to happen.

She'd sleep in her car before doing that. She had a credit card full of funds, a heart full of regrets back in New York and a possible sister to meet in Texas. She turned her head to the west and stared off in the direction of the Alamo and tuned in to the confusion roiling in her usually uncluttered mind.

She didn't want to discover that Texan grandmother had room for one more. She didn't want Sheriff Jed Jackson to be right.

Because his being right about that might cast a different light on other decisions she'd made about coming here. About keeping Jessica Calhoun's extraordinary letter secret from everyone but her mother. From her siblings. From her twin—the other Patterson so immediately affected. Maybe more so than her because Matt was their father's heir.

She drew in a soft breath.

Or maybe he wasn't, now.

Dread washed through her. Poor Matt. How lost was he going to be when he found out? The two of them might have lost the closeness they'd enjoyed as children but he was still her twin. They'd spent nine months entwined and embracing in their mother's womb. Now they'd be lucky to speak to each other once in that time.

She didn't always like Matt but she absolutely loved him.

She owed it to him, if not herself, to find out the truth. To protect him from it, if it was lies, and to break it to him gently if it wasn't.

A sigh shuddered through her.

It wasn't. Deep down Ellie knew that. Her mother's carefully schooled candor slammed the door on the last bit of hope she'd had that Jessica Calhoun had mixed her up with someone else.

Of their own accord, her feet started taking her back towards her car, back towards the one last hope she had of staying in Larkville. Back towards her vision of kindly grandmothers, open stoves and steaming pots full of home-cooked soup.

Back to the Alamo.

There were worse places to wait out a few days.

'Well, well…'

Ellie's shock was as much for the fact that the big, solid door opened to a big, solid man as it was for the fact that County Sheriff Jed Jackson had no reason to wear his sunglasses disguise indoors.

For a man so large, she wasn't expecting eyes like this. As pale as his faded tan T-shirt, framed by low, dark eyebrows and fringed with long lashes. His brown hair was dishevelled when not covered by a hat, flecked with grey and his five-o'clock shadow was right on time.

Coherent thoughts scattered on the evening breeze and all she could do was stare into those amazing eyes.

He slid one long arm up the doorframe and leaned casually into it. It only made him seem larger. 'I thought you'd have gone with Nan's Bunk'n'Grill out of sheer stubbornness,' he murmured.

Ellie tried to see past him, looking for signs of the hand-hewn craft and that pot of soup she'd convinced herself would be waiting. 'You're staying here?'

No wonder the tourists of Larkville couldn't find a place to sleep if the locals took up all the rooms.

His dark brows dipped. 'I live here.'

She heard his words but her brain just wouldn't compute. It was still completely zazzled by those eyes and by the butterfly beating its way out of her heart. 'In a B & B?'

'This is my house.'

Oh.

She stepped back to look at the number above the door. Seriously, how had she made it to thirty in one piece?

'You have the right place, Ellie.' Ellie. It sounded so much better in his voice. More like a breath than a word. 'This is the Alamo.'

'I can't stay with you!' And just like that her social skills fluttered off after her sense on the stiff breeze.

But Texans had thick hides, apparently, because he only smiled. 'I rent out the room at the back.' And then, when her feet didn't move, he added, 'It's fully self-contained.' And when she still didn't move... 'Ellie, I'm the sheriff. You'll be fine.'

Desperation warred with disappointment and more than a little unease. There was no lovely Texan nana preparing soup for her, but he was offering a private— warm, as her skin prickled up again at the wind's caress—place to spend the night, and she'd be his customer so she'd set the boundaries for their dealings with each other.

Though if her galloping heart was any indication that wasn't necessarily advisable.

'Can I see it?'

His smile twisted and took her insides with it. 'I'd wager you wouldn't be here if you'd found so much as an empty washroom. Just take it. It's clean and comfortable.'

And just meters from you...

She tossed her hair back and met his gaze. 'I'd like to see it, please.'

He inclined his head and stepped out onto the porch, crowding her back against a soft-looking Texan outdoor setting. She dropped her eyes. The house's comforting warmth disappeared as he pulled the door closed behind him and she rubbed her hands along her bare, slim arms. This cotton blouse was one of her girliest, and prettiest, and she'd been pathetically keen to make a good impression on Jessica Calhoun.

She hadn't really imagined still being outdoors in it as the sun set behind the Texan hills.

She followed him off the porch, around the side of the house and down a long pathway between his stone house and the neighbors'.

It was hard not to be distracted by the view.

Her fingers trailed along the stonework walls as they reached the end of the path. Jed reached up and snaffled a key from the doorframe.

'Pretty poor security for a county sheriff.' Or was it actually true what they said about small-town America? She couldn't imagine living anywhere you didn't have double deadlocks and movement sensors.

As he pushed the timber door open, he grunted. 'I figure anyone breaking in is probably only in need of somewhere safe to spend the night.'

'What if they trash the place?'

He turned and stared at her. 'Where are you from?'

The unease returned and, until then, she hadn't noticed it had dissipated. She stiffened her spine against it. 'New York.'

He nodded as if congratulating himself on his instincts. He looked like he wanted to say something else but finally settled on, 'Larkville is nothing like the city.'

'Clearly.' She couldn't help the mutter. Manhattan didn't produce men like this one.

She shut that thought down hard and followed him into the darkened room and stared around her as he switched on the lights. It was smaller than her own bathroom back home, but somehow he'd squeezed everything anyone would need for a comfortable night into it. A thick, masculine sofa draped in patchwork throws, a small two-person timber table that looked like it might once have been part of a forge, a rustic kitchenette. And upstairs, in what must once have been a hayloft...

She moved quickly up the stairs.

Bright, woven rugs crisscrossed a ridiculously comfortable-looking bed. The exhaustion of the past week suddenly made its presence felt.

'They're handcrafted by the people native to this area,' he said. 'Amazingly warm.'

'They look it. They suit the room.'

'This was the original barn on the back of the building back in 1885.'

'It's…' So perfect. So amazing. 'It looks very comfortable.'

He looked down on her in the warm timber surrounds of the loft bedroom. The low roof line only served to make him seem more of a giant crowded into the tiny space.

She regretted coming up here instantly.

'It is. I lived here for months when my place was being renovated.'

She was distracted by the thought that she'd be sleeping in Sheriff Jed Jackson's bed tonight, but she stumbled out the first response that came to her. 'But it's so small…'

His lips tightened immediately. 'Size isn't everything, Ms. Patterson.'

What happened to 'Ellie'? He turned and negotiated his descent quickly and she hurried after him, hating the fact that she was hurrying. She forced her feet to slow. 'This will be very nice, Sheriff, thank you.'

He turned and stared directly at her. 'Jed. I'm not the sheriff when I'm out of uniform.'

Great. And now she was imagining him out of uniform.

Unfamiliar panic set in as her mind warmed to the

topic. It was an instant flashback to her childhood when she'd struggled so hard to be mature and collected in the company of her parents' sophisticated friends, and feared she'd failed miserably. Back then she had other methods of controlling her body; now, she just folded her manicured nails into her palm and concentrated on how they felt digging into her flesh.

Hard enough to distract, soft enough not to scar.

It did vaguely occur to her that maybe she'd just swapped one self-harm for another.

'You haven't asked the price,' he said.

'Price isn't an issue.' She cringed at how superior it sounded here—standing in a barn, out of context of the Patterson billions.

His stare went on a tiny bit too long to be polite. 'No,' he said. 'I can see that.'

Silence fell.

Limped on.

And then they both chose the exact same moment to break it.

'I'll get a fire started—'

'I'll just get my bags—'

She opened the door to the pathway and the icy air from outside streamed in and stopped her dead.

A hard body stepped past her. 'I'll get your bags, you stay in the warm.'

His tone said he'd rather she froze to death, but his country courtesy wouldn't let that happen.

'But I—'

He didn't even bother turning around. 'You can get the fire going if you want to be useful.'

And then he closed the door in her face.

Useful. The magic word. If there was one thing Eleanor Patterson was, it was useful. Capable. A doer. Nothing she couldn't master.

She took a deep breath, turned from the timber door just inches from her face and stared at the small, free-standing wood fire and the basket of timber next to it, releasing her breath slowly.

Nothing she couldn't master...

The night air was as good as a cold shower. Jed's body had begun humming the moment he opened his door to Ellie Patterson, and tailing those jeans up the steep steps to the loft hadn't reduced it. He had to work hard not to imagine himself throwing the Comanche blankets aside and plumping up the quilt so she could stretch her supermodel limbs out on it and sleep.

Sleep. Yeah, that's what he was throwing the blankets aside for.

Pervert.

She was now his tenant and she was a visitor to one of the towns under his authority, a guest of the Calhouns. Ellie Patterson and feather quilts had no place in his imagination. Together or apart.

She just needed a place to stay and he had one sitting there going to waste. He'd dressed it up real nice on arrival in Larkville and had left the whole place pretty much intact—a few extra girlie touches for his gram when she came to visit, but otherwise the same as when he'd used it.

It might not be to New York standards—especially

for a woman who didn't need to ask the price of a room—but she'd have no complaints. No reasonable ones anyway. It was insulated, sealed and furnished, and it smelled good.

Not as good as Ellie Patterson did, but good enough.

He opened her unlocked car to pop the trunk.

He'd watched her rental trundle off down the long, straight road from the Calhoun ranch until it disappeared against the sky, and he'd wondered if he would see her again. Logic said yes; it was a small town. His heart said no, not a good idea.

The last person on this planet he needed to get mixed up with was a woman from New York City. That was just way too close to things he'd walked away from.

And yet, he'd found himself volunteering the Alamo in her moment of need, the manners his gram raised him with defying his better judgement. He'd been almost relieved when she so curtly declined his help.

As he swung her cases—plural—out of the rental's trunk, he heard the unmistakable sound of Deputy protesting. A ten-second detour put him at his front door.

'Sorry, boy, got distracted. Come on out.'

Deputy looked about as ticked off as a dog used to the sole attention of his owner possibly could, but he was a fast forgiver and barrelled down the porch steps and pathway ahead of Ellie's cases.

In the half second it took to push the door to the old barn open, he and Deputy both saw the same thing. Ellie, legs spread either side of the little stove, hands and face smudged with soot, a burning twig in her hand. He only wanted to dash to her side and wipe clean that porcelain skin. Deputy actually did it. With his tongue.

Ellie gasped.

Jed barked a stiff, 'Heel!'

Deputy slunk back to his master's right boot and dropped his head, sorry but not sorry. Ellie scrabbled to her feet, sputtering. There was nothing for him to do apart from apologise for his dog's manners and place her suitcases through the door.

As if he hadn't come off as enough of a hick already.

Then his eyes fell on the work of modern art poking out of the fireplace. He stepped closer.

'I've never made a fire.'

He struggled not to soften at the self-conscious note in her voice. It was good to know she could drop the self-possession for a moment, but he wasn't buying for one moment that it was permanent. Ms. Ellie Patterson might be pretty in pastels but he'd wager his future she was tough as nails beneath it.

He didn't take his eyes off the amazing feat of over-engineering. An entire log was jammed in there with twigs and twisted newspaper and no less than four fire-starters. And she'd been about to set the whole lot ablaze.

He relieved her of the burning twig and extinguished it. 'That would have burned down the barn.'

She looked horrified. 'Oh. Really?'

Deputy dropped to his side on the rug closest to the fire, as though it was already blazing.

Dopey dog.

'Less is more with fires....' Without thinking he took her hand and walked her to the sofa, then pressed her into it. He did his best not to care that she locked up like an antique firearm at his uninvited touch. 'Watch and learn.'

It took him a good five minutes to undo the nest of twigs and kindling squashed inside the wrought-iron fireplace. But then it was a quick job to build a proper fire and get it crackling. She watched him intently.

He stood. 'Got it?'

Her colour surged and it wasn't from the growing flames. 'I'm sorry. You must think me so incredibly inept. First the cows and now the fire.'

He looked down on her, embarrassed and poised on his sofa. 'Well, I figure you don't have a lot of either in Manhattan.'

'We have a fireplace,' she started without thinking, and then her words tapered off. 'But we light it with a button.'

Well, that was one step better than 'but we have staff to do it for us.' Maybe she knew what she was talking about when she teased him about being the Calhouns' butler.

'I'm sure there's a hundred things you can do that I can't. One day you can teach me one of those and we'll be even.'

Her blue eyes glittered much greener against the glow of the growing fire. 'Not sure you'd have much use for the intricacies of delivering a sauté in arabesque.'

'You're a chef?'

His confusion at least brought a glint of humour back to her beautiful face. 'Sauté onstage, not on the stove. I'm a dancer. Ballet. Or... I was.'

'That explains so much.' Her poise. The way she held herself. Those amazing legs. Her long, toned frame. Skinny, but not everywhere.

The lightness in her expression completely evaporated and he could have kicked himself for letting his eyes follow his thoughts. 'What I mean is it doesn't surprise me. You move like a professional.' Her eyebrows shot up. 'Dancer, I mean.'

Deputy shot him a look full of scorn: way to keep digging, buddy!

But as he watched, the awkwardness leached from Ellie's fine features and her lips turned up. The eyes that met his were amused. And more than a little bit sexy. 'Thank you, Jed. I'm feeling much less self-conscious now.'

So was he—stupidly—now that she'd used his name.

He cleared his throat. 'Well, then… I'll just leave you to unpack.' He glanced at the fire. 'As soon as those branches are well alight you can drop that log on top. Just one,' he cautioned, remembering her overpacked first effort. 'As long as you keep the vent tight it should last awhile. Put a big one on just before you go to bed and it should see you through the night.'

'I'll do that now, then, because as soon as you're gone I'm crawling into bed.'

'At 7:00 p.m.?' Why was she so exhausted? It couldn't just be the steer, even for a city slicker.

She pushed to her feet to show him the door. 'I think my week is finally catching up to me. But I'm going to be very comfortable here, thank you for the hospitality. You've done your hometown proud.'

It was on the tip of his tongue to tell her Larkville wasn't his hometown, but she didn't say it to start a conversation, she said it to end one.

He moved to the door, surprised at how his own feet dragged, and whistled for Deputy. 'Sleep well, Ellie.'

His buddy hauled himself to his feet and paused in front of Ellie for the obligatory farewell scratch. She just stared at him, no clue what he was expecting, but then his patient upward stare seemed to encourage her and she slid her elegant fingers into his coat and gave him a tentative rub. She released him, and Deputy padded to Jed's side and preceded him out the door.

Jed stared after the dog, an irrational envy blazing away as she closed the door behind him. He pulled the collar of his shirt up against the air's bite and hurried back to his house. It was ridiculous to hold it against a dog just because he'd been free to walk up and demand she touch him. Her sliding down his body earlier today was a heck of a lot more gratuitous than what just happened in the barn.

Yet… The way her fingers had curled in his dog's thick black coat… Her eyes barely staying open. It was somehow more…intimate.

Deputy reached the street first, then paused and looked back at him, a particularly smug expression on his hairy black, tan and white face.

'Jerk,' Jed muttered.

Who or what Ellie Patterson touched was no concern of his. She was the last kind of woman he needed to be staking a claim on, and the last kind to tolerate it.

But as he put foot after foot up that long path—

way towards his dog, he'd never, in his life, felt more like rushing back in there and branding his name on someone—preferably with his lips—so everyone in Larkville knew where Ellie Patterson was coming home to at night.

Stupid, because the woman was as prickly as the cactus out on the borderlands. Stupid because she lived in New York and he lived in small-town Texas. Stupid because he wasn't interested in a relationship. Now or ever.

He turned and stared at her door.

But it wouldn't be the first stupid thing he'd done in his life.

Deputy looked at him with disgust and then turned back to the front door of the cottage and waited for someone with opposable thumbs to make it open.

Not half the look Ellie would give him if she got even the slightest inkling of his caveman thoughts. This was just his testosterone speaking, pure and simple.

Men like him didn't belong with women like her. Women like Ellie Patterson belonged with driven, successful investment bankers who made and lost millions on Wall Street. Men like him belonged with nice, country girls who were happy to love him warts and all. There was no shortage of nice women in Hayes County and a handful had made their interest—and their willingness—clearly known since he arrived in Larkville. And right after that he'd made it his rule not to date where he worked.

Don't poop where you eat, Jeddie, his gram used to say, though she generally referenced it when she was trying to encourage him to clean his room. But it was good advice.

His gut curled.

He'd ignored it once and he'd screwed everything up royally. Sticking faithfully to this rule had seen him avoid any messy entanglements that threatened his job or his peace of mind ever since he'd arrived in Larkville three years ago.

But abstinence had a way of creeping up on you. Every week he went without someone in his life was a week he grew more determined to only break it for something special. Someone special. That bar just kept on rising. To the point that he wondered how special a woman would have to be to meet it.

Deputy lifted his big head and threw him a look as forlorn as he felt. It was exactly what he needed to snap him out of the sorry place he'd wound up. He flung himself down onto the sofa, reached for the TV remote and found himself a sports channel.

In the absence of any other kind of stimulation, verbally sparring with an uptight city girl might just be as close to flirting as he needed to get.

If she didn't deck him for trying.

Chapter 3

Given how many five-star hotels Ellie had stayed in, it was ridiculous to think that she'd just had one of the best sleeps of her life in a converted hayloft.

She burrowed down deeper into the soft quilt and took herself through the pros and cons of just sleeping all day.

Pro: she wasn't expected anywhere.

Pro: she wouldn't be missed by anyone. No one would know but her; and possibly the sheriff, although he'd almost certainly be out doing sheriffly duties.

When was the last time she just lay in? While all her classmates were keeping teenage hours, she'd spent every waking moment perfecting her steps, or doing strength training or studying the masters. Even when she was sick she used to force herself up, find something constructive to do. Anything that meant she wasn't indulging her body.

Now look at her. Twelve hours' rest behind her and quite prepared to go back for another three.

What had she become?

Her deep, powerful desire to pull the blankets over her head and never come out was only beaten by the strength of her determination not to. She hurled back the toasty warm covers and let the bracing Texan morning in with her, and her near-naked flesh protested with a thousand tiny bumps. Even the biggest log she'd found in the woodpile couldn't last this long and so the little room was as cold as…well, an old barn. Bad enough that she'd broken a cardinal rule and gone to bed without eating anything, she'd stripped out of her clothes and just crawled into bed in panties only, too tired to even forage amongst her belongings for her pajamas.

More sloth!

She pulled one of the blankets up around her shoulders and tiptoed over to her suitcases, the timber floor of the raised loft creaking under her slight weight. The sound reminded her of the flex and give in the dance floor of the rehearsal studio and brought a long-distance kind of comfort. They may have been hard years but they were also her childhood. She rummaged to the bottom of one case for socks and a T-shirt and dragged them on, then slid into her jeans from yesterday, her loose hair caressing her face.

No doubt, the people of Larkville had been up before dawn—doing whatever it was that country folk did until the sun came up. There was no good reason she shouldn't be up, too. She looped a scrunchie over her wrist, pulled the bedspread into tidy order, surrendered her toasty blanket and laid it neatly back where it belonged, then turned for the steps.

Downstairs didn't have the benefit of rising heat and it had the decided non-benefit of original old-brick flooring so it was even chillier than the loft. It wasn't worth going to all the trouble of lighting the fire for the few short hours until it got Texas warm. Right behind that she realised she had no idea what the day's weather would bring. Back home, she'd step out onto her balcony and look out over the skyline to guess what kind of conditions Manhattan was in for, but here she'd have to sprint out onto the pavement where she could look up into the sky and take a stab at what the day had in store.

She pulled on the runners she'd left by the sofa, started to shape her hair into a ponytail, hauled open the big timber door…and just about tripped over the uniformed man crouched there leaving a box on her doorstep.

'Oh—!'

Two pale eyes looked as startled as she felt and the sheriff caught her before momentum flipped her clean over him. All at once she became aware of two things: first, she wasn't fully dressed and, worse, her hair was still flying loose.

Having actual breasts after so many years of not having them at all was still hard to get used to and slipping them into lace was never the first thing she did in the morning. Not that what she had now would be of much interest to any but the most pubescent of boys but she still didn't want them pointing at Sheriff Jed Jackson in the frosty morning air.

But even more urgent… Her hair was down.

Ellie steadied herself on Jed's shoulders as he straightened and she stepped back into the barn, tucking herself more modestly behind its door. She abandoned her discomfort about her lack of proper clothing in favour of hauling her hair into a quick bunch and twisting the scrunchie around it three brutal times. That unfortunately served to thrust her chest more obviously in the sheriff's direction but if it was a choice between her unashamedly frost-tightened nipples and her still-recovering hair, she'd opt for the eyeful any day.

Of the many abuses her undernourished body had endured in the past, losing fistfuls of brittle hair was the most lingering and shameful.

She never wore it loose in public. Not then. Not even now, years after her recovery.

Jed's eyes finally decided it was safe to find hers, though he seemed as speechless as she was.

'Good morning, Sheriff.' She forced air through her lips, but it didn't come out half as poised as she might have hoped. The wobble gave her away.

'I didn't want to wake you,' he muttered. Four tiny lines splayed out between his dark eyebrows and he glanced down to the box at his feet. 'I brought supplies.'

She dropped her gaze and finally absorbed the box's contents. Milk, fruit, bread, eggs, half a ham leg. Her whole body shrivelled—the habit of years. It was more than just supplies, it was a Thanksgiving feast. To a

Texan that was probably a starter pack, but what he'd brought would last her weeks.

'Thank you.' She dug deep into her chatting-with-strangers repertoire for some lightness to cover the moment. 'Cattle mustering, fire lighting and now deliveries. County sheriffs sure have a broad job description.'

His lips tightened. 'Sure do. In between the road deaths and burglaries and domestic violence.'

She winced internally. Why did every word out of her mouth end up belittling him?

But he moved the conversation smoothly on. 'You were heading out?'

'No, I just wanted to see the sky.' That put a complex little question mark in his expression. 'To check the weather,' she added.

'You know we get the Weather Channel in Texas, right?'

Of course she knew that. But she'd been trusting her own instincts regarding the weather for years. On the whole she was right more often than the experts. 'Right, but I'd rather see it for myself.'

Wow, did she sound as much of a control freak as she feared?

His stare intensified. 'As it happens, meteorology is also on my job description. Today will be fine and eighty-two degrees.'

Ellie couldn't stop her eyes from drifting upwards to the streak of cloud front visible between the overhanging eaves of the two buildings.

He didn't look surprised. If anything, he looked disappointed. 'You really don't trust anyone but yourself, huh?'

She lifted her chin and met his criticism. 'It smells like rain.'

He snorted. 'I don't think so, Manhattan. We've been in drought for months.'

He might as well have patted her on the head. He bent and retrieved the box, then looked expectantly towards her little kitchenette. No way on earth she was letting him back in here until she was fully and properly dressed and every hair was in its rightful place. She took a deep breath, stepped out from behind the door and extended her arms for the box.

'It's heavy…' he warned.

'Try me,' she countered.

Another man might have argued. The sheriff just plonked the box unceremoniously into her arms. It was hard to know if that reflected his confidence in her ability or some twisted desire to see her fail.

She fixed her expression, shifted her feet just slightly and let her spine take the full brunt of the heavy supplies. It didn't fail her. You don't dance for twelve years without building up a pretty decent core strength. Just for good measure she didn't rush the box straight over to the counter and, since it was doing a pretty good job of preserving her modesty, she had no real urgency. 'Okay, well… Thanks again.'

B'bye now.

He didn't look fooled. Or chagrined. If anything, he looked amused. Like he knew exactly what she was doing. The corners of that gorgeous mouth kicked up just slightly. He flicked his index finger at the brim of his sheriff's hat in farewell and turned to walk away.

She could have closed the door and heaved the box over to the kitchen. She probably should have done that. But instead she made herself take its weight a little longer, and she watched him saunter up the pathway towards his SUV, law-enforcement accoutrements hanging off both sides of his hips, lending a sexy kind of emphasis to the loping motion of his strong legs.

Then, just as he hit the sidewalk—just as she convinced herself he wasn't going to—he turned and glanced back down the lane and smiled like he knew all along that she was still watching. Though it nearly killed her arms to do it, she even managed to return his brief salute by lifting three fingers off her death grip on the heavy box in a *faux*-casual farewell flick.

Then she kicked the door shut between them and hurried to the counter before she had fruit and ham and eggs splattered all over her chilly barn floor.

Jed slid in beside Deputy and waited until the tinted window of his driver's door was one hundred per cent closed before he let himself release his breath on a long, slow hiss.

Okay…

So…

His little self-pep talk last night amounted to exactly nothing this morning. One look at Little Miss Rumpled Independence and he was right back to wanting to muscle his way into that barn and never leave. No matter how contrary she was. In fact, maybe because she was so contrary.

And, boy, was she ever. She would have hefted all one hundred and twenty pounds of Deputy and held him in her slender arms if he suggested she couldn't.

But she had done it. Thank goodness, too, because a man could only stare at the wall so long to avoid staring somewhere infinitely less appropriate. It wasn't her fault he'd had a flash of conscience while jogging at 6:00 a.m. about how empty the refrigerator in his barn conversion was. Her mortification at being caught unprepared for company was totally genuine.

So she might be snappish and belligerent, but she wasn't some kind of exhibitionist.

Which meant she was only two parts like Maggie, he thought as he pulled the SUV out into the quiet street. Maggie and her sexual confidence had him twisted up in so many knots he could barely see straight by the time she'd worn him down. It was never his plan to date someone in his own department but it was certainly her plan and Maggie was nothing if not determined.

But he was practically a different man back then. A boy. He'd taken that legacy scholarship straight out of school and gone to the Big Smoke to reinvent himself and he'd done a bang-up job.

He just wished he could have become a man that he liked a little bit more.

Still…done was done. He walked away from the NYPD after fifteen years with a bunch of salvaged scruples, a firm set of rules about relationships and a front seat full of canine squad flunky.

Not a bad starting point for his third try at life.

One block ahead he saw Danny McGovern's battered pickup shoot a red intersection and he reached automatically for the switch for his roof lights. Pulling traffic was just a tiny bit too close to Ellie Patterson's jibe about the kinds of low-end tasks she'd seen him run as sheriff but, if he didn't do it, then that damned kid was going to run every light between Larkville and Austin and, eventually, get himself killed.

And since one of those fine scruples he'd blown his other life to pieces over involved protection of hotshot dumb-asses like McGovern, he figured he owed it to himself to at least try. He'd been negligent enough with the lives of others for one lifetime.

His finger connected with the activation switch and a sequenced flash of red and blue lit the waking streets.

Time to get to work.

Chapter 4

Ellie pulled her knees up closer to her chest, cupped her chamomile tea and listened to the sounds of the storm raging over Larkville. The awesome power of nature always soothed her, when the noise from the heavens outgunned the busy, conflicting noise inside her head—the clamoring expectations, her secret fears, the voice telling her how much better she should be doing.

The sky's thundering downpour was closer to mental silence than anything she could ever create.

Her eyes drifted open.

The crackle of the roasting fire was muted beneath the rain hammering on the barn's tin roof but its orange glow flickered out across the darkened room, dancing. The flames writhed and twisted in the inferno of the stove, elegant and pure, the way the best of the performers in her company had been able to do.

The way she never had. Despite everything she'd done to be good enough, despite sacrificing her entire childhood to the God of Dance. Her entire body.

One particularly spectacular flame twisted in a helix and reached high above the burning timber before folding and darting back into itself.

Still her body yearned to move like those flames. It craved the freedom and raw expression. She hadn't really danced in the nine years since walking away from the corps and the truth was she hadn't really danced in the twelve years before it. The regimented structure of ballet suited her linear mind. Steps, sequences, choreographed verse. She'd excelled technically but, ultimately, lacked heart.

And then she'd discovered that one of her father's corporations was a silent patron for the company, and what heart she had for dance withered completely.

The place she thought she'd earned with brutal hard work and commitment to her craft… The place she knew two dozen desperate artists would crawl over her rotting corpse to have…

Her father had bought that place with cold, hard cash.

Two air pockets crashed together right overhead and the little barn rattled at the percussion. Ellie didn't even flinch. She shifted against the sofa cushions to dislodge the old pain of memory. She'd run from that chapter in her life with a soul as gaunt as her body, searching for something more meaningful to take its place. But she didn't find it in the thousands of hours of charity work she put in over the past decade raising funds for Alzheimer's research. And she didn't find it in the company of some man. No matter how many she'd dated to appease her mother.

And—finally—she opened her eyes one morning and realised that her inability to find something meaningful in her life said a whole lot more about her than it did about the city she lived in.

The rolling thunder morphed into the rhythmic pounding of a fist on her door, though it took a few moments for Ellie to realise. She tossed back the blanket and hurried the few steps to the front door, taking a moment to make sure her hair was neatly back.

'Are you okay?'

The sheriff stood there, water streaming off his widebrimmed hat and three-quarter slicker, soaked through from the knee down. A bedraggled Deputy shadowed him.

Surprise had her stumbling backwards and man and dog took that as an invitation to enter. They stepped just inside her door, out of the steady rain, though Jed took off his hat and left it hanging on the external doorknob. He produced a small, yellow box.

'Matches?' she said, her tranquil haze making her slow to connect the dots.

'There's candles in the bottom kitchen drawer.'

'What for?'

He looked at her like she was infirm. 'Light.' Then he flicked her light switch up and down a few times. 'Power's out.'

'Oh. I didn't notice. I had the lights out anyway.'

Maybe people didn't do that in Texas because the look he threw her was baffled. 'You were sitting here in the dark?'

Was that truly so strange? She rather liked the dark. 'I was sitting here staring into the fire and enjoying the storm.'

'Enjoying it?' The idea seemed to appall him. He did look like he'd been through the wringer, though not thoroughly enough to stop water dripping from his trousers onto the brick floor of the old barn.

'I'm curled up safe and sound on your sofa, not out there getting saturated.' He still didn't seem to understand so she made it simpler. 'I like storms.'

Deputy slouched down in front of her blazing fire and his big black eyes flicked between the two of them. Jed's hand and the matchbox still hung out there in space, so Ellie took it from him and placed it gently next to the existing one on the woodpile. 'Thank you, Sheriff. Would you like a coffee? The pot's just boiled.'

Colour soaked up Jed's throat, though it was lessened by the orange glow coming from the stove. Had he forgotten his own woodpile came with matches?

'Sorry. I thought you might be frightened.'

'Of a storm…?' Ellie swung the pot off its bracket and back onto her blazing stove, then set to spooning out instant coffee. 'No.'

'I'd only been home a few minutes when the power cut. I had visions of you trying to get down the stairs in the dark to find candles.'

Further evidence of his chivalry took second place

to inexplicable concern that he'd been out there in the cold for hours. 'Trouble?'

He shrugged out of his sheriff's coat and draped it over the chairback closest to the heat. 'The standard storm-related issues—flooding, downed trees. We've been that long without rain the earth is parched. Causes more run-off than usual.'

The kettle sang as it boiled and Ellie tumbled water into his coffee, then passed it to him. He took it gratefully. 'Thank you.'

She sunk back into her spot on the sofa and he sat himself politely on the same chair as his dripping coat. Overhead, the storm grizzled and grumbled in rolling waves and sounded so much like a petulant child it was hard not to smile.

'You really do love your weather, don't you?' he said.

'I love...' What? The way it was so completely out of her control and therefore liberating? No one could reasonably have expectations of the weather. 'I love the freedom of a storm.'

He sipped his coffee and joined her in listening to the sounds above. 'Can I ask you something?' he finally said. 'How did you know it was going to rain?'

She thought about that for a moment. Shrugged. 'I could feel it.'

'But you know nothing about Texas weather. And it was such a long shot.'

'Intuition?'

He smiled in the flickering firelight. 'You remind me a bit of someone.'

'Who?'

'Clay Calhoun.'

Her heart and stomach swapped positions for a few breaths.

'Jessica's father. That man was so in touch with his land he could look at the sky and tell you where a lightning bolt was going to hit earth.'

Awkwardness surged through her. Clay Calhoun was dead, just a legend now. Getting to know the man at the start of all her emotional chaos was not something she expected when she came to Texas. Yet, there was something intensely personal about discovering a shared... affinity...with the man that might be her father.

Was. She really needed to start digging her way out of denial and into reality. Her mother had virtually confirmed it with her bitter refusal to discuss it. And Jed had just reinforced it with his casual observation.

Maybe her weather thing was a case of nature, not nurture. Her Texan genes making their presence felt.

She cleared her throat. 'Past tense?'

He shifted his legs around so that the heat from the stove could do as good a job drying his trouser bottoms as it was doing on his dog. 'Yeah, Larkville lost Clay in October. Hit everyone real hard, especially his kids.'

Some harder than others.

He turned to look right at her. 'I thought that might be why you were here. Given Jess's recent loss. To bring condolences.'

'I'm...' This would be the perfect time to tell someone. Like confessing to a priest, a stranger. But for all she barely knew him, Jed Jackson didn't feel entirely like a stranger. And so, ironically, it was easier to hedge. 'No. I… Jess is helping me with…something.'

Wow… Eleanor Patterson totally tongue-tied. Rare. And exceedingly lame.

'Well, whatever it is I hope it can wait a few weeks? Jess won't be back until the end of the month, I hear.'

It had waited thirty years; it could wait a couple more weeks. 'It can.'

He stood and turned his back on the fire to give the backs of his calves and boots a chance to dry off. A light steam rose from them. His new position meant he was five-eighths silhouette against the orange glow. Imposing and broad.

But as non-threatening as the storm.

'Have you eaten?' he suddenly asked, his silhouette head tilting down towards her.

Even after all these years she still had a moment of tension when anyone mentioned food. Back when she was sick it was second nature to avoid eating in public. 'No. I was planning on having leftovers.'

Though her idea of leftovers was the other half of the apple she'd had at lunch.

'Want to grab something at Gracie May's?' he asked, casually. 'Best little diner in the county.'

The olive branch was unexpected and not entirely welcome. Was it a good idea to get friendly with the locals? Especially the gorgeous ones? 'But you just got dry. And won't her power be out, too?'

'Right. Good point.' He launched into action, turning for the kitchen. 'I'll fix us something here, then.'

'Here?' The delightful relaxation of her stormy evening fled on an anxious squeak.

He paused his tracks, cocked his head in a great impression of Deputy. 'Unless you want to come next door to my place?'

How did he manage to invest just a few words with so much extra meaning? Did she want to go next door and sit down to a meal with Sheriff Jed Jackson? Surrounded by his cowboy stuff, his Texan trappings? His woodsy smell?

Yes.

'No.' She swallowed. 'Here will be fine. Some guy delivered enough groceries for a month this morning.'

His smile did a good job of rivaling the fire's glow and it echoed deep down inside her. He set about shaving thin slices of ham from the bone and thick slices of bread from the loaf. Then some crumbly cheese, a sliced apple and a wad of something preserved from a jar labelled Sandra's Jellies and Jams.

'Green-tomato jam. Calhouns' finest.'

That distracted Ellie from the sinking of her stomach as he passed a full plate into her lap and sank down onto the other half of the suddenly shrunken sofa. She turned her interest up to him. 'Sandra Calhoun?'

'Jess, technically speaking, but a family recipe.'

Her family's recipe. That never failed to feel weird. For so long her family had been in New York. She picked up her fork and slid some of the tomato jam onto the corner of the bread and then bit into it. If she was only going to get through a fifth of the food on her plate, then she wanted it to be Jess's produce.

Jed was already three enormous bites into his sandwich and he tossed some ham offcuts over to Deputy, who roused himself long enough to gobble them up before flopping back down.

She risked conversation between his mouthfuls. 'The Calhouns have quite a presence.'

'They should. They're Larkville's founding family. Jess's great-great-granddaddy put down roots here in 1856.'

'And they're…well respected?'

The look he threw her over his contented munching was speculative. 'Very much so. Clay's death hit the whole town hard. They're dedicating the Fall Festival to him.'

'Really? The whole thing?'

'The Calhouns practically ran that festival anyway. Was fitting.'

'Who's running it now?' With Sandra and Clay both gone, and all the kids away?

'Jess and Holt will be back soon enough. Nate, too, God willing. Everyone else is pitching in to help.'

She filed that away for future reference. 'What happens at a fall festival?'

He smiled. 'You'd hate it. Livestock everywhere.'

Heat surged up her throat. 'I don't hate cows…'

'I'm just teasing, relax. Candy corn, rides, crafts, hot-dog-eating competitions. Pretty much what happens at fall festivals all over the country.'

She stared at him.

His eyebrows rose. 'Never?'

The heat threatened again. 'I've never left New York.'

'In your entire life?'

She shrugged, though she didn't feel at all relaxed about the disbelief in his voice. 'This is my first time.'

'Summers?'

Her lips tightened. 'Always rehearsing.'

'Family vacations?'

'We didn't take them.' The way he'd frozen with his sandwich halfway to his mouth got her back up. 'And you did?'

'Heck, yes. Every year my gram would throw me and her ducks in her old van and head off somewhere new.'

The ducks distracted her for a moment, but only a moment. 'You lived with your grandmother?'

His eyes immediately dropped to his plate. He busied himself mopping up the last of the jam.

She'd grown up with Matt for a brother. She knew when to wield silence for maximum effect. Jed lasted about eight seconds.

'My parents got pregnant young. Real young. Dad got custody after Mom took off. Gram was his mother. They raised me together.'

Mom took off. There was a lot of story missing in those few words. If only she didn't respect her own privacy so much—it necessarily forced her to respect his. 'But your dad wasn't in the van with you and the ducks every summer?'

'He worked a lot. And then he—' Jed cleared his throat and followed it up with an apple-slice chaser '—he died when I was six.'

Oh. The charming cowboy suddenly took on an unexpected dimension. Losing your parent so young…

And here she was whining about having too many parents. 'That must have been tough for you to get over.'

'Gram was a rock. And a country woman herself. She knew how to raise boys.'

'Is she still here in Larkville?'

The eyes found hers again. 'I'm not from Larkville, originally.'

'Really?' He seemed so much part of the furniture here. Of the earth. 'I thought your accent wasn't as pronounced as everyone else's. Where are you from?'

'Gram was from the Lehigh Valley. But my dad was NYPD. He met my mother while he was training.'

New York. Her world—and her hopes at anonymity—shrank. She moderated her breath just like in a heavy dance routine. 'Manhattan?'

'Queens, mostly. He commuted between shifts back out to the Valley. To us.'

'And he's the reason you became a cop?'

'He's part of it. He, uh, died on duty. That meant there was legacy funding for my schooling. It felt natural to go into law enforcement.'

Died on duty. But something much more immediate pressed down on her. 'You studied in New York?'

His eyes hooded. 'I lived and worked in Manhattan for fifteen years.'

Her voice grew tiny. 'You didn't say. When I told you where I was from.'

'A lot of people come from New York. It's not that remarkable.'

So she just asked him outright what she needed to know. 'Do you know who I am?'

That surprised him. 'Why? Are you famous?'

His cavalier brush while she was stressing out didn't sit well with her. She took the chance to push her plate onto the footstool next to them. 'Be serious.'

He stared at her. Doing the math. Consulting his mental Who's Who of New York. She saw the exact moment that the penny dropped. 'You're a Patterson Patterson?'

She stared back. 'I'm the oldest Patterson.' By six minutes.

Or...was. Charlotte was now. Wow. That was going to freak her middle sister out when she discovered it.

He chewed that over as thoroughly as his supper. But his inscrutable expression betrayed nothing. 'Wish I'd known that before I rescued you from the steer. I might have kept on driving.'

Not what she was expecting. Nervous wind billowed out the sides of her sails and was replaced by intrigue. 'Why?'

Tiny lines grew at the corners of his eyes. 'Your father's politics and mine differed.'

Ellie sat up straighter. 'You knew him?'

'Nope. Didn't need to.'

'Meaning?'

'Meaning some of the circles he moved in weren't ones that I had a lot of time for.'

Defense of the man she'd called father for thirty years surged up. Despite everything. 'If you were really from New York you'd know he hasn't moved in any circle for the past two years.'

'I came here three years ago. Why? What happened?'

She wasn't about to discuss her father's Alzheimer's with such a vocal critic. And—really—what were the chances he'd truly cut all ties and not even kept up with what was happening in the city he'd lived in. 'He's been unwell.'

'I'm sorry.'

'Why? You didn't like him.'

'I didn't like his politics. There's a difference.'

'Even if he lived and breathed his politics?' To the exclusion of all else? At least that's how it felt, although his increasing detachment to his two oldest children started to make more sense since she opened Jess's letter.

His eyes grew serious. 'I know what it's like to lose a father. So I'm sorry.'

He did know. But did he know what it was like to lose one three times over? Her father was no longer her father—first in mind, now in fact. And her apparent biological father was dead.

'Look at us having a real conversation,' he joked lightly after the silence stretched out like Deputy in front of the fire. The storm had settled to a dull rumble.

She'd failed to notice it easing. How long had they been talking?

His eyes fell on her plate. 'You going to eat that?'

For everyone else, eating was just a thing you did when you got hungry. Or at parties. For her, eating was something personal. Private. She took a slice of apple and then slid the rest over to him. He started to demolish it.

'What made you leave New York for Larkville?' she asked, nibbling on the sweet fruit.

Instant shutdown.

She watched it happen in the slight changes in his face. But not answering at all would just be too much for his Texan courtesy. 'The politics I told you about,' he hedged.

There was something vaguely uncomfortable about thinking that her family was responsible for anyone up-rooting their life. Even by association. She scrabbled around for a new topic. 'What about Deputy?' The dog lifted his horse's head on hearing his name. 'Is he a New Yorker, too?'

Dogs were apparently neutral territory because Jed's face lightened. 'Born and bred.'

'You said you and he had a deal? About how he be-haved. What did you mean?'

He shifted more comfortably on the sofa. 'Deputy had some...behavioural issues when I got him. Our agree-ment was that he got to spend his days with me if he could manage his manners.'

'He's a rescue?'

'He was a canine-unit dropout.'

She looked at the big brute sleeping happily on the floor and chuckled. 'What do you have to do to flunk being a guard dog?'

'He wasn't trained for guard duty. Unit dogs were used for detection—drugs, firearms, explosives, fire, bodies.'

'Locating the dead?'

Jed nodded. 'Others are trained to take supplies into dangerous situations or to recognise the signs of trauma and approach people in need of comfort and therapy.'

Ellie glanced at Deputy—all fur and teddy-bear good looks. 'He'd be good at therapy. Is that what he did?'

Jed shook his head. 'He was a tracker, tracing criminals through the back alleys and sewers,' he said. 'He was good, but he…was injured.' His eyes flicked evasively but then settled on Deputy again. 'Couldn't earn his keep.'

Ellie had seen the police dogs working with their human partners on Manhattan's streets. 'What happens to the ones that can't work?'

He stretched his leg out and gave Deputy a gentle nudge with his boot tip. 'The lucky ones end up with me in a town full of people that spoil him. Hey, boy?'

Deputy's thick tail thumped three times, four, against the timber pile…but the rest of him didn't move. The boot kept up its gentle rub.

So Sheriff Jed had a big, soft heart. Why did that surprise her? 'Well, he's fortunate he met you, then.'

'Depends on how you look at it,' he muttered.

She shot him a sideways look.

Suddenly Jed was on his feet flattening his hand in a signal to Deputy to stay put. 'I should get going. Storm's easing. I'm going to leave him here with you tonight.'

Here? With her? The half-baked dog certainly looked content enough, but…would he be so compliant once his master had gone? 'That's not nec—'

This time Jed's hand signal was for her. It said don't argue. He snagged his dry coat off the chair back. 'You'll feel more secure with him here.'

'In what universe?' The words slipped straight from her subconscious to her tongue.

Jed chuckled. 'You didn't have dogs growing up, I take it?'

'We had a cat. And it was pretty standoffish.' Her mother loved it.

'Think of it as an opportunity to bond, then.'

Bond? With a hundred-plus pounds of wet dog? 'What if he needs to...?' She waved a hand to avoid having to use the words.

'He's already...' Jed imitated her gesture. 'Just let him out quickly before bed. He knows where to go if his bladder's full.'

'What if it's raining?'

'Then he'll get wet. Or hold on until morning. Seriously, Ellie. It will be fine. He'll just lie by the fire and help you ride out the storm.'

'I don't need help. I like storms, remember?'

He wasn't going to take no for an answer. Who knew, maybe the sheriff had a hot date tonight and wanted a dog-free zone. She looked over at Deputy, who lazily opened one eye and then closed it again.

Okay, so she was a dog sitter. Stranger things had happened...

She followed Jed to the door. He turned and looked down at her.

'Well, thanks for supper, Ellie. I appreciate it.'

She shrugged. 'You made it.'

He wasn't put off. 'You humoured me.'

'I didn't mind the company.' Though she'd not realised she was craving any until she had his. 'It was... nice...talking to you.' And, strangely, that was true.

He stared down at her for an age, a slight frown in his voice. 'We should do it again.'

Or…not. Deep and meaningful discussions were not her forte. 'Maybe we shouldn't push our luck?'

His sigh managed to be amused and sad at the same time. 'Maybe so.' He snaffled his hat off the doorknob. 'Night, Ellie.'

'Good night, Sheriff…' He turned and lifted one eyebrow at her. 'Jed. Good night, Jed.'

And then he was gone. She watched his shadowy form sprint up the path in rain half the strength of earlier. Even knowing he was just next door she felt a strange kind of twinge at his departure. Enough that she stared for a few moments at the vacant spot he'd just been in. But then the cool of the night hit her and she backed inside, closed the door and then turned to look at her house guest.

Deputy was sitting up now, his thick tail wagging, a big doggie smile on his face. Looking like he'd just been waiting for the party pooper to leave.

'Good boy…' she offered, optimistically.

His tail thumped harder.

'Stay.'

The big head cocked. Ellie took two tentative steps towards him. He didn't move. Two more brought her parallel to him in the tiny accommodations and two more after that had her halfway to the kitchenette. Still the dog didn't move.

Maybe this would be okay.

She reached for the kettle and filled it again with water, then turned back to put it on the cast-iron stove.

There was nothing but air where a dog had just been. Her eyes flicked right.

Deputy had made himself at home on the sofa, stretching his big paws out on Jed's beautiful hand-crafted throw and looking, for all the world, like this was something he was very accustomed to doing.

'Off!' she tried.

Nothing.

'Down?' Not even an eye flicker. She curled a hand around his collar and pulled. Hard. 'Come on, you lug…'

Nada. Eventually she gave up and just squeezed herself onto what little dog-free space remained on the sofa.

And there she sat as the tail of the storm settled in for a long night of blustering, the golden glow of the fire lighting her way, her own breath slipping into sync with the deep heavy canine ones beside her.

And as the minutes ticked by she didn't even realise that her hand had stolen out and rested on Deputy's haunches. Or that her fingers curled into the baked warmth of his dark fur.

Squeeze…release. Squeeze…release.

Or that her mind was finally—blissfully—quiet.

Chapter 5

The tapping on his door was so quiet Jed was amazed it cut through the three hours of sleep he'd finally managed to grab. Ninety minutes after leaving Ellie's, he'd been called out again to assist with a double vehicular out towards the interstate and then he'd just rolled from one stormy night task to another until he finally noticed the light peeking over the horizon and took himself off the clock.

Never a good look, the county sheriff driving into a post because he was so tired.

Unfortunately, dragging his butt out of bed just a few hours after falling fully dressed into it really wasn't high on his list of things to do on his rostered day off. He yanked the door open. Deputy marched in with a big grin on his chops. The woman behind him wasn't smiling.

'He slept on my bed!'

'What?' It took Jed a full ten seconds to even remember he'd left his dog with Ellie last night. Bad owner.

'Deputy. He helped himself to the other side of my bed. Made himself right at home.'

Deputy? The dog who'd staked out the mat by the fireplace in his house? The dog raised to live in a kennel? The dog that'd been so slow to trust anyone? 'What have you done to him?'

Her fine features tightened. 'I didn't do anything. He climbed up after I'd gone to sleep. I woke up in the middle of the night to his snoring.'

Jed turned. Deputy thumped. 'Opportunist,' he muttered. He turned back to Ellie, rubbing the grit from his eyes. 'Maybe he was scared of the storm. Or maybe the fire burned out.'

Her delicate fingers slid up onto her hips and it only made him more aware of how someone could have curves without seeming curvy.

'Or maybe he's just a terrible, undisciplined dog,' she suggested.

'That seems a bit harsh…'

'He was on my bed.' Those green eyes were trying hard to look annoyed.

'It's a big bed, there's plenty of room for two.' Not that he actually knew that from experience. He'd had it to himself the entire time he lived in the barn. Her coral lips opened and closed again wordlessly and he realised she actually was genuinely scandalised. Time to be serious. 'Did you ask him to get down?'

Whoops. Wrong question. Determination flooded her face.

'He ignored me, Jed. He's uncontrollable. No wonder he flunked out of the canine unit.'

The instinct to defend his old pal was strong. Flunking out of the unit was never Deputy's fault. 'Well, now… That's not true, watch this.'

He took Deputy through his paces, sitting, dropping, staying, presenting a paw. He responded to every command exactly on cue.

A pretty little V formed between her brows. 'He didn't do that for me.'

'I guess he doesn't recognise your authority.'

'What do I need, a badge?'

The outrage on her face was priceless. Maybe princesses from the Upper East Side were used to their name automatically carrying authority? Where he came from—and where Deputy came from—respect was earned. He ran tired fingers through his hair, tried to restore some order there. 'You just need him to accept that you come above him in the pack.'

Her whole body stiffened, and he thought he'd be in for an earful, but then her face changed. Softened. Slim fingers crept up and clenched over her sternum. 'I'm… I'm part of his pack?'

The unexpected vulnerability shot straight to his chest. 'Sure you are. You shared a den.'

She stared at Deputy, a haunted fragility washing briefly across her face. 'But he thinks he's boss?'

'Not for long.' Jed snagged his coat off the rack and swung it on, before her confusion weakened him any further. 'Come on. I'll show you around Larkville.'

Sleeping in your clothes had some advantages. First, he was fully dressed and much more able to just walk out the door than if she'd caught him in his usual morning attire. And second, being in uniform helped legitimise what they were about to do. Appear in public, together, on an early morning stroll. Not that it would stop certain tongues from wagging.

'We're going for a walk?'

'Exercising a dog is one of the fastest ways to show it where you fit in the pack.'

'I'm going to walk him?' He might as well have said they were going to jump from a hot-air balloon. 'But he's huge.'

Jed pulled the door shut behind them and slid the snout harness over Deputy's eager nose. 'Dogs. Horses. Cattle. They're all the same. Just get their heads pointed where you want them to go and they'll do the rest. Every command you give him will reinforce your dominance.'

Her brow folded. 'I don't want to dominate him.'

'I'm not talking about him cowering at your feet. I'm talking about him trusting you to be his leader. Respecting your choices. Believing in you.' He thrust the lead into her unprepared hands. 'If he pulls, stop. When he stops pulling, go again.'

And so it began…two of the most entertaining hours he could remember having. Ellie was a natural student; she remembered every single instruction he gave her and applied it consistently. In no time Deputy was glancing to her for direction as they moved through the streets of Larkville.

Even Ellie loosened up. And that was saying something. 'How did you learn this?' she asked.

'I had dogs, growing up. But the boys at the canine unit are the real specialists. I learned something new every day.'

The words were out before he even thought about it. Dangerous words.

She gently corrected Deputy when he pulled in the opposite direction and then brought her eyes back to him. 'You worked for the canine unit?'

Sure did. Not that he usually told anyone about it. His only course now was to give her some information, but not enough. Definitely not everything. 'I headed it up. For my last couple of years in the NYPD.'

That stopped her cold and Deputy looked back at her impatiently. She glanced at the stars on his shoulder. So, because he'd had rank in the city he was instantly more credible?

'Changing your opinion of me?'

'I… No. It kind of fits. I should have guessed it would be either the dogs or the mounted squad.'

It fits? Was he that much of a country hick in her eyes? 'Both those units are sophisticated operations.'

'I don't doubt it.' She looked puzzled. 'But I'm wondering why you'd trade working with dogs for working with people. Here.'

She made his old job sound so idyllic. He could hardly tell her that he'd had as little heart for his job as

Deputy did at the end there. 'More like trading a desk and filing cabinet for an SUV and a radio.'

'You missed active duty?'

'I missed a lot of things.' The easy days pre-promotion—pre-politics—particularly. The days when his responsibility didn't get people killed. 'I like policing in the county. It's more…personal.'

'Sheriff…' On cue, two older ladies nodded their elegant hairdos at him and failed miserably at disguising the curiosity they sent Ellie's way.

He tipped his hat. 'Miss Louisa… Miss Darcy…'

They walked on. Ellie was still looking at him sideways. She really had that New York knack of tuning out everything around her. 'But just as political, I'm guessing.'

'I don't mind politics if I agree with it.'

She narrowed her eyes. 'Politics is just a game. You just have to know how to play it.'

And just like that the enjoyment evaporated right out of his morning. 'I'm not interested in playing it,' he said flatly.

Her laugh sprinkled out across Larkville's still-quiet streets. 'No one likes it, Jed. You use it.'

He threw her a look. 'Speaking from experience?'

'Right people. Right dinners. Right connections.' She shrugged. 'Money follows.'

His laugh was more of a snort. 'What does a Patterson need more money for?'

She tossed back her head and her eyes glittered. 'Oh, you know… World domination, buying out crippled economies and selling their debt to hostile nations, that sort of thing.'

He wanted to believe that. It fitted very nicely with the picture of her he had in his head. The picture that allowed him to keep her at arm's length. They walked on a few paces.

But he couldn't help himself. He had to know. 'What do you really need it for?'

Right in the corner of his eye he saw her tiny smile. She meant it to be private, but it speared him right between the ribs. He'd just pleased her.

'I fundraise.'

'For?'

Deputy's jangling collar was the only sound for a few moments. 'For research into Alzheimer's disease.'

Ah. 'Your father.'

Again, more silence, then her voice came lower and breathier. 'You'd think with all the money at our disposal we could have bought him a cure, huh?'

The contrast between the very public place they were having this discussion and the incredible pain in her voice hit him low in the gut. He got the sense that it wasn't something she usually spoke of. Just like him and his New York years. He thought about his own father—how a full police escort failed to get him to hospital quick enough, and all their departmental resources later failed to bring the shooter to justice. How he'd had to learn to live with that reality growing up. 'It's not always about money. Or resources.'

That was the irony. Everything else on this planet revolved around resources.

'Well… I'm hoping that my work might make a difference to someone else's father someday.'

Shame curdled in his belly. Her words weren't for show or effect. Suddenly the wicked stepsister of his mind morphed into a gentle, hardworking Cinderella. He'd always considered that those on the lucky side of the privilege rat race had some kind of advantage that people on his side could only dream about. Some magical shield which meant their hands weren't being forced every other day. To make decisions they weren't happy with. To make compromises with the lives of others.

But all the money in the world literally couldn't save Cedric Patterson.

He stopped and slid his hand onto her forearm. 'Don't give up,' he murmured. 'Science changes daily.'

Ellie stared down at the masculine hand on her arm as a way of avoiding the intensity she knew would be in Jed's eyes. It was only a touch, but it stole the oxygen from her cells. She wanted so badly to believe him, believe in him. It had been so long since she'd been able to confide in anyone, and trusting Jed sort of happened by accident.

Jess Calhoun's secret weighed on her like stocks. Would it compromise the universe if she just told one person that her father was not her father? If she tried to talk through the confusing mess of emotions that discovery had left her with? The deeper reasons as to why a stupid dog accepting her into his pack had nearly had her in tears?

She lifted her eyes and opened her mouth to try.

'Jed! Hey. Didn't know you were on duty today.'

A fresh-faced young woman with thick auburn hair met them in the middle of the sidewalk, greeted Jed with a brilliant smile and Deputy with a thorough scratch behind the ears. The dog's eyes practically rolled back in his head and he leaned his full weight into her legs.

Jed's seriousness of a moment before evaporated. 'Sarah...'

Ellie immediately stiffened at the affection in his tone and the way he met the woman's cheek effortlessly for a kiss. She was very friendly with both man and dog....

'Was out on calls all night,' he continued. 'Heading home soon.'

Ellie stared at him. He'd been out all night? And she'd barged in at the crack of dawn. Why didn't he say?

'Oh, poor you.' Her eyes drifted to Ellie. She thrust out her hand. 'Sarah Anderson.'

'Sarah's born and bred in Larkville,' Jed hurried to say, belatedly remembering his manners.

No wonder he was distracted; Sarah was a natural beauty, all willowy and classic even in running pants and sweats. Feminine curves were somewhat new to Ellie and she knew hers didn't sit quite as well on her. She slid her hand into Sarah's. 'Ellie Patterson.'

'You're new in town?'

'Just visiting.' Jed said it before she had a chance to.

'You know you'll have seen everything Larkville has to offer by the time you've finished walking Deputy.'

First-name basis for the dog, too? Ellie looked from Sarah to Jed. Then she put on her best cocktail-party face. 'It's a beautiful town, I love the antique stores.'

'Oh, my gosh, I know! Have you been to Time After Time down on Third? Probably Larkville's best.'

Jed threw his hands in the air. 'If you ladies are going to talk antiques Deputy and I might go find some breakfast...'

'Sorry, Jed.' Sarah laughed, then turned her focus back to Ellie. 'If you're in town for a bit maybe I can introduce you around, scour the markets with you on Saturday?'

I'd like that. That's what someone polite would say. But until she understood a bit better what Sarah's relationship with Jed was—and until she'd examined why she cared—her personal jury was out. 'Sure, great.'

The brunette turned her keen focus straight back onto Jed. 'I have a favor to ask. I've taken on the volunteer co-ordination for the Fall Festival and I'm looking for extra hands.' Before Jed could take more than a breath she barrelled on. 'I know you have your hands full in the lead up to the event with permits and stuff but I'm thinking more...nowish...to help with the planning. Darcy and Louisa have withdrawn their services given the unpleasantness over last year's bread bake. I'm caught short.'

'Unpleasantness?' Ellie risked.

'They didn't win,' Sarah answered, in perfect sync with Jed. 'How about it?'

'What would I be signing up for?' he hedged.

'Don't suppose you know what a Gantt chart is?'

Jed's blank stare said it all. 'Something you use to measure fish?'

The laugh shot out of Ellie before she could restrain it. Both sets of eyes turned on her.

'Okay, Manhattan, what's a Gantt chart?' he challenged.

'A project-planning tool. Helps you to schedule your resources. Project your timeline.'

Sarah stared at her like she'd grown enormous, iridescent wings.

Awkwardness cranked up Ellie's spine. 'I used it for fundraising,' she muttered.

'Do you have project-planning experience?' Raw hope blazed in Sarah's eyes.

'I'm only visiting.' Except that wasn't strictly true. She had no fixed return date. And she was going to get bored with nothing to do…

A deep voice pitched in. 'Bet the two of you would get a lot done in two weeks.'

She threw Jed a baleful look.

'Could you?' Sarah only got prettier as excited colour stained her cheeks. 'We'd probably get a month's worth done.'

But Ellie's natural reticence bubbled to the fore. She barely knew Sarah. 'This was supposed to be a holiday…'

'Jed!' Sarah flung her focus back on the suddenly wary-looking sheriff. 'Jed will make up for any time you lose helping Larkville pull its Fall Festival together. He can show you the highlights after work. Introduce you to people.'

'Oh, can I?'

Sarah trundled right over his half-hearted protest. 'And you'll meet people on this project, too.'

That's exactly what she was afraid of. Just because

she schmoozed and smiled in the ballrooms of Manhattan didn't mean she enjoyed it. She was kind of happiest on her own.

Jed didn't look all that pleased about it, either. 'Sarah... I think Ellie—'

'Okay, look, my final offer. One week, a few hours a day, and I will personally teach you to line dance. Texan dancing lessons from a real Texan. What do you say?'

Should she tell her that she'd danced for the joint heads of state in her time?

But Sarah's enthusiasm was infectious. And there really weren't enough stores in Larkville to keep her amused for long. And how hard could a fall festival be after some of the top-line soirees she'd pulled off since giving up dance?

'Okay, one week...'

That's as far as she got. Sarah squealed and threw her arms around Ellie's stiff shoulders and then did the same with Jed. He didn't look like he hated it, particularly. But—interestingly—neither did Ellie. And that was quite something for someone uncomfortable with being touched.

'How can I contact you?' Sarah rushed.

'She's at the Alamo.'

Sarah's eyes said *oh, really?* but out loud she just said, 'I'll come for you early Saturday morning. We can strategise after we've stripped the markets bare of antiques.'

'Sounds great.' Every breath she took was one further away from anonymity. First the sheriff and now Sarah.

The awkwardest of silences fell and Sarah's focus

darted around them before returning. 'Have you heard from Nate, Jed?'

Even Ellie could read between those innocent words—see through the bright, casual smile—and she'd never met Sarah before. To his credit, Jed answered as if she'd just asked him the time. 'Not since the funeral. No news is good news when it comes to the military.'

'I guess.' A deep shadow ghosted over her dark eyes. 'Well, Deputy's going to pull Ellie's arm off if I don't let you two get going. See you Saturday, Ellie? Take care, Jed.'

They farewelled Sarah and she jogged off, continuing her run.

'Thank you for helping Sarah out.'

Ellie shrugged. 'I'm going to need something to do with my time. Might as well throw a party, right?' She hoped she wasn't as transparent as Sarah had just been. She really wasn't in the mood for celebrations. 'You don't need to give up your time to show me around. I'm happy to help, no strings attached.'

'I don't mind doing my bit. I like Sarah, she's had a rough time these past few years.'

She studied him closer. Liked Sarah or *liked* Sarah? But the thoughtful glance he threw down the street after her had nothing more than compassion in it. Rough times were something she could definitely empathise with. Maybe that's why she'd felt so instantly connected to the bubbly brunette.

'Breakfast?' Jed hinted. The second mention in as many minutes. 'Gracie will let us eat out in her courtyard with Deputy.'

Did all country towns revolve around the social nexus of food? She lifted her chin. 'Sure. I'd love a coffee.'

'I should warn you, Gracie's coffees come with obligatory berry flapjacks midweek.'

Great.

She glanced at Deputy. Maybe she could sneak hers to him. He'd be a willing accomplice for sure.

Jed wasn't kidding about the flapjacks. They didn't order them but a steaming stack came, nonetheless, and no one else around them looked the slightest bit surprised as theirs were delivered.

Ellie stared in dismay at the fragrant pile. 'Are they free?'

Jed laughed. 'Nope. Standing order. Flapjacks on weekdays, full fry-up on the weekends. Gracie believes in promoting her specialties.'

And reaping the profits. Gracie May had a fantastic sales angle going here, and the locals clearly thought it was charming. 'Nice scam,' she muttered.

Jed laughed. 'Totally.'

She selected herself the smallest of the fluffy discs and spooned some fresh, unsweetened berries onto it. Jed heaped his plate high. 'Come on, Ellie. You can't function all day on that.'

He might be amazed how little a body could function on, although—to be fair—it never was proper functioning. 'I'm not exactly going to be burning it off strolling Larkville's streets.'

He watched her as he chewed his first big mouthful. She sliced her pancake into eight identically proportioned strips and then folded the first one carefully onto her fork and then into her mouth. Ignoring his interest the whole time.

'You eat like a New Yorker,' he said as soon as he was able.

He didn't mean that to be an insult. He couldn't know what it really meant to survive in the world of professional dancing. 'When I was dancing I would have probably just had the berries.' If she had anything at all.

'Seriously? On the kind of stresses you must have put your body through?'

'Dancing's a competitive industry. We all did whatever we could to find that balance between strength and leanness.' Smoking. Exercising.

Starving.

Jed nudged the half-ravaged stack towards her. 'Live a little.'

Ten years ago she might have literally recoiled as a plate of food was shoved towards her like that. Sitting calmly in the face of it was extraordinary progress and knowing that bolstered her confidence. Every day she was reminded how far she'd come. And she was proud of it, given she'd done it practically alone. But this was going to keep coming up if she didn't head it off at the pass.

She took a deep breath. 'Food and I have a…complicated relationship.'

That stopped the fork halfway to his mouth. 'Meaning?'

'I've taught myself to look at food purely as fuel for my body. As the total sum of all its nutritional parts.'

He glanced at the pancake pile. Then back at her. 'You don't like food?'

She smiled. 'I like good food, but I don't eat it because it's good. I eat it—just what I need of it—because it's nutritious.'

His eyes narrowed. 'Are you one of those organic, bio-birthed, grown-in-a-vacuum kind of people?'

She laughed and it felt so good. Most people wouldn't speak so casually about this. 'I actually don't mind where it comes from as long as it's good food.'

'Healthy?'

'Bio-available.'

'To your body?'

'Correct.'

She'd never felt less understood. Sigh. But it wasn't from a lack of willingness on his part.

'That is complicated.'

'I know.'

'Does your whole family eat like that?'

'No.'

'So where did it come from? I'm interested.'

Was he? Or was he sitting in judgment? Sincerity bled steadily from his gaze. But talking about her past wasn't easy for her.

She pushed her plate away. 'I had a few problems, when I was younger. Part of my treatment was to come to terms with the role food plays in our lives.'

The policeman in him instantly grew intrigued. She saw it in the sudden keenness of his expression. But the gentleman won out. He let it go. 'And you came to the conclusion that food is only about nutrition?'

She shrugged. 'That's its primary function, in nature. Cows don't eat straw because it tastes good, they eat it because it's what their bodies need to run on. It's fuel.'

Excellent, a cowboy analogy. Way to condescend, there, Ellie!

But he didn't bite. 'You don't think a steer would appreciate the sweet tips of spring shoots more than old summer grass?'

'They might. But that's just a pleasure thing. They're actually eating it for the energy.'

He stared at her. 'Got something against pleasure?'

The way the word pleasure rolled off his tongue, the way he leaned in slightly as he said it, sent her skin into a prickly overdrive. And it threw her off her usual cautious track. 'It took me ten years to believe that food wasn't my enemy. Just getting to the point of accepting it as fuel is more than I once thought was possible.'

That shut him up.

Heat immediately began building at her collar as she realised what a big thing that was to dump on someone who was just making polite conversation. But he didn't look away. He didn't shy from the awkwardness that poured off her in waves.

She watched him put the puzzle together in his mind. And it looked like it genuinely pained him.

'You have some kind of eating disorder?'

'Had.' She lifted her chin. 'I'm better.'

This is where he'd hit her with twenty questions, grill her for the gruesome details that people loved to know.

Can you ever truly be better after anorexia?

How low did your weight get?

Is it like alcoholism, something you manage forever?

Yes, pretty low, and kind of. She readied herself to utter the stock-standard answers. But Jed just flopped back in his seat and considered her.

'Good for you,' he said, then got stuck back into his pancakes.

Ellie blinked. 'That's it?'

He glanced back up, thought hard for a moment and carefully reset his fork on his plate. 'Ellie, I've been expecting people to take me at face value since I arrived in Larkville. It would be hypocritical of me to do anything other than accept you for who you are. Or were.'

Gratitude swelled hard and fast in her ever-tightening chest. Acceptance. Pure acceptance. This is what it looked like.

'Just like that?'

'Just like that.' His eyes dropped back to his flapjacks. 'Although I would like to make you dinner tonight.'

The ridiculous juxtaposition of that statement with what she'd just revealed caused a perverse ripple of humour. 'Why?'

'Because I reckon someone needs to induct you into the pleasures of a well-cooked, well-presented, just-for-the-hell-of-it meal.'

The idea should have made her nervous, but it only made her breathless. 'And you're that someone?'

'Who do you think does all my cooking?'

'Uh, Gracie May, judging by the number of times you've mentioned her.' And by the fact they knew exactly how he took his coffee, and had his own hat hook by the door.

'Fair call. But Gram taught me how to cook. I might surprise you.'

He already did, in so many ways. She took a breath. 'Okay. But make sure it's been grown in a vacuum.'

Silence draped like a silken sheet after they'd finished laughing. Jed called for the check. Ellie used the moments that followed to gather her thoughts and to finish her solitary pancake. Dinner was almost a date. It had been a long time since she'd even been on a date, let alone actually wanted to be there.

She'd done it because it was expected.

Her mother's horrified reaction when she gave up dancing was very telling. As if she'd just thrown in the most remarkable and appreciable thing about herself. So she'd done her best to find in herself some other marketable value at the ripe old age of twenty-one, but she'd spent so long in her determined battle to dance she really didn't have a lot of other skills. Organising fundraisers was something she was good at but it wasn't going to make her a career. Certainly not a fortune. Not the way a good marriage might. So she'd dated banker after stockbroker after up-and-coming media mogul. Year after year. She'd bluffed her way through an endless series of meals, held her emotional breath at the end of the date lest the good-night kiss become too much more and tactfully extracted herself from the most persistent and slick operators.

And she'd felt nothing. For any of them.

To the point that she wondered if all sexual sensation had withered along with her muscle mass. Was that the lasting damage her doctor had warned her so constantly about?

Yet, here she was going positively breathless at the thought of a man putting on an apron for her. Doing something just for her. Not because he wanted to get into her pants or wanted her name or her money, just because he thought she might enjoy something he had to offer. Something he enjoyed.

They paused at the entrance to Gracie May's alfresco courtyard. 'I'm going to give Deputy a proper run before heading home for some more sleep,' he said. 'You'll be okay to find your own way back?'

She nodded, intrigued and absurdly breathless. 'What time should I come round tonight?'

'I'll pick you up at six.'

'But you're right next door.'

'Ellie…this is step one in "food is more than just kilojoules." If we're going to do this we're going to do it right.'

A ridiculous lightness washed through her. 'At six, then.'

He smiled, and it soaked clean through her. Then he lowered his voice. 'Wear something nice.'

Chapter 6

Jed dropped the heat on the simmering rice and turned to survey his little cottage. Not perfect but tidy enough. He wanted lived-in and welcoming, not spotless and cold. Deputy snoring by the fire sure helped with the lived-in part. So did his pre-loved Texan furnishings and the original 1885 fixtures.

He glanced at the antique clock face and frowned at how short a distance the little hand had moved since he last looked. Tension had him as tight as an arthritic old-timer.

What had possessed him this morning to offer to cook Ellie a meal—after what she'd just told him? A lush dinner for two was not exactly the easiest route to arm's length for him and nor would it be the easiest of experiences for her. She'd be under pressure to eat whatever he prepared. She might end up hating it.

And him.

But the words had just tumbled from his lips as she laid her soul bare over pancakes. Maybe it was the sleep deprivation. Maybe it was the tremulous defiance in her expression after she let it slip about her past. Maybe it was his total inability to think of anything else but helping her while she sat across from him.

And then the words were out. He was committed.

Six o'clock crept marginally closer.

The crushing pressure to do something spectacular weighed down on him. He wondered if she had any idea how long it had been since he cooked for someone. Dates had been sparse enough in the past few years—but to have someone inside his home and to prepare a meal for them...

Someone like Ellie...

He felt like a rookie around her. Just a little bit in awe. She wasn't getting any less striking with the passing days. And she was knocking down his misconceptions one by one.

Not quite the princess he'd thought.

Not quite the charmed life he'd imagined.

In fact, he could only imagine how uncharmed her past must have been. He knew enough about eating disorders to guess which one she'd had and to imagine the damage that would do to a young girl's body. And mind.

Not that you'd know it now. She was slim but healthy, toned, curves in enough places, her skin and eyes clear. He only got the briefest of looks at her hair that first morning, dropping off her supplies, but it was natural and golden enough to make him wonder why she punished it by dragging it back all the time. If she'd been sick when she was younger, did she have a clue what a spectacular comeback she'd made? Maybe not, judging by the whole food-is-fuel thing. That was just…

He wanted to say weird but it was obviously what she'd needed to get healthy. So it had worked for her. And he was the last one to judge anyone for doing what they needed to do to get by. But, boy, what she was missing out on…

He gave the rice a quick stir in its stock base.

Ellie Patterson liked to know where her boundaries were. She liked things as well lined up as those flapjack pieces she'd carved so precisely. Her carefully pressed clothes, her librarian's hair, her preference for seclusion. Knowing what he knew now, he could only imagine how tough she must have found the whole situation with the steer.

Yet, she'd been impulsive enough to come to Texas without checking whether Jess Calhoun was going to be home. That meant she was capable of spontaneity. She just needed the right trigger.

What was your trigger, Ellie?

She'd still never said what her business with Jess was. Not that he could ask. The whole nosy-cop thing still stung. She just wasn't used to how they did things in Texas. And why would she be if she'd never left Manhattan?

The more he got to know her, the less like Maggie she became. Similar on the surface, but Maggie was con-

fident from her cells up—overconfident quite often—
whereas he had a sneaking suspicion that Ellie's perfect
facade masked something quite different.

Quite fragile.

The two hands of the clock finally lined up and cut
the clock into perfect hemispheres.

Showtime.

'Stay,' he instructed Deputy, then threw a jacket over
his shirt and jeans. Casual enough not to freak her out,
dressy enough to show some respect. Two seconds later
he was out the door and turning down her laneway.
Twelve seconds after that—including some time to make
sure his shirt was tucked in—his knuckles announced
themselves on her door.

His door. But amazing how fast he'd come to think
of it as hers.

Like she'd always lived there. Thank goodness she
hadn't. He couldn't imagine managing this attraction he
felt for longer than the few weeks still—

'Hey.'

The door opened and filled with designer heels and
long, bare legs. His eyes trailed up over a knee-length
blue cotton dress, hair disappointingly pulled back hard
but this time captured in a braid that curled down onto
her bare shoulder and curved towards one breast like
an arrow. His heart hammered harder than his first day
on duty.

'You'll need a sweater' was all he could manage.

'Really? Just to run next door?'

'Better safe than sorry.' And better for him so he
could string more than clichés together over dinner. He

shook his head to refocus while she reached for the light cardigan hanging by the door. The stretch showed off more of her dancer's tone.

'Okay. Let's go.'

Either the brisk air was getting to her or this felt as weird for her as it did for him, because there was a breathlessness in her voice that gave her away. And made him think of other ways she might get breathless.

Okay...! Shutting that one down. Was he doomed to behave like a kid around her all night? He sucked in a lungful of evening air and told himself this was just a one-off. It wasn't a date. It wasn't the start of anything.

It couldn't be.

'So... Am I overdressed?' She glanced at his casual jeans and frowned. 'I can change.' She even faltered and half turned back for the house.

He slipped an arm behind her to prevent her retreat. 'You're perfect, Ellie.' And she was. The dress was so simple and so...fresh.

So not New York.

'I got this in Austin.' The woman was a mind reader. 'I drove in earlier. I didn't really bring anything appropriate with me.'

With two bulging suitcases he doubted it, but he liked that she'd gone into a fashion crisis for him. And then as rapidly as the thought came to him he shoved it away.

This wasn't a date. This was a...demonstration.

'Good choice,' he said, and hoped the appreciation didn't sound as gratuitous in her ears as it did in his.

They turned the corner and his hand brushed her back as he guided her in front of him. She flinched at the contact. When he was younger he would have chalked that up to a physical spark, but her hasty steps forward told another story. His touch made her uncomfortable. That killed any fantastical notion that she was breathless about this dinner.

She was just plain nervous.

He paused on his porch and indicated the outdoor sofa. 'I'll just set the risotto to simmer and then we're heading out. Make yourself comfortable for a few minutes.'

Deputy dashed out and went straight to Ellie. Her hand went absently to the thick of his fur. So it wasn't all touch that she was averse to.

Just his.

He found the lid for his pot and dropped the heat down to almost nothing. Gram taught him the best way to slow-cook rice but it needed an hour longer than he'd left himself. Hopefully Ellie didn't mind a late supper. New Yorkers always ate late. It was one of the things that used to bug him about Maggie. He wanted to eat half the furniture on getting home; she wanted to wait until the streets grew more lively.

'Okay, let's go.' He pulled his front door shut behind him.

She stared at him. 'Wasn't tonight about a meal?'

'It was about a meal appreciation. Part of appreciation is anticipation.'

'In other words you're going to make me wait?'

'Not good with delayed gratification?'

She smiled, tightly. 'Are you kidding? Self-denial is what I specialised in.'

'Right. Well, then, I'll ask you to trust me. Would it help if I told you we were heading over to the Double Bar C?'

She stood. 'We're visiting the Calhouns?'

'Just their land. Their foreman, Wes Brogan, is going to meet us at the gate.'

'So we just…roam around on their land? Dressed like this?'

He smiled as he opened the SUV's door for her. 'We won't be roaming. I have a specific destination in mind. But I figured you might be curious to see a bit of the Double Bar C.'

'Yes. I'd love to. Now I understand the sweater.' She climbed in, neatly evading his proffered hand.

Deputy was most put-out to be relegated to the back seat and his harness meant he couldn't even stretch his head forward for a compensatory scratch. But a car trip was a car trip and he was happy enough to stick his head out the back window and snap at the trees whizzing by.

Ellie watched him in her side mirror. 'I can't imagine him in the canine unit.'

He glanced over his shoulder at his old friend. 'The thing with Deputy is that he's a real obliging animal. That made him easy to train and super-responsive in the field. He loved being on task and he had a fantastic nose.' He brought his eyes back to the road ahead of them. 'He was our first choice for tracking. His size was a deterrent for perps, but he was next to useless in close contact. He just didn't have the aggression we needed.'

'Is that why he flunked?'

It had to come up sooner or later. Jed chose his words

carefully. 'He never really flunked, it was more of a...
retirement situation.'

She smiled. 'Really? He got his 401(k) and gold
watch?'

He hissed under his breath. Had he really thought he
could only half explain? 'Actually he had some trauma
in the field. He never really recovered from it.' True yet
not entirely true. The truth was too shameful.

Her smile faded immediately and creases folded her
brow. She sat up straighter. 'He was hurt?'

'He got beaten, Ellie. Pretty bad.'

She spun around in her seat and looked back at Deputy, so content and relaxed now. Jed's own mind filled
with the images of how they'd found him down by the
river.

Her eyes came back to him, wide and dismayed.
'Who would do that?'

'Bad guys don't discriminate. Deputy could have led
us to them.'

'What about his...person. Where was he?'

His stomach tightened into a tiny, angry fist. He
cleared his throat. 'She... His handler.'

'Where was she?'

Shame burned low and fierce in his gut. 'She was
right there with him. But she was...in no position to
stop them. When it was over he dragged himself to her
side and wouldn't leave until she did.'

In a body bag.

Those clear blue eyes filled with tears. 'Oh, my
God...'

Nice date conversation, stupid! He tried to wind it

up, as much for his own sake as hers. Those were not days he let himself revisit. 'After that he had trouble with close conflict, which made him a liability in the team. He was retired. But he was miserable doing the PR rounds and there were no openings for therapy dogs. I decided to take him in with me.'

'And he's okay now?'

'About the most action he sees with me is car chases and some casual steer mustering.' Which brought him nicely back on topic. 'Wes was grateful you called the fence breach in the other day. Saved his team a lot of time. He was happy to do this return favor.'

The sadness in her eyes lifted just a bit but he noticed she kept casting her eyes back to Deputy in her mirror. As though his physical trauma was something she could relate to.

'Well, I'm glad those hours on the rooftop were valuable for someone!'

The gates to the Double Bar C were perpetually open and Jed cruised on through and followed the well-maintained road for about a mile, then threw a right and headed on up a much less groomed track.

Up ahead the Calhouns' foreman waited for them near a rusty, wide-open gate. The padlock swung free in his thin fingers.

'Wes.' Jed pulled the SUV up to the gate opening.

'Sheriff.' Wes leaned his forearms on the lowered window and dropped the padlock through it into Jed's hands and smiled. Not his mouth, his eyes. 'Lock up when you're through?'

'Sure will. Wes, this is Ellie Patterson from New

York City. Ellie, Wes Brogan, he's been foreman here on the Double Bar C for near as long as either of us has been alive.'

'Right grateful for your help with the stock on Monday, ma'am.' He dipped his broad, battered hat and did a good job of not looking curious at seeing his sheriff not only out of uniform but with a woman. At night. Alone.

Ellie leaned forward. 'You're welcome. I hope they were all okay?'

Jed stifled a snort and waited for Wes's reaction. Brogan was proud of his stock *en masse* but he didn't have a lot of time for the intellectual talents of cattle individually.

'Damned fool livestock were just fine. Was the fence came off second best.'

Ellie sagged back in her seat.

'Why don't you leave Deputy Dawg with me, Sheriff,' Wes offered. 'He can mix it up with some of the hands till you pick him up from the homestead. Then he won't get in your way up at the mine.'

It was crazy to think of a dog as a chaperone but having Deputy along made this whole thing feel less like a date and more like an outing. Leaving him behind threw everything into a new light. But saying no would only raise more speculation in Wes's shrewd hazel eyes. 'He'd enjoy that, thanks, Wes.'

Deputy leapt—literally—at the chance to get out of the car and visit with Wes. He was still running the older man in circles as Jed rumbled the SUV up and over the hill. The side of his face tingled and he knew Ellie was staring at him. He met her speculative gaze.

'Mine?' she queried. 'We're going hunting for gold?'

Of course she didn't miss Wes's slip. 'Part of the Calhoun fortune was made on mineral rights,' he said simply. 'The Double Bar C is dotted with speculative mines going back a century.'

Her brows dropped. 'And you thought a dress and heels would be appropriate attire for exploring an old mine?'

The image made him smile. If there was a woman to pull that off it was Ellie Patterson. He had a feeling she'd tough out any situation with finesse. 'We're not exploring it, exactly.'

'What are we doing…exactly?'

Here we go… Make or break time. He'd come up with this idea in that crazy, anything's possible, just-before-you-fall-asleep moment after he collapsed back into bed this morning. Seemed to him that Ellie lived her life trussed up in expectations and New York niceties and he wondered what she would do if she let go of all that, just for a moment.

Let herself just…be.

But this could go only two ways.

He took a breath and just leapt right in. 'How do you feel about bats?'

Chapter 7

'Bats?'

Ellie stared at Jed. He didn't seem to be joking so she dug a little further. 'Baseball or vampire?'

Those gorgeous lips twisted. 'Just regular bats.'

'I…' Was this a trick question? But he looked serious enough. 'I've seen bats before, feeding high over Central Park.' She almost dared not ask. 'Why?'

'I want you to see one of Larkville's most amazing sights.'

'You must have a low opinion of your town if a bunch of bats in an old mine is one of its highlights.'

'That's not a "no."'

'I'm not going to say no or yes until I know exactly what you have in mind.'

He stared at her long and hard. 'Can I ask you to trust me? I don't want to spoil the surprise.'

Any surprise that had bats in it couldn't be all that great. But this was Texas, her genetic home, and he was looking at her with such optimism...

He pulled the SUV up on a ridge top and pulled the handbrake on hard.

'I'm trusting you that this won't be bad, Jed.' She hated that there was a quaver in her voice as she stepped out of the vehicle.

'It's not bad. And I'll be right here with you.'

Her body responded to his low promise in a ripple of shivers.

The sun was half hidden behind the hills and ridges of Hayes County but Jed left the SUV's headlights on for illumination. They pointed across the void where the earth dropped clean away.

'If we're here for sunset we should have driven faster,' she joked, not entirely comfortable with having no idea what they were doing.

'Trust me,' he murmured, close behind her. 'Just let something happen to you, not because of you.'

Ellie's breath caught. That sounded awfully intimate. And he was standing pretty close. In the heartbeat before she remembered how hard she found physical contact, her body responded to his words with something that almost felt...sensual.

You know...if it had been in anyone but her.

The sun seemed to pick up momentum the further it sank.

'See that opening down there?' He pointed down into

the void while they still had any light at all and she squinted her eyes to see what he meant. 'One of the region's biggest colonies of free-tailed bat roosts in there.'

'It's a long way down,' she whispered, still transfixed by his closeness.

'Not a problem. We're not going to them...'

Almost as he said the words she caught a momentary glimpse of a small black shape cutting across the stream of light coming from the SUV. She gasped. 'Was that a bat?'

'Keep watching.'

A second black shape shot across the headlight beam. Then another. Then another. Crisscrossing the shaft of light like big, dark fireflies.

'Those are scouts,' he said, closer again to her ear. But the magic and mystery of the evening had taken hold. She forgot to be sensitive to his proximity.

'What are they scouting for?' she breathed.

'To see if it's safe.'

'Safe for what?'

She heard his smile in the warmth of his words. 'For the colony to hunt.'

And then it happened. A surge of small black shapes formed a wave and rose towards them from below. The raw sound of so many flapping wings made her think of a flood surge. She stumbled back, right into Jed. He held steady.

'You're safe, Ellie,' he said, low into her ear so she could hear him. 'They can navigate around individual blades of grass, they're not going to have any problem missing us. Just let it happen.'

Just let it happen.

How many times had her soul cried back in dance training after her instructors promised her it would happen if she just let it come—the magical, otherworldly sensation of letting the dance completely take over. She watched it happen in her fellow dancers, she watched the joy on their faces, and she wanted it for herself.

But no matter how her soul had bled it had never just happened for her.

Just like the rest of her life.

The bats drew closer, moving as a single body, and the first members flicked past her a little too close for comfort. She flinched away from them and reached behind her to curl Jed's shirt in her anxious fingers.

'You're okay.' His arms crossed down over her shoulders to keep her still. But nothing felt more unnatural than to stand here on the very edge of a precipice while a tsunami of wild creatures enveloped her. Every part of her wanted to rush back to the safety of the vehicle. Surely she could watch it from there?

More bats whizzed past, and then more—the closest managing to miss the two of them by an inch, until she felt like they were being buffeted by a hurricane of tiny wings, whipping close enough to feel the tiny sting of disrupted air against her skin and hair but never actually touching her.

The wave kept coming, thicker and deeper until the air around them seethed loudly with life.

'There's two million of them in there,' Jed half shouted as the windstorm from twice that many wings hit her.

The sheer scale of the life around them sent her senses spinning off into the dark sky. She felt small and insignificant against such a powerful collective mind, but safe and so very present.

Two million creatures knew she was there. Two million creatures were taking care not to hurt her. Two million creatures were relying on her not to hurt them.

Being frightened suddenly felt…kind of pointless. But she wasn't ready to be alone up here.

She slid her arms up between Jed's still crossed over her and then ran her hands along his forearms until they curled neatly within his. His fingers threaded through hers and anchored there so that the two of them formed their own, primitive set of wings.

Ellie carefully unfolded their joined limbs until they were stretched as wide as the bats' must be. Still the tiny black shapes did nothing more than buffet them as they surged past and up into the Texan dusk. She lifted her left arm—and Jed's—and then her right, a flowing exploration, testing the bats' sonar skills. They continued to miss her by the shallowest of breaths.

Incredible lightness filled her body until she felt certain she could take lift on the bats' air. She bent and swayed amidst the flurry of bats and closed her eyes to just feel the magnitude of the power in their numbers. Her hair whipped around her face, coming loose of its braid in the updraft caused by their exodus.

Jed stepped back slightly and dropped her right hand.

Anchored to him by her left, Ellie stepped ever closer to the drop of the ridge—ever closer to the tempest of tiny mammals coming over its lip—and she stretched her body up and out blindly, feeling the music of their flight, the melody in their subtle turns and shifts. Seeing the mass of bats as they each must: through their other senses.

Twisting as the airborne fleet did felt the most natural and right thing in the world. She used Jed's strong hold as a pivot and twisted under his arm in a slow, smooth pirouette as she'd done a thousand times onstage. But it had never felt this right onstage. Or this organic.

This...perfect.

She bent and she straightened and she moved with the flow of the bats—inside the flow—her eyes closed the whole time, predicting their intent in the mass of the flight. Being part of it.

Was this it? Was this what real dancers experienced when they hit that special place where everything just came together? When they let their minds go and just felt? She was eternal. As old as the planet and as young as a baby taking its first breath. Every synapse in her body crackled with life.

The whole time she was tethered to earth by Jed's touch, by the warmth of the intense gaze she could practically feel against her skin.

She danced. Sensual, swaying and shifting, and reaching out on the precipice, letting her body have its way.

Finally, the density of the bats around her lessened, the flurry of their millions-strong zephyr dropped, the sounds of their flight faded. Until only the last few laggers whizzed past.

And the only sound left was Ellie's hard breathing.

Her eyes fluttered open.

She stared out across the empty void of the dark Calhoun gully and felt the exhilaration slowly leach from her body. She missed it now that she'd finally— finally!—had a taste. But, deep down, her heart pulsed with joy that she was capable of feeling it at all. Utter sensual freedom. Infinite possibility.

After a lifetime of believing otherwise.

'Ellie?' Jed was as breathless as she was.

A dark heat surged through her and swamped the last vestiges of golden glow. What had she done? Dancing like that in front of a man who was virtually a stranger. It was like suddenly realising you were naked.

But she was nothing if not resilient. She turned and used the move to twist her fingers out of his. Ready for his laughter.

But he didn't laugh; he stared at her, silent and grave. 'That was—'

'Not what you were expecting, I'm sure.' She forced the levity into her words. Better to laugh first...

'—amazing.' His face didn't change. His focus did not move. 'I was going to say that was amazing.'

She stared at him, searching for signs of condescension. 'I just...' What could she say? How did you explain one of the most moving moments in your life?

'Why are you crying? Are you hurt?'

Unsteady fingers shot to her cheeks. Sure enough, they were wet.

'No.' Not outwardly. 'But that was—' the most free she'd felt in her entire life '—so beautiful. So wild.'

He stepped forward, arms open to comfort her, and

she couldn't help the learned response of her body. She flinched.

Jed froze.

His voice, when it came, was thick. 'Is it being touched in general you don't like...or is it just me?'

Chapter 8

She'd hurt him.

After he'd done this amazing and lovely thing for her.
After he'd not judged her at all this morning when she
dumped her whole illness on him.

'It's not you.' She shook her head, and golden strands
flew all around her. Trembling hands went immediately
to the destruction that was her carefully braided hair. Between the sideswipes of four million tiny bat wings and
her own twisting and rolling, it was a complete wreck.
She fumbled trying to tuck the largest strands back in.

'Why don't you just take it out?'

Her eyes shot to his. As if she hadn't made enough
of a fool of herself tonight, getting freaky about her hair
would be the final insult.

'No, I'll just...' Her fingers moved more quickly,

shoving and tucking, but it wasn't easy, reinstating the prison after the freedom of just moments before.

'Ellie…' Jed's hand slid up onto hers, stilled it. She forced herself not to snatch it away. 'Don't make it all perfect again. Don't undo everything you just experienced.'

She didn't want to. Deep inside she longed to just let it loose, or leave it wild and shambolic like right now. 'What must it look like…?'

'It looks like you just took a ride in the rear of a World War Two fighter, or galloped hard across all of the Double Bar C.' His eyes held hers, penetrating. 'It looks good.'

She stared at him, trapped in the intensity of his stare. His hand slipped off hers and slid down to the small band holding her braid in place. He closed his fingers over it but didn't pull.

He waited for her.

She took a breath, still locked in his gaze and whispered, 'I don't wear it out.'

'Why not? It's beautiful. Amazing colour.' He stroked the hair sticking out from under the band. For a bunch of dead skin cells they certainly came alive under his touch.

Beautiful? Hardly. 'It was a symptom…of my illness. For so long it was brittle.' For so long she was too ashamed to let people see it. 'And it fell out in patches.'

'Not now,' he assured her, slowly sliding the band down and curling it into his fingers as it slid off. 'It's healthy and strong. Like you are.' He worked the bottom of the braid loose, his fingers gentle but a little bit clumsy. The braid unwound more.

It was his clumsiness that stole her breath. It was his clumsiness that stilled her hands when she burned to disguise her shame and pull her hair back into a ponytail.

He was as nervous as she was.

For her this was a major step. What was his excuse?

He let gravity do most of the work, but he helped it along by arranging her long tresses around her shoulders as the braid finally gave way completely.

Ellie stood stiff and ready for some kind of reaction from him.

'Why did you give up dance?'

The unexpected question distracted her from the discordant sensation of having her hair unbound and free in front of someone.

'What I saw just now…' he continued, 'and the fact you made yourself sick to be good at it. It makes me wonder why you'd give it up.'

Tonight had been way too monumental for her to be able to retreat to her usual private shell. She was unravelled in more ways than one. She answered as honestly as she could, despite her very cells crying out for her not to.

'Not eating was never really about dancing,' she confessed, and then wondered where the heck she went next. Brown eyes just watched her. 'But professional dancing was a good environment for a sickness like that to go unremarked. Everyone was hungry in those dressing rooms, everyone was lean, everyone was exhausted all the time.' She felt it now, just for talking about it. The cell-deep fatigue they all danced through six days a week.

'It certainly wasn't conducive to me getting better, but I didn't leave because of it.'

'Then, why?'

Her eyes dropped. Would he understand? Or would she just sound like the precious princess he thought she was? Only one way to find out.

'Turns out the Patterson trust was a major benefactor of the company I danced for. My father donated six figures every year to it.'

'So he was proud of what you did?'

Her smile even felt token. 'I traced his contribution back in the company's annual reports. It started the year I was recruited.' She cleared her throat. 'Just before.'

His eyes said more than any words could have.

The old shame sat heavily on shoulders that had felt so light just minutes ago.

'He bought you in?'

'When I was feeling particularly glass half-full I'd imagine he saw how hard I was working and wanted me to feel validated.'

'Did you?'

She thought about that. 'At first. It had been my dream for so long. But the harder I trained the further behind everyone else I slipped. The more I saw what they all had that I was missing.'

'What was that?'

'Passion,' she snorted. 'Heart.'

His eyes blazed. 'I don't believe that.'

She tossed her head back. 'Are you a regular at the ballet?' Colour peeked out above his collar. 'So trust me to know where I sat in the company food chain. I loved the logic and the certainty of choreography but I lacked spirit.' Her breath shuddered in. 'I made a great chorus member, but I was never going to be a principal.'

'You threw it in because you didn't get to be the star?'

Even after just a few days she knew when he was being provocative for effect. He had to recognise by now how little she liked being the center of attention.

She smiled. 'No. But my father bought my spot. And I knew how many real dancers had earned it. Their chance. I decided to let one of them have it.'

Angry colour crept up his neck. 'You gave up your childhood for it. You gave up your health. Don't tell me you hadn't earned it.'

'I didn't want it all that much, it turned out.' She shrugged. 'It was everything I knew growing up, something I could excel at, something I could be technically proficient at. That proficiency probably would have kept me there until my body literally couldn't do it but, in the end, I couldn't face being reminded of my lack of passion every single day.'

'No. Not after what I just saw.'

'Earlier today I might have disagreed with you on that point,' she murmured. 'But with what I felt just now...' She turned and stared down at the old Calhoun mine. Then she brought her eyes back up to his and pressed her fist between her breasts. 'Maybe you're right. Maybe there's passion in here...somewhere...just looking for the right voice.'

Maybe? Jed watched Ellie's blue eyes glitter in the low light thrown by his SUV. Was she serious? Underneath the neatly pressed outfits and perfectly groomed hair, the woman oozed sensuality, but obviously didn't know it. The way she'd danced as the sun set… He'd never seen anything as moving. How someone could be one hundred per cent focused and one hundred per cent absent at the same time. Off…somewhere… otherworldly.

He recognised the feeling, though it had been a long time between sensations. He'd had it back when he was a kid and learning to horseride with his dad. The first time he'd galloped—petrified but exhilarated—alongside the man that he admired and respected so much. The man who only came home to him from duty on weekends and whose time and attention on those days was the whole world to a boy of six years of age. It was a feeling that had had to sustain him for a very long time after his father died.

Until he eventually forgot how it had felt.

Until years passed between incidences of remembering it.

He almost envied Ellie the experience she'd just had except for the fact that his own body had responded vicariously to her complete immersion. He'd seen her experiencing the thrill for the first time. He'd felt it in the tight grip of her fingers, the way she wanted to fly away from him but didn't at the same time.

It fed a need in him that he'd barely acknowledged. It stirred his blood in a way that probably wasn't helpful out here in the privacy and dark. Under a rising moon. This whole night had gone a totally different direction than he meant. He hadn't prepared himself to feel…drawn.

He cleared his throat. 'I have a confession to make. I brought you out here to show off a bit of Larkville, to help you see that the country has its merits, too. And to get you loosened up a bit so you might enjoy dinner rather than viewing it as something to be endured. But I'm glad that it has affected you so strongly,' he continued. 'And I'm thankful I could experience a little bit of it, through you, too.'

They stared at each other wordlessly for moments. The growing awareness in her gaze intrigued and frightened him at the same time.

'You still up for dinner?' he risked.

For three hard heartbeats he thought she was going to say no. But then she tossed back that hair she was so ashamed of and took a deep breath.

'Depends,' she said, and Jed realised he'd do just about anything at all to keep this connection they'd unexpectedly formed between them alive a little longer even if it was a mistake. It had been too, too long.

Her eyes twinkled. 'Will there be bats?'

No bats.

But something delicious was bubbling away on the stove when they walked back into Jed's cottage half an hour later. They'd had to pry Deputy away from the men lazing around the Calhoun hand quarters—he was in his doggie element—but he was happy enough to be back in front of his own fire now.

So was Ellie.

'Sure gets cold fast at night here,' she said.

'Yep,' Jed agreed. 'As soon as that sun sinks behind the mountains...'

Excellent. Talking about the weather. A new social low. Conversation had been pretty sporadic since returning from the Double Bar C but, for the life of her, Ellie couldn't manage anything more fascinating.

When had she got this nervous? And why?

'Give me ten minutes—I'll just serve up...' Jed cleared his throat. 'Washroom's through there if you want to freshen up.'

She did, but there'd be a mirror in there and if she looked in the mirror there was no way she was walking out with her hair hanging loose around her shoulders. And given how Jed would almost certainly feel if she came back with it perfectly pulled back, Ellie figured it would be best all round not to go in at all.

Plus it felt pretty good having it down. Kind of... risqué.

Her eyes automatically went to Jed, but she dragged them away when she realised what they'd done. Risqué and Sheriff Jed Jackson didn't belong together in the same thought process.

At all.

They went instead to Deputy. Much safer territory. He was such a good-natured dog. She'd thought he was just plain dopey but he couldn't have been to make it into the canine squad, even as a tracker, if he wasn't smart. They had to be pretty focused and resilient. Her heart squeezed... Though apparently every dog had its breaking point.

Just like humans.

Whatever kind of a dog he used to be he approached life much more simply now. She certainly understood that desire.

'Ready?'

Jed pulled up two seats at the timber breakfast bar. Then he added a bottle of wine and two glasses to the two steaming bowls already there.

'We're eating here?' she queried.

'Yup. A meal doesn't have to be fancy to be good.'

She frowned at him. 'I feel like I need to let you know I've had good food before. Despite my—' idiosyncrasies '—rule.'

'Good dining is about so much more than the taste.' He held one of the two tall seats out for her to perch on. Then he held an empty glass up and raised an eyebrow. She nodded—barely—and he splashed two inches of white wine into the glass. She wiggled more comfortably on the seat, starting to enjoy the pageantry of this meal, coming as it did so close on the heels of one of the most exhilarating experiences of her life.

'Texan wine?' she tested.

'Naturally.'

He slid a plate towards her and she took an anxious breath. But he'd been careful; she had a bit of everything on her plate but nowhere near the quantities on his. He wasn't out to overwhelm her. She appreciated that.

She peered closer. 'What is this?'

'Cuisine à la Jackson. Texan ribs, risotto and salad.' He smiled. 'A tribute to my past and my present.'

She could see something Mediterranean in the colour of his skin and eyes, bleached by generations of cold Atlantic winters. That side of his family came endowed with old legend and crazy anecdotes and he shared some of them as Ellie tried the moist risotto and the tangy salad. But when she got to the lone rib on her plate she hesitated.

'Just like Texans do,' he said, anticipating her question. 'With your fingers.'

'I don't think I've eaten with my fingers since I was four,' she joked, lifting the rib to her mouth.

'About time you rediscovered the art.'

Ellie tentatively wrapped her lips around the sticky goodness.

Her eyes rounded at the divine taste. 'Ofmigof...!'

Ribs were good. Really good. Rib muscles were constantly being worked out just breathing, so it made sense they'd be lean and tender. That meant that they got a tick in her 'good fuel' box. But in this case they also got a tick each in the boxes marked 'yum' and 'plain fun to eat.'

She nibbled her way along one piece of bone, then licked her fingers individually. Jed reached over for the flat-iron pan the ribs had come out on, his muscles bunching under his shirt. He tonged another one up and lifted an eyebrow.

She only hesitated for a moment. 'What's it cooked in?'

He placed one more rib on her plate and shook his head. 'Old Texan secret.'

'Come on. I'm more Texan than you are—'

Ellie hid the accidental slip-up behind his full laugh. A mistake like that was not like her, she was normally so guarded with her words. She glanced at her wine— only an inch missing. How relaxed had the bats made her? Or was it Jed?

In the end she barely noticed the passing of time, or food over her lips. The conversation roamed all over the place and she was most rapt by the accidental snippets of information about the Calhouns—any one of her sisters or her brothers. Her Texan sisters and brothers, she allowed, thinking of Alex and Charlotte and Matt. Though Matt was as Texan as she was, technically.

Then, barely realising it had happened, she found herself curled up on a sofa just like her own, a cup of steaming hot cocoa in hand. Cocoa. The drink that got no ticks in any of the boxes except the one marked 'sigh.'

'Jed, I have to admit—' and admitting she was wrong took some doing '—this has been a pretty awesome evening.'

'Even the food?'

'Especially the food. I never quite got why people insisted on eating when they got together but...' She looked at him curiously. 'It's kind of nice. Relaxing.'

'That's the cocoa.'

She barely had the energy for more than a low chuckle. 'Right. That must be it.' She shifted more comfortably on the sofa.

'So you didn't hate it?'

She stared at him, recognising genuine anxiety flirting at the back of his careful expression. 'On the contrary. I'm not sure when I've ever been this relaxed and comfortable with someone. Thank you.' She ignored the squeezing sensation deep inside.

'Are you thanking me for dinner? Or for being comfortable to be around?'

She tipped her head onto the thick-stuffed top of the sofa and let it rest there. 'Both?'

Confusion battled it out in his silent gaze. 'For what it's worth, the feeling's mutual. Though I wouldn't have expected that when I first met you out on the road to the Calhouns'.'

She groaned. 'You got me at an especially difficult time. End of a long drive, a bad week.'

'Drowning in steer.'

Ellie laughed. 'And the steer.'

'Why the bad week?'

Could she tell him? She wanted to—a lot—but until she'd spoken to Jess it really wasn't her secret to share. How ironic since she *was* the secret.

She leaned over and placed the last of her hot cocoa on a side table Jed had dragged over next to the sofa. Then she brought her eyes back to his. 'Back home I'm…expected to uphold a certain standard. A level of output. It's a crazy kind of pace.' Though it's quite handy when you don't think you have much else of a life to lead. 'But add a few emotional upheavals to the mix and it all gets a bit overwhelming.'

Upheavals—suitably broad and non-specific.

'Who expects it? This standard?'

She blinked at him. 'Everyone. I'm Eleanor Patterson.'

'You say that like you're the First Lady, with obligations to the whole country.' He shifted his leg slightly to point the soles of his shoes towards the fire and it brought him a hint closer to her. 'Define "everyone"?'

'My parents. My brother and sisters. The people who count on me to work their events, to attract a crowd, to make them money.'

'What about you?'

She frowned at him. 'What about me?'

'Do you have high expectations of yourself?'

'I do. But not unrealistic, I don't think. I have a good idea of my strengths and weaknesses. It's not all bad.'

Suddenly his gaze grew more intense. 'Throw me a couple of strengths.'

When had he moved that close? 'Okay. Well… People call me driven. Focused. Tireless. They're all good things.'

'Depends how you look at it.' Jed stared steadily at her. 'You don't look tireless to me. You just look tired.'

For absolutely no reason, the compassion in his lined face was like a sock to her guts, robbing her of air. Her chest squeezed in, collecting into a tight, painful ball. She held his eyes.

'I'm exhausted,' she confessed. Exhausted by life. Exhausted by faking it. Exhausted by all the angst and worrying over something she couldn't control in any way.

Like whether or not she was a Calhoun.

He turned his body front on to her and took her hand between his.

It wasn't a come-on. It was humane compassion, pure and simple, but it wasn't something she could let herself do. She pulled her hand free and then, without meaning to speak, words were leaving her lips. It suddenly seemed extra important to her that Jed understand it wasn't him she was afraid of touching.

'I don't like physical contact because I was always so self-conscious about how I must feel to people,' she blurted. 'How frail.'

How skeletal.

He didn't react, but she was starting to expect that from him now. Jed Jackson was a man who was careful to think before he spoke. Plus the deep shadows in his gaze gave him away. 'You don't want to seem fragile?'

'I'm supposed to be strong.'

He slid one hand along the back of the sofa and his eyes were steady on hers. 'You can't be strong all the time. It's okay to ask for help.'

His body language was obvious, his message clear. He was there to lend her strength if she wanted it.

But she had to come to him.

She stared at the big barrel of a chest just a foot away from her, imagined resting there. How had they got there, the two of them? At the place that a virtual stranger could ask her if she wanted to absorb some of his apparently endless strength and the place that she was actually considering doing it.

But there they were and it didn't feel weird, just... foreign. She hadn't had someone touching her in a long time but it had been even longer since she'd been the one to initiate contact. Beyond the necessary courtesy with the necessary people. Beyond her sister's life-sustaining hugs that she only allowed because it was Alex. Beyond the quickly evaded clinch at the conclusion of the endless first and only dates she went on to make her mother happy.

Heart hammering, her eyes slid to the soft denim shirt covering his broad chest. It did look extremely comfortable. And it was so close.

She was as slow to move as trust was to come but, once she started, momentum took over. She reclined into the sofa back, against the length of Jed's arm, her breath suspended the entire time.

He did nothing. No words. No actions. He didn't trap her within the curl of his arm or force some kind of intimacy for which she wasn't ready. He just sat quiet and undemanding and understanding as she grew accustomed to the feel of someone's body against hers.

'There's a reason I took Deputy in with me,' he rumbled from next to her. 'More than just him needing a home.'

His pause wasn't an invitation for her to speak, it was an opportunity for him to gather his thoughts. Something about the slight stiffness in the body pressed so warmly against hers told her that he was rewarding her vulnerability with one of his own.

Making this easier for her by making it harder on himself.

Ellie inched in closer to the crook of his arm. Why she thought such a tiny gesture would bolster him... Yet, it seemed to work.

'Police presence was massively increased in Manhattan after the 9/11 attacks,' he started. 'The NYPD got an influx of new recruits wanting to make a difference, to defend their city. For a while there we had rookies coming out of our ears but, by the time I was promoted to the canine unit, the enthusiasm to serve had waned, yet the required service level stayed high.'

He stared into the fire.

'As captain of the unit it was my job to oversee training and rosters and staff development as well as dealing with budgets and resources and procedures. It was my job to deal with the expectation of management, too. Sometimes those two things didn't fit together at all.'

'Expectations and resources?'

She felt his nod in the slight shift of his torso. 'I made some decisions that I wasn't all that comfortable with.'

Ellie changed the angle of her head so that she was looking up at him. Mostly into that gorgeous jawline. 'Did that include Deputy Dawg?'

The hard line of his jaw flexed. Pronounced creases formed between his brow. 'Deputy's handler... Officer O'Halloran. She and Deputy were inseparable, she was as good a trainer as Deputy was a tracker, but she was no more suited for the front line than he was. I knew that even if she didn't. I knew she was misplaced from before she'd even arrived in the section.'

'But...?'

'But reassigning her would have meant my team was down by one and the others had already carried her for the weeks it takes to train up a new handler and dog pair. And it would have compromised our output at a time we were being hammered for results.'

He paused for so long, Ellie thought maybe he'd changed his mind.

'So I sent her out while we scouted other units

for likely replacements. Despite knowing she wasn't ready—that maybe she never would be. I exposed her and Deputy to risk before they were ready.'

Ellie's breath tightened in response to the sudden tension in Jed's body and she remembered his earlier words. 'The waterfront.'

'She died there, Ellie. And Deputy was beaten half to death defending her. And both of those shames were on me. My lack of judgement. My haste.' He swallowed again. 'My weakness in not standing up to the game-playing and the bull dust from higher up the food chain.'

'You were doing your job,' she murmured, though it wasn't a whole lot of consolation.

He threw up his hands angrily. 'My job was to look after my team and my district and make informed, care-ful decisions. Not to throw a rookie to the wolves.'

His frustrated outburst over, his hands dropped back down and one fell lightly onto her shoulder, but Jed was so lost in his memories he didn't even notice. And, for the same reason, Ellie couldn't bring herself to protest. Plus the small and surprising fact that she didn't en-tirely mind it.

'Is that why you quit the department?'

'I let that team down as badly as I would have let Deputy down by leaving a working dog to rot in some public-relations role. Me stepping aside made way for someone who deserved the stars on their shoulder.'

'That sounds vaguely familiar,' she murmured, lift-ing her eyes to seek out his. He dragged his gaze back from the spot on the far wall he'd been pinned to and lowered it to stare down his cheekbone at her.

His thick lashes fringed a thoughtful expression. 'It's not the same.'

'No, it's not. But it's close. Sounds like we walked away for similar reasons.'

That caused more than a few moments' silence. 'I'm happiest out in the field interacting with people and doing an honest day's work,' he finally said.

'Ditto, as it turns out. Minus the job.' She laughed. 'And the people.'

His smile transformed the shadows in his gaze into contrasting highlights for the sudden lightness there. He nudged her sideways. 'You're not so bad with people once you get warmed up, Ellie Patterson.'

All this time she'd thought pressing into someone like this would be uncomfortable and exposed. But she only felt warm and somehow restored. If Jed was to pay the slightest attention to her body pressed against his, she knew he wouldn't feel stringy muscles and vacant hollows under his fingers. He'd feel flesh and curves and…woman.

Teenage Ellie would never have been able to conceive of a day she'd feel proud of her convex butt and actual bust. But she did right this second.

She felt…desirable.

Brown eyes caught and held hers. Jed's pulse kicked visibly against his skin as his strong, honest heart sped up. Her shallow breathing betrayed the fact that hers matched it exactly.

His gaze dropped to her lips.

'Well.' She cleared her throat. 'Deputy's a lucky Dawg to have ended up with you.' She averted her eyes before he could read too much into her glazed expression.

Jed sat up straight and then used the dying fire as an excuse to break the contact between them. Embarrassed heat surged up her body as he stood and selected a large log piece to add to the embers.

And the moment—so surreal and rare—was well and truly lost.

Ellie stood. 'Thank you for a great evening, Jed.'

'Have I changed your mind about food being more than just nutrition?'

'You've change my mind about a few things, actually.'

Speculation filled his careful gaze. 'Really?'

'But my jury's still out. One good experience doesn't undo the lessons of a lifetime.'

Did he even know she was only partly talking about food now?

He grabbed a spare coat from his stand and helped to drape it around her shoulders. 'That sounds like a carefully disguised opening for a repeat performance.'

Did she want to do this again? Did she want to risk exposing herself to Jed? For Jed? 'You set the bar pretty high tonight. It's going to be hard to beat.'

He paused with his hands on her shoulders and spoke from behind her. 'Is that a challenge?'

She turned and stared up at him and hoped everything she was feeling wasn't broadcast in her eyes. 'Maybe.' Then she turned for the door and opened it herself just to prove she was a modern woman. But secretly she'd loved how he'd so naturally helped her into his coat. How he'd held the car door for her. It gave her an idea of the kind of thoughtful man he'd be in…other ways. Awareness zinged in the air around them as she stepped out into the bracing cold.

Jed followed close behind.

'Walking me back, too, Sheriff?'

'I picked you up, I see you home.'

How many of those New York dates had even bothered to wait while she hailed a cab? Not counting the ultimately disappointed ones who assumed they'd be getting in it behind her.

'Personal rule?'

His voice shrugged. 'Just good manners.'

But as her doorway loomed so, too, did the moment she'd struggled with her whole dating life. The moment she had to hint—or just blurt outright—that they weren't getting inside her wing of the Patterson home. That they weren't getting inside anything else, either. The few that had actually gotten as far as her door weren't there because they were chivalrous; they were there because they were persistent or amazingly thick-skinned. Or presumptuous.

Jed was there because… Well, because she'd been far too busy being aware of his smell and the deep sound of his voice to get busy planning her exit strategy. So here she was just steps away from her door and she had no choice but to wing it.

She turned on the ball of her foot and Jed lurched to a halt to avoid crashing right into her.

So…good night! She opened her mouth to utter the words.

'Don't forget Sarah's coming for you on Saturday.' Jed's pedestrian reminder threw her off her game completely. So did the fact that he was just standing there staring placidly at her. Not making a single move. Implying that she wasn't going to see him again.

'Coat,' he said, when she just stared her confusion up at him.

'Oh…' She shrugged quickly out of his warm jacket.

But the tiniest of smiles played on his face and she wondered if she was being played, too.

'See you on the weekend, maybe,' he said as he folded his jacket over his arm and turned to walk away, casual as you like.

Where were the corny lines? The grasping arms? Ellie reached behind her to open her door, but irritation made her rash. 'You're not going to make sure I get in okay?'

He turned three-quarters back and threw her a glance so simmering it nearly stole her breath. It fairly blazed down the darkened path. 'Do you really think that's a good idea?'

Every molecule of oxygen evacuated through the walls of her cells and escaped into the night. His dark gaze held her, even at this distance.

He wanted in. If she just stood back and opened the door to her little house, he'd be in there in a flash, sweeping her up as he went. Realising was as shocking as discovering she almost—almost—wanted it to happen. After so many years of wondering whether she'd starved the sensuality right out of her, coming to terms with two arousing experiences in one evening was going to take some processing. And she couldn't do that with company.

No matter how tempting.

But it took her so long to make her lips and tongue form the necessary shape, Jed had turned the corner and was gone by the time she whispered, 'No.'

Instead the word breathed out and tangled with the frost of the cold evening and was gone.

Just as her better sense apparently was.

Heads he'd go for it, tails he'd cool it.

Appropriate, really. Heads meant he was completely out of his mind. Tails meant he should tuck his tail between his legs and run a mile.

The moment he was out of Ellie's view earlier he'd kept walking right on past his front door and taken himself for a quick, restorative sprint around the block. Three blocks, actually. Better than a cold shower any day.

He paused at the bottom of his porch steps, before his heavy footfalls gave him away to his sleeping dog.

His version of heads or tails involved his trusty companion. When he opened the front door, Deputy's head would either be facing the fire or his butt would. There was a fifty-fifty chance of either.

Deputy could decide.

Given he apparently couldn't.

Jed bunched his fists into his pockets and hunched his shoulders against the cold, one foot poised on his bottom step. The third option, of course, was to do nothing. She would be gone in a few weeks. He could tough it out that long. But doing nothing didn't feel all that possible. Ellie had a way of wheedling under his defenses if he wasn't actively patrolling them.

Course, if he dropped them altogether it wouldn't be a problem.

Princess ballerinas from New York City didn't meet the definition of Ms. Right and they had another great thing going for them.

They were transient.

Passing through meant *won't get attached*. Passing through meant he could explore this bourgeoning something without risking the expectation of more. Pinocchio could live like a real boy for a few weeks. Flirt and seduce and romance a woman the old-fashioned way.

Except faster.

Three days ago he would have said he wasn't interested in being some New Yorker's holiday fling, but Ellie Patterson had taken him by surprise. He'd clicked with her. He was definitely attracted to her. And she intrigued the hell out of him. There were much worse ways to spend a few weeks than getting to know someone like that.

A couple of weeks wasn't long enough for either of them to form any kind of permanent attachment. But it was long enough for him to give his romancing skills a healthy workout. It wasn't really about sex, per se, but it most definitely was about the hot, vivid feelings that came with the getting-to-know-you phase. He missed that.

The question mark.

The flirting.

The touch.

The kissing.

The chase.

He really wasn't into casual relationships. He'd tried a one-night stand—necessity and raging hormones being the mother of invention—but he'd been unable to have another, his mind not able to go through with a repeat performance even if his body was willing. Which it wasn't, particularly.

So he took up running instead and he pounded out on the pavement all the frustration he felt from doing the whole Zen-monk thing for so long.

Three years of virtual abstinence.

But there was nothing casual about the way his body responded to Ellie's when she was around. There was nothing casual about the way he'd opened up and told her about New York, though he hadn't come close to connecting all the dots for her. And there was nothing casual about the look she'd thrown him just before they left his house.

The look that was part gratitude, part curiosity, part awareness and part just plain sexy. And a whole lot complicated. The beginning of something he had no business to be encouraging.

Something he'd surrendered a right to ever expect.

And so that was why he was delegating this one to the universe. Or to Deputy, more rightly.

If he walked inside and Deputy was toasting his big shaggy butt, that could only be good news. He'd just run more. Exercise Ellie right out of his system. Go back to having a nice, straightforward, uncomplicated, monastic existence. His body would forgive him—eventually.

Though, if he pushed open that door and Deputy's big black and tan head was hot from radiant heat... His body wouldn't have to forgive him. He could spend the next few weeks together, inducting Ms. Ellie Patterson into the wonders of her own body.

Deputy—or rather the universe—could decide. It couldn't do a worse job of his life than he had.

He took the steps quietly.

Turned the handle. Paused. Gave himself one last chance to change his mind. To reconsider whether Ellie Patterson with her New York independence, her burning need to control things and her disinclination to touch him, might end up being the committing type. Totally the wrong type for him.

His fingers twitched on the doorknob.

Nah.

He pushed into the room and reached for the light switch. Deputy lifted his head, his big, brown half-asleep eyes blinking slowly. Away from the fireplace and towards the door where his master stood.

Jed took a deep breath on a weird kind of fated feeling at the same time as his body went into mourning.

Tails.

Probably just as well. He could do without the entanglement.

Chapter 9

A whole new day without Sheriff Jed Jackson...

Already that felt so weird. But it had to be a good thing, right? Given how badly she craved his company. Anything that felt that good simply couldn't be good for you. Denying the craving was one step closer to mastering it.

Ellie frowned.

Except that's pretty much the path she'd been on when she got so sick. Denying her hunger, denying the needs of her body. Mastering it. A daily show of control in a world where she felt she had very little.

Sarah was still speaking but she barely heard the words. She'd done that a lot in the couple of hours they'd been together. Even more in the three days since the bat date.

So… What was the right thing to do? Indulge the craving or deny it? Neither one seemed ideal. Unless… Maybe it was like an inoculation—allow a tiny bit under your skin so that your body could build up defenses.

A little Jed…but not too much.

'Is what possible?' Sarah said, glancing at her as she pulled her car into Jed's street.

Ellie's head snapped around. 'What?' Had she spoken aloud?

Sarah tipped her pretty face. 'You know. If I hadn't been through much worse in my life I might be developing a complex right about now. I get the feeling you haven't really been with me all morning.'

Head flooded up Ellie's throat. 'Sure I have.' Um… 'You were talking about parking for the festival?'

Sarah smiled. 'I was. Ten minutes ago.' Her eyes grew serious. 'Are you okay, Ellie? We can talk festival another day if you like?'

Self-disgust curdled the tasty afternoon tea they'd just had. 'No, let's do it now. I'm fine. Just distracted. I'm sorry.'

Sarah pulled on her park brake right out front of the Alamo. 'Don't be sorry. I'm the one strong-arming you into this. With your background I figure you could do this with your eyes closed. I just didn't actually expect to see that in play.'

Ellie laughed at the image. It was pretty apt. 'God, I'm sorry. I've been pretty present-absent today.'

'So what's on your mind, Ellie? Maybe I can help?'

'Uh…' No.

'Seriously. I know we've been kind of thrust together today but you've been good enough to listen to me talk—' she grinned '—kind of. This is my opportunity to give back.'

Ellie stared. She didn't do girl talk. Not with strangers. And even if Sarah didn't feel much like a stranger, confidence wasn't something she gave lightly. Yet her amber eyes were so open and so intent…

'Have you…' She stopped and tried again, encoding it. 'What are your views on inoculation?'

Sarah scrunched her face. 'Like immunisation?'

'Right.'

'Humans or livestock?'

Ellie laughed. 'Human.'

Those sharp eyes narrowed. 'Oooh, human singular?'

Damn. 'No, I—'

'Never mind, never mind.' Sarah waved the intrusion away. 'I'll just answer it on face value. I am—' her eyes drifted up and to the right '—pro-inoculation.'

'Why?'

She shrugged. 'Because how can you know how your body is going to react to something you've never had any experience of?'

Ellie stared at her. Speechless.

Somehow, despite the worst analogy in the living world, Sarah had managed to actually answer it in a way that was both meaningful and which resonated for her. Ellie could guess what her body would do around Jed, based on previous experience, but until she actually tested the theory…

'We're not talking about foot-in-mouth disease, are we?' Sarah dropped her voice.

More heat. More awkwardness. But she couldn't help herself and a laugh broke out.

'We're not,' she answered, seriously. 'No.'

Sarah stared, visibly battling with something. 'Is it… Are we talking about Jed?' Her expression was virtually a wince. She clearly didn't want to be wrong. Unless she didn't want to be right? But she was saved from the hideousness of asking as Sarah rattled on. 'Fantastic, if we are. Jed's way too good a catch to be going wanting.'

Ellie glanced at her left hand. 'Aren't you single?'

Sarah flushed. 'Now. Yes. But Jed's not…my type.'

Really? A man like that? Wouldn't he be everyone's—?

Oh.

There was someone else for Sarah. And just like that it all made sense. Her warm affection for Jed in the street. Her high opinion that leaked out in a few things she'd said about him this morning. Her total disinterest in him any other way than platonically.

'He'd have to be some kind of guy… Your type.'

'He sure would,' Sarah said, the tiniest of smiles playing around her lips.

What could she say that wasn't stupidly patronising? Not much. So she just nodded, smiled and said, 'Good luck with that.'

'Thank you. Nice try with the deflection, by the way.'

'Rats, I thought you might fall for that.'

'Afraid not. So, back to Jed.'

Ellie glanced nervously into the street as if he might be conjured by their low whispers. 'No, really, let's not.'

'Back to inoculations, then. What are your feelings on the issue?'

Ellie took a deep breath. 'I might be coming around to your way of thinking. But it's not without risk.'

'The best ones never are.'

So much more risk for her than for most people. So many hurdles to overcome. Was Jed worth it? Ellie frowned.

Sarah adopted her strictly business tone. As if sorting things out between herself and Jed was part of the Fall Festival planning. 'Well, he's a regular at the Association Hall for the monthly mixer. He doesn't really dance but given half the single women there come to see him, I'd say they definitely think he's worth taking a chance on.'

A dance. It had been so long since she'd danced for pleasure—if you didn't count the indiscretions of a few short nights ago. But she didn't want Sarah focusing on Jed any more than she already was.

'Who do the other half go for?'

Sarah smiled. 'Holt Calhoun. Not that he'll be there and not that he goes often, but no one wants to miss the one dance he actually comes to.' She shook her head. 'He sure got his brother's charisma.'

Ellie frowned. 'His brother's…?'

Nate?

Sarah blinked; those wide eyes flared a tiny bit more. It was the first time Ellie had seen her anything less than fully composed. She stuttered, 'His father's—Clay Calhoun.'

Awkward silence fell.

Well... Wasn't that the most Freudian of slips? And wasn't that the most furious of blushes. But given how amazingly gracious Sarah had just been about Jed and the whole bumbling inoculation analogy, she was hardly going to repay it by making the other woman uncomfortable.

'Sounds good,' Ellie lied, clambering out of the car. 'Will you be there?'

Sarah smiled and climbed out after her. 'You betcha.' But not for Jed and not for Holt Calhoun. So maybe it was for the line dancing? 'It starts at sunset with a side of beef on a spit.'

A sea of brown, grousing cattle filled her mind. Back on her first day in Larkville she'd have happily consigned any one of them to a rotisserie, but with the benefit of distance and a few personal introductions she felt a whole lot more warm and fuzzy towards the poor dopey creatures. 'A whole side?'

Sarah threw her a curious look.

Ellie pulled herself together. 'I think I just smacked headlong into a big-city double standard. I guess I can't complain about someone throwing half a cow on the barbecue when I happily ate Jed's marinated ribs three nights ago.'

Sarah laughed. 'Get used to it, honey. Out this way they call it "bustin' a beast." Enough for half the town and one of Jess Calhoun's fresh-baked biscuits each.'

Right. Yet another reminder about why she was really here. 'Calhouns again. Seems like they're everywhere I turn.'

'The Calhouns founded Larkville and they practically own it still. You can't move without running into one of their businesses or their animals. Or one of them.'

What would she say if she knew she was walking with one?

'By the way...' Sarah murmured, following Ellie down the laneway to her door. 'Ribs? Seems like you're doing just fine with that inoculation, huh?'

'Ellie...'

Amazing how a single male utterance could whisper so many things. Relief. Confusion. Foreboding. And only the last one made a bit of sense given what had passed between them last.

Caution wasn't the reaction she'd hoped for when she lifted her knuckles to his door, but she had a theory to test. And, given she was already so far out of her comfort zone by being here at all, she had nothing to lose by proceeding.

She stood taller in his doorway. 'I came to take you up on your offer to show me Larkville's highlights.'

His eyebrow twitched but he didn't let it go any further. The effort of keeping his expression neutral showed in the sudden line of his mouth. 'Sarah's offer?'

His words could not have been a clearer reminder that it was their friend and not he that had committed him. She figured she was supposed to be feeling some level of shame right now for making him go through with it. Possibly even graciously relenting and scurrying back to her front door.

Screw that. She had a point to prove to herself.

She was still a tiny bit tetchy after checking her email

this morning and realising there was still nothing from Jessica. And she was a lot tetchy that Jed hadn't so much as said hello since that steamy moment at her door four nights ago. A lifetime!

'Wrong side of bed this morning, Ellie?' She turned her distraction up to him. 'You're forming your own Grand Canyon between your eyebrows there. Something on your mind?'

You.

'No. I'm fine.' Habit got the better of her. 'Is now a bad time?'

His mind was busy behind his careful eyes. But when it finished flicking indecisively between yes and no, it settled on no. 'Happy to be out on a beautiful Sunday showing off my district. Besides, I owe Sarah. She was really welcoming when I arrived.'

In her head she reached out and shoved him in the chest just to jolt that careful beige mask from his face. Wednesday night he looked like he wanted to eat her whole, now he was only doing this for a friend? 'You know I'd help her anyway.'

That earned her the first hint of the Jed from the top of the Calhoun ridge. His eyes landed on her softly. 'Yeah, I know you would.'

'Okay. What time should I come back?'

He reached inside and grabbed his jacket from its peg and whistled for Deputy. 'Now's as good a time as any.'

Don't do me any favors. She followed him out into the street where his chariot awaited. His lips shifted slightly as he walked alongside her and she wondered—again— if she'd muttered aloud.

They rode in silence and Ellie busied herself looking at the architecture in the streets they passed. It was easy to see where 'old Larkville' began and ended in the switch from earthy colours and stone construction to brighter timbers and cladding on the more modern buildings.

Twin bells clanged as Jed pulled the SUV under a sign that said Gus's Fillin' Station. 'Just need gas,' he said unnecessarily, and then didn't move.

Over to her right a weathered man sauntered towards them. 'Fill her up, Sheriff?'

'Thanks, Gus.'

'Wow,' Ellie said, watching the man go about his business. 'An honest-to-goodness service station. I thought these were legend.'

Jed laughed. 'You really need to get out of New York more.'

For a man well past fifty, Gus certainly had superhero hearing. 'Pfff... New York,' he grunted as he passed back along the vehicle to slop a window-washer in its bucket.

Jed half winced, as though this was an argument he should have predicted.

Ellie leaned out her window just a bit. She'd always believed in calling someone's bluff. 'Something wrong with New York?'

'Don't go there, Ellie...' Jed murmured through the wince. 'I was hoping to show off the good things about Larkville.'

Gus shuffled around the front of the SUV and took his time slopping the windshield with soapy water.

'What's right with it? Noisy. Smelly. Dirty.' Every word accompanied a strong swipe of the rubber blade across Jed's side of the glass.

Ellie smiled. It was hard to take such blatant prejudice to heart. 'When was the last time you were there?' she asked brightly.

Steely eyes peered up from under his battered old stetson. 'Back in eighty-one. Gave someone a ride.'

'Eighteen eighty-one?' she said under her breath, and then, much louder, 'A lot has changed in three decades.'

'Would want to,' Gus muttered.

He crossed to her side of the SUV and sudsed up her side a little too zealously. But, as he drew long streaks of clean across the soap, his eyes found hers.

His motion faltered. His black pinpoint pupils doubled in size.

Some kind of prescience nibbled low in Ellie's gut.

He finished what he was doing, then crossed around to her side again, replaced the gas spout in the bowser and appeared at her window. The smell of old-school tobacco wafted with him. 'How old are you?'

'Gus—' Jed sounded literally pained as he passed a bill via Ellie and into Gus's wrinkled, sun-spotted hand.

'Just a question, Sheriff.'

Ellie hurried to head off the inevitable condescension. 'I'm thirty years old. So, yes, I do remember New York from when I was a child. I know for a fact it's changed.'

But Gus wasn't even thinking about New York City any more. His head tipped. 'You look mighty like her.'

Ellie's gut clamped. The oxygen in her lungs sucked into a void.

'Who?' Jed stepped in smoothly when it was obvious she wasn't going to.

'The woman I gave a ride to the Big Apple.'

Her mother mentioned she'd lived briefly on the Calhoun ranch. Stood to reason she would have been into town. Met Gus, maybe.

Ellie forced what little air she had left in her lungs up and past her voice box. She tried to pick a fight to distract him. 'Are you suggesting all women from New York look the same?'

Gus frowned. 'I'm sayin' that you look just like her.'

'Come on… You remember some woman you gave a ride to thirty years ago, Gus?' Jed tried to be the voice of reason. But he glanced at Ellie, too.

She didn't take her eyes off Gus. Exposure suddenly blazed bright, possible and totally unexpected. 'Hard to forget this one. She wasn't here for long but she had a big impact on the town.'

Desperate to end the conversation before it went any further, Ellie turned to Jed. 'Shouldn't we get going?'

'Keep the change, Gus.' Jed put the car straight into gear.

Gus stood back and Ellie wasted no time in smiling briefly and then raising her tinted window pretty much in his face.

He could add rudeness to New York's list of failings.

'I'm so sorry about that, Ellie.' Jed's apology was immediate; they hadn't even bumped out of the gas station yet. 'He's obviously confused.'

Ellie grunted. 'He seemed pretty sharp. Was the New York thing a dig at you or at me?'

'Not me. No one knows my background and that's how I like it.'

'I can see why.'

He rubbed both his temples with one hand, then refocused on the road. 'Would it help if I said ninety-eight per cent of Larkville isn't like that?'

'Would it be true?'

He chuckled. 'There's a reason stereotypes get started. You just met one.'

She was relaxing more and more every meter she got from Gus's Fillin' Station. 'It's fine, Jed. I shouldn't have taken the bait.'

'He's grown too accustomed to speaking his mind. Not many people stand up to him. Certainly not on first acquaintance.'

'Go me, then.' She glanced at him, looking for signs he was patronising her, but his expression was totally open for the first time today. It was the only reason she risked a personal question. 'So...seriously? No one knows your past?'

Trees whizzed by. 'A trusted two. The rest haven't asked, though I'm sure there's been indiscriminate internet searching.'

She stared at him. 'Yet you told me.'

'I did.' Silence. 'Figured you shouldn't be hanging out there all alone on the revelations front the other night.'

So he did at least remember the other night. 'Well, thank you. You can be assured of my confidence.'

His eyes darkened. 'If that's a very formal way of saying I can trust you, I already know that.'

Would he, if he knew how many secrets she was

keeping? Not exactly relevant to national security—lies by omission. As he'd almost found out just now.

She shook the trepidation free. 'So, what's on the agenda today? More bats?'

'I thought you might like to see the aquifer where it bubbles to the surface.'

Chuckling let off a tiny bit of the tension she'd been carrying since opening the door to his textbook indifference. She let it come. 'Another highlight on Larkville's social calendar?'

He shrugged and glanced at her. 'Since when were you all that social?'

'Point.' Besides, he'd be there. And that had taken a dangerously short time to being all she really cared about. She held his eyes longer than was sensible, or safe while he was behind the wheel. At the very last moment, something changed right at the back of them. Something realised. Something…decided. Then he turned back to the road.

'Tell me about your family,' he said after a moment of silent driving. 'Something I couldn't guess.'

The words *Which family?* hovered on the tip of her tongue. He'd never guess that. 'I'm a twin,' she offered optimistically.

His head snapped around. 'There's another woman like you in the world?'

The genuine appreciation in his eyes flattered her stupidly even as he tried to wipe the evidence of it from his expression. 'Boston, actually. And, no, a brother. Matthew.'

'Twins...' He spent a moment getting his head around that. 'You must be close.'

Ellie frowned. 'I... We used to be. When we were younger. But Matt changed right about the same time I quit dancing. Kind of went underground. Lost his joy. I'm closer to my baby sister, Alex.'

She sighed, thinking about how much easier all of this would be with Alex here. Jed glanced sideways at her, drawn by her sorrow.

'I miss her,' she explained.

'She's back in New York?'

Ellie shook her head. 'Australia. But might as well be the moon for how far she seems.'

'That's tough.'

She smiled at his transparent attempts to identify. 'Says the only child.'

He chuckled. 'I can empathise. Gram's too old to travel much now. I miss her.' His lips tightened briefly. 'So there's just the three of you and your folks?'

'Four.' If you didn't count the Calhouns of which there were also four. 'Charlotte's in the middle.'

'And what's she like?'

Ellie glanced at him again. 'Are you really interested or are you just being polite?'

'I never had—' He frowned. 'Families interest me.'

Ellie's heart squeezed. No siblings, no mother, virtually no father. Family dynamics would be a curiosity.

'Charlotte marches to her own beat. Never tethered by convention. We're very different.' And not always that close because of it. But Charlotte and Matt... Charlotte's lightning-streak intelligence fitted perfectly with Matt's dark thundercloud.

'You walked away from dance. You fought your way back to health in secret and alone from what I can gather. You don't think that was sufficiently outside the square?'

She stared at his profile. 'Do two acts even count in a lifetime of conforming?'

'They do if they're significant enough.'

Maybe she and Charlotte had more in common than she'd thought. 'That's high praise from the man who gave the establishment the finger.'

He thought about that as he took the SUV out onto the highway. 'Don't canonise me just yet, Ellie. It took me a long time to be brave enough to leave New York. I might never have if—'

If…?

'Why did you finally do it?'

His gaze shadowed immediately and his eyes unconsciously went to the rear vision mirror. They drove on in silence.

The incident where Deputy got hurt?

Eventually Jed pulled the SUV back off the highway onto a road that had seen better days. A road with a big Authorised Personnel Only sign on it.

'Do you know where you're going?' she asked.

'I'm authorised. And I'm authorising you.'

They fell back to silence. Blessed silence. Something she'd come to really appreciate about Larkville. And about Jed. Here, no one needed you to fill every waking moment with contribution. Saying nothing was okay. Being in your headspace was okay.

'Wow. The rain's really brought her up.'

Jed craned his neck to see the wetland they were approaching. It sparkled and glittered under the mid-morning sun and small white and black birds flitted across its surface. 'Texas has been in drought for so long, but Hayes County practically sits on top of a deep aquifer and this is one of only a few places it comes to the surface. This soak's usually more marsh than wet-land, though.'

She'd seen evidence of the drought as she'd driven south across the state. Crunchy fields, brown stretches, stock clustered around trucked-in water.

Deputy woke from his back-seat snooze and pressed his nose to the glass. Moments later Jed was hauling his door wide and the dog was out and off, sniffing around the edge of the water.

'It's so pretty,' she breathed.

'Seemed appropriate,' he said. Ellie glanced at him to see if he was making a joke but his eyes weren't on her, they were lost out on the water. As though he didn't even realise he'd spoken.

After a few moments he turned back to her. 'So, two younger sisters and a twin brother. Where does Ellie Patterson fit?'

She took a breath. 'I'm not sure she does.' Or ever did. Accepting that was the key to her eventual recovery. Just as not fitting had been the cause. Only now she had a much better idea of why that was.

'Can I ask you a question?'

He turned.

'Your gram… Have you never thought of bringing

her to Larkville?' He glanced at his feet. 'If she's your only family I imagine you're hers, too?'

His sunglasses shifted slightly as his focus moved up to her eyes. 'All her friends are in the Valley. I wouldn't move her unless I had something for her to come to. Grandkids. More family.'

'You don't consider you're enough?'

His shrug looked uncomfortably tight. 'I work all the time. Why would she want to be here?'

'Because she loves you? She could make friends here, too. Maybe hook up with Gus.'

Jed's laugh startled some nearby birds out onto the water. 'Lord, that's an awful image. The damage that the pair of them could do over a few beers…'

He glanced after Deputy to make sure he was behaving himself in this wild place. Ellie stepped closer to the water. Closer to him.

You shouldn't be alone.

That's what she was trying to get at. Trying hard not to say. Because it was ludicrous she would want to. 'Then maybe you should get onto finding a wife and having some kids. Then you can bring her down. Have all your family together. You're not getting any younger.'

Huh. When had she grown so fond of families?

His eyebrows both rose. 'Uh…'

'I'm not… That's not an offer or anything.' Her laugh was critically tight as heat rushed in. Although suddenly it didn't seem quite so ridiculous. But something in his suddenly wary stance told her it was. Very much so.

Old self-doubt rushed back.

The permanent few lines in his brow doubled and

his hat tipped forward slightly. 'I try not to mix business with pleasure.'

Curiosity beat embarrassment. 'Meaning?'

'Meaning I prefer not to date where I work.'

'Never?'

He shook his head.

Wow. That took some discipline. But how amazingly liberating. To be able to not date if you didn't want to. 'I wish my mother subscribed to that theory. She's so busy trying to marry me off—'

His face snapped around to hers. 'To who?'

'To anyone,' she laughed. 'The highest bidder. Apparently my true worth lies in my Patterson genes.' Except—it suddenly hit her—Fenella Patterson had to know that her oldest daughter didn't carry one single Patterson gene. Maybe that didn't matter when it came to high finance. 'When I quit dance she decided that my only course left in life was to become someone's trophy wife.'

Jed snorted.

'I know. Crazy, right? Unsurprisingly I haven't been all that successful.' She squeezed the words out through a suddenly tight throat.

The sounds of Deputy snuffling around and ducks quacking broke up the awkward silence.

'Ellie…' A warm hand on her shoulder turned her more fully back to him. She hadn't even realised she'd turned away. 'I meant that I couldn't imagine a woman like you settling for being someone's trophy wife.'

Heat spread up her throat. 'Oh.'

'You assumed I was saying I don't think you're worth trophy status? Or attractive enough?'

She forced her eyes away, out to the sparkling blue water. Maybe there'd be a miracle and the aquifer would surge up and wash her away from this excruciating moment.

'Can you literally not see it?' he murmured.

The open honesty in his voice beckoned. Her heart thumped. She slowly brought her gaze back around. 'I spent a really long time doubting every part of myself, Jed. And I know how I must have looked to people back then. It's hard to forget that.' And to forgive herself for letting it happen.

'Back then.' He stepped closer. Removed his sunglasses so that she could drown in his eyes instead of the aquifer. 'You're not that girl any more.'

'I'm still me inside.'

He stopped a foot away. 'Take it from a man who never knew you before a few days ago, Ellie, and who doesn't hold those past images in his head. You are—' he struggled for the right word and her heart thumped harder at the caution in his voice '—arresting. You might have detoured on your path to beautiful but you're unquestionably here now. Has no one ever said that before?'

The back of her shirt collar was fast becoming a furnace.

'Or did you just not believe them?'

She took a breath. 'They would have said anything.'

'You think they were just trying to get into your bed?'

'My bed. My inheritance. My seat on the board of Daddy's company.'

He stared at her. 'Wow. That's a horrible way to live.'

She shrugged.

He stared. And stepped closer.

'So, what happens when a man who isn't interested in your money or your name tells you you're beautiful? Do you believe him?'

'I don't know.' She swallowed, though there was nothing to swallow. 'Words are easy.'

'What if he shows you?' He closed the final inches between them, paused a heart's breath away. 'Would you believe him then?'

Words couldn't come when you had no air. Ellie stared as Jed blazed sincerity down at her and the moment for protest passed. Then he lowered his head, turned it so that his hat wouldn't get in the way and stretched his neck towards her.

'I'm supposed to be staying away from you,' he breathed against her skin.

Her head swam; making sensible words was suddenly impossible. 'Whose idea was that?'

Sensuous lips stretched back over perfect teeth. 'Deputy's.'

All she had to do was shrink back, like she had a hundred times in New York on curbsides, in doorways, under lampposts, in elevators. The good-night moment of truth. Step away, mutter something flippant and flee into the night. But, as Jed's broad silhouette against the midmorning sun bore down on her, both his hands out to the side as he made good on his promise not to touch her, Ellie couldn't bring herself to evade him.

Euphoric lightness filled her before her chest tightened.

She didn't want to escape. She wanted Jed to kiss her. And she wanted to kiss him back.

'What does he know?' she whispered. 'He's just a dog.'

He continued his slow sink, his body twisting forward so that only one part of them was going to touch, his eyes gripping hers the way his hands were careful not to. A tiny breath escaped his lips and brushed hers a bare millisecond before their mouths met.

His lips were soft and strong at the same time. Dry and deliciously moist.

Heat swirled around the only place they made contact, and Ellie's head swam with his scent. His warm touch grew stronger, pressed harder, fixing her to him as though they were glued. She moved her mouth against his, experimenting, tasting. Exploring. He reciprocated, meeting her stretch halfway.

She made the tiniest sound of surprise low in her throat. Her stretch? But, sure enough, she stood tipped forward on her toes using every bit of her ballerina's balance to make sure their lips didn't separate. Jed's breath coming faster excited hers. His lips opened more, nibbling gently, then smiling into the kiss.

She leaned into his strong body.

Initiating contact was as good as giving him permission. Two large hands slipped up and into her hair where it hung over her shoulders, working their way up to the twin combs that kept it neatly back from her face. He slid them free and let her thick hair fall forward over both of them, and he deepened the kiss, his lips and his teeth parting and his tongue joining the discussion.

Ellie's entire body jerked, breaking away from him. Jed's kiss was so much more than she might have imagined but she'd never had someone kiss her like that—never let them—and her body reacted before her head could.

'I'm sorry—'

He didn't seem the slightest bit put-out. Though his pupils were the size of saucers. 'You didn't like it?'

It wasn't really a question. He seemed very clear on the impact his kiss had on her. His own chest was heaving, too. He just wanted her to deny it.

But old habits died too hard. 'I thought you didn't mix business and pleasure?' she hedged, desperately trying to manage the sudden tumult of emotion.

He blew a controlled stream of air through tight lips, getting himself back under full control. Like she should. 'You're from out of state.'

Guilt surged up fast and intense. Technically, yes. Would he have kissed her at all if he knew she was a Calhoun? 'But I'm your customer at the Alamo.'

'Consider this your eviction notice.'

He was having too much trouble getting his breath back for her to take him at all seriously. A rare sensation flooded her body—a rush at having his obvious and intense interest focused on her, and a tingly kind of awe that she wasn't hating it.

On the contrary.

Power surged through her disguised as confidence. She chuckled. 'That won't be necessary. If you're happy to abandon your principles the first time you get a girl next to a romantic lake—'

'Wetland.'

'—then I'm willing to be your accomplice.'

His eyes grew serious. A silent moment passed. 'Can I touch you again, Ellie?'

It was impossible to know where dread finished and anticipation started in the complicated breathlessness that answered.

She forced herself to inhale. 'Depends. What did you have in mind?'

'I'd just…' He frowned. 'I'd like to hold your hand. And just stand here for a little bit.'

Gratitude very nearly expressed itself as tears. Two firsts on the same day. Her first proper, toe-curling kiss, and the first time anyone had asked her permission about her body.

Ellie took a breath and held out a surprisingly steady hand. Jed curled his palm around it and threaded his fingers through hers and let their combined weight sink it down between them. She turned out to stare at the water. So did Jed.

And they stood there.

Like that.

For maybe ten silent minutes.

Jed's steady heat soaked through into Ellie's tense fingers and, bit by bit, her nerves eased, until she could genuinely say she liked it. It was quiet and mutually supportive and—a tiny smile stole across her face—who knew holding hands could be so sensual.

'Would you like to go to a dance tonight?' The words were out before she even realised she'd thought them.

Jed's chin dropped to his chest and he chuckled. 'I've been standing here working my way up to asking you the exact same thing.'

She tossed her loose hair back. 'Snoozers are losers.' Where was this incredible…lightness coming from? Since when did she flirt so unashamedly?

Since now apparently.

'I get to take you to out.' He smiled. 'That's not losing.'

She smiled up at him and fought her body's instinctive desire to protect itself. Like Jed never meeting someone if he didn't go outside of his county, she'd never find the sort of closeness she craved if she didn't lower her shields from time to time.

Clearly this wasn't going to be forever—Jed had basically said so—but she'd been waiting her whole life to feel what she was feeling now. She'd just about given up on it. So she wasn't going to take that for granted.

'You do realise it will involve dancing,' he teased.

'Sarah still owes me line-dancing lessons.' And she would die for a chance to dance with a real Texan sheriff.

'Larkville is an amazing place,' she said softly, her eyes looking out over the water. It was almost as if Larkville Ellie and New York Ellie were different women. Cousins. Maybe she would have grown up to be a totally changed person here, with the Calhouns. A woman with a great relationship with her mother, her siblings. A woman who was free to be wild and crazy if she felt like it. A woman who wasn't at war with her body. Then again, if she had, would she have been available when Jed came strolling into town three years ago? Or would she have hooked up with some cowboy and have a dozen kids and a double mortgage by then?

Meeting him and not being able to have him. Impossible to imagine.

Yet she had no trouble at all imagining herself sitting on a porch rocker with Jed's kids at her hip. It was disturbingly vivid. And most unnatural, for her.

'I'm so glad I met you.'

There. It was said. Six short little words but they communicated so much.

She extracted her hand from his under the pretense of finding a stick to throw for Deputy. He exploded into ecstatic life and bounded after it, before bringing it back to her on wet paws. She threw it again. In her periphery she saw the shadow pass over Jed's angular features before he masked it.

Ellie Patterson—Ellie Calhoun—was a work in progress and she had been since she first started to get well. If Jed couldn't deal with baby steps, then he wasn't the man she thought he was.

The man she secretly hoped he really was.

The man that was going to be hard to top when she went back to New York.

Assuming she went back at all.

It all rested on how Jess and her other siblings felt about her arrival. But they contacted her; they invited her down to the memorial festival for Clay Calhoun.

They opened the door to her and Matt becoming a part of their family.

But what if that was just a one-off, 'love to see you at the festival but then go on back to New York' kind of thing? What if she'd badly misinterpreted Jess's letter. There was a big difference between 'come visit' and 'come stay.'

She glanced at Jed as he got into the throwing game with Deputy and chewed her lip. Of course, staying and being a Calhoun would kill any chance of something more happening with Sheriff Never-Mix-Business-with-Pleasure. But there wasn't a whole lot she could do about it now. That die was cast the moment she got in her rental car and headed south out of New York.

Actually, it was cast thirty years ago when her mother first did.

Her stomach sank. Mind you, not staying was going to do the same thing. Jed left New York far behind him three years ago.

There was something just a little bit tragic about the haste with which her body accepted that she might have to walk away from Jed. Like it was conditioned to being denied.

There was only one way to fix that.

She glanced at the strong back and shoulders playing tug of war with one-hundred-plus pounds of dog and wondered if she had the courage.

He wasn't promising forever but he could change her life for now. They had two more weeks.

And 'for now' started this evening at the Larkville Cattleman's Association mixer.

* * *

It was just like something she might have seen on a movie. Or a Texan postcard. The residents of Larkville tricked up in their newest stetsons, their shiniest boots and their tightest jeans. Little miniature cowboys and Miss Junior Corn Queen wannabes running around between the legs of the bigger, adult versions and the rest perched on hay bales stacked around the old hall. Chatting. Laughing.

Pointing.

She was a bit of a spectacle since she'd arrived with Jed who, it seemed, was generally spectacle enough himself—at least with the women present—but no one looked so surprised that she believed her arrival was totally unheralded.

Clearly the gossip vine had done its job.

On walking in, Jed went straight into public-officer mode, greeting people, asking about their barn conversions and their heavy-equipment licenses and their wayward teenage sons, and Ellie trailed politely alongside smiling and nodding and shaking hands just as she had at so many New York events. She was well accustomed to arrival niceties with strangers and to being the one everyone showed interest in—a Patterson at their party—so the speculation she was fielding from all angles didn't really faze her.

But it bothered Jed.

It took her some time to register the way his spine seemed to ratchet one notch tighter every time someone asked for an introduction or every time they didn't ask but their badly disguised curiosity drifted to her.

Jed's lips tightened as another beaming face made a beeline for them.

She couldn't hide her chuckle. 'I'll get you a drink.'

Whether he wanted one or not, she knew from personal experience that one's fingers couldn't twist with anxiety while they were otherwise occupied negotiating a glass. In his case, maybe holding a beer would allay those tense fists he was making and releasing down by his denim-covered thighs.

The Starlight Room in New York or a Cattlemen's Hall in Texas, people were people no matter what zip code they came from. There was one sure way to end all the speculation... Feed the beast.

She put on her game face and marched straight up to the bar, faking it one hundred per cent.

'What can I get you, darlin'?'

She threw a blinding smile at the man behind the bar and earned herself a slightly dazzled expression in return. 'Hi, I'm Ellie Patterson. Can I have a sparkling water please? And a light beer for the sheriff.'

Within minutes the whole place would know who she was, that she wasn't cowed by the pointing, she wasn't going to get drunk and do something scandalous, and that she was here—officially—with their sheriff. For some reason all those things felt enormously important to get settled straight up.

Especially the last one.

Her eyes went to Jed through the crowd and she could tell by his rigid posture that things weren't improving. Sure enough, two pairs of eyes flicked her way for a heartbeat. Only one pair looked comfortable.

She made herself smile at them and then turned casually back to the barman who was finishing up her order. These people might find out later that she was a Calhoun and so she wanted their first impression of her to be a worthy one. And if Jed was having some kind of change of heart about coming here tonight...

His problem.

'Miss Patterson...' The man slid her two drinks and a few bills. From darlin' to miss in twenty seconds. Mission accomplished. She slid the considerable change straight back to him and earned herself his loyalty as well as his appreciation.

'Ellie!'

Sarah! 'Thank goodness,' she muttered under her breath. Just because she was used to living life under the microscope didn't mean a moment's relief from it wasn't welcome. She leaned in for an air kiss.

'Forget that, Ellie, you're in Texas now.'

Two slim arms were around her, hugging hard, before she even had time to think about what was about to happen. The air left her in a rush. But Sarah looked completely unaffected when she pulled back and launched straight into a run-down of what they'd missed in the half-hour since the dance started and the progress she'd made on planning the Fall Festival. Most of it meant nothing, in fact most of it washed right over her because she was so busy concentrating on how very pleasant that hug had felt and how very little the universe had imploded because of it.

Maybe she was as normal as anyone else now. If she let herself be.

The novelty of that stole her breath.

'I'm so glad you came. I have an agreement to make good on. Line-dancing lessons in exchange for your event-management services.'

Ellie tuned back in fully. 'I was a dancer for ten years, Sarah,' she confessed belatedly, and wished she'd just said it back when it was first suggested. 'Ballet.'

Sarah took the surprise in her stride. 'Ballet? Pfff... you don't know what dancing is, woman! Come on.' She dragged Ellie by the forearm across the room where Jed now stood talking to an elegant woman. 'Excuse us, Mayor Hollis,' Sarah interrupted brightly. 'We need to borrow the sheriff for a bit.'

Jed immediately turned his focus on to Ellie. 'Mayor, this is Eleanor Patterson visiting from New York City. Ellie, Mayor Johanna Hollis.'

Ellie knew how this went. She passed Jed his beer and reached her free hand forward. 'Mayor, I've been enjoying your town very much.'

The mayor knew how it went, too. Her smile was professional but tight enough to suggest she thought she was being patronised by the city slicker. 'Thank you, Eleanor. We're very proud of it.'

That should have been it—niceties exchanged—but Ellie felt a burning need to make sure Johanna Hollis knew she meant it. 'I've been reading up on the architecture in this part of Texas. You have some amazing stone facades still standing. I gather not all towns are as committed to retention as Larkville is?'

A different light blinked to life in Mayor Hollis's eyes. And in Jed's. 'No—' she turned more fully towards Ellie '—you would not believe how hard it is to convince people to maintain our heritage...'

The mayor warmed to her topic and Sarah was momentarily distracted off to one side. Ellie specifically ignored Jed's eyes burning into her in favor of showing the mayor her courtesy.

'Sheriff,' Mayor Hollis finally started when the conversation about Larkville's masonry frontages drew to a comfortable close. She turned a smile on him that was four parts maternal concern and one part admiration. 'I'm so pleased you've found yourself such a lovely and informed lady. I was beginning to despair for you ever settling down.'

Jed disguised his discomfort behind taking a sip of beer. Ellie only noticed because she'd had her share of that awful, neutral expression in the week she'd known him and she'd already learned to read the tight discipline of his muscles.

'Sarah,' he ground past his rigid jaw, ignoring the comment entirely and drawing his friend's focus back to them. 'Did you want something when you came over?'

'Yes! I need you and Ellie. Time for those dancing lessons I promised. I'll see you out there.' She snaffled the mayor's attention on the subject of the Fall Festival and the two of them turned away.

Jed actually glanced around for escape.

Okay...

Ellie placed her half-drunk sparkling water next to Jed's barely touched beer on a sideboard and touched his arm. He pulled it away carefully. But she toughed it out and found his eyes. 'You've never been seen in public with a date, Jed. Did you not expect a level of community interest?'

Or should she be flattered that he'd wanted her here enough not to be swayed by that?

'It's not their interest that concerns me...'

'Then, what?'

Emotion warred behind cautious eyes. 'People think we're together.'

She straightened. 'We are together.'

His frown was immediate. 'We're together, but not...' She lifted her eyebrows as he floundered, but stayed silent. 'You know... Together.'

'Jed—'

'You were practically working up a platform for public office with the mayor just then with all the talk about preserving Larkville's heritage. What message does that send?'

She glared at him. 'It says I have good manners. Not that I'm hunting for real estate.'

Dark conflict ghosted across his eyes. Her mind served up an action replay of every single instance that he'd taken such care to introduce her as just visiting. Tonight. Before tonight. And right behind that was the realisation that the only particularly public thing they'd done was walk a dog and have pancakes. As though by being private he couldn't be held accountable for what else happened between them.

'What are you really worried about, Jed?' She frowned. 'That they might think there's more to our relationship or that I might?'

Frustration hissed out of him. 'Ellie...'

But she knew she was on to something. Every single one of her insecurities triggered, but if she gave in to the fear she'd never let herself feel like this again. So she tossed her hair back and echoed the smile she'd given the barman. Every bit as bright and every bit as fake.

'They're just curious, Jed, they're not queuing up to witness a marriage certificate. Lighten up. Dance. The next time you bring a woman to a mixer—' she took a deep breath at the unfairness of having to say that '—it will barely cause a ripple.'

His eyes lifted long enough for her to spot the doubt resident there. He sighed, but he couldn't keep the tension out of his voice.

'You're right. I'm sorry. Let's dance.'

Line dancing was much harder than it looked from the outside. Even for someone trained in movement. It took Ellie a few minutes to get used to the requirement to anticipate the steps so that they finished on the beat instead of starting on it—more military than musical—but, before long, the repetition and string of steps started to feel pretty natural.

She was pleased that it was a non-contact sport on the whole because touching Jed right now was not high on her wanted list, not while she was still so fresh from his overreaction to the mere thought of being connected with her. Men would have fallen over themselves for that impression back home.

Not that he was most men. If he was she wouldn't be in this position.

'Well, darn,' Sarah said over the music from right

next to her. 'You're a natural. Looks like I'll have to find something else to trade you for your time.'

The best part of ballet for her had always been choreography—building complicated dance sequences from established balletic steps. Line dancing was the same in principle. Even dancing in file didn't feel that foreign; she was well used to the ranks of the corps.

Jed moved in perfect sync with everyone else who clearly knew this music a whole lot better than she did. Not flashy but not awkward, either. Just...proficient. And perfectly in time. Exaggerated swagger in his steps, and more hip sway than was healthy for her already-straining lungs.

She glanced at him sideways.

He was watching her move. Both of them trying so hard not to look too interested in the other. She made herself remember that she was mad.

Her cheeks warmed with exertion and her heart thumped steadily. Much more of a workout than she might have imagined. Around them, people whooped and clapped and threw in the occasional 'yee-haw' as they danced, but Ellie's focus kept drifting back to Jed's eyes.

He may be incomprehensible at times but he was still just as attractive and intelligent as the man she'd kissed just hours before. She dropped her lashes and smiled, concentrating on the movement of his feet to stop her losing her place.

And possibly her heart.

They danced like that—ignoring each other and becoming increasingly aware of each other for it—for thirty minutes straight. But it flew past. At last, the band slowed the pace up onstage. Sarah turned to her from her other side as everyone clapped and started moving off.

'I'm going for a drink,' she panted. 'Be right back.'

Ellie's feet went to follow but she was stopped by a warm hand on her forearm. 'Dance, Ellie?'

Jed never dances. Sarah's words echoed in her mind.

Her heart, only just beginning to settle, lurched back into a breathless pattering. There was an apology in his deep brown depths and more than a little regret. It made her breast even tighter.

'We just did.'

He pulled her gently towards him. 'Oh, no, that was fun but…this…is dancing.' He stepped in close and slid one arm slowly around her waist, giving her time to get used to his touch. Around them, others did the same.

'Won't this just draw more attention to us?'

'That horse has bolted.' He smiled, pulling her closer. 'Right about the time you started moving to the music.'

In heels she would have been eye to eye with him. Pity she'd kicked her shoes off once the line dancing hit full speed. As it was, she had to lift her eyes slightly to see into his. She stared at his chin instead, though it was disturbingly close to his full bottom lip. Her breath caught.

'What dance is this?' she asked, as if that made the slightest difference to whether or not she wanted to be back in his arms.

'Texas slow dance.' The way he said it…with that tiny curl in his voice. He made it sound sinful.

Their neighbors shuffled left and right, some glued

together like teenagers, some father-daughter pairs with little pink-pumped feet balanced on their fathers' boots, others with a respectful, first-public-dance distance.

Like theirs should have been.

Jed pulled her into him and lifted one of her hands up to his neck. The other he collected in his big palm and threaded his fingers through hers. The arm around her lower back tightened.

'Relax,' he murmured into her hair. Then his feet started moving.

A middle-aged woman who'd stepped up with the band started crooning the lyrics to 'Cry Me a River.' Slow and sensual. Deep and moving. She looked like she tossed hay bales by day. It was amazing the secrets some people had.

Maybe Ellie didn't hold them all herself.

Her muscles loosened in increments as Jed swayed her from side to side, and she did her best to anticipate his moves.

'Let me lead, Ellie.' Soft and low against her ear. 'Let go.'

Letting go meant so much more to her than he knew. He was asking her to undo the habits of a lifetime. The fears and hurts. But if there was a man to be holding her up while she let go, Jed was it.

She let herself be distracted by the feel of his denim thighs brushing against her soft skirt, by all the places she fitted neatly into him. Their bodies constantly rubbing.

'That's a girl.' He grinned. 'You might even start to enjoy it.'

His gentle words teased an answering smile out of her. She let herself lean into him a tiny bit more.

Jed led Ellie around and around in a small arc, taking care not to dance her into anyone else, to protect her from the accidental physical contact he knew would rip her out of the happy place she was slipping into.

Synchronised. Swaying. Lids low. Breath heavy.

In fact, every part of him felt heavy—lethargic yet excited at the same time. Somewhere at the back of his mind he knew he should be worrying about what message this might send her but, right now, his world began and ended with the woman in his arms. He'd sort the rest out later.

'How are you doing?' he murmured.

'Mmm…'

She was practically asleep in his arms. On Ellie, that was a good thing. It meant she trusted him. Enough to drop her guard and let herself relax. Be mortal.

He hadn't planned on creating a dance-floor sensation tonight. He'd planned on keeping his separation of the six-degree variety for both their benefit. Ellie didn't need her emerging awareness trampled all over by a man with no intention of honouring it the way it should be. But somewhere between 'God Bless Texas' and 'Cactus Star' her energy and presence affected him in a way he was still scrabbling to understand. It wasn't just the catlike movement of her long body—although that undoubtedly drew the attention of more than one male in the room—and it certainly wasn't the high-energy, synchronised moves. That only got him thinking of all the other ways the two of them could be synchronised.

It was her focus. Her determination to do the best job she could, even at something as ridiculous as line dancing.

Ellie Patterson had a big, flashing perfectionist gene. And an equal part of him responded to that. He found capability pretty attractive. It was right up there with intelligence and compassion on his list of must-haves. And Ellie had all three in multiples.

All the more reason to stay the heck away from her.

'Ellie?'

Thanks for the dance, Ellie...

There's someone I need to speak to...

If you'll excuse me...

'Mmm?' Her head was nestled in right next to his now, and the warm brush of air from her barely formed response teased the hairs on his neck. Excited them.

'The band's taken a break,' he whispered. It was the best he could manage just then, though he knew he should have been walking away. Fast. Her head lifted enough to turn towards the now-empty stage and then her eyes tracked the band members making their way towards the bar.

'Oh...' She straightened awkwardly and he hated being the trigger for the return of carefully controlled Ellie. A deep something protested with a rush of sensation that tightened his hold.

'Or we could just stay here, dancing.' Drowning.

Her head lifted fully. Her skin flushed. The space between them increased. 'No... I could use a drink.'

He crossed with her back to where their drinks still waited, warmer and flatter now, loath to let her go but so aware of how many curious eyes were trained on them again following their slow dance. He kept a gentle hand at her back to let her know he was there, and to let everyone watching know anyone messing with her was messing with him. Even that felt like a mistake. But it stayed glued there of its own accord.

She paused to slide her heels back on and somehow that act signaled the end of relaxed, free Ellie.

He wasn't ready for that to happen.

'We should get going.' The words were out before he thought about what they meant.

She turned to look at him. 'Already?'

'You want to stay?' The question was so very loaded, she'd have to be blind to miss it. He wanted her out of this crowded fishbowl. To get her alone somewhere that they could talk, get to know each other.

God help him.

She stared at him, weighing up her options. 'No,' she breathed. 'I don't.'

It took fifteen long minutes to edge their way around to the exit, making polite conversation all the way. The departure conversations were more excruciating than the arrival ones because there wasn't a person there who had missed the floor show he'd just put on and he knew he'd set himself up for that. Ellie departed first, ostensibly to use the restroom, but on completion there she turned left instead of right and was gone. He gave it a few more minutes, for appearance's sake, and then followed her out to his truck. Fooling no one, probably, but at least he'd made an effort to protect her privacy.

He knew his own was already lost. But that was a

small price to pay for moments more of the heaven he'd felt on that dance floor.

'Hey,' she said as he tumbled into the driver's seat, her eyes vivid in the moonlight. 'Thought you might have got snared again.'

There was only one person he was ensnared by. He turned to her, not prepared to make polite small talk. If he was going to hell he didn't want to waste a moment. 'Ready?'

'Yup.'

Home was a two-minute drive. Deputy was ecstatic that they were home so early and only took a further minute to dash outside and lift his leg against the nearest cypress tree. Jed used the time to throw another log on the dwindling fire.

'I feel like I've missed so much of normal life,' Ellie mused from the shadows. Her arms wrapped around her even though the cottage was warm.

'What do you mean?'

'I didn't go to my first party until I was twenty-two and that was a full-on New York soiree. To represent the family.'

He lowered his long body into the sofa, trying hard not to look as desperate as he felt. Trying hard not to feel it. 'Nothing before that? At all?'

'Not a party. Not a celebration. The occasional end-of-season dance after-party but they tended to be serious kinds of affairs. Lots of sitting around being introspective and deep. Most people had to be up early for rehearsals on the next performance. I was always studying.' She uncrossed her arms. 'So this was my first hoedown.'

He chuckled. 'It wasn't a hoedown. But it was fun. Did you enjoy yourself?'

She studied him across the space and he couldn't have been more aware of how not close she was keeping herself. But at least she smiled. 'I think I did.'

He struggled for easy conversation, to take her mind off the fact they were alone in his house with a bed just a few feet above them. 'Why did you work so hard as a kid? Dancing. Studying.'

Confusion riddled her voice. 'To be good at it. To get good grades.'

'Did you need good grades to be a dancer?'

She frowned. 'Not especially. I guess I wanted…a fallback.'

'In case you didn't make it?'

'My parents had expectations.'

'They expected you to have good grades?'

'They expected me to work hard. I wanted to have good grades.'

'Why?'

Her frustration showed in the flap of her hands. 'Because that was what I did. I was good at things. Why the inquisition?'

He kept his cool, stayed reclined, relaxed. Though what he really wanted to do was drag her out of the shadows into the furnace of the fire. Of his arms. He regretted drawing her attention to the absent band back in the dance hall. They might still be entwined now if he hadn't spoken. 'Just trying to decide who you wanted to prove something to.'

'No one.' It was too immediate. Too practiced. Her eyes flickered. She waited a moment and then whispered, 'Me…maybe. I just wanted to do well.'

'What would have happened if you hadn't?' he asked.

'They would have been disappointed. So would I.'

'They wouldn't have loved you anyway?'

She inched closer to him. To the fire. Eventually she perched carefully on the very end of the sofa. She pressed her hands in her lap. 'Let me paint you a picture. When I was twenty-one, a couple of days after I resigned from the company, I heard my mother talking to my father, bemoaning how I'd shown such promise earlier in my life.'

Jed's stomach squeezed in sympathy. 'Past tense? Ouch.'

'They never would have verbalised it but I felt that expectation my whole life. Mostly coming from my mother. The necessity to prove myself. To earn my place in the family through excellence.'

'You didn't have to earn it, you had a birthright.'

'I was a fraud.' Sorrow saturated her features.

It was his turn to frown.

'I was Eleanor. The capable one. The flawless one.' She looked at him. 'It's what they wanted to see.'

'You're not a fraud, Ellie—'

She turned pained eyes to him. 'I'm not a Patterson.'

He sat up straighter. 'What?'

'My mother was already pregnant when she met

my—' She pressed her lips together. 'When she met Cedric Patterson.'

Hurt for her washed through him. There was nothing he could say to that.

'I felt so vindicated the day I found out—that all those feelings I had weren't just neuroses. There was a reason I felt like I didn't belong.' Her bitter laugh betrayed the tears thickening her words. 'Because I didn't.'

He was up in a heartbeat, scooting along the sofa and gathering her into his arms. She came willingly. 'No, Ellie...'

'I was so angry with her, Jed. I'd been through so much, struggled alone for so many years because she made it clear that failure wasn't an option. Just in me and Matt. Nobody else. Not Alex. Not Charlotte.' She shook her head. 'Maybe she thought he'd renounce us the first time we made a mistake.'

'Was your father that kind of man?'

She was silent for a moment. 'She must have feared he was.'

He paused, wondering how much of this scab to scratch off. 'Did he know?'

He felt her nod against his shoulder. 'Always. Two little cuckoos in his nest.'

'Ellie...' He turned her chin up to look her in the eye. It broke his heart to see them full of tears. It made him want to wrap her in his arms and protect her forever.

Forever?

The intensity of that shook him. He pulled back a little. 'He chose you. To raise you and to love you.'

Her shrug was sharp. 'We were a package deal. He wanted my mother.'

Compassion settled in his gut. Who was he to say what motivated Cedric Patterson or didn't, or what kind of a father he'd been to Ellie? What experience did he really have with parents? Ellie was the one who'd had to live the life, deal with it as best she could.

And it had nearly ruined her.

'I guess I understand, then, why you feel such an intense need to control things.'

'I don't.' But it was so patently ridiculous even her own protest was half-hearted.

'Then why aren't we naked in front of that fire right now?' He needed to shock some life into those suddenly dead eyes. It worked, two green-tinged blue diamonds flicked up to him. Heat flooded her cheeks. But she'd been nothing but honest with him since they'd met.

'That's not about…control…exactly.'

Sure it was. 'Then what's it about?'

She smiled, a poignant sort of half effort. 'I'm not sure you appreciate how rare it is for me to feel this way.'

He narrowed his eyes, a stone forming in his gut. 'What way?'

'Attracted. Comfortable.' She took a deep breath and twisted upright against him. She locked gazes with his, though there was fear behind the bold words. 'Desirable.'

Chemistry whooshed around them but it tripped and tumbled over heavy boulders of reality. Ellie wasn't like other women. She didn't operate on the same plane as everyone else. She had no real experience with men, from what he could gather, yet here he was offering her a good time but not a long time.

Jerk.

Yet beneath all the chivalry, a really primal part of him tipped his head back and howled that she trusted him with her soul and her body. Could he really walk away from that?

Regardless of whether or not he was worthy of it.

He shut that part of him down and refused to look closer. 'Ellie… You know what you're saying? Is this something you really want to do?'

She met his eyes. 'I'm thirty years old, Jed. Old enough to make my own decisions. I'm ready.'

He knew he was. He'd been ready from the moment he met her out on the road to the Calhoun ranch.

He settled her more comfortably against him and cupped both sides of her face, staring into her eyes intently. They sparkled with provocativeness and defiance. So much so he almost bought it. But her own words echoed in his head in the half a heartbeat before he let his lips touch hers.

'Fraud,' he breathed against her lips. 'You're terrified.' She was nowhere near okay with this.

'A little.' Her eyes smiled where her lips couldn't. 'But I feel safe being terrified with you.'

Unfamiliar emotion crowded in, wanting to awaken her and protect her at the same time. He knuckled a loose thread of hair away from her face. 'I don't want to hurt you, Ellie.'

And he would. Because that's what he did. He couldn't be trusted with hearts.

She lifted her face. A dozen thoughts flickered across her expression and he wasn't quick enough to grasp any of them. 'I don't want to be like this forever.'

'Like what?'

She stared at him, long and silent. Then finally she whispered, 'Broken.'

Compassion flooded up from that place down deep he wouldn't look, washing away any hope of him doing the rational, sensible, smart thing. Part of him rebelled against that, stormed at him that healing her was not his job, that it was not conducive to the kind of short and sharp relationship he wanted. But the primal part shoved past those concerns and spoke directly to his soul.

Ellie needed him. Ellie wanted him.

And he wanted her.

He wasn't a fool. He knew tonight wouldn't be the night that he really got to know her. And he didn't want it to be. With Ellie he wanted to take it slow.

They mightn't have long but they could make it count.

The raging, warning part of him slammed itself against the casing of the box he kept it in way down deep. He ignored it. There were a dozen reasons this was a bad idea but, for the life of him, he couldn't think of one strong enough to stop the motion of his body as he swung his legs off the sofa and pulled her upright with him.

For some reason—despite everything that happened in New York with Maggie and despite the kind of man he was—he'd been gifted this beautiful woman and her courageous soul.

He wasn't going to throw the opportunity away.

Ellie saw the decision in Jed's gaze the moment he made it and the reality of what she was about to do hit her in a flurry of sharp nerves. She swallowed hard. 'How do we…start?'

His fingers against her jaw eased some of the flurries. 'What about where we left off?' he breathed.

Already she was half hypnotised by the new intensity in his heated gaze. The hunger. 'The dance or the lake?'

'The best parts of both.' He took three steps towards the fire. Then he pulled her into his arms for another slow dance.

She tipped her face up. 'We have no music.' It was a pathetic attempt to head off the inevitable, even if she wanted it. And she really, really did.

His eyes softened. 'Let go, Ellie. We'll dance to the rhythm of the fire.'

And so they did, shuffling left and right in the cozy space between the stove and the sofa. Jed trailed his fingers up and removed her combs, freeing a tumble of hair. She let herself enjoy the sensuality and anticipate his next touch.

'Okay?'

Her heart pounded against her ribs. She nodded.

On they danced, Ellie sliding her arms around his waist and curling her nervous hands into his shirt. His fingers travelled up and down her spine, stroking her once again into the comfortable place she'd been back at the dance.

It didn't take long.

Warm breath teased her jaw, her neck, as his lips dragged back and forth across her blazing skin. She leaned into his caress and slid one hand up under his hair, then—finally—turned her face towards his.

Their blind lips sought each other out.

And then they were kissing. Soft, sweet. Hot, hungry. Slow, lazy. Every part of her body throbbed with a mix of uncertainty and yearning. Sensory overload. Jed's strong arms kept her safe and created a place where she could explore and discover without fear. Desire washed through her starved cells, fast and tumbling.

He breathed her air and fed her in return. She felt the hammer of his heart against her own chest and knew it wasn't uncertainty, like hers. It was passion.

Jed wanted her. And he cared enough to take it slow.

He cared.

Guilt shoved its way up and into her consciousness just as he slid his hand around to her ribs so that his thumb sat just below her breast. Her skin tingled then burned where his skin branded hers. She tried to focus on the new sensations he brought.

Then his thumb brushed across the tip of one breast.

'Wait…' Ellie tore her lips from his. 'Just wait…'

His breathing was as strained as hers. 'Too fast?'

'I need to—' she stepped back and pressed her fingers to her sternum '—I need a moment.'

'It's okay, Ellie. Take your time.'

Distress tumbled through her. He was being so kind. 'No. Not that. There's something I need to… Before we go any further.'

She had to tell him. She should have already told him. A dozen times.

He collected her frantic hands and brought them together, in his. 'Take it easy, Ellie.'

'I need to be honest with you, Jed. I owe you that.'

It was such a risk. She knew how he felt about—

'Honest about what?'

She stared at him, wide-eyed. Her feet tipped on the very edge of no return. 'Ask me who my father is.'

He blew out a strained breath. 'Unless you're about to tell me that we're actually related, I really can't see how—'

'Ask me, Jed!'

Her bark shut him up. He stared at her, his mind whirring visibly amidst the confusion in his eyes. He took a deep breath. 'Who is your real father, Ellie?'

She stared at him, sorrow leaking from every pore. Wondering if she was throwing away any chance of ever feeling normal again. Wondering if she was throwing away her only chance at happiness.

But knowing she must.

She took a breath. And told him.

Chapter 10

Deputy slamming full into him couldn't have done a better job at knocking the air clean out of Jed's body. He stood, frozen, and stared at her.

'You're a Calhoun?'

'It's why I'm here in Larkville,' she whispered.

Visiting Jess. He'd not let himself quiz her further on that once he got to know her. It was none of his business then. But now...

'You're a Calhoun.'

He stepped back, a deep, sick realisation growing in his gut. She was here to meet them. He knew the Calhouns; there was no way they wouldn't ask her to stay, to bring her into their care. He regulated his breathing to manage the roar building up inside him.

She'd say yes; why wouldn't she? He'd never met

a woman crying out more strongly for somewhere to belong.

She'd say yes and she'd never go back to New York.

'I wanted you to know, before we—' Ellie swallowed '—went any further.'

Further? His body screamed. He'd gone quite far enough. Yet nowhere near where he wanted to be. He lifted his eyes and stared at her. 'I thought you were only here for a few weeks.'

Her face pinched. 'I know.'

'But you waited until now to tell me?'

'I didn't know if…this morning was a one-off, an accident…'

'You think my tongue just fell into your mouth?'

She winced at his crude snipe. 'I'm sorry that you're shocked but it wasn't my secret to tell.'

'So why tell it now?'

'Because we were about to…'

'What?' Do something irretrievable?

'Go further,' she whispered.

He searched around for something to hang his anger on rather than hating himself for being stupid enough to let this happen. He knew how hard she was searching for something more meaningful in her life. Yet he'd let himself want her anyway. To need her. And that scared the hell out of him. 'You could have told me this morning. At the dance. Any time before this.'

On some level he knew he should be grateful she spoke up now and not even later. But he just wasn't capable of more than a raging kind of grief. Ellie was a

Calhoun. That meant she wasn't just passing through; she was about as forever as it came.

Her colour drained more. 'Yes. I should have.'

His snort damned her. 'You think?'

It was her wince and Deputy's quick slink away around behind the sofa that told him his voice was too loud. His anger was really disproportionate to what she was supposed to be to him—a casual thing—but it was burbling up from deep inside him just like the soak did from the aquifer.

Confusion only made him madder. 'That's it, then. We're done.'

The pale shock left Ellie's skin, pushed aside by her own angry flush. 'Why? Why does it make any difference to us now? Either way I'm out of your life in a week.'

'You're part of my town's biggest and most influential family. You couldn't be more off-limits to me.' He clung to that like a lifeline. It was better than risking exposing the truth.

'Why? Just because of your rule…?'

Her pain burned him harder the more he tried to ignore his body's response to it. She had no idea what she was stumbling towards. 'My values, Ellie.'

She frowned, half confusion, half distress. 'I thought…'

He threw his hands up, frustration eating at the body that just moments ago was humming with sudden and long-absent life. 'What? That you were different? Special?'

Her gasp was like a reverse gunshot.

She did—he could see it in the hurt awakening in her eyes. She thought he might make an exception for her. For them. She didn't understand that it was bigger than whether or not he wanted to make an exception.

Deputy peered out from behind the sofa at the sudden silence, the whites of his eyes betraying his anxiety.

'You know how big a deal this was for me, Jed,' she whispered. 'To get myself to this point.'

Shame gnawed hard and low. But so did the raging frustration of who she was. And what that meant. And the fact she'd effectively lied to him. He flung open the door to the stove and stabbed at the crumbling coals.

But this wasn't really about her keeping secrets. This was about grief. His grief that Ellie was now so thoroughly and permanently out of the question. There was no way he was risking her in any way. And since he couldn't be trusted…

His body screamed at the denial and his soul echoed it softly.

That betrayal of his own heart outraged him even more.

He didn't want to look into her eyes and see the growing emotion there, her growing connection. The dream of the cartload of kids they'd have tumbling over a greying Deputy or Ellie grown round and healthy with new life inside her. Even if secretly—desperately—he did.

He'd been down this road before and it didn't lead anywhere good. A woman wanting more. A man wanting less.

He needed her to walk away. Fast. And she wasn't going to do that unassisted.

He mentally brought out a revolver.

'Why did you tell me now?' he gritted, loading an emotional bullet into the barrel.

'Because it was the right thing to do,' she whispered.

'It was the safe thing to do.' He loaded another for good measure. 'That way you wouldn't have to step outside of your comfort zone at all. When things got heavy.'

'Jed—'

Her chest rose and fell faster and he forced himself to forget how the curve of that flesh had felt under his fingers just moments ago. Soft and innocent. Vulnerable.

He'd betrayed someone else's vulnerability once…

Her eyes glittered dangerously. 'Why are you being like this? After everything I told you, did you seriously imagine that my past wouldn't still raise its head? It's going to take some time—'

'We never had time, Ellie.' He spun the barrel and snapped it into place. 'That's what you didn't understand.'

'I know. But it's a start.'

'The start of what?'

Confusion bled from her beautiful eyes.

His voice dropped. His pulse throbbed in the lips that were about to hurt her so badly. 'What we were about to start would mean more to you than any other woman I know.'

Her nod was barely perceptible.

'That's not something you'd do lightly. Yet you were willing to do it, with me, for just a few short days?'

'I… Yes.'

'Because you hoped for more?'

'No. You've been very clear.'

Liar. He could see the hope even now, shining brave and bright. And terrible. She wanted more. 'Then, why?'

Her entire body stiffened. 'Because I thought that it might just be the only chance I ever have. To feel like this. I wasn't going to give that up.'

Her only chance. Forever? The responsibility of that pressed its force outward from the dark place inside. He didn't do forever.

He lifted the emotional gun and fought to keep his hands steady.

'Right man, the right conditions,' she went on. 'I can't imagine that happening again. Not for me.'

Anxiety twisted up live inside him. 'What conditions?' What was she expecting?

Ellie's arms crossed her body. 'Trust. Patience. Commitment.'

Panic tore its way out of that box deep down inside. Somewhere distant—far, far away from its angry tirade—he knew that she didn't deserve this. But he couldn't stop it.

He lined her up in his sights. 'I haven't offered you a commitment.'

'I know. You've been painfully clear.' Her voice thickened. 'Why is that?'

She was going to fight back. Intense pride warred with disbelief, but he pushed it away. 'Commitment doesn't come on tap, Ellie. I have to feel it.'

Her face blanched and those slim arms tightened around her torso, steeling herself for the blow. 'You don't feel anything?'

'I feel something.' He wouldn't lie to her but he wouldn't string her along, either. He was no one's Prince Charming. It didn't matter how much he felt. Nothing good could come of her wanting him. 'But it was never going to be happy ever after.'

She withered before his eyes and breathed, 'Is that so inconceivable?'

And there it was.

The disappointed awakening. Hope dashed. Fear realised. Heart broken.

All the things he was best at. Self-loathing burned in his gut. 'I know myself, Ellie. I'm not the committing type.'

'Ten days ago I wouldn't have said I was the kissing type. Yet here we are.'

Did she need it spelled out? He disengaged the safety on the gun she had no idea she was facing. 'I don't do commitment, Ellie.'

'You've committed to Deputy. To Larkville,' she argued, holding her own. 'So you're clearly capable of it. Is it just women?'

Ready...

'Don't do this, Ellie.'

'Why not? My flaws are so clearly up for discussion, why can't yours be?' She tossed her hair back.

Aim...

'Look, we gave it a shot, it didn't work out. It happens.'

She clenched her jaw and locked eyes with him. 'I imagine it happens to you a lot.'

His finger trembled on the trigger. 'What's that supposed to mean?'

Deputy dropped his snout flat to the floor and cast anxious eyes at them both, whining, as Ellie gave as good as she got.

'It means that limiting yourself to meeting women outside of the county when you have no intention of going out of it is a convenient way to ensure that no relationship is ever going to work out, don't you think?'

She was fighting for her life and—God help him— he was starting to fold. He urgently fortified his resolve. The more she fought him the more he was going to hurt her.

'You have a problem committing to women,' she cried. 'Just admit it and let's deal with it.'

He closed his eyes. 'Why does it have to be a problem? Why can't it just be because I don't want you?'

...*Fire.*

Her sharp intake of air was the only clue that he'd struck her way, way down deep. Where she was the most raw and exposed.

A prideful woman would have walked out. A bitter woman would have railed at him. A vengeful woman would have struck back. But Ellie just lifted her chin, to hide the devastation at the back of her defiant eyes.

'Is that true?'

Self-disgust burned and he spun away tossing the useless gun far away. 'We've shared a few kisses, Ellie. And now you're asking me for a commitment. That's not normal.'

Silence stretched out.

And out.

Deputy crawled closer to them on his belly.

Not normal.

Ellie had to make herself breathe. Jed probably had no idea how much more that last accusation hurt than any of the other things he'd said since this beautiful evening started to go so very, very wrong. All she ever wanted was to function like everyone else. To love and be loved just like everyone else.

Was that really so much to ask?

But she wasn't like everyone else. She was all back to front. She needed the trust and respect and surety of a man before she could even do the simple things that usually fostered trust and respect and assurances.

Like hand-holding.

Kissing.

Touching.

No wonder it had taken her thirty years to even find one. What were the chances of ever finding another?

Jed prowled around his tiny living room, his expression so crowded it was unreadable. 'Believe me, I'm just saving us both a lot of time. The novelty of your physical response to me would have worn off sooner or later.' He crossed his arms across his chest and clenched his jaw until it was pale. 'You're a good person, Ellie, but I'm not interested in a relationship with you. And I don't think you'd be interested in anything less with me. What else is there to say?'

She stepped forward. 'Jed…'

He barked his frustration. 'Ellie, I don't know how to be clearer. My life is complicated enough without having to make allowances for a high-maintenance princess with body issues.'

She froze.

Having her life—her illness—so summarily dismissed burned much more than it should have. She'd guarded herself her whole life against the judgment of others. And her own. But, sometime in the past two weeks, she'd lowered those shields. Opened herself up to hurt.

And this is what hurt felt like. Amplified a thousand per cent by love.

She stumbled against the arm of the sofa on the realisation.

Love.

Oh, God, was that what Jed could see in her eyes? Had she let it show? Somewhere between rescuing her from raging cattle, helping her fly with the bats and dancing with her as if they were making love she'd fallen head over heels for Sheriff Jerry Jackson. The woman who thought she wasn't capable of feeling it.

Of all the moments to realise she was wrong, discovering it just as he was rejecting her was the cruellest blow of all.

Her whole body ached.

Love.

That was a mistake she'd be careful not to make again. Not if this was how it felt.

'I need to go.' The words came out as a croak. She turned and stumbled for the doorway. Deputy cringed and ducked as she passed him, then he circled around her, his shoulders low and tail tucked between his legs.

Exactly how she felt.

'Ellie—'

She yanked the door open.

'Ellie, wait…'

Not compassion. Not from him. Not now. She couldn't bare it. She turned back—heartsore—and said the only thing she knew would hurt him.

'That's Ms. Calhoun to you, Sheriff.'

It hit its mark with shocking accuracy and every bit of colour drained from his tanned face. She was too numb to feel any triumph.

She turned and lurched down the pathway to her own little haven, leaving the door gaping behind her as wide as her chest cavity.

Drinking was almost pointless.

It didn't even feel good. Like the calluses that formed on his weapon fingers during training, or the ones that formed on his thumb in his pen-pushing years, the liquor he'd hit so hard after losing Maggie only formed a hard, impenetrable casing over his stomach and his heart that meant he never got drunk…

He only ever got numb.

He resettled his cheek on the old leather cushion.

Numb was good enough.

He lay on his front on the sofa, head turned to the side, eyes lost in the orange glow of the dying fire he couldn't be bothered stoking.

Thinking.

Trying not to.

It had been hours since Ellie had stormed out of his

house and he'd raged across the room and slammed the front door shut behind her. What followed was three hours of pent-up grief and denial. Latent stuff left over from New York that he'd never fully expressed. It had to be. He'd not let his emotions get that firm a hold on him...ever. The whole lot liberally lubricated with the bourbon he kept for when his gram visited.

He'd stopped short of breaking stuff but only just. He had too much respect for his inherited furnishings and the many lifetimes they'd endured before his. Much harder lifetimes than his, too—war and drought and hardship and loss.

Real, unimaginable, barely survivable loss.

So he'd slammed and cursed and raged around instead, lecturing himself at half volume and doing a damned fine impersonation of his training sergeant until his legs got sore from being upright.

And then he'd fallen into this exact position and not moved for the next hour. The luminosity of the fire held him transfixed. It glowed exactly the way Ellie's eyes had as she'd stared up at him, offering herself.

Back when she was still in his arms.

He'd done the right thing. If he said it enough he might even start to believe it. He wasn't about to repeat the mistakes of his past and stay with someone out of a sense of duty, because they needed him. That wouldn't do anyone any favors, especially someone as damaged as Ellie.

He got a flash of the extra damage he'd done tonight—patently reflected in her traumatised expression—and clenched his fists. Better a short, sharp pain now than longer and much worse later.

Before he really hurt her.

Then right behind that he got a flash of the same expression on the face of Maggie's sister. She'd taken it on herself to clutch his hand by way of support, surrounded by all his girlfriend's family and friends in their funereal black, as he heard over and over how happy Maggie had been with him and how in love they'd been.

He'd stopped in at a liquor store on his way home.

Limiting yourself to meeting women outside of the county when you have no intention of going out of it is a convenient way to ensure that no relationship is ever going to work out, don't you think?

He did think. He'd been very cautious all this time to justify it that way. But Ellie had torn that careful excuse wide open and called it for the BS it was.

He'd been so close to telling her what had really happened in New York. What kind of a man he really was. But something had stopped him. Maybe he thought Ellie would understand.

And he didn't deserve understanding.

And he sure as hell didn't deserve her acceptance.

So he'd pushed her away with everything he had, and he'd done as thorough a job as he did with everything. You don't keep people at a distance for years without developing some powerful strategies. Never committing, never letting yourself feel.

You've committed to Deputy, to Larkville.

His vow to his dog was more about atonement than anything else. As long as Deputy was alive and well—as long as he'd salvaged something worthwhile from that train wreck of a situation in New York—then he didn't have to look too closely at his own demons.

His eyes rolled sideways to Deputy's mat expecting to see the big lug stretched out in his usual position. But the mat was vacant.

Jed lifted his head. Squinted into the corners of the room.

Silence.

He pushed to his feet. 'Deputy?' He swung the bathroom door open, then took the steps up to the loft by twos.

'Deputy?' Loud enough to be heard by a sleeping dog but not so loud that he'd wake Ellie next door.

Nothing—from this cottage or the old barn.

Raw panic seethed through him and he had a sudden vision of slamming his front door closed. What if Deputy had gone out for a nature break and he'd locked him out? He sprinted back down the stairs and flung the door wide, emerging coatless into the chilly, empty street.

He gave the whistle command that Deputy had been trained to respond to—a dog never forgot that primary signal, no matter what—and then held his breath for the *galumph* of approaching feet.

Still nothing.

Nausea washed through him and his mind served him up a fast-action replay of his fight with Ellie as it must have looked from a fragile dog's perspective. The moment where he slammed that front door closed. The noise he was making for the hours that followed. If Deputy had come home, it would have scared him off again.

Ellie…

His body called straight out for her. Ellie would help him. She would hold him together as he lost it. She'd keep him grounded as his past fears threatened to rise up and swallow him. Because she had more strength than she realised and maybe he didn't have as much as he liked people to believe.

If ever there was a woman to understand weakness, wouldn't it be a woman who'd battled her own dragon and survived? A woman who knew the many aspects of fear by their first names? If ever there was a woman who could help him, wouldn't it be Ellie Patterson, with her insight and compassion and courage?

But that spoke of so much more than just wanting her.

That was needing her.

And he didn't do need. Needing was not something you could come back from.

He gave it a moment more, then dashed back inside and reached for his coat and police-issue flashlight. Hadn't Deputy been let down by humans enough times? And now he'd consumed too much liquor to even get behind the wheel and find him fast. Self-reproach oozed through the surges of adrenaline.

Dogs. Hearts. Souls.

He was so right not to trust himself with anything fragile. But still he burned to find Ellie and beg her help. Not just for Deputy's sake, but for his own. Failing someone that needed him again would send him back to that place he'd been three years ago. To a much worse place than he'd let himself go because—all this time—he'd been holding on to his one, furry reminder of New York like a talisman.

As long as he could love that stupid dog, then he could love. He caught himself on her doorstep just as his knuckle rapped once on the timber. He pressed his hand flat on the wood to stop it knocking again. Rousing Ellie to help him was not something he should be doing.

It was three in the morning.

He'd just evicted her from his life.

He curled his fingers into the flaking paintwork. And he couldn't bear to see her face when she realised what little care he took of things that he loved.

He pushed away from her door, turned back up the laneway and switched on his flashlight, then jogged out into the cold night.

Chapter 11

'Leaving so soon?'

Ellie dragged her tired eyes back from the place on the horizon she'd let them drift and turned her head to the man wiping his wrinkled hands on an oily cloth. She'd vowed only yesterday never to bring her car to Gus's Fillin' Station, yet here she was. Fillin' up.

But she just wanted gas. She so wasn't in the right emotional place for another stoush with someone. Last night had spoiled her for courage for…pretty much ever. And she had as little energy and drive for a fight as she had at the height of her sickness.

She'd lain awake for hours after storming out of Jed's place. She'd lain awake and listened to him through the paper-thin drywall between his cottage and hers—pacing, slamming, cursing. The intermittent yet all too fre-quent *clank-clank* of glass on glass.

She'd lain awake, crying silently in the darkness for his pain as much as her own, and trying desperately to divine the truth from every footfall, every slam, every muttered phrase that she couldn't quite make out.

Barely breathing past the hope that the next noise she heard would be pounding on her front door to make all the pain go away.

Dying by degrees every time it wasn't.

And then beating herself up for having dared to dream.

Only when Jed had raged himself into an exhausted silence had she let herself follow, tumbling into the only place pain had never followed her.

Oblivion.

Even then she'd dreamed of one short, tortured rap on her door.

'I have to get back to New York,' she lied, dragging her gritty focus back to Gus. Although technically not a lie. She couldn't stay here to wait for Jess. So home was pretty much the only place she could go.

The path of least resistance. Letting down Sarah was easier than staying in Larkville and seeing Jed every single day. Running out on Jess was easier. Going home to face the mother she'd so cruelly stormed out on—the mother who'd lied to her daughter her whole life—was definitely easier.

And that was saying something.

Everything was going to be better than staying in

Larkville with a man who didn't want her. Or worse, didn't want to want her.

'Got yer business seen to?'

'No.' Not that her business was any of his.

He nodded, and watched her surreptitiously from the corner of his vision. Finally, he bent down to her, placing both hands on the edge of her lowered window. Her heart clenched.

Here it comes.

'Reckon I owe y'all an apology.' Her eyebrows lifted as he hurried on. 'An' I don't do that very often or very easy so let me just get it out.'

Something in Gus's awkwardness spoke to her. Maybe it was the soul of one misfit calling to another.

'You took me by surprise yesterday, sitting there all calm and unexpected. You reminded me of someone else and it put me out of sorts.'

Ellie smiled inwardly at how much this apology sounded like him blaming her.

'Anyways, my reaction didn't really belong to you, so I'm sorry if my actions caused offence.'

She smiled, though it wasn't without effort. The last thing she felt like being today was civil, but she'd changed since getting to Larkville; opting out of dealing with the world was no longer an option.

'Thank you, Gus. I'm sorry I let it get to me.'

That should have been that, but just as he was about to step away, he rounded back, looking a decade younger. Yet older at the same time. 'Your mother. Was she ever in Larkville?'

She could play innocent, she could lie, she could do

any number of things that would send Gus back into
his office scratching his head and wondering until the
day he died. Or she could treat him better than she'd
so recently been treated and put him out of his misery.
Because, she wasn't sure why, but she knew unquestionably that this man was miserable way down deep inside.

She nodded. 'Fenella Groves, back then.' Or Calhoun, really.

He kept his feet but for one moment she feared he
wouldn't. His knuckles whitened on her lowered window. 'I thought so. You look so like her. Sound just
like her.'

'You knew her?'

'Yes. For the short time she was here. A lovely
woman. How…' He slid his hat off to reveal thinning
grey hair. 'How is she?'

He feared she was dead, it was all there in the way
he clutched his hat respectfully to his chest in readi-
ness for the worst.

'She's fine. Healthy, happy, busy with my father's
business.'

His eyes lit up. 'A New York businesswoman. I should
have guessed.'

Drive away, Ellie. But something wouldn't let her.
The chance to salvage something valuable from this trip
loomed large. 'How did you know her?'

'Through Clay Calhoun. We was friends and he and
Fenella was—' his eyes shaded '—friends.'

He's guessed. Not guessed that her mother was
pregnant when he drove her seventeen hundred miles
to Manhattan, necessarily, but that Ellie was here be-

cause of Clay. She should have figured; it was too big a coincidence in a country this size. She met his speculation head-on. 'I came to meet Clay's children.'

'They're all away.'

'So I gathered. I'll come back another time.' But as soon as the words were out she realised she might not be able to. Even for the Fall Festival. Jed would still be here.

Silence fell. Dirty boots shifted on the tarmac surface. Ellie glanced at the clock on her dash. 'I should get going.'

Gus stepped back. 'Right. Sure. Y'all drive carefully.'

But old pain was resurrecting in his eyes. Something was hurting him. And Ellie didn't want to be responsible for more pain in under twenty-four hours. She blew out a breath. 'Unless… Do you sell coffee?'

'Better than Gracie May's,' he bragged, relief live in his voice.

She sighed, glanced in her mirror at the empty road that led back towards the Alamo and then pushed open her driver's door. Minutes later she was seated at the cramped little counter inside the store filled with car polishes, air fresheners, snacks and magazines, cupping a coffee she didn't really want between her hands.

But at least it went some way to warming the hollow, cold place that was her heart.

'How well did you know my mother?'

Gus frowned. 'Well enough. The three of us spent some time together. She was the talk of the town being squired around everywhere with two such good-looking young men.' He chuckled at his own wit.

Her mother...firmly in the center of the spotlight? 'I'll bet.'

'Don't you go sassin' the woman that gave you life,' he scolded and, astonishingly, Ellie felt some shame. 'Weren't her fault she was cut from such different cloth to everyone else. Everything she did was interestin' to folks around here. Won't be no different with you.'

'Except I won't be staying long enough to make an impression.'

'Heard y'all made an impression last night at the dance.'

Her heart sank. 'If by "impression" you mean "spectacle," then, yes, I probably did.'

They'd danced close enough and slow enough to ignite a dozen rumors.

Gus busied himself cleaning his counter. 'Weren't no surprise to me when I heard. Y'all looked right cozy when I last saw you. I told him so when he came through this morning, too—'

She hated the way her heart lurched at that news. 'Jed was here?'

'Not for long. Searched round the back, lookin' for that mutt of his.'

Ellie sat up straighter, her chest tight. 'Deputy?'

'Not the first time he's slipped his collar. Won't be the last. He's probably getting himself a second breakfast with Misses Darcy and Louisa.'

Probably. It wasn't her right to worry about Deputy or Jed any more. Not that it ever had been, apparently. She forced her mind onward.

'So you drove Mother home to New York?'

He snorted. 'Not what she most preferred, but only choice she had.'

Ellie paused midsip. 'She didn't want to go back?'

'She didn't want to admit defeat to her folks. She'd burned a fair number of bridges coming here at all. Marryin' without their approval.'

So she returned with her tail between her legs. Just like me. And a belly full of babies, thankfully not like her. How much more awful must it have been, discovering that? Her mother must have had strength she'd never seen.

Or just never looked for.

'Do you know why she went back?' Ellie studied him, watching closely for a reaction.

She got none. He just shrugged wiry shoulders. 'She wouldn't stay in the same town as Clay and have to face him every day.'

Every day. Just like Jed.

'And he never went after her?'

'Clay was a proud man. Proud of his heritage and his business. It never sat right with him that he'd picked a woman who couldn't settle here in the country. Whom he couldn't make happy. Whom he couldn't give children to.'

Ellie nearly gasped. 'She told you that?'

'Not on your life. She'd have never spoken about him like that, even to me. But he told me. After she'd left. About how desperate she was for offspring and how none ever came.'

'He got over her quick enough. From what I hear Holt

Calhoun is my age.' She surprised herself by feeling actual, genuine umbrage on her mother's behalf.

She knew how she'd feel if she heard Jed took up with someone from last night's dance the moment she was out of the picture. That he was kissing someone else in front of his fire just days after she'd stumbled down his steps.

Gus wiped down his spotless counter one more time. 'Weren't no shortage of women eager to have her place. Turns out any fertility issues didn't lie with Clay. He got himself the heir he'd been wanting so bad after just one night with Sandra. Once that was done, there was no question he'd marry her as soon as the divorce papers came through.'

So he couldn't reconcile with her mother even if he'd wanted to. But that didn't explain why he never acknowledged her and Matt. Why wouldn't he at least seek them out? 'He got the family he always wanted.'

'Yup.'

'And my mother got hers. Just not together, I guess.'

'Love don't hardly ever strike two people equally, Ellie.'

Her mind went straight to Jed.

Was it really that simple? Had she let all the new and overwhelming feelings she'd had since coming here skew what she felt for Jed? Had she misread the level of his interest? What experience did she have to call on? Sudden heat joined her aching heart.

Just how much of a fool had she made of herself?

'Well, thanks for the coffee, Gus.' Despondent, Ellie

pushed up and away from the counter and turned for the door. The bell above it tolled. 'I'll tell Mother you asked after her?'

His head shot up, his eyes grew bright and keen. He looked like asking after her was just the first of a hundred things he wanted to say to her mother.

'That would be a kindness. Thank you.' Gus cleared his throat again. 'So when do you leave Larkville?'

'Right now. That tank you just filled will get me halfway home.'

His brow folded. 'Now?'

'Got a long drive.'

'Before seein' Jess?'

'She's on her honeymoon.' He even told her that; did he have a touch of her father's Alzheimer's?

'Sure, but she's back this morning. Her best friend, Molly, mentioned it yesterday.'

Ellie's heart leapt in her tight chest. 'Today?'

'A week early. Something to do with her boy getting homesick. Would be a shame if you missed her.'

Imagine if she hadn't come to Gus's station to top up her rental. She would have left Larkville and probably passed Jess Calhoun on the way out of town. 'Yes, it would. Thank you, Gus, I really appreciate that.' She threw him a gentle look. 'It really was a pleasure meeting you.'

And in his understated Texas way he agreed. 'Mutual.'

Then she was out the door, back in her car and lead-footing it in the direction of the Double Bar C.

* * *

She almost, almost didn't miss it. The dark shape that lurched out of the bushes on the side of the high-way feeder and darted across the front of her rental. First cows, now wolves. How many wildlife incidents was she destined to have in Larkville?

Maybe the cows had been a sign. Maybe she was supposed to turn back there and then that day? Maybe she'd just been too slow on the uptake and everything that happened afterwards with Jed was the price she paid for staying.

Except—despite the awful end—it was hard to regret meeting him. To know that such a man existed, that such new parts of her existed… They had to be worth every-thing that followed. No matter how awful.

She kept her foot steady on the brake as the dark shape dashed out of her periphery. Behind it, like a con-sciousness shadow, came recognition.

'Deputy?' She craned her neck back to see into the bushes on the other side of the road where he'd headed. 'Deputy Dawg!' she called out the open window.

Maybe it was the formal use of his full name, maybe it was because she was a voice he vaguely knew, or maybe it was just because they'd had that one special night crammed into her bed together, but after a mo-ment of breathless silence his big horse head poked back through the bushes and wild eyes stared at her as she climbed out of her car. She looked both ways for traffic and then crouched.

'Come on, boy!'

He didn't hesitate. He rushed straight towards her,

his tail slinking between his legs as he approached, his ears flattening. The first things she noticed were the terror in his eyes, the wet of his thick coat and the muddiness of his paws. The next thing she noticed was the pace of his heart.

He shoved his wet body against her and lifted a sopping paw against her crouched hip.

'What are you doing out here?' she queried, wrapping her hands around his shoulders and snagging his collar. His body was roasting, and drool hung off his usually dry chops in strings. His gums were pale in the split second she saw them, and a series of anxious whines issued from the back of his throat.

Deputy was stressed. Really stressed.

Had he been hit? Injured?

She glanced left and right again to make sure they were still traffic-free. A semi could come along any moment and find a car, a woman and a dog taking up their lane.

'Come on.' She opened the back of the car and gestured for him to jump in. He did so with an unseemly amount of haste and then sat, trembling top to toe, crowded in amongst her suitcases.

'Where's your dad, boy?' His big head cocked at the sound of her measured voice and he seemed to relax just a hint. 'Oh, you like me talking to you, huh?'

Deputy blinked, refocused, came back to the same plane as she was on.

Yeah, he did.

So she started a gentle monologue as she slipped the rental into gear and pulled forward on the highway. 'I don't have your dad's cell number or I'd call him.' More head cocks in her rear vision mirror. 'I can't call 911, boy. Even for you.'

She thought fast as he *humphed* back against her luggage, relaxing further. 'But we're so close to the Calhoun place. Why don't we go there? They'll have his number. And we'll ask Wes to take a look at you, hey? You like Wes, he's a good guy, and you like the Double Bar C, I know....'

On and on she rambled, as Deputy zeroed in on every tone and nuance of her voice and inched back down the stress Richter scale. She told him about meeting Gus Everett and about Jess's letter and how her mother had loved Clay Calhoun enough to betray her family's wishes and marry him. Enough to uproot her city life and move out here.

'Must have taken some courage, huh?'

Deputy tossed his head up and smacked his lips clean of the prodigious amount of drool. It was almost an agreement.

Courage. Though it was hard to know whether it took more courage to stay or to go.

'But then she left...' How bad had things become between the newlyweds that she was willing to bail so soon on their marriage?

Ellie knew, firsthand, how deficient she felt just for having her aversion to touch. The hundred different ways the world had of reminding you that you didn't measure up. How much worse must it have been for her mother to believe she was infertile when the man she loved wanted an heir so very much?

At least she had Jed in her corner helping her, not judging.

Had being the operative word.

A sudden realisation shimmied through her. Whether or not Jed had withdrawn his interest in her, he could never withdraw the difference he'd made to her soul. And to her body. She could never—would never—go back now that she'd tapped into that passion inside of her.

Jed gave her that.

Yet here she was running away rather than staying and toughing it out. But didn't it take two to work things through? And could she even face him knowing how awfully she'd misread his interest?

'I've messed things up, boy.' She groaned and Deputy cocked one brown eyebrow. 'I said things I shouldn't have. I hoped for things I shouldn't have.'

He just blinked at her.

She turned at the Calhouns' access road that she'd first met the cows on. 'He's a good man, your dad. Got his share of issues but nobody's perfect.'

By the time she pulled under the big entry statement to the Double Bar C she'd offloaded her entire childhood onto the poor old dog, who'd dropped to his elbows some time back and now his eyes were drifting shut. But they shot open as she pulled her car up to the Calhoun homestead.

That big tail began to thump.

Ellie's own tension eased. Maybe he was going to be okay, after all.

Up ahead a handful of people were unloading luggage from a fancy truck. Ellie recognised Wes Brogan immediately, and the ranch hand she'd spoken to on her first visit to the Double Bar C. Next to them, a tall, dark-haired man with killer bone structure looked up from the back of the vehicle.

Ellie pushed her door open.

Up on the homestead porch the door swung open and a young boy dashed out, skipping down the steps and running over to the man whose eyes were fixed so firmly on her arrival. Behind the boy, a blonde, willowy woman stepped out of the house.

Ellie's breath caught.

Jess.

Suddenly she became critically aware of her appearance. Barely groomed from her desperate exit this morning and patches of damp and mud and dog slobber where Deputy had leaned on her and pawed her. Ordinarily she'd have been mortified that this was going to be Jessica Calhoun's first impression. But Deputy's needs came first. There was no time for preciousness. And besides, something essential in her had changed since arriving in Larkville.

She turned and pulled open the back door of the car and the whole car lurched as Deputy leapt out. Wes Brogan's eyes flared wide. The boy dashed forward, squealing. The tall man snatched him up before he could get far.

'The sheriff's been tearing the county up looking for you,' Wes said in a loud voice, coming towards her.

Ellie's breath caught, low in her throat. 'Me?'

Wes laughed and his eyes dropped to her side. 'Deputy Dawg.'

The breathlessness hardened into a lump and embarrassed heat soaked up her neck. She forced speech past it. 'He's... I'm not sure what's happened to him. I found him on the highway. He was in a bad way.'

Wes instantly sobered and barked over his shoulder for the younger hand. 'Cooper! Grab Misty's kit and clear us a space in the tack room.' Then he lifted his eyes back to hers and said quietly, 'I'll check him over, Ms. Patterson.'

'Ellie, please...' Ugh. All so hideously awkward. And none of it really mattered anyway. She'd be gone in a few minutes.

Some fuss and bustle and all three men and one very tired, miserable dog disappeared for some much needed care. The surprise must have still shown on her face after they all trooped off because a soft, polite voice spoke right behind her,

'Deputy's part of the family around here.'

Ellie's back muscles bunched. She took two deep breaths before turning around...and her eyes met a pair so similar, yet different, to her own. There was absolutely no question of their owner's identity.

'Jess.'

Jessica Calhoun's pretty face folded in a frown. Ellie could see her trying to place this newcomer who'd arrived with their sheriff's dog. But just as she thought to introduce herself, Jess's eyes widened and her lips fell open on a gasp. 'Are you...?'

'Eleanor Patterson.'

'Oh, my Lord—' Long slim fingers went to her chest and her eyes welled up dangerously. 'Oh...'

'I'm sorry to take you by surprise,' Ellie rushed.

'No! Molly told me someone was looking for me in town. I had no idea...'

The two of them stood awkwardly, their respective hands dangling uselessly at their sides. Ellie said the first thing that came to her. It was the least poised and professional she'd ever been but also the most honest. Another thing she'd learned to be.

'I don't know what to do.'

Jess's nervous laugh bubbled up. 'Me, neither. Can I, um... A hug?'

Old whispers instinctively chorused in her head and she grasped for a legitimate excuse. 'I'm filthy—'

Jess laughed properly this time. 'You're on a working ranch. Everyone's dirty here.' She stepped forward, undeterred.

Ellie knew this moment counted more than any other she'd ever have with her half-sister. She tamped down the whispers, held her breath and stepped into Jess Calhoun's open embrace.

Warm, soft, strong arms closed around her, and Ellie felt her body flinch on a rush of emotion.

Good emotion.

Jess hugged just like Alex. The discovery brought tears to her eyes.

The hug went on just a bit too long but neither one wanted to be the one to end it. Eventually Ellie pulled away but kept her hands on her half-sister's arms. 'This is so...'

'Odd?'

She laughed, sniffing back tears. 'But good!' she added lest Jess think she wasn't cherishing every moment. 'There are four of you.'

Oh, no, she was rambling.

But Jess knew she was talking about Calhoun offspring. She smiled. 'I know. And two of you. Twins!'

They stared again.

'I'm sorry I came without checking,' Ellie said.

Jess shook her head. 'Don't be. It was quite a bombshell I dropped on you. I'm sorry I wasn't here.' She pressed her fingertips to her coral lips and shook her head. 'I can't believe I have a big sister.'

Ellie laughed. 'And a big brother.' Matt may not be here but he deserved to be counted into this moment.

'Holt's going to freak out…not being the oldest any more.' Her laugh then was pure delight, yet Ellie could tell it came from a solid and dedicated affection. Her eyes went to the little boy who peered around his mother's legs.

'And…do I have a nephew?' Ellie breathed.

'Oh! Brady Cal—' She caught herself. 'Sorry, still getting used to that… Brady Jameson, I'd like you to meet your aunt Eleanor.'

Ellie reeled back. 'My goodness that makes me sound a hundred years old.' Then she bent down and shook a very serious Brady's hand. 'Call me Ellie.'

'You sure don't look a hundred,' he said, pumping her hand formally.

Everyone laughed then and the silence no longer felt awkward. 'So…the letter…'

'Do you want to see it?' Jess was quick to offer.

'No, not right now. I don't need a letter to know the truth. I can see so much of Matt in you. And maybe a bit of me.'

'I thought the same thing. The rest of you must be your mother?'

'I look a fair bit like her, yes.' Much to poor Gus's distress.

'She was very beautiful, then.'

This time, accepting the compliment—believing it— wasn't quite as hard as it once would have been. Maybe Jed had helped her grow accustomed to that, too. Or… just grow.

'She's quite a legend in our household. This mystery first wife we could never ask about.'

Ellie grimaced. 'She's pretty ordinary in real life.' Except that wasn't true any more. Fenella had walked away from a man she loved, pregnant with his children, and built herself and them a whole new life. That took amazing courage. So did maintaining her stiff New York veneer when Ellie had blurted the fact of Clay's passing to her. She wondered how she would have reacted if someone threw news of Jed's death at her so carelessly.

She owed her mother a really long conversation. And several apologies. Starting there.

'I think I have a photo in my phone if you'd like to see it.'

Jess answer was immediate. 'Oh, I would.'

'I'd love to see a picture of your father if you have one?'

One beat. Two. 'Our father, Ellie.'

The niggling hurt of disloyalty to the man who'd raised her sharpened its teeth. Honesty compelled her. 'That's going to take a while to sink in.'

Jess's eyes darkened with compassion. 'I'm sure.'

'He never...' She paused, wondering how heartbroken Jess still was about her father's death twelve weeks ago. 'He never told you about us?'

Jess stared at her. 'Ellie... He never knew. He never got the letter.'

Everything whooshed around her feet. 'Not at all?'

Oh, her poor, poor mother. That was going to break her heart.

The crunch of vehicle tires on gravel drew their eyes around behind them. Her gut squeezed harder than a fist as she turned.

Speaking of broken hearts...

'Sheriff!' Brady called, and dashed over to the now-stationery SUV.

Jed's empty eyes hit Ellie's almost immediately but that careful nothing had always been his particular talent. He slid them to Jess's instead. 'I wasn't far away when I got Johnny's call. Where is he?'

Jess waved him in the direction of the tack room. Brady followed him.

It wasn't reasonable to be surprised—or disappointed—by his intense focus on the dog he felt so responsible for. But his barely cursory glance still hurt. She forced her attention back onto her half-sister.

'Sheriff Jackson,' Jess explained. 'Deputy is his dog.'

'I know.'

'Oh, you already met him?'

'I was staying in his barn conversion. He's shown me around town a bit.' Her heart squeezed. *I fell in love with him.*

Jess looked bemused. 'I'm surprised he didn't say hello.'

So it wasn't just her who saw nothing but a passing glance in that moment. 'Just anxious for Deputy, I'm sure.'

'Are you okay, Ellie? You've gone quite pale.'

She forced her lungs to inhale. 'Yes. This has been quite a morning, that's all.'

'Sheriff Jackson doesn't need our help, buddy.'

Jess turned to the striking man emerging from the tack room with a protesting boy in his arms. He was easily more handsome than Jed, but Ellie felt nothing but aesthetic appreciation for his beautiful angles and stunning complexion. He was fire to Jed's earth.

And earth appealed to her so much more.

'Ellie, this is my husband, Johnny Jameson. Hon, this is Eleanor Patterson.'

The way she only put the tiniest of inflections on the surname told Ellie she'd been the topic of quite a few conversations.

Light grey eyes widened and Johnny extended a hand. 'Ms. Patterson, it's a real pleasure to meet you.'

She took it without hesitation. 'Congratulations on your marriage.'

The newlyweds looked at each other with such focus then; the passion and love between them stole Ellie's breath and hurt her already bruised heart.

That's what she wanted. Someone to look at her like that.

'Thank you,' Johnny said, all courtesy.

'How's Deputy?' she asked when what she really wanted to know was how Jed was. Did he hurt like she did? Did he feel anything at all? Or had he already exorcised all trace of her from his system.

'He's good now that the sheriff's here. Apparently he's been missing since last night.'

'Last night? But he—' She snapped her mouth shut. She could hardly admit that Deputy was right there when she was kissing Jed. Although then she had a flash of the dog cringing as they argued and of her bolting from the house and leaving the door wide open. Guilt swamped into the empty place inside her.

'Oh. Poor boy.'

'He'll be okay. He's had a rough run in life and he's easily spooked these days.'

He doesn't deal with conflict well, Jed had once told her. Like two members of his pack tearing each other to emotional pieces.

Behind them, all three men and one infinitely more relaxed dog emerged from the stables.

'Is he okay?' she asked Wes, specifically, determined not to give off any unhappy waves while Deputy was around. Jed's eyes finally fell on her but he didn't speak.

Her chest ached.

'Right as rain,' Wes said. 'Or he will be when he gets home. Cooper gave him a quick once-over with a brush for the mud on his fur. Sorry about your suitcases, Miss Patterson.'

Jed's head snapped up, then around to the still-open rear door of her car. Exhibits A and B were on plain view complete with muddy paw smears. Finally his brown eyes came back to her and this time he couldn't hide what burned there.

Betrayal.

'You were leaving?' Jess gasped. 'Imagine if we'd missed each other!'

You were leaving? Jed's dark eyes accused.

She faced Jess. 'Lucky Gus told me you were back. I was on my way over here when I found Deputy.'

Finally Jed found speech. 'Why didn't you let me know?' he asked, low and deep. 'That you'd found him.'

Why are you leaving? It was all there right between what he was actually saying.

'You're welcome,' Ellie said, pointedly, her eyes fixed on him. 'The Double Bar C was closer. I thought Deputy might need some first aid.'

They stared at each other, a crackle of pain reaching from her to him. Jess's eyes flicked between them and then to her husband, wide with concern. For a heartbeat Ellie truly thought that maybe she'd dissolve into tears here in front of her new family and the Calhoun hands. And Jed. She willed her body not to.

And some miracle—or maybe years of dominating it—meant it listened.

Jess broke the silence. 'Ellie, why don't you stay for brunch, if this is the only chance we'll have to talk? We can swap those photos. You, too, of course, Jed.'

'Thank you, Jess, but I should get Deputy home. Get him settled back in. Maybe another time?'

Would it be that easy? He'd just leave and that would be that? Ellie's breath grew shallow.

Not easy. Not at all.

'Sure, Sheriff,' Jess said. 'I'm glad everything's worked out okay.'

If you didn't count a broken heart and some hurtful truths.

'Yep.' He curled his fingers into Deputy's coat as she had so many times. 'Something like this sure makes you think about what's important.'

His eyes flicked to her again as he said that, but then he turned, gave them all a Texas wave and signaled for Deputy to follow him to his vehicle. Ellie watched him go, wondering if that long-legged lope and those square shoulders would be branded in her mind forever.

She stared, unblinking, to make sure they would be.

As they turned for the house, Wes Brogan muttered, 'He's a good man, that sheriff. Most people would have shot that dog.'

Johnny grunted. 'Jed's not the sort of man to give up that easily when there's a bit of hope.'

Those words anchored Ellie's feet to the ground. Her whole body lurched to a stop and the air in her lungs made a word all of its own volition. Was she giving up too easily? Was there truly not even a sliver of hope for her and Jed?

'Wait—'

He was going to disappear from her life not knowing if she didn't do something.

Brown eyes and grey looked back at her. 'Ellie?' Jess said.

Um… 'I'm just going to need a couple of minutes. Can I meet you inside?'

Jess's head cocked in a great impression of Deputy, but her eyes flicked for a heartbeat over to where Jed walked away. 'Sure, just let yourself in the front door and follow your nose through to the kitchen.'

'Thanks.'

She hadn't sounded that breathless in years. Since she'd come rushing out of her first-ever dance class busting to show her parents what she'd learned. Wow, those sure were innocent days. Who might she have become if she'd taken up tennis instead of ballet?

A burned-out tennis player instead of a burned-out dancer probably. She couldn't go on blaming her childhood for everything. Those years were long behind her. What she did now was what counted.

Right now.

She pivoted on one foot and then sprinted off after Jed, refusing to call out to him. Hoping to preserve some modicum of dignity. He was loading Deputy into his vehicle when she caught up.

'Jed,' she puffed.

He stiffened, but finished securing Deputy into his harness before turning. He nodded like he was passing her in the street. 'Ms. Calhoun.'

The words coming back at her the way she'd flung them at him were exactly the insult he intended.

Her tension coiled so far up inside it threatened to strangle her. 'Can I speak to you?'

'You are.'

Now that she had his full attention she didn't know where to begin. 'I talked to Gus today.'

Not what he was expecting. One eyebrow lifted under the brim of his hat.

'He knew my mother. How she came here, why she left. How hard that was for her.'

Despite what had happened between them, Jed was still a decent man. If he felt any impatience at her bumbling beginning his country manners didn't let it show. 'You didn't know?'

'I knew that she left, not why. She couldn't tell me.'

He frowned. 'Bad?'

'She believed she couldn't give Clay an heir. They ended their marriage over it. And she left feeling inadequate. He let her leave feeling about as inadequate as a woman possibly can.'

Jed suddenly realised which way the wind was blowing and he straightened two inches. But his eyes didn't go back to their careful neutrality. Maybe there were some things he couldn't hide.

'These past two weeks have been life-changing for me, Jed. You may never understand the difference knowing you has made for me.'

'Ellie—'

'Don't worry, I'm not going to make a scene or put pressure on you. I just wanted to thank you.'

'Thank me?' He frowned. 'Why?'

She looked down at her strappy sandals, covered in Calhoun dirt. 'Everything in my life started spinning wildly a month ago. My father is not my father. I'm not a Patterson. My Fifth Avenue mother was married to someone else and lived on a ranch. My sisters aren't my full sisters…' She wrapped her arms around her front. 'I arrived here feeling…disconnected to everything and wondering where I belonged.'

She took a breath. 'And then I met you. And you were like…a rock. Predictable and sure.'

Offense flirted on the edge of his silence.

'But at the same time you were a surge I had to go with or get buffeted. Like the bats in the gully. Every moment with you challenged me and made me really look at myself. At the person I've let myself become.'

His gaze dropped to his steel-capped boots.

'I've developed so many strategies in life to keep from having to face the reality of who I've grown into, they've become excuses.' Every word was harder to get out, every breath tight. 'Dance was an excuse for not eating. But not eating was about controlling my body, controlling something in my environment where I felt otherwise invisible.' She twisted the fingers of both hands together. 'Studying or rehearsing all the time, that was an excuse, too. My distancing myself from relationships was about hiding my disorder from people who might notice it.'

She took a shaky breath. 'Not touching anyone was about disguising my internal deficiencies. Blaming it on something external was just an excuse.'

His eyes closed briefly. 'Ellie, you don't have to do this—'

'I do. I do, Jed, because I'm lucky. I won't be leaving Larkville like my mother did, believing I'm inadequate. You showed me what I have inside me and I will always be grateful for that. Whether or not you wanted me, ultimately, I know you wanted me at least for a moment.'

She took a breath and he pressed his lips together, almost as if to stop himself speaking.

'But more importantly,' she said, 'I wanted you. I know now that I'm capable of that. So…that's it really. Just…thank you.'

He nodded, his eyes intense.

She turned back for the house.

'You were right when you said I told you about being a Calhoun to stop us getting physical,' she said, spinning back around just as he pulled the door to his SUV open. Stalling, and they both knew it. Her eyes fixed on his. 'But it wasn't because I didn't want you touching me.' Her voice cracked. 'I can't imagine being touched by anyone else. I can't imagine wanting to touch anyone else.'

Jed's lips pressed tighter together.

'But I will. And if I don't, well…so be it. But I want to explain because I don't want to drive out of town leaving you feeling inadequate, either.'

His laugh was so very cowboy and so very awkward it warmed her heart. He no longer had a prayer of hiding the pain in his gaze.

She took a really deep breath. 'I've never…' How was she even having this conversation? 'My whole adult life I thought I couldn't…'

She closed her eyes and remembered the bats. Remembered how that felt. Then she opened them and remembered how he felt. 'I was petrified of how you were making me feel. Totally out of control. My body reacting in complete contravention of my will. I've never felt that before.'

Jed the good man wasn't far away. 'That's the best part, Ellie.'

'Look at what I did to myself to maintain control growing up. You think I did that by choice? It's not a conscious thing. It's something I'm going to have to work on.' She curled her nails into her palms to stop herself reaching out. 'I get that we're not going to happen. I'm still leaving today. I just want to leave with us both understanding what happened between us. How it went so very wrong. Because up until then I thought things were going pretty right.'

The distant keening of cattle filled the silence.

'You're still leaving?'

She turned back and stared at him, no energy or heart for more.

'What about Jess? You came to get to know her.'

She summoned some words. 'I came to find out who I was. Mission accomplished.' At least she knew, now, who she wanted to be. 'I'll stay in touch with Jess by email.'

'And Sarah, the Fall Festival—you're just going to dump her?'

It sounded so much uglier when phrased like that. Defensiveness washed through her and tangled with the exhaustion. 'I can help her from New York. Come back in October for the big event.'

Maybe.

He stepped closer. 'Visit once a year? Is that what you want?'

She took a sharp breath and met his eyes. 'That's what I can manage. You've helped set me on a new path but I'm not a masochist. I won't find it easy coming back in the future.' She swallowed. 'Maybe finding you with someone else.'

His eyes echoed her pain. 'You think I'm going to do that?'

Her breath caught, but she fought hard not to make assumptions about what that meant. She'd done more than enough of that since arriving. 'According to Sarah you're Larkville's Most Wanted. I think you'll have no choice.'

'What if I don't want to be wanted by one of them?'

Her heart shrivelled. 'You'll figure it out,' she said instead, the best she could offer. She turned to walk away again.

'I'm not a good man, Ellie.'

The raw pain in his voice brought her back. 'Says who?'

'Says me.' He stared at her, and something indefinable shifted. Right at the back, in the space between blinks. 'Not wanting to get involved with someone where I live was not just about avoiding relationships. It's because I had a relationship with someone I worked with once and it didn't end well.'

Oh.

Had she somehow imagined that he'd been as loveless as she all this time? Or had she just not let herself ask?

'A woman in my unit. Maggie. We were together for five years.'

Her heart twisted. Five years? That didn't spell commitment issues. So maybe it truly was just her?

He'd tried to tell her.

'Why did you break up?' She didn't want to know, and yet she had to.

'We didn't break up,' he gritted. 'She died.'

Shock and empathy responded to the pain bleeding off him. All this time she'd been battling a ghost that she didn't know existed.

'We'd been together in another division, careful to keep things on the down low. Most people didn't know we were a couple. Maggie followed me over to the canine unit when I was promoted.'

The idea of Jed—her Jed—loving someone else. Spending time with someone else... Five years. It felt impossible.

'My superiors would have transferred one of us out of the unit if they'd twigged. So I worked hard to treat her like everyone else.' His eyes flicked away. 'Too hard.'

Her silence was a question in itself.

'She begged me to let her go out before she was ready. Not to make a big deal about it in front of the team. She wanted to be equal.' He turned half away from Ellie. 'Thing was if I'd truly been treating her equally I would have grounded her and let her deal with the fallout.'

'She went out?'

'And she died. And Deputy got beaten.'

Ellie gasped. 'Maggie was Deputy's handler?'

He looked across the seat of his car at the dog that'd looked up when he heard his name. His head nodded, brisk and small.

'I'm so sorry.' The urge to touch won out. She slid her hand onto his arm. 'You loved her.'

The bleakness in the eyes he turned up to her took her aback. 'That's just it. I didn't love her.'

Maybe someone had to live with it to recognise it in others, but Ellie suddenly wondered how she'd never seen it in him before.

Blazing, damning shame.

'Oh, Jed…'

'Five years, Ellie, and I kept her at arm's length the whole time. So much so she had to chase me from department to department to stop me slipping away.' He swallowed past the pain. 'I dishonored her the whole time. Deep inside. Overcompensating for the love I just didn't feel.'

'Why did you stay together?'

'Because she adored me, because she'd put our relationship ahead of her own career so many times. Because she was willing to take whatever I could give her.'

Ellie felt sudden and cell-deep empathy for the woman who had tried so hard to win Jed's love. Who'd died trying.

The pain in his eyes told her exactly how deeply he felt that, too.

'Being together was the perfect excuse not to be with anyone else. Work was the perfect excuse to keep things superficial. To manage Maggie's expectations.'

Excuses. Didn't that sound familiar?

He turned to her, self-loathing blazing in his eyes. 'That's the kind of man I am, Ellie. That's why I know I can't commit no matter what I feel for you. You deserve someone who's capable of loving you with everything in them.'

Deputy's heavy sigh punctuated the silence. Was he afraid they were going to start fighting again? Ellie fought hard to keep her body language relaxed. 'You're not that man,' she whispered.

He turned to her suddenly and pain glowed real and raw in his plea. 'Then who am I?'

She shook her head. 'A man who's been really hurt in his past. A man who protects himself from loss before it can happen.' She took a breath. 'You're the male version of me.'

Jed stared at her, pain giving way to confusion.

'Do you think your Maggie would blame you for what happened to her?'

His answer was a frown.

'Do you think she would blame you for not loving her more than you could?'

'I blame me.'

'I don't,' she breathed. 'Not for her.' She bent lower to stay connected to eyes that suddenly dropped to stare at the dirt. 'And not for me.'

And it was true. She could no more blame Jed for not loving her the way she needed than she could blame Deputy for falling to pieces at the sound of raised voices.

But she could love him.

And she would.

And she wouldn't hide it.

She curled her hand around his arm, touching him. Letting every feeling and emotion and hope run through her body and into his. Letting her know she accepted him.

He shrugged her hand free and she slid it back on, refusing to let him back away again.

'I can't love you, Ellie.' His volume betrayed his pain. 'Not the way you want.'

Her heart hitched. *Can't*. Not *don't*.

'Why?'

'Look what I did to the last person who loved me.'

'She would forgive you, Jed.'

He shook his head, not hearing. Not wanting to. 'You can't know that.'

'I can know it, because I know you. And because I love you like she did. And I know that I would forgive you if I had the chance.'

He stared at her, eyes roiling with a mix of pain and confusion.

'Give her the chance,' Ellie pleaded, and slipped her fingers in between his. 'Forgive yourself so that she can, too.'

He stared at her, the options tumbling visibly in his gaze, and then—exactly like the houselights used to come on after she'd been lost in the depths of a performance—the shadows leached out of his eyes and he almost blinked in the sudden brightness of hope.

And in that exact moment, Deputy chose to nudge his wet, cool nose into the place their hands entwined. He'd moved more silently than a dog his size should ever have been able to and he blazed his wide, dark, loving eyes straight up into Jed's.

It was Maggie's forgiveness.

And his own.

And it broke the last of Jed's strength.

Ellie slid her arms around him and let him bury his face in her neck. His hold tightened hard around her, hard enough to last them forever. Ellie didn't care how many of the Calhouns might be watching out of the window. She was through with worrying about appearances.

'Stay.' The word croaked against her neck, but Jed's tight arms reinforced it. And the four tiny letters carried a universe worth of meaning. 'I don't want you to leave.'

She pulled back a little. 'I can't stay.' Not without being certain.

He cleared his throat and lifted damp eyes. 'Remember the bats? The way I stood behind you on that cliff top and kept you safe while you danced? How scared you were?'

Her chest threatened to cave in. Those memories would be the ones replaying on her deathbed in a half-century. She pushed the words through her tight throat. 'Of course.'

He paused and there was confusion in the dark depths of his eyes. But it was greatly outweighed by something new. Something she'd not seen there in all the time she knew him.

'I'd be willing to do that again, to help you heal.'

She scrunched her forehead. 'With the bats?'

Intensity blazed down on to her. 'With me. And with you.' His fingers rose to trace her jaw. 'Slowly. Until you're ready to feel yourself fly again.'

His meaning finally dawned on her and her lungs cramped. 'Are charity cases part of your job description?'

He smiled down on her, and didn't let her hide behind sarcasm. 'I want you to stay, Ellie. With me.'

She refused to let herself hope. Old habits died way too hard. 'Just like that?'

He stroked the hair from her face. 'No, not just like that. Feeling like this absolutely terrifies me.'

She could see the uncertainty live and real in his eyes. But it wasn't alone. Something else flanked it, keeping it at bay. It shifted and flirted at the edges of his gaze, ducking and weaving just out of view so that she couldn't quite place where she'd seen it before.

'Feeling like what?'

The golden threads between her eyes and his were enough to let a little piece of his soul cross over. 'Like my world will end if I let you drive away today.'

Her breath faltered and her chest tightened as he took her hand, pressed his fingers to hers and returned her own words from last night to her. 'But I wouldn't feel safe being terrified with anyone else, Ellie.'

Every old instinct she had urged her not to allow this hope. But something newer overruled that. The same something she saw fighting the fear in his eyes. And in a moment of intense clarity she suddenly knew where she'd seen it before.

Just now—in the look passing between Johnny and Jess.

In the look she must be blazing up at him now.

Love.

Jed would keep her safe while she learned to accept every part of herself. She'd do the same until he could recognise the feelings he harbored. Understand them. She absolutely would.

He lowered his mouth until it was just a breath from hers and his hat blocked out the sun. 'It's been so fast, Ellie, it's hard to trust. But if this isn't love, then God help us after another week together.'

It was love, for both of them. Inconceivable and miraculous. She knew that way down deep in the oldest part of her soul, the part that held all her truths. And she so badly wanted to be in the room the moment it finally dawned on him.

'I want to stay,' she whispered against his mouth. 'I want to feel like that again.'

He touched his lips lightly to hers and her soul sang. He nibbled the corner of her mouth and then turned it into a fully fledged kiss. A searing kiss. They were breathless when they pulled apart.

That rich, golden glow now consumed his eyes. There was no fear.

'The bats, Ellie? That feeling? I give you my word, that was only the beginning.'

Chapter 12

The bats were only the beginning. It took a scandalously short number of weeks for them to discover, tucked up in her comfortable loft bed, they could reach a place Ellie never imagined actually existed. A safe place. A place where the feel of their two bodies moving in sync was the most poetic and seductive kind of dance ever.

Jed was patient and gentle and forceful and strong in just the right amounts and he let her fly when she needed to and shelter when she had to.

When she wasn't with him, she hung out with Jess or Sarah, and she'd started teaching ballet to the local schoolchildren and, thanks to a bizarre request from the eighty-year-old Misses Darcy and Louisa, to Larkville's senior ladies. Now she taught three times a week.

And it meant she was dancing again.

She still loved her solitude, but alone had so quickly come to mean just her and Jed and Deputy. The word had failed to apply to Ellie by herself because she just didn't feel alone any more even when she was.

Jed kissed his way from her thumb, up her inner arm to the crook of her elbow, and then murmured against her strong pulse there. 'I have something to ask you.'

She matched his gravity. 'Okay.'

'Gram's coming down next week.' She pushed up onto her elbows. 'I wanted the two most important women in my life to meet.'

She stared at him. For Jed, that was quite a pronouncement.

'I'd like that.' But then something occurred to her. 'Where will she stay?'

'Right here in the barn.'

'Then where will I stay?'

His face grew serious. 'I thought that you could move in with me.'

Ellie's lungs refused to inflate. 'Just while she's here, you mean?'

He took her hand in his and absently played with her fingers. It was the least casual casual thing he'd ever done.

What was happening here?

'Sure. Or we could keep the barn for her visits. Or if one of your family visits.'

She sat bolt upright and the covers dropped to her waist, leaving her naked and exposed. That no longer troubled her. In fact, she positively adored the way his face and body changed in response to hers.

'Just so I'm clear...' She swallowed past the lump which grew low in her throat. 'You want me to meet your gram and you want me next door with you? For good?'

His eyes sobered. 'I do. And so do you.' He leaned in and traced her collarbone with his lips. 'It's in the special laugh you reserve just for me and the fact you let my dog sleep on your feet in front of the television...'

'He's very warm—' Ellie started, her natural instinct to protect herself creeping through.

He smiled against her lips. 'It's in the way that you touch me and that way you let me touch you. You love me.'

'That's hardly a newsflash.'

His kiss grew more ardent before he tore himself away. 'It's funny...'

Lack of oxygen dulled her capacity to keep up with his mental tangents. 'What is?'

'You hated this body for being weak, but I love it for being so strong. Strong enough to get you through.' His eyes darkened and lifted to hers. 'To get you to me.'

She cleared her suddenly crowded throat. 'You... love it?'

The wonder in his face didn't change. 'Every part of it.' His eyes locked on hers. 'Every part of you.'

Ellie's heart raced her mind. He looked so casual lying there talking about the weather one moment and the next—

Joy contributed to the gentle spin of the room but caution still ruled. Because he still hadn't said those all-important three words. Not exactly. And she knew him to be a man of his word.

When he said it, he'd mean it.

'I'd sort of hoped to do this somewhere more memorable,' he frowned.

More memorable than in his arms after a morning of beautiful intimacy? Did such a place exist?

He took her hands. Both of them.

Her breath froze.

'You've been so strong, Ellie. And so patient while I worked my complicated way around to this.'

She still hadn't breathed.

'Everything before you felt slightly off kilter but I just didn't know why. Everything since that day with the cows has felt…right. Colours got brighter. The air got fresher.'

Words to die for but she hoped it wouldn't be literal, from oxygen deficiency.

'I love you, Eleanor Patterson-Calhoun.'

Elation, gratitude and adoration tingled under her skin and she worked hard not to throw herself straight into his arms. The moment she had the words, she realised that she'd known them all along. 'Would you have said that if your grandmother wasn't coming to stay?'

'You think I'm declaring love to free up a bed for a tenant?'

She smiled and nudged his shoulder. 'I think you'd say anything to get me to move in with you out of wedlock.'

'Who said anything about out of wedlock?' His eyes devoured her metaphorically and then his lips repeated it literally. When he finally released her he said, 'How would you feel about a fall wedding?'

The earth stopped revolving. 'You're proposing?' Such short words but so very hard to get out.

He took both her hands. 'Ellie… Believing I was worthy of your love was the tough part, marrying you is a no-brainer. If you'll say yes.'

Yes. Oh, two hundred times, yes! She was so ready to love and be loved for all the world to see. 'We'll need a long engagement.'

He flinched, just slightly. 'So you can be sure?'

'I am already sure,' she said, holding his eyes with hers. 'But if we upstage Clay's memorial Sarah will skin us both alive.'

They laughed until the smiles turned to kisses.

'And one thing…' she said, emerging for breath. 'That's Eleanor Patterson-Calhoun-Jackson to you, Sheriff.'

A fire burst to life deep in his eyes and he pulled her back onto the bed before twisting over the top of her.

'Jed,' she laughed from under his weight, 'your gram's going to be sleeping here…'

His powerful arms shoved his hard, naked body out into the cool morning air, leaving her with ringside seats to the breathtaking view.

'That does it. I'm packing your things,' he said. 'You're moving in right now.'

Dearest Alex,
I'm sorry I've been so lax in writing. Though I know you'll forgive me when you understand why.

*I'm really not sure what part of this letter will
stun you most. That I'm engaged to a spectacular man whom I love and trust beyond either of
our wildest dreams, or the other news I have yet
to share.*

*But first the man... I know you'll only skip
down to that part anyway.*

And out it all came.

Jed. Deputy. Larkville.

Her entire second family and the Fall Festival. The
amazing personal leaps she'd made since arriving and
how, for the first time, she felt whole. Whole! Not like
she'd rattle if she shook her head hard enough. The hard
truth she was going to have to tell Matt and her concern that such bad news would be better coming from
Alex, or Charlotte.

The ink flowed over the linen weave parchment, her
handwriting still as practised and careful as ever.

*Love's a funny thing, Alex, the more you have, the
more it seems you can fit in.*

*So, no matter how many secret siblings I turn
out to have, you remain—and always will—the
sister of my heart.*

Please come, if you can, in October.

I cannot wait for you to meet Jed.

xx

Ellie

'Hon, Holt's only back for a few hours. Given you're the guest of honour do you think we should get going?'

He was so handsome, and so impatient. And so beautifully, wonderfully hers. She pressed a seldom-used number in her contacts and held up two fingers to Jed, apologetically.

'Sorry,' she mouthed.

He smiled and shook his head.

A man answered and she brought the phone quickly back to her ear.

'Hi. Matt...?' She kept her eyes on Jed. He looked so proud. And so in love. And so very, very certain.

Pretty much everything she felt.

'Matt, it's Ellie...'

* * * * *

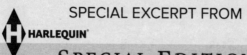
How hadn't he heard her first knock?

And then she saw the carrier on the chair next to him. He'd been rocking it.

"What on earth are you doing to that baby?" she exclaimed, nothing in mind but to rescue the child in obvious distress.

"Damned if I know," he said loudly enough to be heard over the noise. "I fed her, burped her, changed her. I've done everything they said to do, but she won't stop crying."

Tamara was already unbuckling the strap that held the crying infant in her seat. She was so tiny! Couldn't have been more than a few days old. There were no tears on her cheeks.

"There's nothing poking her. I checked," Collins said, not interfering as she lifted the baby from the seat, careful to support the little head.

It wasn't until that warm weight settled against her that Tamara realized what she'd done. She was holding a baby. Something she couldn't do.

She was going to pay. With a hellacious nightmare at the very least.

The baby's cries had stopped as soon as Tamara picked her up.

"What did you do?" Collins was there, practically touching her, he was standing so close.

"Nothing. I picked her up."

"There must've been some problem with the seat, after all…" He'd tossed the infant head support on the desk and was removing the washable cover.

"I'm guessing she just wanted to be held," Tamara said. What the hell was she doing?

Tearless crying generally meant anger, not physical distress. And why did Flint Collins have a baby in his office?

She had to put the child down. But couldn't until he put the seat back together. The newborn's eyes were closed and she hiccuped and then sighed.

Clenching her lips for a second, Tamara looked away. "Babies need to be held almost as much as they need to be fed," she told him while she tried to understand what was going on.

He was checking the foam beneath the seat cover and the straps, too. He was fairly distraught himself.

Not what she would've predicted from a hard-core businessman possibly stealing from her father.

"Who is she?" she asked, figuring it was best to start at the bottom and work her way up to exposing him for the thief he probably was.

He straightened. Stared at the baby in her arms, his brown eyes softening and yet giving away a hint of what looked like fear at the same time. In that second she wished like hell that her father was wrong and Collins wouldn't turn out to be the one who was stealing from Owens Investments.

Don't miss
An Unexpected Christmas Baby *by Tara Taylor Quinn,*
available November 2018 wherever
Harlequin® Special Edition books and ebooks are sold.

www.Harlequin.com

HARLEQUIN®

SPECIAL EDITION

Life, Love and Family

Save **$1.00**

on the purchase of ANY

Harlequin® Special Edition book.

Available whever books are sold,
including most bookstores, supermarkets,
drugstores and discount stores.

Save **$1.00**

on the purchase of any Harlequin® Special Edition book.

Coupon valid until December 31, 2018.
Redeemable at participating outlets in the U.S. and Canada only.
Limit one coupon per customer.

52616059

5 65373 00076 2   (8100)0 12393